The image of his bloodied father swaying on his hellish tether returned. Jubal sat at the cave's opening, his head buried in his hands.

"A firearm is only as good as the brain of the person holding it. Right, Pa?"

"Well, you remembered my little quote, son," he said with a laugh. "But let's see what else we can come up with today that might hold you in good stead these coming years."

Walking deep into the woods, the elder Jubal Young taught his son the finer points of riflery. He finished by saying, "If you've learned anything, let it be primarily this. Never, ever, point this weapon at a human being. You hear me? Even in jest."

Jubal still remembered his father's final words that day. He thought it ironic that the one thing the older man had warned against had come to pass. When Jubal had aimed at a human being, it had not been in jest, it had been in a threatening manner, a terrible deadly moment.

He would never be free of it now.

This title is also available as an eBook

GENE HACKMAN

PAYBACK AT
MORNING PEAK

A NOVEL OF THE AMERICAN WEST

Pocket Books

New York   London   Toronto   Sydney

Pocket Books
A Division of Simon & Schuster, Inc.
1230 Avenue of the Americas
New York, NY 10020

First Pocket Books paperback edition July 2011

POCKET and colophon are registered trademarks of Simon & Schuster, Inc.

For information about special discounts for bulk purchases, please contact Simon & Schuster Special Sales at 1-866-506-1949 or business@simonandschuster.com.

The Simon & Schuster Speakers Bureau can bring authors to your live event. For more information or to book an event, contact the Simon & Schuster Speakers Bureau at 1-866-248-3049 or visit our website at www.simonspeakers.com.

Cover Art by Bill Anton
Designed by Esther Paradelo

Manufactured in the United States of America

10 9 8 7 6 5 4 3 2 1

ISBN 978-1-4516-2356-7
ISBN 978-1-4516-2358-1 (ebook)

To my wife, Betsy.
Without her work and patience,
this book would be but a passing thought.

ONE

Jubal hiked with abandon through the mountainous forest, cradling the Colt slide-action rifle in his slender arms, proud his father had seen fit to allow him use of the small-bore .22. Not quite eighteen, he was just under six feet, nearly as tall as his father, and did his best to dress like him: whipcord pants tucked neatly into calf-high boots. Two rabbits he'd shot that morning hung from a leather-tooled belt around his waist, a gift from pa. He thought of cleaning them himself but decided he would let ma take care of that little chore. He imagined her proud face when he returned home with them. Rabbit stew would be a welcome change from the tough buffalo meat cured in the family smokehouse.

He thought of his sister Prudence, pouting earlier today when ma had told her to stay home, shuck peas, and tend the fire.

"Jube gets to have all the fun!" she'd said.

"Miss Prudence," ma had replied, "you're only four-teen, and it's best you tend your chores." Strict but fair.

Jubal didn't mind the company of his sister, though, as they had much in common. Much to Mother Young's concern, Pru often ventured alone into the forest to hunt berries and wildflowers.

The boy topped Morning Peak, seeing Colorado stretching out to the northern end of New Mexico's San-gre de Cristo Mountains. A late afternoon sun warmed his chapped hands while he marveled at the painted landscape, aspens shimmering as their new spring leaves caught the sun. To the west he could just barely see his family's cabin, nestled into a meadow lined with fir and limber pine. A gray smoky haze from the log structure filled the small valley, and he knew Pru had been doing her job with the fire.

The wind changed, and Jubal's eyes widened. There was too much smoke. He noticed unusual movement around the house and heard eerie sounds of strange, jubi-lant voices floating up through the dense valley.

His reaction was immediate. Gripping the rifle in front of him to clear the way, Jubal broke into a dead run and began to close the hefty distance to the cabin. He tore through thickets down the canyon, sharp branches ripping at his leather coat as he plowed through the brush.

Minutes later, he stopped within shouting distance of the compound, his legs on fire with exertion, his lungs needing air.

A pile of bright gingham fabric lay on the earthen courtyard. *Like a body.* The clothing looked to be his mother's, her dress cloth flapping with the breeze. Pru's horse, Butternut, lay near the well, her legs thrashing as a rush of blood flowed from her neck.

Jubal counted five men riding on horseback in the courtyard, with several more stirring around the outbuildings and barn. They all seemed determined to celebrate, shouting as if they had achieved a great victory.

Trying to control his breathing, the boy slumped behind a massive pine. He wanted this day to start over, wanted to forget the body in the yard, wanted only to run, but Pa would skin him if he didn't stand as a man.

Where *was* pa?

Jubal took several more deep breaths. He moved to his stomach and started to crawl. He'd gone only a few feet when he rolled onto his back, fighting panic, his nose stung by the sharp and disagreeable scent of burnt flesh and manure.

He had to keep moving. Rising, he darted between a stand of scrub oak, then bellied down and once again crawled, hiding behind the scattered chamisa.

Laughing and drunk, the men staggered around the toolshed and outhouse. One dark-skinned fellow looked different, wearing a feathered, flat-brim leather hat with a bright yellow braided string running under his chin. He carried a bow across his back and a quiver with arrows attached to his belt. He looked familiar, the way he carried himself. The whole raft of them seemed related.

Jubal's thoughts drifted to more pleasant times. The family together, Pru laughing at his jokes, his parents sharing secrets. When was that? A lifetime ago. He forced himself back to the present. He had work to do.

He looked down at the rifle. He'd killed animals for

food, but could he kill a man? He shifted on the rough ground. Maybe it didn't matter.

A wail came from the barn, growing louder as Jubal crept closer through the thicket. He caught a glimpse of the two-story structure's exterior.

And then he saw his father.

Jubal, Sr., hung from a pulley outside the hayloft, arms stretched high above his head, legs dangling above the wicked flames of a fire. Charred remnants of his clothing and strips of skin swung from his chest. A chunk of red cloth, which Jubal recognized as his father's bandanna, had been stuffed into his mouth. A man with a filthy poncho wrapped around his shoulders tossed hay from the loft onto the torturous blaze.

Jubal's pa was near to death, his bare legs burned. Blood matted his neck, arms, and chest.

Then the wailing stopped, the body swaying like a pendulum. Jubal stared, looking for recognition. His father's lips were moving. With each group of words, a nod, then he would begin again. He gazed at Jubal. Did he speak? Did he call out, "Save yourself"? His eyes rolled toward the smoked sky, once again the same litany, but this time the head drooped, the shoulders and legs relaxed. The body settled into its trusses.

Jubal chambered a round in the .22, raised it, and took a long, dreadful moment to pray. His head pressed hard against the rifle's breech. He wiped the moisture from his eyes, adjusted the rear sight, and shot his father in the head.

The sound, though muffled by the crackling fire, still startled the fire-tending Mexican. He turned toward the noise as Jubal stood and pumped another round into the Colt. Trembling, he fired, his bullet catching the man in the lower stomach. The man dug his hands under his heavy leather belt, searching, then doubled over as if looking for something on the ground.

Jubal's second shot pierced his head just above the cheekbone, dropping the man like a rock from a high place.

The boy slumped to the ground, watching the remains of his father swinging from the barn. "Help me, Pa. What have I done?"

Fifty yards off to his left, two men, their hair pulled tautly into braids on the sides of their heads, dragged tied bundles of his mother's and father's clothing. They soaked the pile of garments in lamp oil and lit it. Trailing the fiery bundle behind a crazed horseman, they made great circles around the house and barn, setting fire to the dry grasses.

"Be the man I taught you to be," his pa had once said to him. He eased to the ground, too frightened to move and yet strangely not seeming to care. Jubal looked down at the two paltry rabbits still hanging from his belt.

The men by the house stopped their whooping to look at the area of the barn, the structure now fully taken by rising flames. The cracking and popping of the dried timbers had partially covered the sound of the small-caliber .22, and Jubal was still safely unknown to them.

He watched as they cavorted in his family's vegetable garden. Others circled the lifeless form of his mother on the ground, making coarse gestures and poking their rifles at the body.

Pru. He hadn't seen her anywhere. *Where is she?*

Jubal started to pick himself up. He was sick with fear and remorse, but he'd do his damnedest.

Crouching low, he sprinted to the edge of his mother's root cellar. There he remained unseen behind the canted door, thinking how easy it would be to slither out of the clearing and into the welcoming shelter of the spruces and whitebark pines that surrounded the homestead—then run for his pitiful life.

A high-pitched scream came from the edge of the woods, beyond the burning barn. Pru was running into the clearing where their mother lay, her bonnet streaming behind her, tangled in her long blond hair. Wildflowers fell from a basket on her arm. She ran like a frightened animal, shouting to her mother.

A horseman spotted her and pursued her across the open field.

Ignoring the other men, Jubal took quick aim with his rifle and pulled the trigger. The shot went awry. The horseman scooped Prudence up in one swift powerful move, gripping her waist and swinging her up beside him. She protested loudly, beating her fists against the man's head and chest.

Jubal had very little chance for a shot now, he was afraid of hitting her. The other men honed in on Jubal's position and fired at him, bullets dancing past his head. He collapsed onto the ground and crept to where he could use the burning farmhouse as cover.

Pru was taken into the tree line from where she had just emerged. He moved along the ground. Once he was at the other side of the farmhouse, he ran into the nearby woods. All of his instincts told him to keep his head down and pursue cautiously, but he couldn't ignore his need to chase the horseman. He had lost his parents. He couldn't lose his sister.

Once in the woods, he could hear Pru's voice coming from several directions, all of her cries amplified by the reverberating valley walls. For some time he searched for her, scrambling from one tree to the next. When he was finally resigned to the idea that the horseman had moved out of the valley, he heard hoofbeats coming from the east. He ran in that direction, only to see a lone rider bolting at a gallop between the trees a hundred yards in front of him.

The man had left Pru in the woods.

Jubal quickened his pace and backtracked from where he had last seen the rider. After a lengthy search, he found her . . . her face bloody from a deep forehead wound, clothing twisted about her body. There was so much, too much blood. On his knees, he pleaded with her to speak to him. He cradled her in his arms and rocked her, trying to coax a spark of life.

The wildflower basket was still looped around her arm. Jubal gently pulled out the leaves and twigs caught in her hair. He combed her soft tresses with his fingers, then used his neckerchief to clean her face of dirt and blood.

"Jube?" She opened her eyes, trying to focus. "Tell pa a man tried to . . . hurt me."

Jubal moved her gently, thankful she was alive. "Shush, now, Pru. I'm here. You'll be all right. Try and rest."

Pru seemed to fall into a heavy sleep, a spot of blood leaked from the side of her mouth. Jubal swung his rifle over his shoulder and lifted her into his arms. They needed shelter, and so he started up the long slope toward Morning Peak.

Nearly half a mile from the house stood a group of rocks the two of them had explored in the past. Boulders as tall as their barn had split off from the cliffs above, and wagon-sized stones had fallen away to the base of these rocks, forming the makings of a cave. Jubal tried to awaken Pru while he scaled the steep terrain.

"Remember the 'Sultan's Castle'?"

"You mean the Emperor of Youngdom?" she answered slowly. "His castle?"

His eyes misted. "Yep, the very same. We're almost there."

As they reached the bouldered cave entrance, Jubal turned sideways with his precious cargo in order to slide through the narrow gap. Once safely inside the rock-sided enclosure, he took off his coat and wrapped his sister in fleece-lined warmth. Just enough light peeked from a V-shaped opening for Jubal to see Pru's ghostly pale complexion. Dry leaves spotted the cave floor and lay in drifts against the wall. A rag doll with a clownlike smile sat on the parched vegetation. It belonged to his sister.

Jubal laid Pru on the bed of leaves and moved the doll to a pile of carefully placed rocks.

"I smell Cotton, Jube."

"What?"

"Cotton, my rag doll I used to play with. I smell her. I dabbed some of ma's lilac water on her 'cause the old stuffing got kind of dank."

Jubal took the cheery doll and passed it under his nose before he laid it next to his sister. Indeed, it smelled slightly of perfume. It had been years since he and his sister had used this stone structure as a playhouse.

"Don't tell ma." Her body heaved a long sigh of pain. "Sorry. Don't tell that I spent time here. Ma would skin me."

Jubal ran his hand softly across her face. "Are you in a lot of pain, sis?"

She nodded and held her hand to her mouth. "Jube . . . I'm not seeing too well." She cried, not like a child, but deep and steady. "My side hurts, just here. I'm bleeding something awful." She tried to touch her rib cage. "Maybe ma's pain potion, under the washbasin. The small purple bottle."

Their mother kept codeine elixir for severe pain, on a shelf in the kitchen. Jubal wondered if he could get to it or if it had even survived the fire. The men must have left the farm by now. There was still daylight, and he could be down to the farm and back in twenty minutes. "Pru, I'm going to try to get you that medicine. Will you be all right for a bit?"

"Ma," she called. "Ma, I don't feel well. I've got deep pain there. A man was with me. Make it go away."

Jubal dropped to his knees.

"Can you get me the man in the moon? He's frowning."

She was delirious. Maybe it would be a good time to get back to the cabin for medicine. She moaned, knees drawn up tight toward her chest, hands dug between her legs. Her forehead was dampened with sweat, her face flushed red. But he was afraid to leave her in such pain.

"Jubal Young, a man-child." She rolled to her side and

reached a hand out toward him. "I wrote a poem for you, Jube."

"I'd like to hear it."

She tried to smile. "I don't think I can remember it all. It's about the land, the animals. . . . I gave the poem to ma to keep for your birthday. She put it away somewhere. I really need ma to help me. It's a lady's kind of thing. Please."

Jubal made up his mind. "Listen to me, Pru. I'm gonna scoot down to the house and I'll be right back. You'll be fine for a few minutes, won't you?"

She nodded, trying to smile.

Rifle in hand, Jubal ran back toward the homestead. The image of his sister lying huddled in misery, her pale face distorted, blurred him to anger. He would kill them all. He felt anguish, dizzy with it. *I will track them to the ends of the earth.*

The men had not left but were spread around the clearing, apparently looking for him. Jubal skirted the tree line and started once again to crawl. He realized the farther he went, the more he would be cut off from his sister. Never mind, he would deal with that later. First, these men.

The setting sun turned the raging fires that were once his home into a fiery pink mist. He took a last glance at the sad bundle that was his mother and continued to the root cellar. With the slide-action Colt steady on the door, he let out his breath and squeezed the trigger softly.

A man with a battered straw hat caught a round in the neck. He dropped his rifle and sat on the ground, both hands swatting at his neck as if shooing a pesky bee.

Gripping his throat, he tried to squelch the bleeding. Jubal slid another bullet into the chamber, aimed, and fired it squarely into the center of his forehead. The man's sweat-stained hat spiraled backward. Arms outstretched in surrender, the renegade seemed to melt into the earth.

The other men scurried down behind his father's overturned hay wagon, several with antiquated, single-shot weapons. Jubal hit the ground as the balled rounds ripped at the earth around him. Forcing himself to be calm, he once again reloaded.

The men called out to Jubal, denouncing him, describing in detail what they would do to him. All the while bullets plowed into the ground close to Jubal.

They continued to fire, one of the younger men skipping over a pile of clothing to charge toward the root cellar. As the man drew a long-barreled .44 from his holster, Jubal's bullet caught him in the chest. Stumbling, he tried to reach Jubal, pounding his pistol at the soft earth. Moving within twenty feet, he slipped to his knees and then slowly eased to his side, as if preparing for a nap.

Several rounds splintered the root cellar's plank door, a long thin piece of wood catching Jubal in the side of the head, opening a wound. For an instant he couldn't see. He wrapped his bandanna around his forehead to stop the bleeding and fired several more shots into the distant hay wagon.

The intense pain from his gashed head gave him some welcome courage. His family had suffered, and this pain seemed to make him one with them. He thought of Pru, her bloody dress, and pa, Jubal Thaddeus Young, Sr., a man striving to make a life for his kinfolk, killed now by his own son's hand. Jubal had a moment when he thought maybe his father would forgive him his death and be proud of him.

Be the man . . . , he would have said. Jubal prayed that it be so.

Jubal rose and heard what he thought was a hornet, then a high whistling sound and a shocking pain in his left hip. An arrow protruded from his body. It had not penetrated the skin of his back but stopped somewhere inside his lower waist. Jubal dropped back down on the native grasses to crawl below a small rise in the earth beyond view.

Scuttling along on his right side, he was careful so the arrow did not catch in the heavy foliage. With all the weapons in play, rifle and pistol rounds eating up the earth around him, Jubal thought it odd he would be hit by, of all things, an arrow.

His mission was too dangerous, and from the looks of the house it would be a miracle if anything survived the fire. He would have to go back empty-handed up the steep trail leading to Morning Peak and Sultan's Castle. But Jubal didn't know what else he could do for his sis.

If these men could track, and he knew at least the man with the bow could, then they would trail after him, but he knew the rocky path so well he was confident they couldn't get around him. He glanced at the farmhouse, it continued to burn.

They would follow.

He wanted them to follow.

Hours had passed since Jubal had first come upon the attack. He deemed himself safe for now, having barely made it out of the bloody grounds of the homestead, inching along on his good hip. Grasping the embedded arrow with his left hand, he clawed and elbowed with his right. The ghostlike image of a tall gray-haired man kept him going. Jubal knew him. He felt as if he were missing something, a reason. It eluded him. The figures darting about his family's property were mere phantoms without motive. His lack of memory, the why of this kept him strangely alert.

Jubal limped across an open meadow. Looking down at the protruding arrow, he thought it must have glanced off his hipbone. The length of it jutted out from his bleeding upper leg like an errant tree branch.

A stand of ponderosa pine lay ahead. He pushed on, glancing back often to see if he was followed. Not yet.

At a cliff overlooking what his sister referred to as "Young's Valley," once again he found his sister's retreat, the small opening where two large rocks formed an inverted V.

The light started to fade as Jubal eased himself into the cave, where he was greeted by the sound of his sister's soft, forced breathing. A strand of light from a gap at the top of the boulders illuminated her pale face.

He felt remorse. His search for the medicine had not only been worthless, but he had also been rewarded with a deep wound.

He watched his sister, wondering what to do next. How to deal with his own fierce pain of the arrow was beyond him.

Prudence stirred. "What would pa say?" she asked. It was almost as if she had read his mind. "Pa once said to me, 'Prudence, when all else fails, simply smile.' It's a little harder done than said. Wouldn't you say, Jube?"

"Pa was full of sayings."

"Was?" she asked.

Jubal was happy to hear his sister once again speaking clearly, but she'd caught him off guard. He tried to cover his mistake. "Oh, I just mean he's always saying these . . . platitudes. I think that's the word. Anyhow, he's funny sometimes, right?"

Quiet for a long time, Pru worried Jubal when she finally spoke. "I'd been picking flowers." Her voice softened. "I think I was running and calling out to ma. Then, a smell like somebody's sweat. Is Butternut okay?"

Jubal didn't answer. He sat at her side, the arrow jutting out of his left hip, the blood flow fortunately stanched.

"A man was mean. He did hurtful things." Her voice began to fade. "I want ma. Please get her."

He wished he could.

Pru raised her clenched fists and made feeble striking movements into the air. She cried out.

Jubal once again stroked her forehead. "Try to relax if you can. It will be better soon." He pushed his arm under her neck and brought her head close to his own. He kissed her softly on the cheek. Her eyes opened wide.

"I love my brother Jubal. He's funny and kind. . . ."

Then she was gone.

TWO

"We should split up, go our separate ways. There's gonna be a price to pay when the law finds out about this." Billy Tauson stood by the burnt farmhouse, his prematurely gray hair in contrast to bits of charred embers clinging on his dark tailored jacket. "Dammit all to hell. I didn't mean for this to get all crazy. Where in Christ's sake is Wetherford?"

The men crowded about, tending to a young wounded cowboy.

"How you feeling, Ty?" one of them asked.

"Poorly. My vision's gone all jiggled. I need something for the hurt. It's getting me down."

The men glanced at one another, pretty sure the youngest of their hearty band wouldn't see another sunrise.

This whole plan had been a debacle from the beginning. Tauson had promised his group of misfits a hearty supper in town and a night of drinking if they would accompany him out to his former ranch and scare the devil out of what he described as "the new tenants."

It had gone all wrong. Instead of hollering and frightening the folks when they arrived, the first thing rowdy Pete Wetherford did was ride down the older man of the farm as he came out of the barn. As the fellow lay on the ground trying to catch his breath, Wetherford tied the man's arms above his head, tossing the end of his lariat over the corbel above the hayloft door. Laughing, he passed the rope around his saddle horn and spurred his horse forward, sending the farmer into the air, kicking and thrashing.

Billy Tauson tried to settle everyone down, but Wetherford's actions had driven the mob wild, and they soon lit the farmhouse ablaze. The woman, Bea, was trapped in a small outbuilding, where Wetherford raped and beat her, then left her begging on hands and knees for mercy as she succumbed to the pleasure of his friends.

Then the shooting from the forest. Tauson had ducked behind a fallen oak. "Whoever that bastard is, he's gotta be stopped. Wetherford, you and your brother Al circle 'round to that fellow's left flank."

Pete looked over his shoulder at Billy. "How's about you and your shot-to-hell cousin Ty kiss my skinny behind?" He snorted at his own remark. "It's that brat bastard son of the farmer. I'm fixing to just lie here and wait the little prick out. Okay, Mr. Boss Man?"

Billy Tauson sucked on his teeth, wishing he had the huevos to call Pete Wetherford out. But for now, he'd wait.

A few random shots came from the woods, and then nothing for nearly an hour.

When Tauson had finally called out that "the little shit skedaddled," there began an onslaught of arguing back and forth on whether to pursue him, but when things finally settled, the men broke out their jugs of rotgut whiskey and began to get even more drunk.

"Who was that damn billy goat?" one of the men called out. "He sure as hell knew how to handle that rifle."

"Never mind about that little bastard," Tauson said, "where's that varmint Wetherford?"

"I'm a Wetherford," said Pete's brother Al, "and I resent your talking like that, Billy."

"Sorry, Al, but what in God's name gets into that brother of yours?"

Al Wetherford was the oldest in the group, which consisted of two Hispanics, Jorge and Oscar, a Ute Indian with a shriveled arm, the two drunks Ed and Robert, the brothers Wetherford, and leader Billy Tauson, along with the wounded young man, Ty Blake.

Tauson shuffled around the devastated farmyard, taking a long pull from one of the jugs. "I told all of you people we were just going to put a scare into these folks, didn't I say that? Didn't I?"

The Ute looked at Tauson. "Crook Arm keeps weapon in rawhides." The tall bronzed Indian grasped his crotch with one hand, the other gripping a jug. "Save child-maker for squaw women." He giggled and did a little dance in a tight circle, still holding himself while he took a deep slug of whiskey. The men stood around with half-smiles, enjoying Crook Arm's dance.

"Well, hell's fire," came a voice from behind him. "That farmer came at us like the clappers from hell. I never seen such a determined bastard." Pete Wetherford walked up behind the tall Billy Tauson.

"Where the hell you been, Petey?" Tauson was careful with him. It wasn't that Pete looked formidable, it was more a sense of compressed energy that you didn't want to mess with.

Pete took in the assembled group. "I been behind your old farmhouse, Billy. Heard everything you said. You got a burr in your saddle about me, boss?" He gave Tauson a mocking smile. "Truth be told, I been washing up. Seem to have gotten a little blood on me." He winked at his brother Al.

Tauson stomped around the sad little vegetable garden. "Why'd you have to do that pile-o'-rags woman out there that way? All crumbled and nasty, lying dead. Why'd you do her like that? We didn't come out here to rape and kill, dammit. I told you that on the way, didn't I?"

"You said a lot of stuff, Billy. Mostly horseshit. You wanted us to be your strong right arm while you poked around like a rooster in heat, lording it over those sodbusters." Pete looked for help from his buddies. "Would you all agree, fellers?"

Most of them kicked the dirt and shrugged their shoulders.

"Now," Pete continued, "who was that little yellow-belly with the .22 rifle? I'd like to do some serious work on that youngster."

The wounded Ty Blake called out to his cousin Tauson, "Billy, get me to a doctor, would you? I'm hurting real bad."

Tauson turned toward him. "We got to scamper into the woods and find that kid with the rifle. Then we'll come back and take care of you, Ty." He called to the men, "Mount up. Let's find that shooter before he takes off and spins a tale to the law."

Al Wetherford spoke up. "Before, you told us we had to split up and hightail it out of here."

"I know what I said, but now it's better if we all hunt out that little rotter so there's no witness to talk about all this."

Pete looked at brother Al and rolled his eyes. His smile toward his boss Billy Tauson was not a warm, agreeable treat. An average-sized man, Pete made up for his lack of height with a wicked sense of self.

Tauson called out for Crook Arm to take the lead. They trailed out of the little valley, heading up toward the towering peak that looked down onto the formerly tranquil meadow.

Pete sidled up next to Al. "This jackanapes needs to be taken down a notch. Always ordering people around, it boils me."

"You signed on for it. What did you expect? By the way, I saw you ride off with that bundled-up flower girl. What happened?"

"We had a quiet wedding in the glade back yonder." Pete grinned. "She professed her undying love and insisted on anointing me with the flower of her virginity."

"Oh, ain't you the elegant talker."

Pete grinned even more.

"Where is she?"

Pete gestured with his thumb. "I suspect she's still lying in that pleasant grassy clearing, gazing at the setting sun, not thinking about a solitary thing."

The group rode on for ten minutes, then dismounted, tied their horses to a fallen tree, and headed on foot up the far ridge of a steep canyon in search of that little bastard.

Stretched out in the dark cave, Jubal tried to sort his thoughts.

What had he done to merit this?

What had his innocent family done?

If he lived through this day, he would seek out answers to avenge his family.

What would his father do?

Be the man he'd taught him to be.

"Yes, Pa, but I can't. I'm scared and hurting. Pru and ma are dead."

Then think on it like this, son. If those varmints catch you, you'll be hurting until hell wouldn't have it.

An image floated across his memory, of his father trussed up outside the barn looking down at him. Jubal tried pulling his knees tight to his chest. The left leg wouldn't go, too stiff.

He had to move, take care of the arrow, make some decisions, rest a bit. He closed his eyes, trailing off. He thought of his mother. What was it she had said? "If literature is to be your guide, Jubal, you could do worse than follow the lead of Cervantes' Don Quixote or Dumas's Edmond Dantès." Together, they had read both classics, his mother constructing a tutorial on character and ethics from *The Count of Monte Cristo. If only I had Edmond Dantès's perseverance.* He dreamt on, envisioning wreaking vengeance on the band of miscreants invading the farm.

He awakened almost immediately. Knowing he would have to do the deed. To suffer the discomfort now instead of the big pain later. He tried not to think on it.

Jubal sat up, running his fingers carefully around the skin of his waist, loosening his belt, remembering again.

Jube, you best inherit this belt now, no sense of me kidding myself any longer, it just doesn't fit.

Moving the long arrow carefully, he searched for the jagged steel head embedded beneath his skin. Each tiny motion brought more pain. Jubal teared up, hearing his father's voice.

You're feeling sorry for yourself, son. Break that damn thing and push the rest of it on through the backside of the soft part of your waist . . . grab up that stick on the ground and bite down hard on it while you do it, so you don't snip off your tongue.

Jubal raised himself to his knees, placing the feathered end of the arrow against the rock wall of the cave. He tried not to think on his mom's suffering, what it must have been like to endure the savage assault, and once again saw his father swinging grotesquely from his tether outside the barn. He deserved this pain. He rested his head against the cool stone. Experimenting with a gentle push against the wall, he was rewarded with an avalanche of sensation. *Deserve it or not, this is hellfire.*

Jubal's willful mind whisked him back to the street in front of the land office, remembering a man's mean-spirited taunting of his father. It came back to him, the ride into town on the buckboard. The family together, Pru asking for soda pop. His mother eyeing a colorful scarf as they passed the general store. He recalled when the tall, gray-haired fellow in front of the land office looked back at his group of friends, the meanest-looking desperadoes Jubal had ever seen.

Now, in the cave, he began, his hands resting on the damp stone. He centered the feathered end of the arrow in a crevice in the wall. Whispering a short prayer, he pushed his body hard against the stone bulkhead, feeling the arrow thrust its way through the skin and out the back side of his waist. He reached down and snapped off the shaft six inches below the feathers, jamming the remains of the stick as far as he could, then reached back and pulled the remaining stem out of his body.

The stone walls blurred. The devil had started a massive fire, and it was licking at his guts. He heard screaming in the cave. It sounded like someone he knew.

THREE

Pete Wetherford was tired, which made him angry. He'd expended all his energy on the raid and his conquest, as he thought of it, of the two women. He trailed behind Indian tracker Crook Arm. "Hey, Chief, how much higher we gonna go? It's dark. A feller could plunge off this damn canyon wall and bust a gut."

Tauson replied for the Indian, "If you don't shut your trap, Mr. Pete, you're gonna get your ass shot off."

"Not by you, boss. Yeah, that would be the day."

"That little cocker kid would have to be deaf and blind not to hear us coming. So let's all shut it down, okay?"

Pete was not only worn-out but had had a snootful of his leader, Billy Tauson. He slowed his pace to let Al catch up. "How you making it, Albert the mountain climber?"

Al leaned against a piñon. "I've either gotta stop smoking or playing with my pud. I can't catch my damn breath."

Pete smiled. Al had never been very fit.

They moved on, the light from Crook Arm's torch flickering through the filigreed pines.

A dark shadow lay across the canyon. Pete could still smell on his clothes the remnants of the girl he'd had in the woods. She'd begged him to stop, which had only heightened his pleasure. Something had come over him as his body pounded against hers. She seemed to symbolize everything he both hated and desired. Maybe he should be feeling bad about what he'd done, but it didn't seem to bother him. He thought if he'd hung around a bit he could have pleasured himself again with her. It tickled him that he was insatiable. It amused him when he remembered the other men in the gang, depleted and slack-jawed, coming from the outbuilding where the old gal lay. Hell's fire, it made him warm just thinking on it.

Perhaps that little missy in the woods was still there pining away for him, wanting him to come back and fulfill her dreams.

"What in the hell are you thinking about, Pete?" Al poked him in the ribs.

"Why you ask?"

"'Cause you're giggling away something fierce. Like a kiddie at a birthday party."

Pete continued to thread his way up the steep trail. "I didn't realize I was laughing out loud. Just having pleasant daydreams on this starlit night. I guess the beast is hungry tonight." He threw back his head and howled.

FOUR

Jubal shivered on the cave floor. He caught himself starting each new thought with, *If only I had. Where would it have led?*

He looked once again at the lifeless form of his sister and eased his own pain-wracked body to the mouth of the cave. He gazed at a dark sky. The moon had yet to rise, with heavy clouds building in the west.

Jubal realized he still held the remaining few inches of the arrow's shaft and steel head. He forced the rod from his hand, his fingers and arms flaked with dried blood. In the distance on the valley floor below, a tiny light wavered like a firefly, dipping but always moving steadily up the far side of the canyon.

Finally, they were coming for him.

The renegades were on the rim of the vast trench opposite him. Once they reached the crest of the mountain, they would come back down and search his side.

The cave entrance was hard to see in the best of light, so their pitch-soaked torch might not catch his hiding place.

But he decided he wouldn't take that chance. The men were at least the better part of an hour before making the turn at the top and starting back down. Jubal had surprise on his side.

His body resisted the movement, but he forced himself to roll back, get his rifle, and slide carefully from the rock-strewn entrance.

Checking that the flickering torch's progress had not increased too much, he started up the canyon rim, not sure just what he would do. The renegade men outnumbered him, but it didn't matter.

The earth had split, creating a hollow angling up the mountain. A number of smaller diagonal ravines on both sides would have a man detour for as much as a hundred yards before snaking back to the rim and continuing upward.

Jubal thought he could entice them to take a shortcut. The men's torches across the canyon disappeared and reappeared as they passed steadily through the trees. They were a determined lot.

Good, let them come.

As Jubal continued up the mountain, he began to devise a trap. A large tree had fallen, bridging a gap at a small ravine. Bare of branches nearly all the way, it would make for a fairly smooth walk, saving time and distance if you had the courage, but a long drop if you slipped.

Now to figure out how to entice the renegades onto this tempting bridge.

He wasn't sure how many there were. He'd counted

five and knew there were more. In the heat of the skirmish he never did get an accurate count of the bastards, but it didn't matter. This was worth a try.

He took the long way around, not trusting his weakened body to the makeshift bridge. On the far side, fading light peeked out between the clouds. He found a prickly bush cropping up thirty or forty feet from the base of the log. He tore a strip of cloth from the waist of his shirt and snagged it onto a branch, turned, and hustled back to the base of the log.

Taking several steps onto the downed tree, he pried a large piece of flaky bark from it as if someone had stepped there. Turning, he leapt painfully back onto the cliff edge and swept away his footprints.

Jubal limped up the steep rise, knowing that any self-respecting native scout who took the time to examine his tracks would find something amiss, but he hoped the turmoil of the chase and the increasing darkness would make them sloppy. Besides, the tracker was more than likely the one who had shot him with the arrow, so he would dismiss any thoughts of "self-respecting."

After a hundred yards, he thought he was close to the summit as the canyon began to narrow. If the men saw him from the opposite side it could possibly take them ten minutes to continue to the top and come back down his side of the wide ravine. Sitting on a rock, he watched the torch blink its way up the mountain. Jubal reckoned the Indian would be leading them. Whether he would take the bait at the log was anyone's guess, but he was hoping at least one of the men would be tempted.

It was difficult to wait. He wanted to shout for the

filthy cowards to come get him, but he resisted the urge. They should be doubtful at first, thinking any noise he made was nothing more than an animal moving in the dark. Then maybe he would give a shout of alarm and perhaps a desperate, noisy retreat.

Pa would say, *Have a plan, son, and be honest with yourself when it goes wayward.* Easier said than accomplished.

The search party's torches suddenly went black. Had they seen him? Or worse, if they continued up, would he know where they were? He strained to see across the dark chasm, but it was too far away to discern movement. They had long since abandoned their horses, the ascent being too rocky and steep. When he finally gave up on seeing them, he heard rocks in the distance being struck together.

Someone had a flint, attempting to relight. After several tries, the makeshift light bloomed again and Jubal could make out bodies gathering. They had continued moving in the dark and were much closer, at least a hundred yards farther up the mountain.

Jubal picked up a stick from the ground and waited, taking slow breaths to force calmness, to deal with the pain in his hip. After a few minutes more, the men were nearly parallel to his spot near the ravine edge, probably forty yards, by a direct line. It was now or never.

He snapped the stick atop his knee with a mighty tug, then dropped behind a large stone.

The torch holder stopped and moved the fiery light in an arc over his head, trying to distinguish the distant sounds and shadows.

Jubal sensed them looking in his direction. Would they think the sound was an animal? They waited, not moving. With difficulty, Jubal pulled his knees as close to his chest as he could, sitting as still as possible. He said a silent prayer that included the souls of his family. Not asking safe passage for himself, wishing only for an opportunity at revenge.

He rose as quickly as his injured hip would allow and made his way back down the mountain toward his bridge, making as much noise as he could without sounding intentional. At one point, he let out a loud cry of pain, his wounds lending reality to his ruse. He skirted the fallen log bridge.

When he finally reached the other side, he could hear them approaching. It sounded as if they were at the summit and on their way back down. He had only minutes as he slid down the far side of the ravine under the log onto a rock ledge. An errant branch he'd seen earlier pointed down. He could hide under its foliage and be ready when the men arrived.

They came with a vengeance, cursing and undisciplined. The pitch-pine torch was held high by the Indian, its glow dancing through the tree branches, casting a pasty, evil pall on the men's faces. They panted, angry, gathering at the base of the log. The Indian held the rag that Jubal had hung on the prickly branch. The gray-haired man took the bloodied cloth from him.

"That little bastard's been hit," the man said. "He can't get far. Let's skirt on around this gully and light out after him."

They started to move.

"Hey, Chief, hold that torch," said another. "I'm gonna save some shoe leather."

"Not good," answered the light bearer.

"Just hold it, redskin."

"I'll go, too, Pete." This from the squat Mexican.

"*Bueno, Jorge. Ándale.*"

They were taking the bait. Jubal had already eased his rifle barrel between the heavy branch above him and the fat part of the log. He stayed below the log, his makeshift lever ready.

As the men took their first tentative steps on the log, Jubal added his weight to the stock of the rifle. The log held steady. In order to get the proper leverage, he would be forced to raise himself just out of his shelter.

He watched as the dancing torch lit the outlines of the two men, who were nearly halfway across. Jubal crouched and applied all of his strength onto the rifle.

With a crack and a groan, the log stirred slightly, rolling a few degrees away from Jubal. Its immense weight caused it to stop, then rock back toward him.

"Jesus Christ, Pete, what did you do?" The Mexican grabbed his friend Pete as they both fell to their knees.

Their arms windmilled in the air as Jubal applied more pressure, working with the momentum of the log. Struggling for purchase, Pete made a grab for the trunk as his buddy yelled, trying to grip the air while plunging headfirst down the chasm. Pete held on for only seconds until his weight forced him to slip around under the log, his fingers digging at the soft bark. Jubal eased back into the foliage, hoping he hadn't been seen.

"You bastard, I'll—" Pete called out to his friends. "Help me, Al. Dammit, I can't hold on. For God's sake. He's here. I can't—"

By this time one of the other men had leapt into action, straddling the trunk and inching his way out to help. Jubal heard the other men shouting encouragement as Pete grasped at the log's decaying bark, trying to swing one of his legs back up and over it. He finally succeeded, gasping for air.

"You gotta git this bastard. Oh, God, help me." Pete had one leg looped over the log, his head flopped back, while his arms hugged the fallen tree like a newlywed. He regarded Jubal upside down. "We did your mother, boy. If I live through this I'll do you, too." There was a sickening sound of bark peeling away from the log as Pete, clawing away with his hands, headfirst began what Jubal thought would be the last long moments of his life.

Jubal listened carefully as Pete fell, grasping at over-hanging rocks and shrubs on the side of the canyon, cursing friends and family on the way down. He also thought he heard him call out "little bastard," but maybe not.

For the first time, the rocky outcropping where Jubal sat seemed perilous. He shivered as a cold wind washed over his skin, and he wondered how much of the man's ranting the others had heard and if they could separate Pete's frantic pleading with his all-too-telling giveaway of Jubal's hiding place.

The men on the other side encouraged Pete's brother, Al, who had also begun crossing on the log, to ease his way back to safety. Jubal was tempted to give his rifle one last tug for Al, but thought maybe he'd done enough for now. He'd get the others later. He eased the rifle out from between the branch and log and waited for them to move on.

A wave of thunder rumbled through the canyon, awakening him. Light cold rain blew through the cave's opening. Jubal had waited nearly an hour after the men left the log bridge before making a move, listening to them argue among themselves until their voices faded in the distance. When he thought they were at least several hundred yards past his cave, he made his way carefully back along the edge of the giant crevasse.

Now water dripped steadily onto his hair from the cave's porous ceiling. He rolled over on the damp earth, a dull, insistent pain radiating through his left side. It came rushing back, the events at his log bridge.

"Jesus, mother of Christ, they both fell. Oh, Christ a-mighty. What in God's name?" Jubal couldn't tell who spoke.

"They're gone. Al, you did the best you could, leave it be."

"Pete was my brother, Billy. What d'you mean, 'leave it be'?"

Jubal heard the sound of breaking leaves and twigs as someone walked away.

"I mean leave it. He was drunker than all hell. Now let's git."

Al groused as he followed Billy and the Indian to a switchback and then proceeded toward Jubal and the rim of the canyon. As they neared, Jubal tried to press himself deeper into the ravine wall.

"What in God's name will I tell ma?"

Tell her that Pete, her beloved son, had just participated in the rape and murder of three innocent people, Albert. Al was standing above the log looking back at the ravine where his brother and his friend Jorge had fallen.

It was all Jubal could do to keep from firing his rifle from below into the man's groin. The barrel was pointed the right way, his finger poised on the trigger. But the others were close by and would be on him in a second. Jubal waited.

He would wait as long as it took. Like Edmond Dantès.

FIVE

Jubal didn't know how long he slept, whether he was actually rested or if his stupor was due to his current predicament. In any case, he would have to move. He looked around the cave, his sister's body lying in the leaf-strewn bier, Cotton cuddled into her right arm where he had placed it. He thought on what she had said at the end, about him being kind and funny. In that last moment, she had been thinking of him, and not of herself.

He thought she, being the person she was, would not have sought revenge, but a sort of salvation for her tormentors. But that was her. He had no such thoughts of salvaging anyone.

Crawling to the edge of the shelter's opening, he gazed at a world of spring torrent. Low in the eastern sky, clouds covered the distant mountains as the sun edged through to wake the dark morning. If the renegades were still looking for him, he should just sit awhile. The rain would have obliterated any tracks left behind. He felt weak.

Stretching out of the cave's opening to wash, he looked to the leaden sky and let the water lash his face. Having taken what he thought was his father's advice to save himself, was he simply trading one immediate hell for a prolonged one?

The image of his bloodied father swaying on his hellish tether returned. Jubal sat at the cave's opening, his head buried in his hands.

"Jube, let's take a stroll, son." Jubal, Sr., had the .22 rifle tucked under his arm. "Your continued hounding of me about this firearm has strengthened my resolve to go slow in the releasing of it. I've said this before, Jube. It's a small-caliber weapon but still very deadly."

"A firearm is only as good as the brain of the person holding it. Right, Pa?"

"You remembered my little quote, son," he said with a laugh. "But let's see what else we can come up with today that might hold you in good stead these coming years."

Walking deep into the woods, the elder Jubal Young taught his son the finer points of riflery. He finished by saying, "If you've learned anything, let it be primarily this. Never, ever, point this weapon at a human being. You hear me? Even in jest."

Jubal still remembered his father's final words that day. He thought it ironic that the one thing the older man had warned against had come to pass. When Jubal had aimed at a human being, it had not been in jest, it had been in a threatening manner, a terrible deadly moment.

He would never be free of it.

Holding tightly to his left side, Jubal raised himself to a seated position. He had drifted off again. The rain had stopped and now a briskness spiked the air, smelling of pine and damp grass. He needed food, not having eaten since the previous day, while on his hunt. He remembered the smoked meat his mother had wrapped in old newsprint, along with a chunk of sourdough bread, and felt a lump rise in his throat. He caught himself and made a vow never to cry again, then immediately realized that making a number of promises to himself didn't change his predicament.

Though his family was gone, he was alive and in good health, except for a crusted wound on his forehead and a couple of jagged holes in his side that appeared to be mending well. Jubal felt better for the moment, having stated to himself a few simple facts. He smiled, thinking about something his pa had said. *A person has to take oneself to the woodshed from time to time. You got to look inside, tell the truth to yourself.* He bundled Pru's body into his arms and edged out of his damp shelter.

Jubal felt no pain on his trip down Morning Peak. Only a quiet sensation in his hip. Pru felt light, like she was a part of him.

The charred remains of the family barn lay in the distance, the house and front yard bordered by a copse of singed cottonwood and ponderosa. Jubal sat down behind a large boulder and took it all in.

As he poked his way through the damp forest, a small strawberry bush yielded a handful of bitterly unique fruit. It reminded him of Pru and ma making a tart strawberry jelly that he so loved. It took nearly the entire morning to make his way to the valley floor. He paused occasionally, listening for sounds of the men, but felt they would have no need to return, since they had already ravaged everything in sight.

Still, he waited, listening to the sounds of the mountain, the whispered leaves and occasional high-pitched calls of the ravens. Young's Valley seemed at peace.

As he approached the homestead, something like music came across his ears. He hesitated, listening. It drifted from an area of the house hidden, from where he stood, by a stand of large pines, then waned. Faint lilting sounds hung in the air. A strong breeze moved the branches of the surrounding trees, and he realized he was listening to his mother's wind chimes, still hanging on what was left of the front porch.

"Jube, what have you done, dear?" Jubal's ma said to his pa.

"Oh, it's nothing, really. Just a poor copy of a thing I saw hanging in McNeil's store. I was going to buy it, but I thought we could use the money best on bacon and salt."

Jubal's father had made the chimes from broken glass, horseshoe nails, and long strands of rawhide. He had hung a worn-out rim from his wife's small garden wheelbarrow horizontally, then strung the glass and hardware with bits of baling wire.

She loved it.

"I'd wondered where my long-lost thimble went." She looked closely at the hanging apparatus.

Pru giggled.

Bea continued, "Hmmm, and there's the other half of those broken scissors. Will miracles never cease?"

The family burst into grins when a breeze kicked up and teased a melody from the glass and horseshoe nails, all clinking together in a delicate symphony. Pru, standing with arms raised, announced the "Young Family's Mountain Orchestra!"

The pile of gingham rags that once were his mother's lay in a sodden mess. The rain had diluted the rust-colored bloodstains. As Jubal made his way to the back side of the barn, he dreaded seeing his father's body.

Half the barn was destroyed, and the fire had finally burned through the rope, depositing his father's broken body on the damp earth. Upon inspection, it appeared as though the renegades had taken their fallen brethren with them.

Jubal sifted through the charred timbers of the farmhouse. A blackened chair in his room, stark among the waste. A trunk with old clothes at the foot of his parents' bed, still intact.

He bathed his wounded side, then wrapped one of his mother's tattered dresses around his waist. He raised it first to his face and wept at the soft scent of his ma's lilac-water perfume. He reprimanded himself for his indulgence and continued to prod around the gutted remains. An oval-shaped tin of talcum powder with an elegant sailboat on the lid reminded him of earlier, better times.

"Tell us about your voyage, Ma." Prudence loved the story of her mother's trip from Ireland.

"Pru, sweetheart, you've heard that story so many times."
"Please, Ma."

Jubal sat in a charred hard-backed chair and stared red-eyed at the oddments of the living room. The roof of the house, gone. The two walls left upright formed an L shape opposite the stone fireplace, standing like a soot-covered gravestone.

"Tell the story, Bea, the children love it."
Jubal could feel his sister's excitement as his mother told of the thunderous storm that hit the good ship Bonne Daye.

"We were all so very sick, near to thirty days at sea. The waves beat terribly against the sides of the boat, tossing us like skirts on a windy-day clothesline. My daddy, your grandfather, said if he lived through this, he was going to put a boat's oar over his shoulder and walk inland and the first person who asked what it was, that would be where he put down his roots."

Jubal loved his father's stories. She loved her mother's.

"Jube, the children want to hear about your exploits. Tell about your fishing days."

"Bea, I was trying to make a living. There were few 'exploits,' as you describe them."

"Weren't you swept overboard once, Pa?" Prudence asked. *"Where was it, off Halifax or someplace?"*

Jubal could still see his father taking time to light his pipe.

"It was off Prince Edward Island, we were a group of four boats. Mostly youngsters like me—"

"Youngsters"—it was hard to believe his father had ever been a young man. And now? He could never get any older.

Jubal poked around in the ashes of his home for several hours. A small round-topped chest, blackened, stood next to his parents' bed, the little steamer trunk's brass lock and fittings holding it together. He opened it and found inside a locket of his mother's. The fire had fused the clasp to the thin chain.

A silver brooch in a half-moon shape had survived intact. Jubal picked it up, rubbed the dust away, and slipped it into his pocket. His mother's Bible, protected in a leather-bound pouch, held papers and old letters stuffed between the pages. Jubal carefully removed the crinkled souvenirs, then placed them back in the leather pouch for storage in the root cellar. The Bible, he decided, would for now accompany him inside his shirt. He discovered a delicate ring Prudence kept in a painted tin box. His father's soot-covered pistol lay in the ashen rubble of the kitchen cabinet, the wood handle partially burned away but the tarnished steel frame of the weapon still in one piece.

"We were snot-nosed youngsters and this ole gal who ran the Blue Heron in Halifax—"

"She ran a blue heron?" interrupted Pru.

"The lady was the proprietor of a drinking establishment called the Blue Heron." Pa smiled. "Audrey was huge and didn't take guff from any of the rowdies. A couple of them got to squabbling, and this . . . Amazon, I guess would be the best way to describe her—"

Pru looked to her mother for an explanation of the strange word.

"Greek mythology, dear. Female warriors."

"Do you want to hear this story or not?"

"*Yes, Jube, dear, please proceed.*"

Pru and Jubal giggled as their father continued.

"*Well, this old gal grabbed these two ruffians by the scruff of their necks and marched them right out the door. When she came back she stood in the center of the saloon. 'Any and all you roughnecks want to get to fussing and fighting in my drinking house, step up.'*" *Jubal, Sr., paused.* "*I still remember the silence that drifted over that room. You could hear a mouse breathing. God a-mighty, she was challenging all of us.*" *He had a faraway, bemused look.* "*Years later when I won that weapon in a poker game, I named it after her.*"

Pru raised her hand to ask a question. "*But, Pa, why does a stinky old gun have to have a name?*"

"*It doesn't really, sweetheart. It was just something that reminded me of a different time in my life.*"

"*A better time?*"

"*No, just different. More hectic, kind of full of youthful troubles and the like. Audrey the Argument-Settler. Never really had to use it in that regard. Fact is, it was never really loaded, but it was always there . . . just in case I ever needed it.*"

In a cracked mason jar in the root cellar, Jubal found a few bullets that had survived. He pocketed them, in case Audrey would need to settle any new arguments.

SIX

He had never fired a pistol. His father's gun had always been treated as a sacred object, kept hidden and rarely taken from its dark sanctuary. Now Jubal held it, moving the weapon slowly in his hands, pleased with its weight. When he pushed the release tab for the cylinder, it opened partially, soot and ash restricting its movement. Jubal shook the gun and blew hard against the machined pieces to clear them of debris. Once open, the cylinder spun freely. He slid six rounds into the awaiting chambers and pushed the apparatus back into place. It seated with a satisfying click.

He carried the pistol at his side and walked the perimeter of the small valley, wishing he could come upon just one of the men who had raided the farm. A noise from inside the tree line startled him. He spun toward the sound and fired, the slug ricocheting off a large rock several yards to the right of where he'd aimed.

The white tail of a fawn retreated swiftly through the thick forest.

Startled, not only at the power of the gun but at the undisciplined response he had to the deer in the woods, Jubal realized he had a lot to learn about Audrey. She was risky, as his father had warned, and needed to be handled with care and respect.

Jubal stood in the open yard in front of the family house, guessing this ruined shell was now his. He would find the rest of the devils who did this, and he would make them explain their reasons, just before they begged forgiveness from their sainted mothers. He would shout to them as they lay on their heathen backs, staring up at him from the bottom of their earthen pit.

He slept in the root cellar, on a bed of straw salvaged from the barn, using smoky patchwork quilt remnants and tattered curtains from the house to keep warm. Everything smelled like smoke.

Awakened by the sound of a high-pitched whinny and approaching hoofbeats, Jubal quickly found his slim rifle. He cracked open the cellar door and listened. If the bastards were back, he would be ready for them.

The hoofbeats grew louder, and a shadow crossed his line of vision. He felt relief when he realized it was Frisk, one of his pa's draft horses. She wandered about, tossing her head, snorting and fractious, her mane singed by fire. Jubal spoke softly and led her by the halter to a tree stump, where he mounted her. He coaxed her several times around the yard. Protesting, she danced in tight circles, but the warmth from her back reassured him. The horse, alive and familiar, was a solid thing he could hold on to. He stroked her neck, gentling her.

Jubal chose a small rise on the north boundary of the valley to bury his family. Frisk, hooked to the buckboard, served as a bearer to transport the bodies.

He dug three separate graves and laid his family to rest. Prudence in the center, sheltered on either side by her parents. He had washed their faces, straightened their clothing, and lowered them into the fresh ground, still moist from the melting winter snows.

He recited from his mother's Bible, and afterward he returned the earth as he had found it.

Jubal loaded the wagon with as much food as he could find, emptying the root cellar of other provisions he thought might be of help. He took his time gathering what was left of the leather tack from the toolshed and put together dried jerky and beets from his mother's larder. His father's rain-soaked hat smelled of damp tobacco. Snapping it several times against his leg, he tried it on and was pleased at the fit. The remains of several burnt-cornered books lay in the rubble. *The Count of Monte Cristo* in the center of the pile had survived. Less fortunate, *Don Quixote,* burned to an almost perfect oval shape, the text in the center of the pages barely readable. Jubal riffled through the scorched pages, stopping occasionally to read snippets of Quixote's pleas. "'. . . my endeavor not to disappoint . . .'" It was as if the character were speaking to him. "'. . . even at the expense of my life, or even more, if more were possible.'" *Strange.* He held the book in his hands. "Wait and hope."

With Frisk hitched to the buckboard, he drove out of

the valley not really knowing where he was going, thinking he should tell someone of this occurrence—who that should be, he wasn't quite sure.

At the crest of a hill, Jubal looked back, the wasted farm standing out in sharp contrast to its verdant surroundings. He was reminded of one of his pa's favorite sayings. *If you can stand on a hill and look back at your land with your arms outstretched, and your land exceeds your fingertips, you're in God's graces, indeed.*

Frisk snorted as if something were in the air. Jubal turned her and proceeded northwest.

After nearly an hour, a trail opened through a pleasant valley, the place where his family had driven through on their last trip into Cerro Vista.

> *Jubal's father guided the team carefully into town.*
> *"Pa, can I get a what's-you-call-it? A sarsaparilla?"*
> *"And a hard candy, if Old Man McNeil has them still." Jubal, Sr., regarded his wife and daughter. "Spend anything your hearts desire, girls—as long as it's under four dollars."*
> *The women chuckled as they dismounted and went into McNeil's, while Jubal, Sr., asked his son to take the wagon down to Blacksmith Charley to have a look at Frisk's right rear shoe.*
> *Jubal nodded, proud to be given the responsibility. "Sure, Pa. Where you off to?"*
> *"I've got to see Will Davis about our land transfer. Evidently nothing important, a few papers to be signed, something about the former owner. Shouldn't be long." With a wave, he stepped down from the buckboard.*

Jubal wheeled the wagon around and pointed Frisk back toward Charley's. As usual, a crowd was gathered at the blacksmith's, the favorite place for locals to hang out and swap stories. "I hear tell he was so fast he could blow out a candle and be in bed before it got dark."

Waving to the storyteller, he asked if Charley was in. "He's in, all right, but that's about it." He made a weaving movement as if drunk, much to the delight of the hangers-on.

After arranging for Charley to have a look at Frisk, Jubal drifted back down the street toward Davis and the land office. He stopped in front of the gun shop to gaze at the assortment of pistols and rifles while hearing the echo of his father's advice. "A gun, boy, is a tool, and only as good as the carpenter using it. Keep it in mind. They're not toys and shouldn't be thought of as such."

Having had his fill of weaponry, he moved on, watching the parade of folks, most of them walking on the sunny side of the street. Opposite the land office, his father stood on the sidewalk facing a tall gray-haired man.

"Hold on, there, friend."

Who was Pa calling "friend"? And why did he say it in that way that sounded like he was trying to be calm?

Jubal's father took a nonthreatening step toward the man, his palms flattened in front of him in a placating manner.

This eccentric-looking dude with gray hair and youngish face wore a black duster and shiny, pin-sharp boots. The unbuttoned coat showed off his striped mauve vest and heavily decorated gun belt. A gray flat-brimmed hat with long braided leather strings kept his headgear secured tight under his chin. Even at a distance, Jubal could tell his eyes were colorless and mean. A number of his friends were gathered behind him. They *seemed disreputable, all mismatched. A couple of Indians, maybe half-breeds, several Mexicans, and four or five white fellows who had adorned themselves with bandoliers draped over their shoulders.*

He turned to survey his hearty band of rebels. One of the most notable, a black-haired desperado with scraggly mustache, kept urging on the leader.

"Kick his farmer's ass, Tauson." The man danced about, showing off for his compatriots. Pulling back his long coat, he cocked his hip to reveal a bone-handled pistol. "Hey, Tauson, let me take care of your light work. You can hold my coat while I trounce that vegetable-peddler."

The gray-haired man took offense at his compatriot's jeering.

"Shut your hole, Pete, I'm busy."

Pete's audacity fascinated Jubal. The man walked half-way across the street backward, arms stretched to his sides as if in mock surrender, pretending to be afraid.

"Oh, sweet Jesus, help me in my hour of need." He put his hands together in the gesture of prayer. "The boss man has spoken and my ass is a-tightenin', Jesus. Show me the way to salvation and temperance."

The rest of the men in the gang enjoyed Pete's antics. Though Jubal, Sr., took a step back, his son thought a part of him wanted to dive into Tauson and pound his face.

A shot rang out, and the fancy wooden ball on the arched top of the land office sign went whistling through the air. Pete spun his .44 around his trigger finger and slid the weapon back into his holster. "You ever seen such shooting, Tauson? Why don't you gun the fellow down? Sooner or later you're gonna have to do it."

Tauson took a step toward the shooter. "Damn your eyes, Wetherford. Stay out of my business. I'll deal with the sodbuster when I see fit." The man turned back to Jubal's father. "You cheated me, mister, that's the square of it. It doesn't matter if it were legal or not."

Jubal's father gazed at the sky in apparent disbelief, then walked away.

The man called out. "I'll have my day, make no mistake about it. Auction or no, you hear?"

Jubal caught his father's attention, who signaled at him with his eyes in a way that said, Stay away. Jubal kept on the far sidewalk as the lanky fellow walked after his father.

"I'll be paying you a visit, farmer. So mind your night prayers."

Jubal, Sr., hesitated, looking as if he wanted to turn and belly up to the man, but instead he walked away, half smiling.

The gang continued to argue on the street, Tauson shouting at Pete. "Dammit all to hell. Wetherford, I told you to stay the hell outta my business, you hear?"

Pete reached down with both hands and cradled his crotch. "Or what?"

"What do you mean, 'or what'?"

"'Or what' means what are you big enough to do, Billy? I was just having a giggle with that farmer." The man yelled toward Jubal and his father. "You want a handful of this, pig-sticker? Say the word and we can do it."

With his hands still cupped around his privates, he started walking to Jubal, Sr., ignoring Tauson, much to the delight of his friends. The more they cheered him on, the more animated his walk became.

"Step away, son," *Jubal's father whispered*. "This bastard is out of control."

A loud command from Tauson slowed the monkey walk. "Wetherford, stop the foolishness and come on back. Now."

Pete turned to face his friends and boss. He giggled and spoke in a child's voice. "But, Da-da, I want to go pee-pee on the farmer man."

Tauson walked away in disgust while Pete turned back to Jubal, Sr. "Do farmer man and his"—he winked at Jubal— "daughter want to play paddy cake with Petey boy?" He was even closer now. Dropping his hands from his crotch, he raised them into fists, chest-high.

"Why don't you leave us alone?" Jubal had never seen anyone act so blatantly foolish. "None of this is any of your business, mister."

Jubal's father reached across to secure his son's arm. "Easy, this fellow's just drunk. He'll be moving along directly." He nodded toward the man. "Won't you?"

Pete hesitated and reached toward his pistol, but his long coat had worked its way from behind the holster and now smothered the six-shooter. Jubal's father lunged forward, grabbing Pete's right hand, driving his shoulder into the man's chest.

They both went down as Jubal scrambled along the ground next to them, grabbing Pete's .44 from under his coat. He held the gun by its barrel, ready to crack the man's head if needed. "Got his gun, Pa."

"Watch out for the rest of them, son." Jubal's father secured Pete with his arm tucked up under his shoulder blade. Jubal watched as Pete's friends started moving down the street toward the fight, the gun hanging limp in Jubal's hand.

A group of townspeople crowded around the two men wrestling on the ground. Shop owners and customers deserted their pursuits to be entertained by the rowdy display in the center of the busy street, cheering on the combatants as if this were a paid circus.

Pete kicked back hard against Jubal, Sr.'s leg and spun around, but his exit was blocked by a knee driven into his groin.

"That should give you something special to hold on to, mister." Jubal, Sr., took the pistol from his son and broke open the breech, emptying the bullets into his hand and tossing them into a nearby water trough.

Pete writhed on the ground, his hands firmly holding his crotch.

Jubal, Sr., bent over him. "Have some respect for others. This land business with your jefe Tauson is never your mind, you hear?" He dropped the pistol in the dirt.

The gathered townspeople cheered, swelling Jubal's chest with pride. As they walked to the blacksmith's shop to retrieve the wagon, his father said, "That was a brave thing you did, Jube. Taking that gun when we were scuffling around on the ground. What would you have done if he'd gotten the better of me?"

"I don't know, Pa." Jubal paused. "It didn't occur to me that I would have to do anything as long as I had the gun."

"Maybe you've got a point." He smiled. "He who has the gun, rules. Unfortunate, but true. Mind you, recognize that things can change very quickly. As I've said before, a gun can be a useful tool, but in the wrong hands, dangerous to a fault."

Pru and his mother were already in the wagon. "Jube, dear, you look a mess," she said to her husband. "What happened to your clothes?"

"I was larking around with some jaybird and tripped and fell." He swung easily up to the wagon seat. "Jube here was a big help. He stepped in and . . . saved the day. Guess I'm getting old, tripping over my big feet." He smiled at his wife and clicked his tongue to the horses.

Jubal wondered what his pa would have done to the guy Pete if he hadn't been there. He suspected it would have ended very differently.

As they made their way back to Young's Valley that evening, Jubal asked his father what had happened.

"Jube, it's a case of a man making a number of poor decisions. Billy Tauson is a scoundrel and he runs with a pack of equally rotten ne'er-do-wells."

Nearly an hour later, Jubal asked his pa if he would mind stopping for a few minutes.

"Sure enough, son. I'm sure your ma and sis would appreciate a rest also."

While the ladies wandered off, Jubal spoke to his father. "Pa, if you look over my right shoulder, back about a hundred yards just inside the tree line, you'll see a horse and rider from town, an Injun. I'm pretty sure he was with the others you were having that set-to with."

Without looking, Jubal, Sr., answered, "My oldest and onliest son has developed a keen sense. Very good, Jube. Yep, he's been following us for near to an hour, and as for him being with that group, you're right again. You'd think if he were a proper scout he would at least not wear such a bright yellow string to hold on his hat. Believe his name is Crook Arm.

Peculiar, in a way. They know where we live, why bother to track us? That jackass Tauson—"

"That's the tall, gray-haired man?"

"Yes, he used to own our plot of land. I expect they're just trying to pester us. One thing's for sure, they can't eat us—that's against the law."

SEVEN

The weathered road came to a fork, one way leading north to Colorado, the other west to Cerro Vista. Jubal was tempted to push on north, but he knew he had to tell his story to the authorities, even though he couldn't truthfully explain the death of his father without getting himself in trouble. His impulse was to ride away from all the carnage.

But he had to do what was right. He veered west toward Cerro Vista.

As he approached the fork, a slight movement off to his left at the edge of the woods startled Jubal. A dappled gray mare grazed along the fringe of the tree line, looking skittish, with her reins looped over the saddle horn. Oddly, her rider had left the horse with the reins untied. Jubal walked slowly to the animal.

"What you doing out here all alone, huh?"

The horse backed away and whinnied loudly.

"She needs water, Mr. Rifleman," came a voice from behind. "Fact of the matter, so do I."

As Jubal turned, he saw a young man who seemed close to his own age lying half propped against a ponderosa. A .44-caliber pistol with dirt caked into the barrel and side rested limply in one hand. The front of his flannel shirt was streaked with dried blood.

"Don't you concern your mind about this here hogleg, boy. It's dirty, but it'll still bust you up to a fare-thee-well, so just hustle back to your buckboard and get me water before I put a round in your chest like you did me."

Jubal recognized the young man as part of the group of renegades back at the farm. The gunshot wound in his upper torso was from Jubal's rifle.

"Get me some water, dammit. Go on, git."

The wounded cowboy seemed weak, and Jubal doubted if he could even pull the trigger, but there was something about his helplessness. Jubal's rifle lay under the seat of the buckboard, his water canteen hung in plain view on the side of the wagon. He hesitated, then retrieved the water and stepped carefully toward the slumped young man.

"Just set it down careful-like, boy. Don't try anything brave, or I'll open *you* up. My name is Ty and I'm a shootist." Trying to muster some bravura, he fell short of a sneer. He held the gun in one hand and struggled with the stopper on the canteen. In exasperation, he threw it at Jubal's feet. "Open it, damn it. Go on."

Jubal opened the canteen and started pouring the contents onto the ground at the renegade's feet. "Set that pistol down or I'll pour all this water out."

The gunman attempted to cock the pistol, trying to show he was still in the game.

As he did so, Jubal swung the canteen by its strap, easily slapping the .44 to the ground. He calmly retrieved the weapon, stuffing it into his belt while Ty slumped in defeat.

Jubal handed the canteen to his enemy. "I ought to let you die of thirst, you bastard."

The wounded man whimpered behind him. "They did me dirt, the scoundrels. Left me for dead," he wailed, full of self-pity. "I rode with those men near on two years, and this is how they treat me. Billy Tauson's my cousin, for gosh sakes. Said he'd come back for me once they caught and skinned you alive, but he lied. I waited a couple hours, then struggled up on Ned here and made it this far before I slipped off."

Jubal turned away.

"Don't leave me. I'll pay you whatever you need. Don't leave. I need some fixin'."

He couldn't leave this person out here to die. Jubal walked to the slumping form, pulled him away from the tree, and wrapped both arms around him to drag him to the buckboard.

The cowboy screamed as Jubal hoisted him into the wagon and slid the gate back into place so the lout wouldn't fall. "Dammit, kid, do you have to be so rough?"

Jubal didn't answer as he tied the fellow's horse to the back of the wagon and clicked his tongue to Frisk while pulling away.

He had to take the swine into Cerro Vista. It would have been preferable to have left him for the wolves, but Jubal knew he wouldn't sleep if he did. But he wasn't sleeping too well as it was, so maybe it wouldn't have mattered.

"I didn't harm your kinfolk back there. Nope, wasn't me. Was Tauson, Petey, and the rest of them. There's a pistolero for you—Pete 'Repeat' Wetherford. He's another story. I tell you, you're lucky he didn't latch onto your butt. He'd a straightened you out, that's for sure. Never seen anything like him. Toughest sumbitch I ever laid these weepers on, ole Pete. Can you maybe dodge a few of them potholes, pard? That little round you put into me is botherin' my breath some, I'm gonna shut up now and rest for a bit. . . ."

The wheels of the wagon seemed to search out the potholes.

"Did you pick up my iron? That piece cost me a pretty penny, accurate 'til hell wouldn't have it. I tell you, son . . . no, I never touched your folks. It was the others. I kept telling them to ease up . . . we just came for payback. Old Billy Tauson got all embarrassed 'cause of your pa. Tauson's the boss of the group. The bastard said we'd just have some fun with you folks 'cause he lost the farm to you all. Got outta hand, I reckon. But most everyone does what Billy says, even Pete Wetherford. Though in a one-on-one Petey would lick him. Except for gunplay, then it's anybody's guess. But old Billy Tauson is just a natural kinda leader, the devil." He grimaced, then immediately started groaning.

They rode in silence for a few minutes before he started up again.

"I figured it were your pa who had the argument, front of the land office . . ." He paused. "That was him, right? He looked to be a good hand. I couldn't hear what he told Tauson, but ole Billy was one sober sumbitch when we all got back together. Come to think on it, so was Petey, your pa twisted his arm right smart. No wonder he was so riled up at the farm. Kept yelling, 'Kill 'em all, boys!' Tauson was running 'round like a sissy schoolteacher. But hell, he started it. In town, I remember he told Crook Arm, the Injun, to trail you back to your ranch. Betcha didn't know that, did you? Ha, ha. I said to them, 'Don't bother the womenfolk, boys. That wouldn't be good.' I can't honestly say whether they did or not. I drift off when things get kinda heavy—"

Jubal gave Frisk some right-hand rein so the wagon wheel would drop into a large hole. It bounced out immediately, followed by the back wheel doing the same.

"Goddammit, can't you drive this cussed thing? If'n I didn't know better, I'd say you were a . . ." He groaned, then picked up where he left off. "I heard the boys a-gigglin' and carryin' on, but as I said, that wasn't for me. No, sir, my mama didn't raise no rape person, huh-uhh, nosirree. I kept telling Petey, 'Pete, it ain't right, I tell ya.' But nobody tells Pete nothing, uh-huh . . . what a guy. Makes me chuckle to think on it. We was all in Abilene, Kansas, and there was this ole gal what could do things with her private parts that would make a body tie up in fits. Well, she didn't shine up to Petey so good—"

Jubal stopped the wagon and slapped Frisk on the rump. She snapped against her traces, shaking the buckboard with a mighty lurch.

"Dammit to hell!"

After the punishing jolt, Ty sniffled and carried on for a while, then finally drifted off to sleep.

After a mile or so, Jubal heard him stirring.

"What would you say, farmer, if I was to simply mount my horse and ride on out of here. What would you say?"

Jubal didn't answer, just gestured with his hand as if to say, *Help yourself.*

"The bed of this wagon stinks. Looks all nasty with blood and shit and stuff. Don't you have a blanket I could put under my head, for Christ's sake?" He snickered. "Yeah, old Petey and I'll be friends 'til the day we die."

"Day before yesterday," said Jubal.

"What'd you say? I didn't understand. I wasn't condoning what Petey does, I simply said we would be—"

"I heard what you said, Ty, and I said, 'Day before yesterday.' That's when you and your friend Petey ceased being friends."

"Why's that?"

"It's baffling. Your bosom pal, Petey, didn't mention you the last I saw him. Oh, he talked about a lot of folks. . . . I could hear him bouncing down the ravine, yelling threats. Your Mexican pal Jorge, his trip was . . . I think the word is 'unencumbered.' Yeah, Petey reached deep into the darkness. Your tough friend managed to go down a list of people he wished to be damned—his mother 'the filthy whore', his father, I think, he described as a 'rotten bastard', and, ah, yes, me. A rotten pup whom his friends, guess that would include you, should castrate. Yeah, Petey might have lived for an hour, maybe. I hope so. I pray the pain enveloped him in hot misery until he breathed his last." The dull pain in Jubal's hip aggravated him. He shifted on the hard buckboard seat.

"I don't believe you," Ty finally said. "Petey dead? Nah. Huh-uh."

"Petey didn't die well, Ty. No, both Pete and Jorge entertained me for several long seconds while they tumbled, shouting their guts out." Jubal tried to rein in his anger but couldn't. "The blood and waste on the wagon floor, by the way, are from my family. If you open your mouth again before we get to town, Ty, I'll let you hop and skip on in to Cerro Vista on your own, agreed?"

"Nobody kills Pete Wetherford." He took an instant. "All right, agreed."

The buckboard creaked its way toward town. Jubal dug his mother's Bible from inside his shirt, wrapped the reins around his arm, and leafed through the worn pages. He tried to recall a quote about weakness his ma used to repeat. He couldn't remember if it was from the Bible or not. He pictured his mother standing proud at the cabin door. "Weakness is—" No, it was "cruelty." "All cruelty springs from weakness," she'd said.

EIGHT

Cerro Vista had a welcoming feel, the locals all pleasantly busy. A man called out to Jubal, "What's you hauling, sonny?" Main Street was lined up with mostly wood-frame buildings, each looking much like its neighbor. A few adobe-style homes dotted the street, but most of them had been converted to boardinghouses or small dry goods stores. The Wicks, a grand Victorian and Cerro Vista's only hotel, stood at the end of the street.

Jubal made his way to the county jail. Built in the pueblo style, it consisted of four small cells constructed with crude metal poles, each area with its own bucket to serve as a privy. A short hallway and wall separated the large open room's barred cubicles from the small office up front.

Jubal tied Frisk to the rail and stepped inside. He found two desks, each with a man behind it, asleep. "Excuse me, Sheriff?"

"What the—" The larger of the two sat up, red of face, with a heavy handlebar mustache. "Don't you believe in knocking on a door before you enter, child?"

"Sorry, sir. The door was open. I just thought—"

The man called out to the other sleeper, "Wake up, Ron. Hell's fire. You can't get no help these days." His attention came back to Jubal. "You look to be somebody what was shot at and missed, shat at and hit." He grinned at his own joke. "What's eatin' at you, laddie?"

Jubal didn't think it funny. "I've got a young guy in my wagon been shot in the chest." He walked toward the door. "He's in a bad way."

The heavyset lawman stepped outside and yelled once again at his deputy. He looked at Jubal's passenger, who had returned to his moaning. Deputy Ron finally came stumbling out the front door, rubbing his face.

"Ron, carry yourself down to the hotel and get Doc Brown here, quick-like."

It wasn't more than five minutes before a harried-looking older man in a suit vest and black string tie came hustling down the street. "Where is he?"

The sheriff pointed toward the back of the open wagon.

The older gentleman examined Ty. "Anybody know how this happened?"

Jubal looked to the sheriff, then back to the doctor. "He was shot."

The doctor continued tending to the pale gunman. "I can readily see that, youngster."

"By whom?" asked the sheriff.

Jubal paused. "Me."

The sheriff watched Jubal. "Ron, climb up on that buckboard. You and Doc here, take that shot-up boy back to the doc's office at the hotel. You hear?"

"I'm on it, Sheriff. Just you watch my smoke."

"Mind my horse, sir." This from Jubal.

The sheriff signaled for Jubal to follow him back into the jail, where he gestured for the young man to take a seat. They sat looking at each other far too long for Jubal's comfort.

"I'm gonna let you think on some things for a minute or so. I'll be tending some 'portant business in the back." He made this sound like a great secret between them. "Okay by you, sonny?"

Jubal looked around the sparse office. A faded picture of an older man with a badge and gun held a strong family resemblance to the sheriff who was "tending business" in the back. A shelf behind the desk held several rifles and a shotgun. Framed documents on the wall proclaimed Bufort L. Morton a stellar public servant. A newspaper article stated the sheriff had been instrumental in the capture of Harry Walls, a desperate wife-beater and chicken thief. *With credentials like that, Sheriff Morton will round up the raiders of the Young family farm in no time at all.*

As Jubal waited, he relived the past two days, not really regretting anything he had done, except the way his father had died. He was caught in a trap of memory as the sheriff's couple minutes expanded to nearly half an hour, until he heard voices coming from the back, where he thought the cells to be.

With an explosion of energy, the big man burst back

into the room. He plopped down in his swivel chair. "You want to tell me about it, son?"

Jubal let out a sigh. "I was hunting up around Morning Peak—"

"And this fellow just happened to step in front of your rifle, correct?"

"No, sir. Not exactly. I'm sorry to say I shot him on purpose."

Morton grew a huge grin. "So you shot him for good reason, but you're sorry you did it. By the way, I assume that's his horse tied to the back of your buckboard, right?"

Jubal couldn't keep up with the sheriff's interrogation. "I was on the mountain and saw smoke rising from our place in the valley, so I ran—"

"Why'd you take his horse? By the way, what's your name?"

"Jubal Young, sir—"

"I better write this down," he mumbled. "Just to keep it straight." He retrieved a sheaf of paper and pen before nodding. "You shot the fellow, then started to run home 'cause you saw smoke, then what?"

"No, sir. I saw the smoke, then once I got down to the farm there were a whole bunch of these renegades hollering around our place."

"Renegades. You mean deserters? Indians? That shot-up youngster don't look to be a 'breed. What do you mean?"

"No, sir. They weren't Indians. Well, a couple of them might have been. The rest were just rowdies pa and I had seen here down by the land office last week sometime."

Sheriff Morton tapped his pen against his worn desk.

"So you came upon these so-called desperadoes and shot one of them, correct?"

Jubal felt his eyes starting to well up. "No, sir. I shot several of them, because—"

"Oh." Morton held up his hand for Jubal to stop. "So this gang of grown men were dancing and carrying on around your farm, you come home from hunting squirrels—"

"Rabbits."

"All right, rabbits, and decide you'd wing a couple rounds at them. What did they do, son, let you take pot-shots? Mercy me, you're gonna have to do better than that. Who were these terrible men, sonny?"

"I don't know all their names. One of the Indians was Broke Arm or Crook Arm, I don't recall." He started to get impatient, but he wanted to get everything straight. "And another, who has gone dead now, was named Pete something. Warefort or Wetherfort."

"You're talking about Petey Wetherford. Know him well. What did Petey have to do with all this? By the way, where is he?"

"Like I said, sir. Dead."

"The hell you say. Petey Wetherford dead? Who did him?"

Jubal remained silent.

"You? Bullshit, son. You killed Petey. . . . How?"

"I lured him onto a log stretching across a ravine. When he was halfway, I shifted the log and he fell. He and a Mexican named Jorge."

"Let me get this right. You saw smoke, there were a bunch a ne'er-do-wells dancing about your farm. You shot one of them—or was it several?—then coaxed the rest of them onto a tree trunk and jiggled them to death."

"Sheriff, you can make light of this if you want, but these people—" Jubal could feel himself getting angry. "These low-life bastards killed my family, dammit."

"So you say. Who saw any of this?"

"Me."

"And who in hell are you?" The sheriff bolted to his feet. "Walking in here with some bullshit story, and getting uppity when questioned. You best tend your behavement. I'll slap your ass behind bars. *Com-pren-de?*"

Jubal acknowledged that he indeed understood and held his anger. "It wasn't all of them on the log, only two. The rest were taking the long way around."

"I don't understand any of that. How did you know their names? They tell you?" The sheriff seemed to be enjoying himself in a mean-spirited way.

"No, they didn't tell me, sir. I heard them talking, and that Billy Tauson, the big gray-haired one, the leader, he's the one my pa had trouble with here in town."

"Damn. This is getting better and better. Why don't you start once more at the beginning and see if you can tell it straight without any storybook? Start with the first one you shot, the feller in back of your wagon."

Jubal closed his eyes and steeled himself to tell the truth. In for a penny, in for a pound. "He wasn't the first one. The first one was out back of the barn where they tied my—"

Deputy Ron burst through the door. "That ole boy didn't make it, Sheriff. Passed on to his reward with a big bubble of blood comin' out his mouth. Nasty. He kept talking right to the end, though." The deputy pulled his chair up close to Jubal. "I gotta get a good look at this gunner, Sheriff. He's a jimmy cracker, I'll tell ya."

Fascinated, the deputy took a hard stare at Jubal, then leaned back. "Doc did whatever he could, then called Father McBride, who happened to be having supper at the hotel. The long and short of it, Sheriff, is that this here snip of a kid you're talking to went on a killing spree."

Morton rocked in his chair. "That's what I'm finding out. This youngster says he killed ole Petey Wetherford and some Mexican up toward Morning Peak."

"Hell, no. Petey? Sheriff, that ain't the half of it. This yehoo kilt his whole damn family."

"I didn't kill my family. The men here in town who had a run-in with my pa did it. Out of revenge 'cause my pa had a disagreement with this fellow Billy Tauson—"

"Hell's fire, you admitted you shot that Ty—"

"When the good Father were giving that ole boy his last rites, I heard him going on about the family deaths, and when the priest asked him who killed the family he said in a rattly voice, 'the son,' and just kept mumbling it over and over. 'The son, the son.' Damn, it were kind of scary. Why would the son do something like that? Lordy."

"He wasn't saying I did it," Jubal blurted. "He was saying *Tau*son. *Tau*-son. Billy *Tau*son. When I came down off the mountain they were all dead." Jubal stopped. *They weren't all dead, were they, Jube?* He knew if he spoke the absolute truth these yokels wouldn't understand him.

The slow, pendulumlike movement of his father swinging in the barn splashed before him.

The sheriff put his feet on the desk. "Ron, I think we

got us a real desperado on our hands. Show our Mr. Young one of our accommodations in back, would you, please? We'll have Judge Wickham look into this in the morning."

Jubal felt as if the sheriff and deputy were having sport with him. Not really believing him, yet maybe wanting to hear his complicated story out of sheer boredom. It had been a mistake to bring the now-departed Ty Blake into this miserable town. But it was either that or leave him to the animals, and he knew he couldn't do that. "Sir, please, if you would just listen. They were burning our farm. When I arrived back from the mountain the place was an inferno. M-my family were lying about, all near to dead," he stammered. "Or, soon to be," he said, mostly to himself.

The sheriff dropped his feet from the desk and towered over Jubal. "What you mean, 'near to'? Were they all dead or what?"

"Yes, dammit, they're all dead . . . now." Jubal couldn't look at the man as Deputy Ron took him by the arm and opened the heavy door separating the office from the four cells.

With a rude shove from the back, the deputy moved Jubal into one of the tiny cells and locked the steel-barred door. "Nighty-night, Storyboy." He laughed as he slammed the solid wood door to the office.

Jubal heard the two men carrying on as if they'd just heard a great yarn. He slumped onto the hard steel cot.

NINE

"Hey, kiddo, you give a girl a smoke?"

Jubal was startled by a female voice with a thick accent.

"What's your name, señor? I am Maria. I've been in this outhouse for two days. They try to say I cheated one of my customers. Is joke on them, señor. I cheat all my customers because I pretend I luff them." She began to hum.

Jubal thought about what he had done to deserve this situation. "I'm sorry, miss. I don't smoke. My father used to, from time to time." Jubal had an image of his father grinning with a long thin cigar clamped between his teeth. "I tried it but it burned my throat. Sorry."

He paced in the cell, not understanding how he had gotten himself into this situation. He finally slumped down on the bunk and buried his head in his hands.

"What's your name, boy?" The woman hadn't spoken for quite some time while Jubal contemplated his fate.

Named after his father, he wondered if a name truly mattered. Presently he was known as "Accused Killer," which had a certain morbid catch to it. Or, to be more exact, "Murderer." But what, after all, is really in a name? "I am Jubal, miss. Jubal Young. You're Maria, correct?" He couldn't see her because of the wall between them, but thought she might be a pleasant person from the sound of her voice.

"My name is Consuela Maria Adelita Gomez, so I just go by Maria. It's more easy. So what's you in for, Jubals?"

He paused. "Can't really say. There was an incident at our place, our farm. It involved my family."

"*Ay, Cristo,* family, they are the death."

How right she was. "The death."

Neither said anything for a while. Then a soft Spanish voice, singing in broken English, filled the dark cell. "Oh, crazy moon, please take my troubled heart away. I sleep under a velvet sky, its clouds wrap my nightly stay. Better times, bet-ter times. *Tiempos mejores.*"

After a while, Jubal heard Maria softly crying. He was at a loss to think of something to say, so he kept to his own, then drifted off to the soundest sleep he'd had in days.

"Get up outta there, cowboy. The judge wants to see you."

Jubal's new day started with Deputy Ron's sour disposition. The door clanged open and Jubal, on shaky legs and with an aching side, wobbled out. He straightened his clothes and rubbed his morning face, taking care not to aggravate the gash on his forehead.

In the office, a pleasant-looking man in his late sixties sat at the sheriff's desk. "Have a seat, youngster, I'm Judge

Wickham. I preside over this county. I hear you've gotten yourself in a spot of trouble, is that right?"

"Well, sir, I thought it was other folks who were in trouble." Jubal hoped the judge had a more sympathetic ear than Sheriff Morton. "If you could let me tell my side of it, sir, I think I can clear everything up."

"We don't have any lawyers or such around here." The judge leaned back in his chair. "So I'm kind of it, son, do you understand? Be honest, but be careful what you say, right?"

"Yes, sir." Jubal turned to Ron. "Deputy, you think I might throw some water on my face so I could wake up a bit?"

"You look fine the way you are, Storyboy. Just turn around there and tend to business."

"I don't think this young man is going to make a run for it, Ron." The judge smiled, then changed his tone. "Take him out front to the pump and let him refresh himself, please."

The grumbling deputy escorted Jubal to the pump and water trough bordering the wood-slated sidewalk, where Jubal spied Frisk tied securely alongside the horse of the newly departed gunman, Ty.

While Jubal doused his head at the pump, Ron dug in his pocket and gave a lump of sugar to Ty's mare. "If you gave that mare the sugar, she'd a bit your hand off for what you done to her boyfriend Ty." He snorted and shoved Jubal back toward the office.

Inside, Judge Wickham looked through his notes. "The sheriff said you admitted shooting the man who died yesterday." The judge scanned the paper. "A certain Mr. Ty Blake, correct?"

Jubal nodded.

"You have to speak your answers, son, so I can write down your response."

"Yes, sir."

"'Yes, sir,' what? 'Yes, sir,' you understand, or 'Yes, sir,' you shot him?"

"Yes, sir, to both, sir."

"All right, sonny. Just start at the beginning and tell me the whole story."

In the telling, Jubal found himself reliving the heartache of the incidents and the thrill of revenge when he was able to pay back some of the despicable acts of barbarism the gang of desperadoes had committed. He tried to keep his voice calm, but it was difficult. He spoke for twenty long minutes, leaving nothing out, except certain pertinent details of how his father had died and the condition of his sister. In the end, he wept openly until Deputy Ron spoke up.

"Shoot, boy. How you gonna prove that palaver? Hell's fire."

"That's enough, Ron."

"But, Judge, it's his word against that ole boy Ty what's-his-name. Besides, we got us a dying declaration from Ty stating that the 'son' did it."

"Why was he there?" Jubal asked, trying to be resolute.

The deputy looked to the judge, who cleared his throat, "Who was where, son?

"Ty. Why was he at our farm? What were he and the others doing there? Send someone out to Morning Peak up that western slope. See if you don't find a couple of them with their noses buried in the rocks. What were they doing on my pa's land? If I killed my family, why would I bring that bastard Ty into town here, can you answer me that? Why? Wouldn't I just have lit out of there and let him rot? Why wouldn't I hightail it up to Canada or someplace? It doesn't make sense. What reason would I have to do such a thing—to bring him in here?"

"There were an ole boy down in Sonora I hear tell that did his whole family in, cousins and all." Deputy Ron looked around the room. "Course, he were Mexican, so maybe you can't rightly tell what he was thinking on."

"Deputy, for Christ's sake, watch your mouth," replied Judge Wickham. "Where's Morton?"

"Over to the hotel, on business, sir."

"Well, pry him out of the bar and tell him to organize some hands to go out to the Young property and find those folks in the canyon. We're going to have to dig up the family also."

"Damnation, Judge. What's to be pleased about stirring with bodies moldering in the ground being eaten on and such? Lordy."

"I suspect you'll do whatever I ask you to do or you'll go back to cleaning spittoons at Sloan's."

Ron stomped out the door, giving everyone his opinion on the way. "By all rights, Judge, that skinny Storyboy ought to be the one digging. He put 'em down there."

After the deputy's clumsy exit, Judge Wickham gathered his papers. "Guess we're forgetting one thing, aren't we, youngster?"

Jubal understood and walked himself back to his cell.

"I am going to hold you to your honor, son, I don't have a key to lock your cell. What say you?"

Jubal sat on his hard bunk. "I'm not going anywhere, sir."

"Mind you don't."

"If you want, Judge, I'll go out there with the posse to tend my family. I'd rather that than leave it to Deputy Ron and Sheriff Morton."

"That might be best. Maybe I'll go along, just in case." The judge tipped his hat.

Jubal wondered what "just in case" meant.

TEN

They left at midday, Jubal driving the buckboard. Ron, grousing about the long ride, kept up a steady stream of chatter. ". . . that feller's name, Martinez. Something like that. Kilt every livin' soul in his family at a get-together, never heard nothing like it."

Judge Wickham sat beside Jubal. "Never mind about that boor, son. There are people aplenty in this world who are honest, sensitive folk." He smiled. "Ron just doesn't happen to be one of them."

Seven of them traipsed up the long uphill grade from Cerro Vista to the Young family farm. The sheriff had insisted the doctor come along to have a look at the bodies. One fellow recruited by the sheriff fell asleep in the bed of the wagon, trying to snore away his hangover. A heavy ne'er-do-well named Tiny rode a small Indian paint that struggled with its weighty passenger.

As they rode into Young's Valley, the sheriff looked

to Jubal, who in turn pointed up to a small rise north of the meadow. Jubal had piled rocks atop the new graves, marking them with simple crosses. The sheriff ordered his boys to get started.

Jubal grabbed a pickaxe and started digging, only to be told by Sheriff Morton to step aside, as he wouldn't be needed. He glanced at Judge Wickham, who shrugged. Morton and Deputy Ron both took shovels, along with the two townies, and started in.

Relieved he wouldn't have to look into the dead faces of his family, Jubal drifted away. He sat with his back to them and gazed down into the valley at the devastated house and barn. It seemed all wrong to be back here. He honestly never thought he would see this land again.

The nightmare kept running, thankfully interrupted by the ignorant ranting of Deputy Ron.

"Lord, what we got here? Damn, Sheriff. They's all laying there like mummies taking a sleep."

"Ron, shut your face." The sheriff walked over to Doc Brown, who watched the proceedings with arms folded over his ample stomach. "Doc, what are you thinking? Wanna get down in there or should we pull them out?"

Jubal rose from his tree-supported seat, trotting across the wide meadow toward the homestead. He didn't want to be around for this.

"Don't be drifting too far off, there, cowboy," shouted Sheriff Morton. "You're not out of the woods yet. Not 'til the doc here tells us how these folk passed. Understand?"

Jubal waved his arm and continued on until he was out of sight. Arriving at the root cellar, he found that the blackened remains seemed sadder now. The sound of birds filled the air, flowers sprouted a kaleidoscope of color, and somewhere out toward Morning Peak a bald eagle echoed his protest into the distant canyon. All the life and beauty served as a contrast, making his family's destruction all the worse.

The entourage finally moved down to the homestead and found Jubal. Everyone had grown more reverential, even Deputy Ron.

"Get up on this buckboard, Storyboy," said Sheriff Morton. "Lead us into that there valley, canyon, or whatever you want to call it, and show us those other folk, what you killed on your so-called bridge."

"We'll not be able to go the whole way with the wagon, sir." Jubal took the reins. "We'll have to walk in the last half mile."

Morton grumbled as Jubal coaxed Frisk up the start of the trail. Once they reached the steepest part of the incline, they secured the horses to the surrounding trees and started hoofing it up the canyon's interior. It took nearly an hour before Jubal thought they were close to being near the log bridge.

"Somewhere here on the west side of the canyon, sir, that's where they fell." He pointed so the sheriff could see the ravine up ahead that dug into the canyon wall.

"You men spread out, take a look-see." The lawman stood rock-still. "Hold it. Did one of you say something? Quiet down."

They all settled.

"There it is again. Ah, hell, it's just a coyote or, no, dammit. Listen."

The wind moving through the canyon whispered in timed gusts, rustling the few trees and shrubs, fanning the prickly dry mesquite. Then Jubal heard it, too. A faint voice.

"Come on up here, fellows. . . ."

The men started moving up the lateral ravine. After thirty yards they heard a stronger plea.

"Give a body some nourishment."

"Lord God a-mighty. Sounds like Petey Wetherford," Deputy Ron said. He called into the ravine, "Where you at, Pete, you rotten ole two-timer?"

Jubal was sure this feeble voice would be the death of him.

ELEVEN

While the group hurried deeper into the ravine, Jubal held back, though he was curious as to how Wetherford would describe having arrived at his present happenstance. By the time he came upon the group, they all stood looking down at the battered form of Pete Wetherford, already spinning his side of things.

"A few of us were hunting, and this damn farmer . . ." He paused. "He seemed downright crazy." Wetherford looked around at the gathering to see how his story was being received. "Screaming about doings the rest of us couldn't understand. Messing with womenfolk, settin' fires. He was loco. Plumb loco."

"How'd you get here all busted up, Wetherford?" Wickham asked.

"Who are you, slick?"

"Judge Wickham of the Cerro Vista County seat. Answer my question, please."

"Well, hell's fire, ole Jorge and I were taking a shortcut down the rim of the canyon, when Jorge slipped and pushed me along with him for one hell of a ride."

Jubal felt an impulse to bust in and expose the truth of Wetherford's made-up tale.

"I grabbed some rock and brush along the way. I don't think the Mexican was so lucky. Give me some water. I'd be obliged."

Jubal stepped forward with his canteen. Now he wanted the man to see him. He opened the cloth-covered water carrier to Wetherford's mouth.

The man took a long pull, then looked up at Jubal. "Thank you, I'm—" Startled, he blurted out, "What the hell?" Pete Wetherford sat up from his resting spot and pointed at Jubal. "I'm gonna kill you, you rotten bastard." He struggled to rise from his seated position.

"Rest easy there, pardner." Judge Wickham held Wetherford off with a heavy hand on his shoulder. "You're not killing nobody anytime soon. We're gonna make a carrier for you and take you down to the wagon." He motioned for several of the men to look for branches to make a bearer for the stricken Pete Wetherford.

Morton stood with hands on hips. "Afore we all pitch in to save your sorry ass, why don't you tell us what you were doing out here in the loneliness?"

With a withering glance at Jubal, the desperado spun more of his tale. "It's like I said. We were all hunting, having a good time, when this brat what's staring so hard at me, his father, I assume it were his father, chased us up here into the hills."

Jubal couldn't restrain himself. "He was already dead and you know it—"

"Let him tell his story, son," interrupted the judge. "Every word out of his mouth buries him further. Go on, Wetherford, tell your tale."

The injured man winced as the two townies lifted him onto the makeshift stretcher. "The reason I blabbed about that youngster was on account he looks like his pa and in my state of pain, I guess I got confused." He paused. "Like I said, we were hunting—Jorge, ole Billy Tauson, several others—when all of a sudden shots were fired." His eyes darted from one rescuer to another. "We all ducked down and called out like proper folk that we were just hunting and whoever was plugging away at us should hold off and let us explain." He stopped for a time, as if reliving the event. "Jorge got real Mexican and insisted on running across this falling tree to get after the farmer." He pointed up to the log bridge. "But I told him to let me go first to try it out 'cause I didn't want nobody to get hurt. He followed me, and then, like I said, he slipped and a week later you all show up and that's about it. I sipped water that were trickling down the rocks or I'd a been a dead one. At night, the coyotes would come yip-yipping, sniffing 'round Jorge's body. Nothing I could do. Soon as the sun went down, damn. It were cold as a well-digger's ass."

Jubal trailed along as Judge Wickham and the group started down the steep canyon. "Other than the part about it being cold, he's lying, sir. My pa was never up here, and I doubt my father ever got a round off during the whole melee. I found his rifle burnt all to heck in the cabin."

They walked a few minutes more. "Can I ask him just one question, Judge?"

The judge nodded. Jubal eased his way alongside the stretcher as they made their way down the steep descent. "First of all, Mr. Pete, it has only been a few days—not a week—that you've been here. Secondly, you say my pa took a shot at you."

Pete grunted, "Yes."

"Was that before or after you hung him from the barn and set him on fire?"

He looked to make sure the sheriff and judge weren't within earshot. Pete hissed, "Recollect what I said up there at the tree, boy? What I did to your mother? I did that to your baby sis, too. And what I promised I was gonna do to you?" His eyes narrowed. "I'll do, in time, as soon as my bones are knitted. I'll be looking for you, boy, think on it."

"How you going to do any of that, Petey? You'll be swinging like a monkey in the breeze for your crimes." Jubal walked away as the group made their way down to the horses.

From back in the canyon, Wetherford called out, but Jubal ignored him.

After trekking down the gully floor to the wagon with Pete, the sheriff and Ron, along with the two townsmen, reluctantly went back up for Jorge's body.

The judge, Doc, and Jubal sat in the shade waiting, none of them wanting to speak. Wetherford continued a nonstop litany, pleading innocence, interspersed with shouts of pain.

"Whoever does me dirt I repay in spades. I'll find a way to . . . Ah, hell, somebody move my leg for me, would you?"

They all looked at one another. The judge finally spoke. "Doc, I suppose we ought to make an effort to move that bastard, don't you think?"

"I suppose it might be the humanitarian thing to do, yes." He made a cursory search into his black bag. "Unfortunately, I'm fresh out of powders that might make him more comfortable." He smiled at his little white lie.

Eventually the judge, Doc, and Jubal carried Pete to the wagon and settled him onto his side amid his loud "you bastards are trying to kill me" protestations. Jubal also ignored the man's "we got ourselves a date, we two," "what's your name, skinny boy" threats. Then they all sat back down and continued to stare out at the darkening expanse.

"Judge, I have my findings, is it all right to speak in front of the accused?" the doctor asked.

"I suppose under the circumstances it's probably fine. Do you want to hear any of this?" he asked Jubal.

Jubal wasn't sure how much he could take, but nevertheless, he nodded.

The doctor took a writing tablet from his bag and read from his notes. "The older woman died of strangulation and had a number of bruises on her body."

Jubal wrapped his arms around his knees and squeezed tightly.

The doctor paused. "She was violated." He spared a glance at Jubal before continuing. "The young girl, your sister?"

Jubal once again nodded.

"She died of multiple injuries, a blow to the head. Ribs cracked, if not broken. Probably bled to death. Violated sexually."

The doctor's words were things he knew, but they were made even more difficult when spoken by outsiders.

"The older man, I assume that was your father, of course passed on due to burns to his body. His was, I'm sorry to say, a painful demise."

The faint sound of Pete Wetherford singing in a taunting fashion came from the buckboard. *"Amazing grace! (how sweet the sound) / That sav'd a wretch like me! . . ."*

The judge got to his feet and hurried to the wagon, calling out to the doctor and Jubal. "You both take a walk into the woods, understand? Do it now."

Jubal and the doctor walked into the heavy forest. They stopped at thirty yards when they heard the loud wailing of Pete Wetherford. It sounded as if the learned judge were beating the hell out of him.

"All right, dammit. I was being foolish. Things got out of hand, we was all drunk. Every man jack o' them was taking part. Why you getting on me, for Christ's sake? I can't defend myself."

"Could that little girl you molested defend herself?"

Jubal heard the judge working Petey over.

"I swear on all that's sacred, I never touched her."

A loud noise, like a tree limb breaking, echoed through the forest.

"I'm a hardworking tradesman, dammit!" Pete yelled at the judge. "Give me a chance to explain!" He paused for a long while. "Yeah, we were all drunk, but the damn farmer started the ruckus. Listen up, Your Honor. I'm just taking a few days off from my job. I'm a family man and a craftsman."

"You said that before. Why did you attack those folks back at the farm?"

"No, sir, you got it wrong about that. I live with my older sister and help her take care of her kids and provide for her. I swear, sir."

Jubal heard the judge's voice but couldn't make out the words. It sounded as if he had gotten up close to Pete.

The judge was holding night court.

The doctor seemed to be in disbelief. "I know that fellow deserves some pain, but Lord God a-mighty." He paced, walking through the dry leaves. "Three murders. How could a soul do that?"

Jubal realized the doctor wasn't really asking him a question but merely reacting to the facts as he knew them. The doctor had missed the bullet hole in his father's head. He hadn't seen it, the burns having hidden the small .22-caliber hole. *Would it have made a difference?* Jubal wondered. *Probably not.*

TWELVE

On the long ride back to Cerro Vista, a number of night creatures sang their peculiar songs. A coyote calling to a mate, owls hooting, nightingales chiming in, and, of course, Pete Wetherford. Alternating between damning the human race and pain-wracked rambling about the judge, he had annoyed everyone by the time the troop arrived back in town.

"Sheriff, will it be all right if the youngster stayed the night in the jail?" asked Judge Wickham. "Without it being locked, of course."

"Why can't it be locked?" Sheriff Morton asked. "He still killed some folks, as I see it. I don't abide rogues in my jail who are on a free ride."

"From the doc's report, and from what I've discerned from our prisoner Mr. Wetherford, I, as a committee of one and the titular head of a grand jury to be convened in the near future, hereby hand down a true bill for our friend Pete for three counts of murder in the first degree. The young man had nothing to do with his family's deaths and you know it. The others who expired—Jorge, last name unknown, and Ty Blake—were shot and felled while performing acts of mischief. That's the way I see it, Bufort."

"Judge, as you say, you're top dog here. Guess you'll do as you damn well please." Both Morton and Ron seemed annoyed. When the group stopped at the jail, the two townies headed toward Sloan's for a drink.

Doc Brown, Sheriff Morton, and Ron took Wetherford to the jail and locked him up. Jubal was escorted to his cell, but his door remained wide open on the other side of the wall from the sleeping Maria. He felt sorry for her. With the sheriff and deputy gone all day, she probably hadn't eaten. For that matter, neither had he.

Jubal stood on the walkway outside the Cerro Vista County Jail contemplating the new morning, a stunning bright spring day, the sky a brilliant blue, the air crisp with a hint of coolness. The day did not match his mood, however, as his back and hip bothered him from sleeping on the hard steel cot. The brightness of the morning, though, convinced him that he should try and make the best of it. He stretched his torso.

Deputy Ron was halfway down the block, lumbering toward the jail with several lunch pails in his hands, probably breakfast. Jubal moved off the sidewalk to the other side of the street, not anxious for his splendid morning to be spoiled by the ignorant lawman.

Sitting on the sidewalk opposite, looking at the jail, he

pondered his next step. Now that Pete Wetherford had been caught, he needed to find the rest of the men who took his family from him, to bring them to the authorities—Billy Tauson, Crook Arm the yellow-stringed Indian, and the others.

"Are you contemplating buying that building, son?" The unexpected voice of Judge Wickham gave Jubal a start.

"Ah, good morning, sir," he said. "No, nothing as complicated as that. I was just trying to decide how to spend the rest of my life."

"Big decisions are not usually made while staring at the outside of a jail," mused Wickham. "On the contrary, jails are made for big decisions to be made inside. For instance, 'I'll never do that again' or 'I've had my last drink' or 'Maybe I better make peace with my Maker.'"

Jubal thought the older man was amusing and stood to shake his hand. "I want to thank you, sir, for the way you handled things yesterday and for having an understanding ear. I wasn't certain anyone was going to believe me. The bast—" He gestured toward the jail, getting ready to categorize the sheriff and his deputy, but thought better of it. "Sheriff Morton and Deputy Ron seemed to have made their minds up about me."

"A small town like this usually suffers from lack of money to hire good people." He looked to Jubal. "But the territory will do the best it can until statehood arrives. I pray it's soon." He paused, and then said, "I realize this is all early days for you to be talking about your situation, and I sympathize with you and your loss, but could an old man buy you breakfast, son?"

"Truth be known, sir, I just ate. But thank you, I'm much obliged."

"When I walked up on you," Judge Wickham replied kindly, "I also saw our mutual friend Deputy Ron carrying breakfast into the jail, so if you 'et,' as Ron would say, it must have been one of our resident long-tailed rodents. What say you?"

"Well, sir, long-tailed rodent is one of my favorite things." Jubal actually did consider the judge's concern to be genuine. "But maybe a second breakfast might be forced down."

Jubal took advantage of the invitation, the relaxed atmosphere at the hotel dining room lessening his self-consciousness. He was pleasantly surprised by the deference paid to the judge by the waitstaff. It was the first time in nearly a week he felt halfway decent.

"Sir," Jubal said after they had eaten, "I noticed you didn't pay after our meal. Do they keep an account?"

"Being as I own the hotel, no. They don't keep an account."

Jubal had never met anyone who actually owned a hotel or anything else of real value, and was surprised to hear that this fairly unassuming man had so much power and wealth. "I'm sorry, I didn't mean to pry."

"No apologies necessary, young man. Let's have a seat in the vestibule and chat a bit."

The room's decor hinted at elegance, but the dark red drapes, heavy wood paneling, and weighty furniture made Jubal recall being in a funeral home in Kansas when he was ten. "Would you mind, sir, if we sat on the porch?"

The judge agreed, and they sat half facing each other in white rockers on the porch. The hotel faced east, and Jubal thought he could see a hint of Morning Peak in the distance. The sight comforted him, yet he still felt apprehensive, not knowing what the older man wanted of him.

Judge Wickham took his time lighting a cigar. "Tell me more about the argument you witnessed in front of the land office, Jubal."

"Sir, it didn't last long. At least what I saw of it. My father—"

"What was his name?"

"Jubal Thaddeus Young, Sr., sir."

"I'm named after my father also. Sometimes it can be a blessing. Sorry, please continue."

"Pa was just talking to this fellow, who I later found out was Billy Tauson. They looked as if they'd been at it awhile. Tauson said something about 'legal or not, it ain't right' and referred to something about our plot of land."

"Could be a number of things. Tomorrow, Monday, we'll talk to Will Davis, try to get an answer to this. Continue."

"He was shouting threats and said my pa should say his prayers, 'night prayers,' to be accurate. I asked my father about it and he didn't want to talk. Said he'd tell me later 'cause my sister and ma were nearby and he didn't want to worry them." Jubal paused. "As it turned out, he never got around to it."

"I'd like to get this cleared up," Judge Wickham said. "I'm sure you would too, right?"

"Yes, sir, I would. I'm going after them, sir. I'll do my

best not to do harm and I'll try to do it proper, but those vandals have to pay one way or the other."

"The thing is, son, I'm not going to allow that until I've thoroughly looked into this. I like you, Jubal, you seem like an honest young man, but I'm going to restrict you from leaving town until everything has been checked out." The judge contemplated his smoke. "I feel you're innocent of harming your family, and as for the other deaths, I believe we can determine them as justifiable. The man Wetherford, who's in jail, said enough that I'm convinced he's one of the perpetrators. Just give me a few days. All right?"

"Yes, sir. Incidentally, Your Honor, just to keep the record straight, Wetherford and my father got into it on the street."

"When was this? On the same day as the fracas with Tauson?"

"Yes. The fellow was acting like a clown, showing off for his pals, and he and my dad ended up on the ground. Pa kneed him in the nether region and that was about it. I'm sure a lot of what happened on the farm came out of that scrap on the street. I think the fellow Pete was mighty embarrassed."

"All right, son. I'll keep that in mind, and remember what I said about sticking close by. No offense, but let the grown-ups handle this, okay?"

Jubal nodded. Tauson and his gang had a lead of several days on him. Maybe a couple more wouldn't matter. The judge seemed a decent sort. For now he'd bide his time.

The judge knocked the ash from his cigar and took a long, satisfying drag. "I apologize for your having to stay at the jail last night, but I needed to chat with you before I offered the following: I have a small accommodation in the back of the hotel where I let some of my help stay. Would you be interested in sharing space with two other workers?"

"Yes, sir, that would be fine." Jubal hesitated. "I hate to sound ungrateful, but would you have room for Frisk, my horse?"

"As long as the other fellows don't mind the smell of horse in the room, certainly." Judge Wickham smiled.

"No, sir. Of course I meant outside." He decided he liked the judge's fine sense of humor.

"We have a corral in back. Frisk is certainly welcome. Jubal, I'll see you in the morning and we'll take a walk over to Will Davis's office, all right?" The judge led him to a small shed in back of the hotel, on the way introducing him to his new roommates, a waiter and a cook.

After saying their goodbyes, the judge seemed perplexed. He took out his turnip-sized pocket watch and opened the gold-plated cover. "There is something else I would like to discuss with you. 'Discuss' may not be the proper word. 'Explain' might be more apt. I love this land and I have great hopes for its promise." The judge fussed with his watch, then pushed it forcefully back into his vest pocket. "Dammit to hell, I'm not an apologizer. I live by a code of ethics, and sometimes that dogma does get bent a bit. Pete Wetherford's confession in the woods isn't worth the time it takes to tell, and like I said, I'm not an apologist. But—and this is the root of the thing—I needed to hear it from that animal's mouth. He is bad, but more importantly, he's bad for this territory, this community. I've talked to Doc Brown and explained my position on my, let's say 'indiscretion,' and he seems to be all right with it—"

"Sir, to relieve your mind," Jubal interrupted, "I was hoping you would have gone even further. When you were striking him, there was a justice-being-served feeling . . . very satisfying."

The judge's confession of the beating still hung in the air. He hooked his thumbs into his vest pockets and rocked quietly back and forth on his heeled boots. He hesitated. "Every man is as God made him and ofttimes even worse." He seemed pleased to be using this quote as an explanation for the Pete Wetherford incident.

Jubal also thought the quote amusing, but for a different reason.

"What, son, you don't know Cervantes?"

"Sir, it's really nothing. With all due respect, as a matter of fact, I studied his writing quite thoroughly with my mother." Jubal waited, not knowing if he should continue.

"And?"

"The actual line is somewhat different."

The judge held back a smile. "So, you're going to take me to school?"

Reluctantly, Jubal recited, " 'Every man is as *heaven* made him and *sometimes* a *great deal* worse.' But I guess it still means the same thing, so my apologies, sir."

"Your apology is not necessary. It is my error. I'll have to watch my step around you, won't I?"

"Truth be known, it's one of the few quotes I remember, probably because ma has a sampler hanging over the dining room table with this same *Don Quixote* line. So I guess I cheated." He also realized he spoke of his mother in the present tense. *Every woman is as heaven made her.*

"You may find what I'm going to say now an odd segue." The judge smiled, still enjoying the fact he had been schooled by this young man. "But I mentioned your situation to my wife and she suggested that maybe you would like to break bread with us some evening?"

Though pleased by the offer, Jubal thought it peculiar, coming on the heels of the judge's rationale about Pete Wetherford's beating. Adults: he couldn't figure them. "I would like that, sir. Just set the date, I'll be there."

"Just a quiet evening, Jubal. You'll meet my family. My wife, Marlene, and Cybil, home from school."

Well, Jubal, thought, a free meal and a family evening with the judge, his wife, and Cybil—probably in pigtails and freckles, just home from school.

The new sleeping arrangement was little more than four walls, but at least it was better than the sheriff's barred confines. Jubal walked back to the jail, unhitched Frisk, and took her and the buckboard to the hotel.

THIRTEEN

The next day, Jubal walked the main street of Cerro Vista, trying to decide how to proceed with his pursuit of Billy Tauson.

Their inquiry at the land office had been of little value. Will Davis told them that because the land had originally been homesteaded, it made for a potentially messy land transfer, and the fact that Tauson had not paid taxes for a number of years further complicated the transaction.

The land, Jubal knew, went to his father at auction. Tauson evidently tried to pay the taxes later, but the transaction had already taken place, and Tauson's complaints of unfair treatment at the land office went unheard.

The judge told Jubal he was well aware of Tauson and his cohorts, they'd appeared in front of him in court on several occasions. "He's a bad one, son. He and the other one over at the jail, Wetherford, drift in and out of these parts from time to time, always getting into the affairs of others."

Jubal thought about asking permission to speak to Wetherford but was almost certain the man would only make threats.

After the judge asked Jubal if his accommodations were comfortable, Jubal offered to repay him the favor by helping with chores around the hotel. Judge Wickham accepted. It pleased Jubal to be given the work of chipping flaking paint off the front porch windows, then refinishing them. Charity bothered him. He didn't know if the judge was just being generous or if he truly needed the help. But the man had treated him well so far. Jubal decided he would not question things too deeply.

After getting tools from the hotel manager, Jubal quickly set to work. It felt good to be busy, like at home. The job kept his mind off recent events, though he was hard-pressed to spend more than several hours without some detail of those times coming to mind. In the afternoon, while cleaning errant paint drops from the porch floor, he overheard two men in lively conversation enjoying the late sun.

"What's the most anyone has done you for?" one asked the other.

"An odd cowhand looking like the devil himself walks into my shop one day and says, 'Yes, sir. I'll have that saddle, the one with the silver buckles.'"

Jubal recognized this speaker as the portly, bald man from the general store.

"That were a fifty-dollar item. I was pleased as punch.

But then he said he only got himself thirty dollars, would I take the rest on a promise? He was hanging with another scrapper I'd seen around town, name of Petey."

Jubal worked on the porch floor even closer to the men.

"So, what the heck, the saddle only cost me twenty-five dollars and I was still in profit for five. I had him sign a note for the balance. What do you know, if I wouldn't see him around town from time to time, and the devil, he'd nod, give me a mean look, and walk on."

"I'll tell you, it wasn't worth getting yourself shot over." The other man smiled. "Where's he from?"

"Don't rightly know. He put a ranch name up Colorado way near Alamosa on the agreement."

Jubal, intent when the name Petey came up, wondered. "Excuse me, sir, I couldn't help but hear about the man who bought that saddle. Was he a very tall man with long gray hair, kind of a dandy, sorta mean-looking?"

"Yep, that's the devil. Why?"

"Oh, no real reason, sir, I just wondered if it wasn't someone I knew. What was his name again?"

"As I remember it was Talson. No, Tauson. Yes, Tauson."

"And he's from Alamosa?"

"Near to some ranch or other. You know him, youngster?"

Jubal paused. "No, sir, I don't."

"If you run into him, would you mention that a certain old man who runs the general store sure could use that twenty dollars he owes?" The men shared a laugh and went back to their gossiping.

Jubal continued his work. Alamosa was a long way to go on sketchy information, but maybe he should consider it. He pictured himself knocking on a ranch-house door and announcing he was there to collect twenty dollars for an old fellow from Cerro Vista, and ah, yes, by the way, could we chat about murderous events that transpired at the Young family farm on April 10 of this year?

The hotel manager and Judge Wickham both appreciated Jubal's work—so much so, they offered him a full-time job. The pay would not be much, but at least it would be steady.

The bid caught Jubal off guard. He liked the judge and didn't really mind the work, and he had also been told not to leave town, so why not? And this was also far easier than farm chores.

But a gnawing still kept after him. He needed to pursue Billy Tauson and his group. He hadn't any idea what he would do once he found them; he would think on that when the time came. After all, they were the mindless ones, the louts and rapists. Why would they have an advantage? Yes, in numbers, certainly, but in terms of righteousness, as his mother would say, "Why should the devil have all the best tunes?" So he took the job—repairing, painting, peeling potatoes—but he didn't plan on keeping it for long.

Several days into his full-time employment, in the evening, just before nightfall, Jubal heard gunshots. He ran around to the front of the hotel in time to see a lone horseman racing down the dirt street. Hatless, with both arms swathed in bandages, the man brandished a long-barreled pistol in his right hand. As he passed Jubal, he fumbled with the weapon, attempting to fire. The bandages and horse reins being too much to handle all at the same time, he managed only a wicked nod of recognition.

Pete Wetherford was out of jail, heading north.

A crowd gathered at the jail, many of them calling out for Doc Brown. As Jubal neared, he heard several women scream and a man shouted that someone had killed the sheriff. Someone else repeated the plea for Doc Brown.

A body lay on the sidewalk, half stretched into the dirt of the street. Sheriff Morton, a puckered hole in his forehead and another in his throat. Both wounds shed blood over his white shirt.

Jubal eased into the office past a half dozen townsmen, all tending a prone Deputy Ron. They had stretched him out on one of the desks, and now several men were holding pieces of shirt and various rags against stomach wounds. The punctures pumped startling amounts of blood onto the office floor.

A trail of blood led to Ron's desk, where the door to the back room had been left open. The deputy must have been in the cell area. Jubal stepped through the portal and eased into the barred confines unnoticed.

He saw Wetherford's open cell door, the key on a large steel ring still in place in the lock.

The sound of someone crying came from the back cell, next to where he had spent the night. As he eased his way down the short hallway, he could see blood splattered in front of the Spanish woman's cell.

"Maria, it's Jubal. Do you remember me?"

"Yes," she mumbled between her gasps. "Can you please to help me?"

"What happened here?"

A long pause. "I don't know."

Jubal stood by the bars, looking at the forlorn woman. She sat on the floor in the corner of the cell, her hands grasping her knees.

"Can I get you water?"

"No, thank you."

Jubal thought the voices in the outer office had gotten even louder, sounding as if they were ready to move Ron. The deputy led the chorus, shouting instructions on how to ease his pain.

Jubal directed his attention back to Maria. "Guess they're helping Ron." Jubal watched for her reaction. "Who shot him? How did it happen?"

"Fat Ron stood there." She pointed to the corner of her cell next to the bars. "Near the wall of the hombre who came to jail all banged up. I, having to do my daily thing."

"Your daily . . . thing?" Jubal didn't know what else to say.

"I was doing him like I did ever'day. Him and stinky-man sheriff."

Jubal still couldn't find the words.

"The hombre next door, Mr. Petey, he reach over to grab Deputy Ron's gun and said to him to open his cell or he was gonna shoot him to death. Well, Ron was soiling himself and unlocked Petey's cell. I beg him to let me out, too, but he just shoots Ron and runs out. It was so loud. Then I'm hearing more *pistola* rounds, then nothing."

Again, Jubal found himself stunned, trying to grasp

how all of this had happened. Even so, in the midst of all the unnecessary pain, Jubal realized there was one thing he could do to help.

Maria continued her moaning but got distracted when Jubal turned the key in her cell door. He swung it open.

"Quietly," Jubal said. "Do you understand? People in the office are tending to Ron. More are outside. Stay alongside me and don't speak."

The diminutive woman nodded and began to creep alongside Jubal as they made their way through the throng. They were lucky to be swept outside as the townsmen hoisted Ron onto a stretcher and whisked him away. Jubal and Maria walked unnoticed into the street.

They made their way along a back alley, and the young woman wept. "Thanks to you, señor. *Muchas gracias.*"

"Do you have a place to stay? What will you do?"

"I have *amigas* who will take me."

Jubal knew there couldn't be much he could say to her. "Good luck to you, Maria."

The woman turned and slipped down a dark lane between two buildings. At the corner she clasped her hands together as if in prayer, called out, *"¡Muchas gracias!"* and disappeared into the shadows.

FOURTEEN

Sitting on the porch of the hotel, Jubal watched people stream past the jail area, there being, he figured, a morbid curiosity about the death of the sheriff.

Bufort Morton had died in the street. He had, much to Jubal's surprise, a family—and, from the reactions of the gawkers, quite a few friends. Or if not friends, acquaintances.

Jubal wondered if he would have to hold himself somewhat responsible for the man's death. If he had simply left his canteen with Ty Blake at the crossroads and ridden off, none of this would have transpired.

He scolded himself for living in the what-if world again. Then he scolded himself again for stalling. He had to make a decision. Not about whether to trail after Wetherford and Tauson, but how to treat Judge Wickham. The man had been forthright with Jubal and deserved an explanation of why Jubal needed to leave. After all, he said he was restricting Jubal to the town until further notice. Otherwise, Jubal could simply pack up and go, although the expression "pack up" might be a bit grand when describing his possessions.

"Why would I consent to lifting my ban on your traveling outside town limits?" the judge asked Jubal. "I have said to you it's still under investigation, your part in all this."

Jubal sat politely, hands clenched in his lap. They were once more on the porch of the hotel. "With respect, sir, I don't believe you think I did anything wrong in the recent . . . tragedy. Am I right?" There was no answer, so he continued. "As I said before, I don't intend to break the law. I am the only one who knows these fellows as a group. I can point them out."

"Good. There's a U.S. Marshal coming up from Albuquerque, should be here soon, and you can describe in detail to him exactly what transpired." He looked at Jubal. "It's true, I don't think you're culpable in these misdeeds, but—and this is important—you should mind your manners, son. I mean that in a number of ways, not just in a legal sense. I have put you on informal status, meaning I have not drawn up a document stating your being bound to this township—a restraining order, if you will. Let's stop beating around the teepee here, son. You're a proper young man. I also believe with the proper education and resolve you could make something of yourself."

Jubal dropped his chin. This act of concern made him uncomfortable. "I'll do as you asked, sir, and will stay in town. Although I don't agree with your order, I respect you and your judgment, and thank you for the encouragement. I know I need additional schooling. When we moved from Kansas, that was pretty much it for any formal book learning. Ma schooled sis and me each day. She taught in Kansas City and when we came out here she set up a curri . . . cure . . . ."

"Curriculum."

"Yes, sir, my sis was very bright. She finished enough reading to have graduated high school, even though she was still real young."

"And you?"

"I completed my studies as far as high school and was given extra reading to do."

"Having been shaken by your last literary revelation of Cervantes, I hesitate to ask. But curiosity rules the day. Such as?"

Jubal hesitated, not sure of the right response. "Melville, sir, he wrote a tale about the sea. My pa was a fisherman when he was young. I don't mean he just went fishing, he fished for a living. Anyway, I liked to read him. Poe was a favorite of my ma's. I liked his stories. 'The Raven,' and the one about the man who was sealed up in a tomb. . . ."

" 'The Cask of Amontillado.' "

"Yes, sir, that one, and, uh . . ." He hesitated, realizing the story of Edmond Dantès had a similar theme to Poe's tale.

"It's about revenge, is that why you like it?"

Jubal blushed. He wasn't sure why he liked that particular story. It did have a bizarre cruel justice to it, but he had read both stories long before the events at the farm.

"Keep reading, son. It's good for the soul."

Jubal wondered if he should mention the long Dumas opus, but maybe for now he would keep the Count and his revenge to himself.

"Have you given any thought to what I asked about you staying on at the hotel as a handyman?"

"Sir, under the circumstances, if I'm not allowed out of the yard—"

"No, no, no. I never said 'not allowed out of the yard.'" He smiled. "I said 'township'—you're a bit provocative, aren't you?"

"Well, no, sir." Jubal now felt confident in his new-found friend. "I don't mean to provoke, I'm much appreciative of your thoughtfulness. I'll stay on as long as you'll have me."

They parted with a handshake.

"Remember what Montressor said to Fortunato?" the judge said as they turned to depart.

Jubal shook his head.

"He said, 'I have my doubts.'" The judge walked off the porch down the newly painted steps. "I am jesting with you, Jubal. They were speaking of a sherry, a fine drink, and whether it was in fact as advertised. It was a subterfuge, a ruse. You say you'll stay, but you say it perhaps a mite too quickly." The judge tipped his hat to Jubal and smiled.

Maybe so, maybe Jubal tended to agree with adults and tell them what he thought they wanted to hear. Was that dishonest? He found himself in peculiar circumstances. He liked the judge and hoped he wouldn't have to disappoint him.

◆◆◆◆

Excitement descended in Cerro Vista the next day when U.S. Marshal Wayne Turner arrived. The man questioned almost everyone who had any knowledge of the Young family killings and the shooting of the sheriff and Deputy Ron.

Jubal took note of him as he arrived at the hotel—a thin fellow dressed in business attire, a dark suit and vest, the gleaming badge tucked just inside his coat. He came and went with a decided self-awareness, which made Jubal anxious as he approached the marshal, who was sitting on the hotel porch having a cup of coffee.

"Good day, sir, excuse me, but I work here." Jubal thought maybe he should mention his employer's name. "For Judge Wickham."

No response.

"He hired me. I do odd jobs and such. I wondered if maybe I could have a few words with you?"

Turner looked to Jubal. "You're the Young family survivor, and are a bit perplexed we haven't spoken, because there's something you feel is important to add to this investigation. The sooner I question you, the sooner you'll feel better about the deaths of a couple of those ne'er-do-wells." He took a sip of his coffee. "Why did you take it upon yourself to shoot those men? Wouldn't it have been more prudent to scamper into town and collect the sheriff?"

Turner didn't wait for an answer, which was good, because Jubal had none. "Youngsters like you are always taking the law into their own hands and the results are always, without exception, disastrous. You're a child trying to be a man. You should be left to your toys. You made a foolish mistake and probably cost several lives.

I've interviewed the deputy and talked to the judge. The deputy puts you square in the middle of all this."

The marshal continued, "The two townsmen who accompanied the lot of you out to the farm said you were standoffish, somewhat excitable. They said you were wanting to get after the victim they found who was hurt, that you wouldn't let him finish his story. Then, while they went back up to retrieve one of the bodies, you beat the hell out of him. An article of intrigue is what you are. You approached me, hat-in-hand polite, with your 'excuse me, I work here, Judge Wickham hired me' bullshit. So what's that supposed to mean? Just because the judge hired you doesn't make you a saint. I'll talk to you when I am good and ready. If you work here, trot inside and get me more coffee."

Jubal took the cup to the kitchen and refilled it, adding sugar and a great glob of his own saliva. With the tainted coffee in hand, he left the kitchen and started toward the porch, but he hadn't even gotten twenty feet when he realized he couldn't do it without regretting it. He went back to the kitchen and put the cup in the sink.

"What's you doing, compadre?" said one of the kitchen workers. "I just saw you pour that."

"I think it's cold, I need to pour a new cup . . . to start over." To start over. What an idea. Was that even possible?

After he delivered the coffee to the marshal, Jubal stood on the porch of the hotel, listening to a trumpeter playing a scratchy spiritual. The musician's lament was followed by a choir of seven singing "Nearer My God to Thee." A flat black buckboard led the sad parade, a pine casket on the bed, festooned with flowers. A man in a battered silk hat drove the two horses in a somber fashion.

A crowd of thirty to forty people trailed the wagon, some singing along with the choir, others holding hand-kerchiefs to their mouths and weeping. At the head of the procession was a woman all in black, with two small children dressed in their finest, walking uncertainly along the dirt street. The youngest of the two had his head pressed hard against his mother's hand. Jubal doffed his hat as Sheriff Bufort Morton took his last, slow ride.

When Jubal returned through the lobby, the room clerk called him over, holding out a folded piece of paper. Jubal opened it.

Jubal,

Please come for a light repast at six this evening, if your busy schedule allows. Turn right on Calle Piñon after the hotel. Three doors down on left.

Regards,
Judge Hiram Wickham

This appealed to Jubal. He could use a good meal.

At precisely five minutes to six that evening, Jubal found himself pacing outside the judge's white picket fence. He had gathered wildflowers in a field behind the hotel and wrapped them in a damp newspaper, and now he looked down at the vivid mix of color forming the haphazard bou-quet, much like the ones filling his sister's basket as she ran across that open field the day she died. Maybe, he thought, that was why he liked them—they were hardy and free like Pru.

"Are you Jubal?" He was startled by a lilting female voice.

He stammered out an answer before having really seen who had called from the doorway. "Ah, yes, ma'am."

A young woman stepped out from behind the screen door into the orange light of the setting sun. "I'm Cybil Wickham. So pleased to meet you, Jubal. Father said you would be coming. Welcome."

This woman was not what Jubal had been expecting. Pleasantly so. "Oh, thank you," he said. "I was just waiting a minute or two. I thought I was late—I mean, early." He hoped the light of dusk hid his now-flushing cheeks. She was gracefully tall, with dark straight hair and a quick, friendly smile, and he desperately wanted her to like him.

Cybil held the door open for him and he started in, then stopped, remembering his manners. "After you, ma'am."

As she brushed past, Jubal held out the bouquet to her. "These poor things were kinda dying to be picked." He fumbled the wildflowers and they fell to the floor. Cybil bent to retrieve the bouquet, but Jubal unfortunately did the same and they cracked heads.

"Oh, my God, ma'am! I'm terribly sorry. Please forgive me, ahh, Miss Wickham."

The girl laughed and reached for the flowers. "Call me Cybil. 'Ma'am' is my mother. May I call you Jubal?"

She could call him anything she wanted, he reasoned, including clumsy and stupid.

The elegance of the house gave Jubal pause. Polished wood floors at the entrance, with a graceful staircase leading to a railed open area with a crystal chandelier. On the walls, oil paintings of faraway cities with boats being steered along river streets. A thick ruby-colored rug led through the long wide hallway toward the back of the house, and to Jubal's left was a full-length mirror encased by an ornate wood frame.

"Your house seems like a palace, Miss Cybil. I've never seen the likes of it."

"Thank you, kind sir." She smiled. "Mother loves Europe, art, all the fine things."

Judge Wickham entered the foyer. He held his right arm pressed against his hip. "The ole rocking chair's got me, I guess."

"My pa has rheumatism, suffers some," Jubal offered. "What I mean is, he had—"

"It's arthritis, son. At any rate, I see you two have met. Jubal, come in and meet my wife."

Mrs. Wickham was an older version of her daughter, trim and sophisticated. She swept out of the kitchen carrying a steaming pot roast on a silver platter.

"You, of course, are Jubal," she said. "Welcome, young man, to our humble abode. Please have a seat while I finish the potatoes and gravy. Cyb, will you see that our guest is comfortable, then give me a hand?"

Jubal wished he had taken more time with his appearance. Dirt-edged fingernails and hair looping over his ears curling inward at the nape of his neck made him feel sloppy in the presence of these people. He decided he would eat, make his regrets, then head for his room in back of the hotel.

Cybil waited until Jubal seated himself, then

disappeared into the kitchen. Judge Wickham sat at the head of the table and shook out his folded napkin.

"I hope you're hungry, Jubal. Marlene's pot roast is delicious."

This "repast," as the judge had called it, was unlike anything Jubal had ever taken part in. Gilded, scalloped-edged dishes. Heavy silverware, napkins with crocheted corners. He was so overawed by the luxury that he didn't really taste the food.

"Cybil has just finished her freshman year at Radcliffe College."

"Oh, Mom. I am sure Mr. Young is not interested in my education."

Jubal fumbled with his fork. "Oh, on the contrary, Mrs. Wickham, I'd like to hear about it. Where is this college, miss?" He turned to Cybil.

"Massachusetts. I'm studying physics. I would have liked to study medicine, but this is the first year of the school, and we pioneers must be willing to sacrifice."

"Oh, Cyb, stop. You know that's not true."

"Daddy, please. Aren't we living in an age of enlightenment?"

The judge dropped his head a bit and looked over his glasses at his daughter. "Are you quoting that Anthony woman, Cyb?"

"Please, Your Honor. May I speak?"

Her father thought this funny, giving her a world-weary gesture to continue.

"First of all, no. I'm not quoting her. I'm merely stating the facts. The Constitution clearly states that all citizens should be deemed equal. There is nothing remotely suggesting that women should be excluded because of their sex."

"Please, dear, your language," Cybil's mother whispered.

"Where would you be if Daddy wasn't a broad-minded, bright, upstanding citizen?"

"What do you mean, dear?" Mrs. Wickham looked to Jubal, who had slouched back in his chair.

Cybil continued, "You were brought up in Europe, where people are relegated to certain ways of life depending on wealth, nobility, birthrights, education."

Her father seemed to be enjoying Cybil's rant. He interrupted in a put-upon strong voice. "Chivalry, brute force, moral power. Right, Jubal?"

He acknowledged the judge, then retreated.

"Excuse my going on at such length, Mr. Young," Cybil persisted. "But wouldn't you agree it's wrong for a son and his so-called aristocracy of sex to be the political master of his mother, as is so prevalent in other countries? Don't you think that's ludicrous, sir?"

"Uh-huh," Jubal answered weakly, having absolutely nothing upon which to base a dissenting vote. The idea of Jubal even being the moral equivalent of his mother was beyond comprehension.

Mrs. Wickham tapped her spoon against her water glass. "Cybil, please. Cyb, darling, do you think this is the proper forum for such talk?"

"I see nothing wrong in Cybil's bombastic proclamations," offered the judge. "You were denied entry to medical school. How does that tie in with this Anthony woman's so-called temperance movement?"

Jubal loved this family's fascinating dinner table discussion but tried to hold his tongue.

"Daddy? You honestly can't see how unfairly that decision came about? I was told that because I refused to state my religious beliefs, if any, my application would be considered incomplete. Do you think that's fair?"

"Why didn't you just put down 'atheist'?" Jubal blurted.

The table went silent. Having spoken out, Jubal now found himself having to defend his position, so he continued.

"I suppose one could argue that would be a lie, but maybe the more important thing is"—he looked around the table, realizing he was in deep—"if you really wanted to be a doctor bad enough, you would do whatever it took." Jubal stopped, thinking maybe he'd piped up at the wrong moment. Once again, a heavy silence. Then Cybil chuckled, followed by her father and Mrs. Wickham. Jubal joined in. Maybe, he thought, an occasional little lie wasn't such a bad thing after all.

Jubal found himself fascinated by this strong, opinionated woman. She was only slightly older than Jubal and yet she had lived away from home for almost a year. He thought of his sister and what she had missed in terms of world experience.

They moved into the parlor, where Cybil served them tea and hard biscuits sprinkled with sugar. She sat across from Jubal on a settee with her mother. "Another cup of tea, Mr. Young?" She tilted her head as if she were having fun with him.

"Oh, no, thanks. I have to work in the morning. It

might keep me up. I could be late." He glanced at the judge and smiled. "I have a tough boss." They all smiled. "I really should be going. But before I leave, could I help with the dishes, Mrs. Wickham?"

They all rose from their seats. "No, that's all right," Mrs. Wickham said, thanking him with a careful, socially polite hug. "Take care."

He thought she was slightly disapproving of him. "It was a terrific dinner and I hope someday to repay you in kind. Thank you again, sir. I am much obliged. Miss Wickham, my congratulations on the sweets, and good luck in school with your studies."

Cybil took his arm. "I'll walk you to the front gate." Jubal's elbow seemed on fire from Cybil's contact, but he could tell she was very much at ease. She opened the gate to let him out.

"I hate to bring this up, but I would feel remiss if I didn't express my condolences on the loss of your family. Father told me of his trip to your farm and the devastation. I can't imagine how you must feel. I know this must sound weak and insipid, but please, if there is anything I can do, just ask . . . will you do that?" She stopped and looked straight at Jubal. "Oh, I almost forgot the flowers." She reached over and kissed Jubal on the cheek. "They were wonderfully appropriate. Hope to see you soon."

Unable to speak, Jubal felt a fool. A stupid schoolboy kind of buffoon, tongue-tied and red-faced. Cybil was almost back to the door before he could utter a "Good night."

He didn't even remember the walk back to the hotel. Though Mrs. Wickham seemed slightly difficult, they were an appealing family. Strong parents, educated, and sensitive. He wondered what Cybil would do with her life. She seemed so sure of herself, smart, and had what he thought to be a rare kind of independence. Would a girl like that ever look twice at him?

FIFTEEN

Night sounds kept Jubal awake. He never quite got to deep, satisfying sleep, but instead was settling on eyes-shut, annoying awareness. Plus he couldn't keep his mind off the ethereal Cybil.

The night was well under way when he was roused by peculiar rumblings. Jubal tried to identify the various noises.

The snoring coming from one of his roommates was soft and rhythmic. A wood board squeaked whenever a breeze passed over the loose windowsill. Somewhere close, a night bird called. In the distance, thunder.

As the storm seemed to find its way ever closer, an itch started in Jubal's mind. It wasn't thunder. It sounded—it felt—as if it were horses.

And they were getting nearer.

Something didn't feel right.

Were the horsemen coming for him? Why would he

think that? Was it simply his ever-present guilt that kept him awake tonight? Why should he feel guilty about anything?

He knew, of course, but it was best left alone.

The hoofbeats trailed away, becoming quieter. Good. Then it sounded as if they turned down Calle Piñon, but why? Nothing there but houses. No bars, no hotels.

Just Judge Wickham's house.

That's when the gunfire erupted. There must have been a dozen shots fired before it all stopped. Then the boom of several shotgun blasts answering back.

Jubal reached under his bed and searched around until his hand settled on Audrey, his father's pistol. He held the weapon up to the weak light from the window and spun the cylinder, checking to be sure it was full and ready. He laid it at the side of the cot and rummaged around for Ty Blake's nickel-plated six-shooter.

He slipped out the shed door, leaving his two drunken companions snoring away.

The night air lay damp all around him. Frisk and several other animals stamped restlessly in the corral, uneasy about the gunshots.

Jubal skirted the hotel and crossed Calle Piñon, where several lanterns had been raised in the various houses along the street. He crouched behind the stump of an oak tree to survey the situation.

The moon was low on the horizon, creating silhouettes of three horsemen. Halfway down the street, their frenetic images stood out against the lighted crescent shape. The hatless one riding a dapple-gray mare he easily identified as Pete Wetherford. The other two men he didn't recognize.

They once again raised their rifles and fired indiscriminately into Judge Wickham's house. Jubal looked behind him at the hotel entrance and spied the outline of several men on the porch, one of them being U.S. Marshal Wayne Turner.

Turner came quickly down the street, hugging the picket fences, dodging behind various trees until he was on the other side of the street. The marshal had no sooner arrived than he called out to the horsemen.

"Drop your weapons. That's an order, I'm U.S. Marshal Wayne Turner, drop those guns."

His order was met with a barrage of gunfire directed at the tree he hid behind. He cursed, then cried out once again to the men. In the middle of his demands the horsemen lit up the night with another volley of gunfire.

Jubal laid his pa's pistol on top of the stump to steady it and took aim at Pete Wetherford, but the men purposely danced their horses to keep from being hit. Finally, one of the riders, on a black horse, came charging up the street past the marshal's position, his horse's reins clamped in his teeth, both hands holding six-shooters. He drove his horse hard all the way to the corner by the hotel before he wheeled around for another run. As he turned, the rider danced his mount under the protection of a large cottonwood.

Jubal shifted his position to the opposite side of the stump, waiting for the horseman to come charging back.

Several gunshots came from the far end of the street, where he had last seen Pete Wetherford. The rider closer to the hotel disappeared from sight. Jubal once again moved, not knowing which side of the stump was safest.

Up the street toward the hotel, Jubal could just make out the slightest movement. The gunman on the black horse had moved his mount onto the tree-shrouded sidewalk and began inching his way up behind the marshal.

"Marshal! Take cover!" Jubal cried out.

Turner hastily scooted around to the other side of the tree and pointed his weapon back toward the horseman. Jubal fired twice into the branches above where he thought the rider to be. His aim was close enough that it seemed to spook the man, who spurred his mount back out into the dirt street. He struggled to calm his horse as it bolted toward the hotel, but he finally reined it in, turned, and came storming back. Jubal fired at him. He came off his horse heavily, bouncing on the hard earth.

The mean-spirited voice Jubal had heard in the mountains at Morning Peak shouted from down the street.

"Al, you okay, brother?"

The lone figure moaning softly in the street didn't answer.

Jubal cupped his hands to his mouth and called out to the two remaining riders. "He's hit bad and suffering. Why don't you come and lend him a hand, you cowardly bastards?" He watched as the two men continued to dance their horses in the shadows of the tree-lined street. He wanted the men to come back. "Come get some redemption, you motherless heathens."

The fallen rider momentarily stilled his sad lament.

"Who's over there?" Turner yelled out from the other side of the street.

"Just the coffee boy, sir," Jubal shouted back. "Tending my chores." He then emptied his pa's pistol at what had now become the two fleeing horsemen, their blackened silhouettes fading down the moon-streaked street.

Judge Wickham had suffered a round to his left shoulder and a grazing wound to the head, which had nearly taken off an ear. He lay on the porch unconscious, losing a great deal of blood.

Doc Brown was already there, and Mrs. Wickham scurried in and out of the house trying to help him, bringing pillowcases for dressings and hot water to clean the wounds. The candlelight flickered off the judge's pale face and made him appear more dead than alive.

Marshal Turner and some of the neighbors crowded around. The lawman looked to Jubal. "You could have hurt someone with your gunplay out there."

"That's what I intended, Marshal." He stood on the grass in the front yard. "They'll be coming for me next."

"What makes you think so? Why are you so damn important?"

"Not important at all, I'm just a nuisance. The hatless one who rode off was Pete Wetherford. The one thrashing about in the street is, I think, his brother, Al."

Indeed, Al was still on his side, pedaling his legs in agony as he gripped his stomach. Several townsmen hung around watching, waiting for him to die.

"Let's get the judge inside, folks," Doc Brown said. "Lend a hand, please." A couple of neighbors along with Jubal and Mrs. Wickham formed a human stretcher.

"On the table, right there." Mrs. Wickham directed the group to the dining room table, where she dispensed with the long white doily and Jubal's fresh-picked wildflowers.

The efficient Mrs. Wickham and Cybil brought several kerosene lamps onto the buffet table at the side of the room. Bent over the stricken judge, Doc Brown reexamined his wounds in the better light. "I have to get that bullet out of his shoulder, it's pressing against an artery and I'm unable to stop the bleeding." He looked up. "Going to need some help, people." He pointed at Jubal. "You there, Jubal, give me a hand."

Jubal went into action as the doctor continued issuing orders.

"See if you can move him over on his right side so I can pack these pillows against his back to keep him steady."

Jubal reached under the judge's neck and with his other arm rolled the man's hip until he was lying on his side.

A soft hand grasped his left forearm. Cybil. She gave him a reassuring glance.

"I'll need everyone to leave the room now, please," Doc Brown said.

Everyone heeded the doctor's words and filed out of the dining room.

"Jubal, could you stay and give me a steady hand?"

"Be glad to, sir."

Mrs. Wickham, who had earlier seemed so in control, retreated to a corner of the room, then to the kitchen, weeping, with both hands clamped securely over her mouth.

"Cybil, dear. Keep that hot water coming, and bring me some washbasins, put them through boiling water. I'll need compresses, long strips of clean bedding about four inches wide, and my case on the front porch. Quickly, now."

Jubal respected the doctor's control of the situation.

"We'll both stay on this side of the table so we won't block the light."

Cybil came back into the room with the doctor's medical case.

"Thank you, dear," Doc Brown said, taking it from her. "While Jubal holds your father's torso steady, grasp your dad's legs to keep him from moving. I'm going to give him some ether so he won't wake up." Doc Brown opened his case and extracted a number of instruments. "Jubal, cut his pajama top away from that shoulder."

Jubal took the scissors the doctor had put nearby and deftly cut away the cotton top, exposing a great deal of blood.

"I'm going to probe into that wound. While I do, I want you to try and keep the opening clear of fluid with these compresses. Can you do that?"

"Yes, sir, I can."

The doctor placed a heavy piece of gauze over the nose and mouth of the judge. "Son, now reach over and let a few drops of that ether soak into that gauze. Careful not to get it on the judge's skin."

Jubal was at the front of the table, where the judge's bloody head was propped on an embroidered pillow. As the doctor bent over the judge's wound, Jubal caught sight of Cybil, biting her lower lip in fear. Jubal winked at her for reassurance and administered the anesthetic.

"Cybil, you can relax now. Your papa is sleeping nicely," the doctor told her. "That's enough for now, son. Grab those cut rags and mop up some of this blood around the wound."

Jubal did so as the doctor continued to search with a long shiny instrument. "I think I've found it. Jubal, hold this while I get my forceps."

Jubal felt the instrument touching something hard.

"Now, as I run these forceps alongside the probe, hold very still or I'll lose the bullet, you understand?"

"Yes, sir."

Jubal suddenly felt a piece of cloth on his forehead. Cybil was wiping his brow, like an angel breathing softly on his skin. She moved on to the doctor and did the same.

He tried shaking it off, the feeling, but it persisted. He needed to concentrate. As Cybil moved behind him, he could smell her bath soap. Green pine or grass, something clean and wholesome.

"I've got it," Doc Brown said. "Cybil, give me that basin. Set it at your father's side." The devilish slug dropped into the basin with a loud *plink*. "Jubal, stuff that gauze into the wound while I hold it open with these forceps."

Blood continued to seep from the gap in the judge's shoulder. Jubal thought Cybil looked woozy.

"Doctor, I need a little time. . . ."

The man looked up. Jubal motioned with his head toward Cybil.

"Sit her down, Jubal."

Jubal wiped his hands and went to her. She wobbled a bit and fell into his arms.

"Here, let me get you seated before you pass out." She felt warm in his arms.

"I'll be fine. It's just, it suddenly felt stuffy here. Maybe some water. . . ."

Jubal took her to a cushioned armchair and went to the kitchen to fetch water. When he returned, glass in hand, Cybil was resting her head on her knees. Jubal gently placed his hand on her dark hair.

"Drink this. Slowly, Cybil." He thought maybe it was the first time he had used her name. It had a nice feel to it, proper and yet feminine. He went back to assist the doctor.

"Keep dabbing that wound while I try to sterilize it, please." The doctor washed the injury carefully, then poured a clear liquid into it from a glass-stoppered bottle. "It will take a half dozen stitches. Then we hope for the best. I can manage now. Why don't you take Cybil out for some air, my good man?"

SIXTEEN

Jubal took the empty glass from Cybil and knelt down in front of her. "The doctor thinks you should get some fresh air." Jubal grasped her elbow and helped her through the kitchen and out the back door. The quarter-moon had traversed the black sky and left their world in darkness.

Jubal returned to the dining room and stood across from the doctor, the room in stark contrast to a few hours earlier. The judge's bloody head and shoulder were just inches from where Jubal had earlier sat enjoying Mrs. Wickham's pot roast. The air was filled with a sharp fetid smell, unlike that during the events at the farm. The brackish taint of blood filled the room.

"As I said earlier, young man"—the doctor kept at his work—"take care of the Mrs. and Cybil. I'll be fine here." He then looked up at Jubal. "One can do only so much. Fate has a way of affecting all of us. You've helped here.

Make nice with platitudes to the judge's wife, comfort Cybil, and go. . . . Thank you again."

Jubal backed out of the dining room and stopped in the kitchen to wash his hands and face. He noticed Cybil in the garden gazing upward, her hands together in a silent prayer.

The kitchen screen door made a grating screech as he stepped into the garden.

"I'm sorry I acted such a fool," Cybil said. "Maybe it's a good thing I won't be going to medical school. I can't imagine what I would do in anatomy class. Thank you for your support."

"It sounds as if your father is going to be fine."

She began to cry. Jubal rested his hands on her shoulders as she slipped softly into his arms. They stood like that in the dark until a voice called from the back porch.

"Cyb, honey, are you out there?"

Jubal noticed Mrs. Wickham silhouetted against the kitchen window.

"Yes, Mom." She walked back toward her mother. "I felt faint seeing all that blood on dad."

"Are you all right now, dear?"

"I'm feeling better. Jubal was kind enough to help me out. It was just so odd. One minute I was fine, then all of a sudden the room started moving."

Jubal moved up next to Cybil. "Doc Brown said he thought your husband was going to be fine, Mrs. Wickham. Is there anything I can do?"

"Ah, no. I don't think so. Cybil, mind the night air, dear. Not to catch a cold, please. I'll wait in the kitchen for you. Good night again, Mr. Young."

"Your mother seems concerned about you," said Jubal. "If you're feeling better, maybe you should go in." He hoped she wouldn't take his advice.

"Oh, it's just mom being protective of me, you know."

Jubal wasn't sure that he did know. "I hope she doesn't think I lured you out into this dark garden."

"Oh, maybe she does. She probably has a lot on her mind." Cybil smiled. She placed both hands on his shoulders and surprised him with a peck on the lips. "Thank you for your help this evening, you are very kind."

They stood staring at each other, then they heard Cybil's mother in the kitchen moving about. The clanging she made with the pots and pans sounded more like a signal than merely tidying up the kitchen.

They continued looking at each other, their mutual attraction beyond understanding, given the circumstances of the evening.

"I feel kind of guilty," said Jubal.

"Why, Jube? We've done nothing wrong."

She had called him Jube. He choked a bit. "My sister called me Jube. . . . There's a part of me that keeps saying it's too soon after the death of my family to feel pleasure. I feel good with you. I should still be suffering." He held her at arm's length. "Penitence must be paid. I have a debt."

She placed her finger gently against his lips. "Do you believe you can see someone for the first time and feel a strong connection?"

Jubal nodded as she continued.

"When I first saw you at the gate, you stuttered something about being late when in fact you were early. Then all through the long meal, even though so much had happened to you in the past days, you were concerned with me. You spoke of my schooling, mom's pot roast, and daddy's arthritis, and how lovely our house was, and on and on." She paused. "I should go in and relieve mom's anxiety. When I said earlier this evening at the gate that I hope to see you soon, I didn't really expect it to be this soon."

They held hands at the back door.

"I'll be gone for a few days," Jubal said. "May I call on you when I return?"

"Yes. I think I know where you're going and why. Please, Jube. Be careful. For me." She turned and passed through the door.

He watched her, then backed away from the house, hoping to catch sight of her through the illuminated windows.

The sky started to lighten in the east as Jubal made his way back toward the hotel.

An hour later, fifteen grown men stood in a semicircle at the foot of the Wicks Hotel stairs listening to Wayne Turner speak. Jubal watched and listened from the fringe of the group. "This is not a lark or game, gentlemen," Turner said. "I want you to understand that. Those of you who choose to go will be deputized and as such will bear all the responsibilities of said office. Any questions?"

"How long you figure we'll be gone?" This from a heavyset man nearly the age of Jubal's father.

"If you're concerned about being away from your families and such, you best not go. We'll be gone 'til we've finished the job, to answer your question." The man nodded as the marshal continued. "Who amongst you have long rifles, a good horse, and a sense of community spirit?"

Most of the men lifted their hands.

"Good, how many are going along?"

There were fewer recruits, but still a fair number.

"All right. The citizens going, raise your right hand and repeat your name when asked." The marshal started reading off an authoritative pledge, which the men dutifully repeated, Jubal included.

Halfway through, Marshal Turner stopped and pointed at Jubal, who had his arm raised. "What in the name of good sense are you doing, shooter?"

Jubal felt embarrassed, suddenly being the center of attention. "I want to be deputized like the rest."

"Are you eighteen?"

"No, sir. But close enough."

"Do you have a rifle?"

Jubal kicked a road apple with the toe of his boot. "I've got two pistols, and I think you could attest to the fact I'm a fair country shot, sir." *The rifle will stay sanctified.*

"Do you have a horse?"

"Yes, sir. Sort of. I mean, she's willing and I'll keep up." Actually, he didn't know if Frisk could keep up. But that wouldn't stop him.

"Get on out of here. Go on, scoot. You'll be late for school."

Jubal slunk away from the group as Marshal Turner continued swearing in the men, at the end of which he gave them instructions on what to bring and to be back in front of the hotel in a half hour. The men dispersed, excited in various degrees. The marshal caught Jubal by the sleeve as he started into the hotel.

"You're not going, boy," he said. "I can't have no gun-happy youngster along. Go on about your business. Get a few years on you."

Jubal objected but was silenced by the marshal's stern attitude. The man swaggered away.

SEVENTEEN

They turned their horses from Calle Piñon and rode out of town. "Dammit all to pieces, Ed. Looks like Al got hit . . . ahh, Christ a-mighty."

Pete Wetherford and Ed Thompson rode like the forces of hell were behind them. Pete continued to cry out his regrets while they fled. They rode for nearly an hour, exhausted and full of doubt, before they stopped by a small creek and slid from their tired horses.

Ed Thompson tried to cheer up Wetherford. "The way old Al went down, I don't think he felt any pain. I know that's not much consolation, but he was surely dead 'fore he hit the ground. He wouldn't have suffered none, that's for sure."

"Yeah, well, we should've hung around instead of chickened our tails out of town."

Big Ed began gathering wood for a fire. "Should we cook up some grub, Pete?"

Wetherford didn't answer but limped down to the creek bed and stared at the reflection of a clouded sky in the slow-moving waters. After a while, he called back to Ed. "Did you see who shot Al?"

"Couldn't really see much. Someone was sneaking along the fence line, but the shot that felled Al came from across the street, looked to me like it might of been that brat we saw on the street the day you got in that scuffle with the farmer. Say, is that the same little bastard from the farm—you know, with the rifle?"

"I'll find that little smartass, and when I do, he'll wish he'd stayed behind the plow." Pete tried to skip a rock down the creek. "Let's saddle up, Ed, and go back into town. What you say?"

"Ah, Pete, it's late. What good is it gonna do? Let it be for a while. I know what you're feeling, but get some rest."

Wetherford's harassed body still had not healed from his fall at Morning Peak. He willed himself to relax, contemplating the events at the canyon, thinking back to his rescue by the sheriff's band of misfits.

At first he'd thought the wolves had returned, and he was more than ready to do his best to decimate their number. But, quietly propped against the slanted wall of the crevasse, he'd heard voices. Faint at first, but clearly human.

He'd called out. "Come on up here, fellows. . . ." He knew he would have some explaining to do and that he would have to be careful. There was a gang of them. Sheriff Morton, Judge Wickham, a couple drifters, and some kid who he later found out was the little bastard with the peashooter. Wetherford recalled the painful trip out of the canyon and his beating by the older man, the judge, whom he hoped he had just killed back in town. It seemed a lifetime getting from the mountainous terrain back to the rickety jail and his incarceration. The doctor had fussed with him once they'd gotten back in town, giving him something for his discomfort. Then, nothing but glorious sleep.

The jail had been a welcome retreat after his ordeal in the canyon. Plenty of water, and the grub wasn't too bad. He recalled his anger at Al and Tauson for not coming back for him. After Pete had gotten out and finally hooked up with Al at Whiskey Creek, Al explained that Tauson had gone on a side journey into the canyon and had told him his brother was dead. So his ex-boss was going to hear some questions that needed answering.

Wetherford had found the Cerro Vista jail fascinating. The sheriff and his idiot Deputy Ron had made the place into their own house of ill repute, which he turned to work in his favor. He had waited for the moment Maria was relieving Deputy Ron's manly tensions.

"I'll have that shooter, Ron." Pete had reached through the bars of his cell into the Mexican girl's enclosure and pulled Ron's pistol from its sagging holster. The deputy's pants were down, his head thrown back, and his arms reaching up high, holding on to the bars. Maria had stopped.

"Gimme back that pistol, Wetherford," Deputy Ron had said, "or you're in a whole hell of a lot of trouble, you hear?"

"Shut your mouth, Ron, and unlock my cell. Do it."

Ron, wide-eyed, had taken the key ring and turned to Pete's cell door. "Can I cover my privates, Pete?"

"Leave them hanging, Deputy. Just do like I say and unlock this cell."

Shuffling with his pants around his ankles, Ron had nervously unlocked the barred door, then stepped back. "Listen to me, Petey. You ain't got no call to blabbermouth any of what you seen here, you understand?" Wetherford hadn't answered as he cocked the pistol and shot Ron in the upper chest.

It warmed his heart to remember Ron, thrashing away on the floor, kicking his feet like it would help distance himself from the pain. Wetherford recalled the sheriff then opening the connecting door, stupidly asking Ron why in the hell he was shooting off his pistol. Funny, Wetherford thought, that Ron was more concerned about people finding out he was having a love bout with a prisoner than he was about a prisoner escaping the jail, while the sheriff's thoughts had to do with what he perceived as an accidental discharge of a firearm. Wetherford chuckled.

Wetherford wrapped his thin blanket tighter around his body. He knew he'd made a mistake in town earlier that night not killing the farmer's son.

He started to drift as a soft, welcoming mist settled over his body. His breathing changed from rapid desperation to a calming, even flow. He remembered the bridge, the cursed log spanning the crevasse. The young guy levering that big old trunk.

He'd felt light for part of the fall, twisting and grasping as his head ricocheted off the base of a hard shrub. Clawing at the side of the crevasse wall, Pete fell, trying to plunge his fingers into the hard-packed clay. His legs slid violently off a rock outcropping as he suddenly grew religious and shouted to the Lord for deliverance. Chamisa that had gotten wedged into a small slit in the canyon wall briefly cushioned his headlong journey as his arms beat like a hummingbird, grasping for purchase.

Wetherford remembered Jorge's screams for help as a small piñon was swept away with his avalanche. A number of boulders, tree branches, and chamisa accompanied him on his downward journey. In the last forty feet, the walls began to slope slightly outward, slowing his sudden stop at the bottom.

Wetherford had taken a sharp breath, causing a sudden stab of pain in his right side. As the shock started to wear off, his whole body vibrated. *If this is death, please, God, let it be quick.*

The longer he had rested, the more intense the noise in his head. He'd lost track of time. Wave upon wave of dizzying pain wracked his body. Then nothing. When he awoke it had been raining. Softly at first, then heavier.

He'd been sure Al would come for him. He lay still, each movement sending lightninglike quivers throughout his body. "Jorge, hey, compadre," he called out. "How you faring?"

He heard only the soft beat of the rain in response.

After what had seemed like several hours, he'd heard a rustling in the brush among the dried mesquite and sage. "Al, I'm over here. Al, where are you, brother? I'm paining pretty good. Stop fooling around."

The disturbance on the canyon floor had continued. Wetherford, afraid of snakes, tried to move his arm to reach for his pistol but his coat sleeve had been ripped inside out and covered his hand.

Wolves or coyotes, he couldn't tell. He could see their vague shapes against the cloudy sky. They seemed to be gathered some twenty feet away, snarling, disagreeing with one another. Wetherford dug the heels of his boots into the soft earth and inched his way backward to the wall of the crevasse. Once sitting up, he was able to reach across with his left hand and unholster his .44. The effort to sit made him dizzy. The animals tearing away at Jorge swayed in front of him. Pete had thought about scaring away the beasts with a round from his pistol, but it occurred to him that allowing them their fill with Jorge would mean they would be less likely to come after him.

He had been certain the Mexican was dead until he heard him scream, as if the wolves in their frenzy had awakened the man's soul. Pete had shivered while the dark shapes snapped and fought the fallen Jorge as the man tried to beat the wolves away.

The feast had gone on for quite some time. Later, a lone animal stared quietly at Wetherford. He raised his pistol and waited. The head of the wolf tipped slightly down, eyes hooded over the dipped brow. Either not able or willing to continue the standoff, she'd trotted back to the depleted corpse of Jorge Morales, sniffed several times, and, after a slow backward glance at Wetherford, moved away.

EIGHTEEN

Twelve riders and the marshal gathered at the front of the hotel.

The sky was now light, with long, soft red streaks trailing east to west against the blue-gray heavens. Without a word, Wayne Turner raised his hand to point southwest. The posse moved at a trot along the street, passing Judge Wickham's house, where Jubal hid, watching as they filed past the corral.

When they were nearly a quarter mile down the road, he moved Frisk onto the trail and followed. He had borrowed a saddle from the barn. Maybe "borrow" wouldn't be the appropriate word. In any case, Frisk seemed at ease with the saddle and with Jubal on her back.

Jubal still had his right hand in the air when Wayne Turner finished his pledge, so he decided that, indeed, he was now a Deputy U.S. Marshal.

They rode for several hours, Jubal trying to keep

proper space between him and the posse. He had promised the judge he would stay in the vicinity and do the "proper thing." So here he was, following a group of men who didn't want him along, knowing in his gut it was all a bone-headed mistake, because they were certainly headed in the wrong direction.

On several occasions, Jubal noted Marshal Turner sending someone back to see who was following, and each time Jubal managed to move out of sight. As the land changed from foothills to level terrain, Jubal noticed Turner had spread his troops in a line abreast, the horsemen thirty yards or so apart, looking for a track.

At one point near midmorning the group gathered for a meeting, and it appeared as if there were dissension among them. Riders pointed accusatory fingers at the man in the center of the circle, U.S. Marshal Wayne Turner.

Jubal stopped on a small rise under a tree to take in the confrontation and was surprised when the whole group came riding back toward him. He started to move, but a shout from the men let him know he had been seen.

They came hard, the marshal leading the way. As they drew closer, Jubal raised his hands in the air. "It's me, Jubal Young!"

When they rode up he could feel the anger from the marshal. "What in hell are you doing?"

Jubal lowered his arms. "Just out for a morning ride, Mr. Turner."

The men gathered in a circle around Jubal. Not finding him amusing, some of them directed their frustration at him. "You're gonna get your ass shot, you know that?

We're out here looking for some desperate souls and here you are, Sunday-mornin' it on that big old plow horse."

"I thought I said you weren't coming along with us," Marshal Turner said.

"You did say that, sir. I think you could also say I wasn't with you. Right?"

"Well, what in hell's name are you doing out here?"

"To be honest, Marshal"—Jubal looked around at the faces, they all seemed like family men—"I guess I was just waiting for you to turn north."

"Why would I do that when the bastards rode out westward?"

"You'd do that, sir, because Billy Tauson is from up around Alamosa, Colorado. Pete Wetherford and anyone left in the gang will probably follow Billy up there."

"Why is that?"

"Because Billy is the leader. I think we scared Wetherford off in town last night. He's probably given up on me and his promise to do me in, at least for the time being." Jubal paused. "I think he's going up Alamosa way."

Marshal Turner slapped the reins on his hands, then ripped into Jubal. "I've told you that you're not part of this group, dammit. I'm not telling you again. Get it?"

"I would have liked to be a part of your posse, Marshal." Jubal pulled Frisk's reins and backed away from the men. "And do this thing in the right way. But so be it, good luck."

One of the men called out to him, "I hear tell there's good hunting up Colorado way, son. Catch yourself some squirrel."

◆◆◆◆

By noon Jubal had backtracked Wetherford and his companion to the place where they'd laid a false trail to the southwest. He zigzagged for several miles, leaning over Frisk's withers, scanning the earth. After another hour they came upon a dry creek bed, and there, plain as a smile on his sister's face, were two sets of fresh horse tracks. The dry gully wound its way east, then back north, then westerly, and then once again toward the north.

A low mesa in front of him would prove a vantage point, and once on top, Jubal could see for miles. The creek bed below indeed snaked through the flat plain but always straightened northward. No need to follow the serpentine trail; he could save time by cutting across the plain and joining up with the creek farther on. Miles ahead, the creek converged into a canyon at the base of the foothills reaching into Colorado.

Jubal pushed Frisk hard, hoping to make up time. Wetherford and his riding partner went to considerable effort trying to hide their intended path. But of course they didn't count on being trailed by Jubal Young.

Clouds obscured the late afternoon sun, and a chilled wind stirred the chamisa as Jubal made his way over the vast open land. Juniper dotted the earth, looking deliberately placed, the growth spaced evenly apart.

To Jubal's right were the Sangre de Cristo Mountains, nearly twenty miles away. Although it was late in the season, he was certain it would snow soon. There couldn't be any doubt those clouds moving from the foothills in the west would be full of moisture.

Lying in front of him, a deep barranca, and just

beyond, a high mesa looming up several hundred feet out of the now-misted sky. He decided he would push on to the east side of the tall plateau, trying for shelter from the oncoming westerly storm. He made it up through a steep crevasse and urged Frisk to hurry on toward the tableland. Jubal wasn't concerned about losing his quarry. He knew Wetherford and friend would be forced to hole up also.

As they neared the base of the broad raised land, he wondered what internal struggle of the earth had produced such an unusual form. The mesa sprouted almost straight up from the flat land leading up to it. On the east side he found slabs of rock that formed a number of structures, one resembling an enormous welcoming archway. Someone had built a now-abandoned lean-to against the easterly wall, a rickety structure to house hay and feed. The entry and interior were wide enough for him and Frisk to slide through and turn around, just as the storm unleashed its fury on the landscape.

He stared out at the howling skies for hours. The snow found small crevices in Jubal's new shelter, the wind swirling annoying flakes around the darkening structure. But he and Frisk were fairly warm and dry. He wondered what Wetherford and his cohort were up to. Would they have had the good sense to look for cover early?

The wind picked up, sweeping across the plain unobstructed. Jubal started a small fire and sat on a mound of hay, contemplating his situation. He felt as if he had several advantages, mostly being that Pete Wetherford didn't know Jubal was on his tail.

But not knowing his exact location bothered Jubal. Perhaps somewhere northwest of Cerro Vista and certainly still south of Alamosa. As he leaned against the weathered side of the shelter, weariness took over and Jubal fell almost instantly asleep.

He was awakened by a sound. The wind? Had Frisk moved? Jubal reached over and clasped the horse's leg between her hoof and first joint. He could feel the animal's pulse—racing. Was there someone close by? Frisk pulled her leg from Jubal's grasp and snorted, pounding her heavy hoof into the darkened earth.

Then a rattle.

Frisk danced about in the confined space. Jubal got out Audrey, then took a small branch from the embers and held it in front of himself, finally spotting the snake close to Frisk's front hooves. The strike, when it came, was incredibly fast, catching Frisk just above the right front hoof.

She pranced about, trying to step on the now-coiled rattler. Jubal fired into the spiraled mass of snake but missed, the bullet ricocheting with a high-pitched whine off a plowshare.

He tucked the gun back under his belt and once again held the smoldering red branch out in front of him. The rattler had retreated back against the rock wall.

Jubal, with his left hand, held the lighted stick as far out from his body as he could get it. Teasing the snake to get its focus on the stick, he reached out to secure the slippery-looking reptile behind its head, but the rattler would have none of it. Hissing a warning by lashing out at Jubal's hand, it struck at open air.

Once again Jubal tormented the snake until he got it to move out of its comfortable form. It slid along the wall for a couple of yards, then once again coiled to take a stand.

Jubal crawled under Frisk's belly and placed his right hand as close as he dared behind the snake's head, then tried to distract it once again with the lighted stick—it made an exploratory strike at the branch, then recoiled and waited. Frisk pumped her left rear leg up and down, trying to find the rattler. The snake struck again, reaching out several feet, nearly half its body length, and finding only air once more. As it again tried to recoil itself, Frisk's heavy hoof caught it squarely on its head.

The reptile thrashed about, then grew still. Jubal grabbed it just below the rattle. Keeping it away from his body, he whipped it out into the storm.

Passing the burning stick close to Frisk's hooves, Jubal looked for and found two bright red spots where she had been hit.

Knowing it would be the death knell for Frisk if he didn't do something quickly, Jubal unsheathed his long-bladed hunting knife and attempted to coax Frisk closer to the fire, but she was still too excited. He propped a glowing piece of firewood into the dirt next to her and once again examined the twin punctures on her lower shin. He held the hair away from the two holes as Frisk continued to try and pull her leg out of his grasp.

Jubal stopped and retrieved several lumps of sugar from his pack and gave a couple of them to Frisk. On his knees, he fed the horse with his left hand, holding the knife with his right, making two deft cuts across the twin holes made by the snake. He then massaged the wounds to help discharge the venom.

As he gently tried to get the wounds to bleed, he felt what seemed to be a small thorn buried in one of the holes. Jubal squeezed until he could pull the object from the wound, feeling a prick on his finger from the thorn's sharp point. He finally got it free and, in the faint light, realized the semi-curved object wasn't a stick or a thorn, but a fang.

Jubal squeezed his finger hard and sucked on the tiny hole. Taking the knife, he split the hole into four sections and once again tried to extract any possible toxin. Taking deep breaths of air as his lips bit down hard on the opening, he sucked out as much venom as he could.

If both he and Frisk were poisoned, they would be in serious trouble.

Miles from a doctor and with the snow mounting, they were at least two days from Cerro Vista.

It took a while for Jubal and Frisk to settle down. If there was one snake, there could be more. But he rekindled the warm fire, did his best to tend their wounds, and now could only sit and wait.

Devilish images disturbed his sleep, waking him several times. If he could only substitute these nightmares with a sweet dream . . . his sister playing in the fields, picking wildflowers, his parents hand in hand, surveying their land. Any good dream would serve.

Jubal and Frisk rousted themselves from their long night, and after he had a breakfast of beef jerky and a tin cup of hot water slightly discolored by a few sprinkles of ground coffee, Jubal gave Frisk grain from the bag strapped behind the saddle. Her breakfast consisted of several cups of cracked corn and oats, much to her liking. Frisk didn't seem to show any aftereffects from her encounter with the snake. As far as his health, Jubal was tired, but not sick. He felt lucky. The weariness he could handle.

The day grew misty, not as thick as the day before but still overcast and leaden. The snow drifted in places as high as three feet, but the wind had swept the balance of the plain clear.

Nearly an hour into their journey north, they started to cross an arroyo when Jubal heard a high-pitched whine that seemed to come from the ravine itself, around a bend, about a hundred yards ahead. They moved cautiously, rounding the turn.

In the middle of a narrow trench lay a horse, its head moving slowly, a bone protruding from its left front leg. It must have stepped in a hole, Jubal thought. He looked ahead at the tracks, only one set of prints leading away, and they were deep. Pete Wetherford and his companion were riding double.

They wouldn't get far in this weather. They had tried to skirt around the drifts piled high against the east wall of the ravine and hadn't put the horse out of its misery, probably so as not to be heard. *So maybe they do suspect they're being followed, but certainly not by a boy.* After examining Wetherford's horse track, Jubal determined they had probably passed that way an hour earlier. The hoofprints in the light snow were just beginning to freeze at the top, where fine crystals had melted to form a soft mound.

He certainly didn't have a choice where the horse was concerned. He felt bad for her and yet he knew a break that severe would never heal even if he could get her to a vet, which he couldn't. He walked Frisk back around the bend and tied her firmly to a juniper, then proceeded back to the stricken animal. There wasn't any rush. The farther away Wetherford and his friend were, the better.

Jubal sat on a large rock, pistol in hand, waiting. Having spent most of his life on a farm, he had a strong affinity for animals and hated seeing them suffer. The mare tried struggling to her feet, her eyes wide with fear. Jubal cradled her large head and gentled her. He then looked to the darkening skies to the west. A flash of light in pewter-colored clouds. Jubal raised his pistol. As the thunder clapped, he fired.

Frisk tramped about where she was tied. As Jubal approached her, he thought he saw an accusatory look, and as he eased into the saddle, she felt a little less welcoming.

NINETEEN

The rain had turned to snow, and Pete Wetherford and Ed Thompson were caught in it. Within minutes, a two-inch blanket covered the open plain. When the weather changed once again, they were well and truly soaked. At long last, a warm breeze coming from the west finally drove away the snow.

"We gotta find a spot to overnight." Ed bundled his coat tighter around his neck. "I'm frozen and sick of packing double."

Wetherford ran his hand around his growth of beard. "Nah, can't you feel that warm air? It's trailing in from Arizona or someplace hot. Why, hell's fire, you'll be stripping off your shirt in no time, bathing in the sun." He tightened his hands around the reins.

Ed flinched as they rode on. To the west they spotted a small fire, and after another hour they came upon a community of Mexicans who had built a number of adobe homes along a meandering stream. They headed toward the village, soon closing in on a number of small pens housing goats and chickens behind modest dwellings.

"Let's pass to the east of them shacks and skirt around, see if there ain't some lonely places farther on," Wetherford said.

"What you mean?"

"It might be there's a house farther out in the country-side that would welcome a couple rain-soaked travelers." Pete winked and gave a short dirty laugh. They continued to circle the dwellings, staying a half mile to the east and north. After a while the adobe huts were not as clustered, then the line of homes abruptly stopped.

"I can't get warm." Ed rubbed his hands together briskly. "Think we left that village wanting for visitors, Pete. Don't see any more houses."

"Bet you're wrong. You have no imagination, boy. There's always some idiot who wants to be different, thinks if he builds his ramshackle house in town he'll be just like the rest of the folks. Nah, old Jose built his place on a little hill close by the river so he could see the relatives' adobe shacks all crowded and nasty in town. Wait and see."

The river took a turn to the north, ran straight for half a mile, then wound back toward the mountains. Perched on a small rise looking down on the streambed was a shack. To call it a house would be exaggerating; it was more of a makeshift shelter.

"*Hola,*" Pete called out as they neared the dwelling. They stopped short of a chicken coop. No answer from the house. Pete tried again. "*Hola. Por favor, comida para dos hombres.*"

"What're you saying?" Ed asked.

"I'm asking for food." He shouted once again. "We have *mucho dinero, señor. Por favor.*"

"There's nobody here, Pete. Let's move on."

"They're here, wait and see. See the couple horses in that corral and the wash on the clothesline? They're here."

They were at the back of the shack. One tiny window looked out toward the chicken coop. "They'll be coming now," Wetherford said.

"Why you say that?"

"Have faith, amigo. Ole Pete wouldn't steer you wrong."

A woman rounded the corner of the house, the river to her back. With her weathered look, it was hard to determine her age, maybe mid-thirties. Her long plain dress was tattered and worn through at the hips and elbows, a denim apron tied around her slim waist. She was handsome in a manly sort of way, legs firmly planted, eyeing the two newcomers. After shaking her long black hair, she raised a Winchester rifle. *"¿Qué pasa?"*

Wetherford, smiling his best toothy grin, worked at making his eyes light up. He raised his hands in exaggerated surrender. *"Comida para mi amigo* and me. I pay *dinero* to you." He pointed to her, took out several coins, and let her see them.

The woman motioned with her rifle for the men to get off their horse. She allowed the weapon to cradle in her arm with the barrel pointed toward the ground as Wetherford held the money out in front of him as a peace offering. The woman stopped his forward progress with a grunt, looking intently at the money.

Once again she motioned with the rifle for the men to dismount. She rounded the corner of the house and pointed for them to sit next to a rounded adobe fire pit. Propping the rifle next to the door, she disappeared inside while Wetherford and Ed warmed themselves next to the fire. Pete still had the money in his hand when she came out with a bowl of beans, rice, fresh masa, and a pan. She cooked fresh tortillas, wrapped them quickly, then heated the beans and rice and handed the food to the men on a long stick with a paddle shape at the end. They ate their fill, Big Ed continuing to ask for more. Wetherford watched the woman intently and leaned over to Ed.

"She don't have no man, no sirree. She's alone. I suspect the master of the house is away, dead, or lying in there sick as a horse. She's lonely."

"Don't do it, Pete." Ed grew nervous. "We got ourselves enough trouble as it is." Wetherford ignored him. "Pete, you listening?"

"I heard you. What is it you think I'm gonna do?"

"I just don't want to be party to no more killing and molesting."

"Who said anything about killing?" Pete rubbed his stomach as if in gratitude. *"Señorita, por favor, muchas gracias."* He handed her the money.

She seemed grateful as she counted it.

"Is possible, to sleep, *dor—dorm—*ah, hell, what's the word for 'sleep'?" He looked to Ed.

"Don't ask me, Pete. I *no hably Españo.*"

Frustrated, Wetherford called to the woman and mimed sleeping, his two hands making a pillow next to his head. He pointed toward the house. The woman shook her head no and went about cleaning up the remnants of the meal. Wetherford dug once again into his pocket and waved more money at her, but she took no notice as she continued her work. The two men finished their food and prepared to leave. The sun was down below the tree line across from the stream, the light beaming through the leaves, making dark patterns on the side of the house.

The woman finished her chores and stepped to the door of the house. *"Adios, muchachos, vaya con Dios."* She grabbed the rifle with her free hand and started through the door.

Pete had his pistol out and cocked it, the sound unmistakable. The woman stopped in the threshold of the door, her back to the men. She slumped just slightly, knowing she would be in for a long night.

The morning sun found the men still packing double heading north. They rode for an hour without speaking. Finally, Ed pulled a canteen loose from his saddlebag and took a long draught. "You seem kinda with yourself this morning. What is it?"

Pete half smiled. "I went against my better judgment with that old gal."

"Really? It sounded like you were having right good sport with her. Kept me awake most of the night."

"No, I don't mean that. I mean the leaving her alive to go to the law." They rode on for a spell, then stopped. "You see that mesa up ahead, half a mile or so?"

Ed looked and nodded.

"Hop off and head up there. I'll meet you later. Probably a couple hours." He laughed in his peculiar way.

"The walk will do you good, cowboy. I gotta go back and take care of business."

Big Ed slid off the back of the horse. "Ah, come on, leave it. That gal did everything you asked, let her be."

Pete ignored him, turned the horse, and started back toward the house by the river.

After a mile, Jubal made his way out of the ravine, thinking it would be too easy for the Wetherford party to be waiting around one of the many turns.

Out on the vast plain once again, he looked to the north. The wind had picked up and the occasional flurry of snow twirled about like small dust devils. Jubal thought he saw smoke miles to the northeast. He couldn't be sure, as the sky and plain were the same gray smudge. He rode onto a small mesa and cupped his hands around his eyes to see where it was coming from. It would appear, then vanish. A movement, and a sound like the wind trying to find its way.

At last a train came into view about five miles away, appearing suddenly out of a gully as it labored its way north. It occurred to Jubal that Wetherford might abandon yet another horse and go north on the train. More than likely, he thought.

It grew warmer and the snow changed to drizzle, then rain. The northern sky was blanketed with streaked vertical stripes of a downpour dominating the vast open panorama to the east toward the mountains. Jubal dismounted and led Frisk over the bank of a steep arroyo with an overhanging large piñon dangling from its edge. The arroyo was eight to ten feet deep and ten yards wide, and provided protection from the deluge.

The arroyo looked as if it stretched for miles, winding its way eventually up into the foothills close by and then into the mountains. Jubal crouched down below Frisk's belly, trying to stay dry. The center of the creek bed began to fill, the gradually slanted floor trickling with just the beginnings of a stream coming off the hills to the east.

Jubal found some joy watching the creek quickly meander through the arroyo, starting first to form a narrow wandering flow and then continuing to expand. To the east about forty yards the arroyo turned and disappeared, debris now beginning to pick up on the far bank where the stream curved.

Jubal was surprised to see a stray coyote hustling along the damp earth in the direction of the running water. It trotted past, intent on its journey, seeming not to notice the horse and huddled rider. Several times, the animal attempted to scale the sides of the arroyo, only to slip back and scamper farther along. It seemed desperate, almost in a panic, its clawing and futile struggle appearing unnatural. Jubal's knowledge of coyotes was limited to hearing them and shooing them away from the farm, but he had never seen one so blindly afraid. Before it disappeared around a distant curve, the animal looked back toward the mountains. Jubal, in his hunched-over shelter, marveled at the mysterious behavior.

The rain continued in strange patterns. It would pelt down hard, making it difficult for Jubal to see more than a couple of yards in front of him. Then it would let up briefly, then shower down again in pea-sized drops just short of hail. Breathing became difficult, almost as if the driving force of the rain had pushed out all the oxygen from the surrounding air. Frisk remained still.

Jubal heard, above the rain, the rumblings of thunder from the east. The downpour lasted for nearly an hour. The stream was full. Jubal wished he could be under the shadow of Morning Peak to see the dark earth being saturated.

The thunder from the hills and mountains seemed to be increasing. The sound, Jubal thought, maybe wasn't thunder—not coming from the sky but down lower through the canyons to the east. At a lull in the torrent, Jubal looked toward the mountains. They had cleared, though it was still overcast in the upper sky and a mist persisted in the largest of the canyons. It seemed to be moving downward. A cascade of water bounded over the edge of a distant cliff, the raging stream packed with trees, limbs, and chamisa rolling like wayward balls down the steep rock face.

The coyote must have sensed something long before Jubal's instincts alerted him. A flood. The water ran off into the canyons and built into a raging wall.

Jubal mounted Frisk and attempted to regain the high ground where they had descended earlier. They made it nearly halfway up the water-soaked wall, then slipped back down. He dismounted and tried leading Frisk up the slippery clay embankment. Each time they would get nearly to the top, but no farther.

The noise became louder. Jubal remounted Frisk and began a hurried, determined gallop west, down the arroyo and away from the now-thunderous onslaught.

After a hundred yards there was still no easy access out of the trench. He knew the farther into the flatland he rode, the more the arroyo's walls would descend, until at last becoming level with the endless plain.

As he rode, the walls did shorten. But as the arroyo turned, it deepened as the valley curved back east toward the mountains. He dismounted and, with the reins in his hand, tried once again to lead Frisk up the steep side wall. She would make it nearly all the way, thrashing with her hind legs for purchase as the wall got steeper. Then, despite Jubal's urging, she would stumble back into the now-ankle-deep water.

The roar from the oncoming flood had gotten impossibly loud.

Ahead, he could see a tributary spurring off to the right. Jubal headed for it. As he neared, a loud prolonged rumbling preceded a wall of water that emptied into the arroyo from the tributary.

He was trapped.

The water carried broken trees, stumps, and branches that drove hard into the arroyo wall opposite the formerly dry tributary. In moments the flood coming from behind Jubal caught up with him and then met the tributary. He scrambled off of Frisk and grabbed her mane with both hands just above her withers as the water whirled them in circles before carrying them down the tumultuous arroyo.

A giant limb from a tree passed wickedly close to Jubal's head. He contemplated latching onto the treelike raft, but decided he would feel best if he survived with Frisk rather than leaving her behind.

They continued their chaotic journey. Between spitting out the brackish water and fending off tree limbs, Jubal had all he could handle, but he continued encouraging Frisk to do her best. The beast's eyes were wide with fear, her legs slowing, she must finally have realized she was floating. A dead squirrel moved past, then a bush of yellow flowers hung up on the back of Frisk's head before drifting away.

Jubal struggled to stay alive.

It once again began to rain.

At last Frisk snorted and seemed to get taller. Jubal realized the earth at least on this side of the arroyo began to ascend upward. Jubal struggled to hold on to Frisk's mane as the animal gradually pulled herself out of the steep ditch. Jubal suddenly found himself standing upright next to a shivering Frisk. They were safe.

On a rise nearby, a copse of piñon looked like a welcoming shelter. Jubal led Frisk by the reins and tied her to a limb. The rain had stopped but the roaring floodwaters continued to carry debris down the arroyo. Jubal sat on the rise and watched as first a small wide-eyed deer came paddling by and later a dead horse floated downstream. It looked like the mare that he had shot earlier, its bloated stomach rising just above the muddy water. It would be many miles before the animal found its final resting place.

Exhausted, he drifted off to sleep under a sheltering pine. When he awoke, he rummaged through his soaked saddlebags. Fortunately, the tin box where he had sealed his matches seemed intact.

He foraged and found a few broken pine boughs. In a small opening in the earth, he found a nest of dry tinder secreted away by varmints. When he lit a match, the twigs and small branches caught, and the larger limbs Jubal had stacked to the side dried quickly. Frisk eased closer to the fire as Jubal swept her hide with a flat piece of wood. The water poured from her long hair. After taking care of Frisk, he took off his clothes and, tying his shirt to a piñon tree branch, twisted it vigorously to wring it as dry as possible. After doing the same with his pants and long underwear, he hung them in a branch above the fire and stood close to the burning wood, dancing naked forward to back, trying to stay warm.

TWENTY

The following morning's sun appeared as if the deluge of the century had simply not occurred, and within two hours Jubal had found the railroad tracks. He followed them for several miles, until he reached a group of stand-alone buildings in the wide-open plain. Signs reading TAOS JUNCTION and DENVER & RIO GRANDE R.R. hung on an old boxcar sitting to the side of the track. Next to the train station were a pair of wagons and a corral with a couple of horses. Jubal slid off Frisk and went up the steps into the railcar. An elderly man tended the desk inside.

"Good day, sir," Jubal said. "I wonder if you could tell me your train schedule."

The man looked down at a booklet. "You just missed the ten-forty to Antonito and on up to Alamosa. Won't be another going that way until tomorrow, same time." The old-timer looked up. "Unless you want to go down south to Espanola or Santa Fe, of course that would be later today, around six or so."

"So the train stops here twice a day, one south, one north."

"Not exactly." The man got up gingerly from his swivel chair and motioned for Jubal to follow him outside. "If we have passengers or freight, we lower that big white ball there."

A tall pole stood adjacent to the track. At the top, an angled board held a sphere nearly two feet in radius, attached by several lines through an arrangement of pulleys.

"Yep, just like a flagpole," continued the man. "If the engineer sees the ball down, he stops the train. Otherwise, he highballs it right on through."

"You say the train that just went through is going to Alamosa?"

"Right you are, son. Should be there around four this afternoon."

"Excuse the questions, sir. But I'm looking for a couple dudes. One of them would have been looking poorly, as if he'd been in an accident, maybe limping."

"Remember them well." He paused. "Rode in asking directions, arguing about whether to take the train on up north to Colorado or not. Damned if they didn't finally just ride off. Heavens to Betsy. They were still dickering when they disappeared over the horizon."

Jubal mounted Frisk. "Much obliged, sir. How far would you say it is to Alamosa?"

"I'd say closer to seventy-five than eighty miles, sonny."

Jubal nodded his thanks. He thought it might have

been better for him if the two men had taken the train, for he wouldn't have to be so on the alert for an ambush. But one takes the sweet with the sour, as his ma used to say.

He reached down and patted his horse on the withers. "Keep a watchful eye, will you, Frisk?"

She snorted as if she'd understood.

They passed through Tres Piedras well into the night. No one was in view, as the small community wrapped itself into a cocoon of sleep. They pushed on through a wide gap in the rock structure.

Frisk was capable of being ridden all night. Jubal figured they would arrive in Alamosa sometime midmorning. Whether or not he himself would be up to the journey, he would find out soon enough.

He felt lucky they had the railroad tracks to follow, the path most of the time paralleling the ribbon of steel heading north. At one point in the middle of the night, Jubal dozed off and awoke to find Frisk had wandered off the path and was standing in a field, head down, joining Jubal in his late-night snooze. He eased off the big mare and walked her back to the trail. They continued like this for a number of miles, Jubal recalling the time when he had walked with his sister Pru alongside the buckboard on the way from Kansas to New Mexico.

"Jube, I'll race you to the top of that hill, where that old tree is leaning out over the road." Prudence skipped sideways along the rutted trail, egging Jubal on.

"What? I don't understand. What do you mean?"

"You know what I mean, Jubal Young. You're just trying to cheat 'cause you know I'm faster."

"*Faster, ho, ho. If you live to be a hundred you wouldn't be as fast as me.*"

"*Ma,*" Pru cried. "*Count it off, one, two, three.*"

Bea, driving the team of horses, yelled, "*One, one and a quarter, one and a half, one and three quarters—*"

Both of the children jumped the gun, and they were off. Pru was fast and Jubal had trouble passing her right at the finish. Under a tree, they both tried to catch their breath.

Jubal had just had his thirteenth birthday. Pru was ten and didn't seem to mind the arduous trip from Kansas City into the "Wild West," as she loved to call it.

"*Ma, can Jube and I explore up over that funny-looking flat hill?*" Pru asked once the two children returned to the buckboard.

Bea gazed out over the rolling hills to the stark-appearing mesa ahead. "*Let's wait 'til we get a mite closer, Pru, so I can see what's what up there.*"

Sometimes on this voyage, Jubal would spell ma, and mother and daughter would walk. They needn't have; it just became a nice change to get out and stretch one's legs.

"*Ma, when will we see Pa? Do you know?*" Pru asked her mother as they walked side by side.

"*When we get there, dear.*"

The two exchanged looks.

"*That's a fairly clever way of asking 'How much longer, Ma' for the hundredth time. I commend you on your enterprising thought, Pru.*"

Pru skipped alongside the wagon. "*What does it mean, 'enterprising'?*"

"*Let's think here for a jiffy. 'Enterprising' means . . . oh,*" *it could mean being ambitious, businesslike, relentless. Kind of like what your pa is doing, Prudence."*

"You mean Pa taking the train to New Mexico while we bounce along in this buckboard? Like that, Ma?"

"No, dear." Bea thought this funny. "Your pa has to make sure his sealed bid for the land we wanted has been properly processed."

"Huh."

"He's a very smart man, sweetheart, and what he has done will be great for this family. Trust me."

Jubal recalled hearing those words from his mother. At that time they were twenty days from Kansas City, and the group of other wagons Jubal, Sr., had arranged for his wife to join in Topeka had not materialized, but Bea Young was a hardy woman and had pushed on with her two young-sters. In the end, they'd made it.

At one point in the long night, Jubal thought he heard the train. After a while, he decided it had more than likely been a combination of night sounds and their echoes through the ravines. For some time, he listened carefully.

They stopped for the night alongside a grassy streambed. They were days into their journey, but it seemed ages since they had left Kansas City. The three members of the Young family stretched out in the buckboard, each with their own bedroll. The hoops that formed the roof of the wagon vibrated with the wind, the canvas cover slapping endlessly against the wood stays.

"Quiz me, Ma."

"On what subject, dear?"

Pru clapped. "Anything birds. Okay?"

"Name six birds of prey whose habitat is mostly North American," Bea said drowsily.

"Eagle, buzzard, hawk, condor, turkey vulture, owl, and the most dangerous of all, the dreaded Latinus Jubus.*"*

They giggled in spite of their sleepiness.

Pru tried to adopt a scary voice. "The Latinus Jubus *is a creature who comes out only at night."*

"Nocturnal."

"Yes, and as I said, it only comes out at night."

"'Nocturnal' is night, dear, speaking of which, don't you think we should go to sleep?"

"Yes, Mother, but Jubal scared me."

"I scared you?" Jubal said. "How in the heck did I do that?"

"You made me make up a name for you that frightened me."

"I didn't make you do any such thing, you did that on your own."

Pru tried to be serious. "But if you didn't look all gawky and birdlike, it never would have occurred to me."

Jubal rolled over in the tight quarters. "Ma, would you speak to your daughter, please? She's loco."

The wagon quieted, and the tired souls gradually drifted toward sleep.

Then, softly from Pru, "The Latinus Jubus *is a night bird, who makes funny sounds and wipes its beak under its wing instead of its handkerchief. It is a slow creature, whose intelligence is matched in the North American climes only by the* Slugus Latimus.*"*

She then whispered a prayer.

Four angels to my bed,
Four angels 'round my head.
One to watch, and one to pray,
And two to bear my soul away.

Jubal missed his sister, a spirit bright and full of life always ready with her quick wit. She had been fond of saying to the family, "When I grow up, I'm going to be a preacher in God's House of Mirth. I'll start each sermon with a 'ha, ha,' and end with a 'hee, hee, hee.'"

TWENTY-ONE

Seeing the evening train come thundering out of the north the previous night, heading back toward Taos Junction, had been exciting, the people on the train moving about as they traveled. Jubal wondered who they were and where they were going. He still had the harsh reality of a long trek ahead of him and bedded down for the night.

He awoke early and walked a fair distance from his campsite. Each day he gave himself the task of strapping his father's shabby holster to his belt and tried to get used to the weight and feel of the weapon.

He suspected that Audrey might have been someone other than the saloon keeper in his pa's earlier life. Jubal would rarely fire the weapon, simply experiment with ways of sliding it from his right-side holster with the least amount of friction. He had to admit that the piece was clumsy and he knew in the end he would be reluctant to use it. But he also knew the quest he had set for himself was full of men who would not hesitate, would relish the opportunity to take advantage of a youngster who was unwilling or not eager enough.

The sky remained a bluish gray for nearly an hour until the sun finally rose over the Sangres. Jubal and Frisk pressed on.

They walked into Antonito at midmorning, still with thirty miles to go to Alamosa. Antonito was a friendly community, and people spoke out sincere morning greetings to Jubal as he tied Frisk to a post outside of Anne's, a GOOD EATS establishment as proclaimed by a small nearby sign.

"What'll it be, cowboy?" The woman looked as if she were the proprietor.

"What will twenty-five cents buy me, ma'am?"

"Not a whole helluva lot. But I guess a stack of pancakes and coffee. That do?"

Jubal nodded. The small place appeared to be the only restaurant in town, crowded with locals having their coffee, gossiping, and getting their day started. The waitstaff consisted of just Anne—a hearty soul who seemed to enjoy what she was doing.

Anne, with a mug of steaming coffee, stopped to chat. "Where you heading for, son?"

"I'm going up Alamosa way. Looking around for some . . . people."

"I've got just the man for you." Anne turned and called into the kitchen, "Bob!"

A bearded man stuck his head out of the partition. "You called, ma'am?"

"Yeah, this young'un is looking for some folk up Alamosa way. Come out and give a neighbor a hand."

"What 'bout the dishes?"

"They'll keep."

The dishwasher came out of the kitchen wearing a bibbed apron with buckskin pants and red flannel shirt, his bald pate set off by a face covered in a tangled red beard. "You from up Alamosa way, son?"

Jubal felt he needed to be careful. "Oh, no, not really. I was just telling the lady—"

"That isn't no lady," Bob whispered. "That's Anne. Just a kidding, she's a nice old gal. . . . So, you're heading north and—"

"Yes, I was telling her I was looking for some people who I'd heard were ranching up around Alamosa."

"I've worked all up through there. Maybe that's why Anne thought I could help you out. What's their names, son?"

Jubal took a quick look around the restaurant. "Oh, well, it isn't that important. I appreciate your concern, sir, but I'll be drifting on. I was just making conversation with the lady, is all. Nothing, really."

The man nodded and went back into the kitchen. Jubal finished his meal, left his quarter on the counter, and went out into the bright sunlight.

At the side of the restaurant, a water trough stood beckoning. Jubal poured a small amount of water from a bucket into the center of the pump to prime it, then ducked his head in the icy water, scrubbing his face and hands. As he was tying Frisk to a steel ring next to the water, Bob came out the back of the restaurant, having a smoke. The man stood silently, then approached Jubal.

"I live up in the mountains most of the year. Time to

time, I come down for a little respite, if you will. I consider myself a fair judge of character and I'd say you're a young man who needs some . . ."—he paused—"help. Maybe even some local awareness."

The man's directness left Jubal uncertain of his words. "All I said to the lady was that I was looking for someone. That's all."

"I been on my own since your age, son. I reckon I know when something's up."

Jubal tried to busy himself by lifting a grain sack off Frisk's back. Finally, he got to the point. "I'm looking for a man named Billy Tauson. Supposed to be working on a ranch up this way. Probably closer to Alamosa."

"Billy Tauson works the Triple C Ranch just east of town. Alamosa, that is. Relative of yours?"

"No, sir, I just need to . . . talk to him."

Bob took out his tobacco and papers and proceeded to roll another cigarette. "I've worked with William F. Tauson. He's a special article, that one. Used to foreman the Triple C a few years back. We had words, he fired my country butt, then beat me out of a month's pay. I said to Billy I'd run into him sometime in this life."

Jubal didn't yet know if he could trust this dishwasher, but he decided to jump in. "He and some of his band of merrymakers set fire to my family's farm, and they did other things as well. I need to make things right with him."

"You don't want to be going up against that bastard alone, son. What's your name?"

"Jubal. Jubal Young, sir," then it all just spilled out. "They murdered my family, my baby sis." He stopped, unable to continue. He tended to Frisk, trying to get ahold of his emotions.

Anne came from the back of the building looking a bit like a mother searching for a lost child. "Bob. You've got chores."

"Duty calls. Stick around 'til this evening and we'll continue our talk. All right, cowboy?"

Jubal nodded. And he had only planned on going in for breakfast.

"Thing about Billy, he's a criminal. Born that way. Works as a ranch hand for a spell, then once he gathers up enough money he lights out and just raises hell. Worked his way up to foreman when I knew him. I hear tell a month after I left he went on a real tear up around Denver. Shot a couple drunks."

They were sitting on a log near a creek. Though they were unfamiliar with each other, Jubal started to be more relaxed around Bob. "He was traveling with a tall Injun, Crook Arm, last I saw him," Jubal said. "Tauson, Crook Arm, another named Pete Wetherford, maybe one more."

"Wetherford I've heard of. Nasty man. Tauson, well, his wife."

"His wife?"

Bob looked down reluctantly. "Folks say she just up and disappeared."

"Disappeared?"

"Well, you know." Bob smiled.

Jubal waited for him to continue.

"I guess the folks in Cerro Vista got to wondering about her."

"Cerro Vista?"

"Yep, that's where they lived. Not in town but up in the mountains east of town, some farm or ranch. Guess after the third or fourth time ole Billy Tauson came into town to stock up on grub and such without his wife, folks got suspicious. Now, I'm not saying that he done her in, I'm just saying what the folks around Cerro Vista were saying. He started raising hell about that time. I heard he lost the property from gambling or taxes or heaven knows. Anyway, that's the long and squat of it. He's a piece a work. Thinks of himself as an intellect. Has a way about him that seems to attract the ornery types like the fellow you mentioned. Wetherford. What's his name? Pete?"

"That's the one," Jubal said.

"Tauson also used to travel with a cousin of his. Kid name of Ty Blake."

"He's no longer with us."

"What do you mean?"

"He and a couple others didn't survive the raid on our farm."

"Your pa must have been right handy with a rifle."

"Yes, sir, he was." Jubal decided he'd leave it at that for the time being.

"What do you intend to do once you find these desperadoes?"

Of all the questions Bob could have asked, that happened to be the hardest to answer. He had thought about it a lot. He reminded himself several times a day that he had promised Judge Wickham, and for that matter Marshal Wayne Turner, that he would turn those bounders over to the authorities—once he found them. "I've made a few promises that I'd do the right thing when the time came. Other than that, I can't say."

Bob picked at a piece of bark from the log. "Okay, and what does 'do the right thing' mean, youngster?"

"Do the right thing" didn't sit right with Jubal. It sounded false. Each time he thought of the potential death of Billy Tauson, Pete Wetherford, and the others, he was reminded of his promises. Had he vowed to Cybil he would do what was "proper"? He didn't think so.

Maybe, like Edmond Dantès, he would reward himself with the gift of life, and his ultimate travails could result in the best life could offer. But the right thing might very well be revenge. The total cleansing of the soul, giving back to a person the right to live. Jubal gazed at the creek as the water moved slowly past. "I suppose the circumstances will dictate that. I'll do what it takes at the time."

"You sound determined enough, that seems for sure." Bob tossed the bark into the nearby stream. The bit of wood drifted down into the bubbling water, hung up on a rock, then found its way free. "Everybody and everything needs to find their own way under God's blue sky. Once you commit to an endeavor like this, you'll ruffle some feathers along the way. Are you prepared for that, Master Young?"

Jubal smiled at Bob's way of describing him. "Yes, sir. More than prepared. I'm anxious and ready. I'll be heading out toward Alamosa in the morning. If you'd be kind enough to give me directions to the Triple C Ranch, I'd be much obliged."

Bob gave Jubal detailed instructions on how to get to

the ranch. They said their goodbyes, Jubal thanking the man profusely.

As night drew near, Jubal prepared his bedroll a little ways outside of town. He hobbled Frisk so she wouldn't drift off, and curled up in front of an inviting fire. He thought a bit on what he had said to Bob about being committed to this endeavor and wondered if, indeed, he was as ready as he let on.

Jubal recalled a saying his mother was fond of. "Chance favors only the prepared."

Morning opened with a hint of yet another late snow in the air. After a thin breakfast of beef jerky and tea, Jubal fed Frisk and headed out north, deciding once again that he would parallel the railroad track. Not far from town, a rider sat at the base of a water tank used by the trains. As Jubal approached, a scrawny mule and a man wearing a coonskin hat drifted out—Bob the dishwasher. Jubal stopped Frisk and the two men regarded each other.

"We haven't really been properly introduced. I'm Bob Patterson, but folks usually call me Ginger," he offered, fluffing his reddish beard. "I've decided to ask if you wouldn't mind company. Would've mentioned it last night, but I needed to speak to Anne to make sure she could get some help at the café. We have a bit of an arrangement, if you know what I mean." He winked. "This is Duke." He slapped the mule's withers lovingly. "Duke and I been pals for a number of years. He don't take a lot of tending and keeps a secret real good. Thought maybe I'd keep you company on up Alamosa way. You never can tell, right?"

Jubal smiled wide. His first legitimate smile in a long time.

"Duke, meet Frisk. She's gentle and loving but packs a heck of a kick."

The two men rode off north, not really knowing what lay ahead. Jubal figured that if Bob was as handy as he appeared, he'd be a welcome companion.

The Triple C Ranch lay southeast of Alamosa at the base of a mountain. It took Jubal and Bob nearly all day to travel the flat plain. They stayed close to the railroad tracks, Jubal still being impressed when the train caught up to them coming from the south. The idea that one could sit in luxury while traveling and enjoying magnificent views felt much like a wondrous dream. He promised himself that one day he would ride one of these splendid conveyances while watching the day gently change before him.

"There's a bluff just south of the bunkhouse," Bob said. "We can lay up there and take a peek at what's going on down below."

Bob had spent the last half hour fretting in his saddle. Jubal wondered if he wasn't a little nervous and suggested they walk the horses to create less of a silhouette. Bob agreed as they climbed a low mesa south of the ranch proper, tied the horses to a piñon, and crawled to the edge of the mesa. They could smell smoke and meat cooking on an open grill outside the bunkhouse.

Bob pulled out a small collapsible telescope from his inside jacket pocket. He scanned the bunkhouse area, where a number of men waited for supper. "I don't see Tauson. It don't mean he isn't there. But ah, yes. There's

Walt Phillips and a couple other hands I knew. But no Mr. Tauson."

They remained still behind the rocks, watching the cowboys having their meal. Just as they decided that their Mr. Tauson and Wetherford weren't going to show, they heard the unmistakable sound of a cartridge being ratcheted into a rifle.

"What's you fellers doing up here?"

When they turned, they found a man in a long rancher's coat training a .30-caliber rifle on them. He held the piece casually, waist-high. A look of recognition came over his face. "Well, Ginger, you came back. What you up to, a little surveying of the land afore you ask for your job back?"

Bob dusted himself off as he got to his feet. "Hello, Mel. How you been?"

"Can't complain, and you?"

"Same as usual. Broke and good-looking." Bob took a few careful steps toward the cowboy with the rifle. "No, I wasn't going to ask for my job back, Mel. We were looking for ole Billy Tauson, is all."

"Were you, now? Tauson ain't here, Ginger. He came in day before yesterday, got some of his belongings, and lit out. Said something about meeting some fellows in Alamosa. That's about it, I guess."

"You can put down that piece." Bob gestured toward the rifle. "We're not going to do anything desperate."

"I'm comfortable just the way I am, thank you."

"Can we mount up and kind of disappear, Mel? For old times?"

He chewed on this a bit and glanced at Jubal. "I reckon

if you was up to no good you'd have done so by now." He lowered his rifle and motioned for them to move on.

When they were comfortably seated on Frisk and Duke, Bob once again turned to Mel. "Do you know where Tauson's headed after Alamosa?"

The man pointed north. "I hear tell Poverty Gulch."

The two men rode in silence for nearly an hour. As they approached the town of Alamosa, Bob finally spoke out. "Not what you might call an auspicious beginning. If I have to say so."

Jubal said nothing.

"Yeah, I'd have to say it was dumb, stupid," Bob continued. "I'd go as far as to say ignorant." They continued through town to the outskirts, where they finally dismounted to let the animals drink at a creek. "I knew better than to ride on in there like a greenhorn. . . . Jesus wept." Bob kicked the earth. "If Tauson had been in camp, what in God's hallowed earth was I gonna do? I ask you, now, what?"

Jubal started to speak.

"No, don't say a word, Master Jubal. I know enough about you to know you'd make some kind of excuse for me, and I appreciate it, but that ain't gonna cut it."

Jubal let it go for a while. "No, I wasn't gonna excuse you, Bob. What you did was stupid."

"Hell's fire, son, you don't have to agree with everything I say. I was trying to be neighborly."

"Sir, maybe that's what you were doing and maybe you were simply fishing."

"Fishing? For what?"

"Compliments, congratulations, condolences, that sort of thing."

"Hold on there, Master Jubal. Yeah, I did a stupid thing and I should have thought it out better afore riding on in there like that, but the truth is, I had company."

They looked at each other.

"I led you up there, trying to be the big man. I apologize. It won't happen again." They shook hands and remounted, riding in silence for half a mile.

"Bob, it's a good thing you knew that cowhand. He seemed a fair sort."

"Yeah, Meldrick was always okay with me."

"I'm glad we talked this out. We need to be a little more careful when it comes to these lawless bastards."

"Agreed."

Darkness got ahead of them, so they built a fire and took in a meal. After tending the animals, Jubal rolled up in his blankets.

Just before falling asleep, he called out to Bob. "How far to this Poverty Gulch?"

After a long pause, Bob answered, "Beats the heck outta me. I was hoping you'd know."

TWENTY-TWO

In the morning, the duo went back to Alamosa in the hopes of getting information about Poverty Gulch. Bob presented a worn map to a local man in charge of the rail depot.

"Poverty Gulch is up north of Cañon City," the man said. "You'd be best to go east through the pass to La Veta." He marked the spot on Bob's map with a pencil. "Then keep the Sangres to your left and head north 'til you're past the Wet Mountains, then you'd be smart to ask from there. I'd say it's the better part of a hundred miles."

Jubal mounted back up to begin this next part of their journey. "This just beats all," Jubal said. "I almost had them in sight and now who knows how far ahead they are? And why are they headed for a place called Poverty Gulch?"

Without answering, Bob ducked back into the depot. He came out a few minutes later, grinning. "Gold."

"Gold?"

"There's been a big find up around Fremont—Poverty Gulch. Close to a certain Cripple Creek that runs through the mountains." Bob still had the smile. "Sounds promising."

"How so?" Jubal remained skeptical.

"It's the kind of place where old Billy Tauson would be drawn to. Lots of new gullible people, plenty of hell-raising, oodles of money."

"Let's go."

It took five days of hard riding for Jubal and Bob to make the trip from Alamosa to Poverty Gulch, and the closer they got, the more would-be prospectors they met on the trail. Some folks came from as far as Chicago and St. Louis to strike it rich.

Bob was a talker, and he talked to them all—when he wasn't talking to Jubal. His favorite topic of conversation was describing the ways of the mountain man.

"Use a few pounds of meat, cut it into strips . . ."

Jubal suffered through Bob's second telling of how to make beef jerky.

". . . add salt, garlic, hot sauce, handful of onion and pepper . . . lay the strips out in the sun to dry."

They rode on, Bob thrilled with his current audience of one. "Tanning is the real art. Lord, it's a process. Soak the hide in water to relax it, then into a lime solution for ten days or so, careful to stir it every day. Then take the hair off. Messy. Soak it again, then add alum and salt. Let it soak again."

Bob's perception of how much his listeners could take was exaggerated.

"After that, stretch while still wet, add sulfonated oil, then rub the devil out of it. Wrap it tight overnight, then smoke it to make it waterproof. See these pants? Hell's fire, you'd never believe I made these myself."

Oh, really?

"You could wade a creek and they'd still be dry inside. Pretty smart-looking, wouldn't you say?"

Bob's worn buckskins had knees that bulged out where the leather had stretched, while the ass end was baggy and thin. "I don't know if I'd call them smart, so much as . . ." Jubal paused, trying to think about a word ma used. "Utilitarian."

"Whatever that means, Master Jubal. I like my trousers." He pointed to his shirt. "I made this too, want to hear about it?"

"I think I've had enough of mountain man schooling for one day, Bob." Jubal smiled. "Maybe tomorrow you could go into fur hats and such."

In spite of Jubal's plea, Bob droned on, entertaining himself with tales of big-game hunting and surviving a variety of outdoor adventures, while Jubal's thoughts drifted south to Cerro Vista and Cybil.

He tried to remember how tall she was. Did their eyes meet without her having to look up? When she wrapped her arms around him in the garden, where was the ribbon in her hair? He recalled the smell of her hair and the warm breath against his throat. She seemed incapable of dishonesty with him. Jubal came back to the present just as Bob finished a long diatribe on the benefits of sleeping outdoors.

After being quiet for a long spell, Jubal heard Bob sniffling. "Catching a death of cold, Bob?"

"Nah, it's nothing."

Jubal looked back at Bob rubbing his eyes as if he'd been under stress. Jubal held Frisk back for a moment to let Bob come up alongside. "Anything you want to talk about, mountain man?"

"Ah, hell, it's silly, really." He took several gulps of air. "I just got to reminiscing about the war, suppose when we were jabbering about sleeping outside and all. Hell's bells, I was just a young'un. Not quite sixteen. Lied about my birthday. I was overgrown for my age." He stopped to blow his nose. "Camped in a grove outside Nashville, near to Franklin. General Thomas's Union troops came at us like hell wouldn't have it. I'd buried my head behind a stump when my rifle flat refused to fire."

Jubal watched Bob, knowing what he said about the rifle was probably a lie.

"I'd killed a couple of blues, and to be honest didn't want no more of it. They shot the living Jesus outta us. We suffered hellish casualties, problem being we were from the same state so you kept hearing of folks you knew or heard about. Hell, in some cases the same little town. Strange what you can feel about a fellow soldier. You can hate the critter, but there's this peculiar closeness. I don't know what you would call it."

"Brotherhood, maybe," Jubal said softly.

"Yeah, so, these two fellows from Murphysboro flat couldn't stand each other, something about a girl. She left one of them. Anyway, the one old boy got gut-shot real bad by a Yankee and his archenemy, think his name was Merle, picked him up and carried him a half mile back to an aid station. Damn."

Jubal reached across the space between them and squeezed Bob's arm. The big man rocked back and forth in the saddle. "I left after that."

"What do you mean, you 'left'?"

Bob took a moment. "Went home, it weren't far, fifty mile or so, Clarksville. Snuck through the lines like a thief. Hid myself in a woodshed on my cousin's farm 'til the end of the war. Onliest good thing came out of that little episode in my life, I taught myself to throw a knife. What else you gonna do, a snot-nosed kid stuck in a shed?"

Jubal listened quietly.

"Shame's a funny thing, Jubal. It were years before I forgave myself for deserting. When you have the living shit scared out of you at such a young age it stays with you, trust me on that." He stopped once again, clearing his throat. He did his best to grin. "Say, want to learn to throw a knife?"

Jubal had very little interest in this, but in deference to Bob's emotional state he agreed to a lesson or two. When they stopped to rest the horses and dine on a couple of beef jerky strips, Bob began showing Jubal the fine balancing art of knife-throwing.

"To keep an even weight on your whole body, you step into the throw. . . ." Bob droned on about balance and speed and the sharpness of the point. Jubal dutifully tried his hand, and surprisingly it became a pleasant distraction.

Toward day's end, Bob asked Jubal if he'd be recognized.

"What do you mean?"

Bob rode on for a while before answering. "Did any of those varmints see you when they raided your farm?"

"Yeah, one of them. Well, maybe a couple. There was a dustup in Cerro Vista earlier with my father, but I don't think Tauson would remember me. Wetherford would, though." Jubal's thoughts drifted back to the night of the log bridge incident and how that cold hard voice told him what it would do to him if opportunity lent itself. "Yeah, he got a good look at me."

"Do you shave?"

"What?"

"Shave. You know, run a blade over your face to take off whiskers. Snip, prune, trim. Shave."

Jubal hadn't really thought much about his appearance for some time.

Bob pulled back on Duke until the two riders were side by side. "You've got what looks to be peach fuzz scattered about your face."

"What are you thinking? We need to change our looks?"

"Yep. What if we clean you up around your cheeks and shave a goatee into that young face? We could darken it with walnut stain. Same with your hair. Cut it short, kinda neat. It'll put some maturity on you. What do you say?"

"I'm game only if you are." Jubal needed convincing.

"What you mean?"

"That old boy Pete Wetherford has never met up with you, but Tauson has. You say you worked for him. Fair is fair, Ginger."

"Ah, hell. Me and my big mouth. Damnation." Bob fiddled with his beard.

They devoted the night before arriving in Poverty Gulch to barbering. Bob looked ten years younger with his ginger-colored beard shorn. He saved a mite of whisker over his upper lip and, with the help of the polished bottom of a tin cup to see his reflection, trimmed it into a neat mustache. Bob's scissors made good work of Jubal's locks. It had been a long time since he'd felt a breeze on the back of his neck. As promised, Bob also darkened the few wisps of Jubal's sparse facial hair with the juice from crushed walnut hulls.

"You look like a desperado with that goatee, son. Here, let's rub a little of that juice into your hair and let it dry."

Jubal went to sleep anxious to see himself, not in the bottom of a polished tin but in a proper mirror.

"Doesn't look like much, does it?" Jubal said as they approached the community. Dozens of shacks and tents dotted the hills, most of them scattered in haphazard fashion along the trail heading into town.

"How long have you had that hat?"

"It was Pa's. Started wearing it right after the raid."

"It's fairly noticeable with those feathers coming out the brim."

Jubal took off the hat and pushed the bright feathers down under the wide band. A brooch of his mother's that he had taken from the remains of the fire came to mind, and he dug it out of his pack. Silver, with several greenish blue stones and small stars carved into the crescent form. He smoothed the brim and bent the front of it up flush with the crown and secured it with the brooch.

"You look like a real hell-raiser, son." Bob eyed him closely. "Yep, a desperado."

"Speaking of hats, Mr. Mountain Man, I can't

imagine anything more distinctive than that animal sitting on top of your head. Lordy."

Bob grabbed the coonskin by the tail and pulled it off his head, cramming it into his saddlebag. He scratched his shiny dome vigorously, then took his sweaty neckerchief and wrapped it Indian-style around his head. "Satisfied?" He grinned like a fool.

"Satisfied."

They pushed on to the center of town, where a group of people and their animals milled about in front of the claims office.

"What do you think, Bob? Should we find a place to bed down?"

The big fellow glanced around, then called out to a man in a fancy suit. "Excuse, sir. Could you direct my friend and me to a hotel or boardinghouse?"

"I could direct you, but it wouldn't do you any good. The town is chockablock full." He rubbed his hands gleefully and continued on his way.

Bob looked at Jubal. "He probably owns a brothel."

Jubal stood high in his stirrups. "Just beyond that row of houses on the street opposite, I can see a row of tents. Let's drift on out that way. What do you think?"

They found a spot near a small stream, made their camp, then walked back into town. The atmosphere was charged with people scurrying about buying supplies and peddlers selling a variety of items on the street. They waited in line at the office for nearly an hour.

"Yes, sir. How can I help?" The man behind the caged portal took a moment to suck on his smelly cigar.

"Just some information, if you please." Bob adopted a

countrified presence. "My friend and I was curious on how to go about making a right proper way to start prospecting. You know, staking a claim—"

"You got to do just that, my man, stake it out right proper," the man interrupted. "The government says you can work twenty acres, but you got to have a map like the one behind me."

The two greenhorns gawked at the wall-sized map displayed behind the man.

"And it's gotta coincide with our chart to be valid. Do you have a location for your claim?"

It was way too early for either Bob or Jubal to be interested in staking out a title. Jubal stepped in and asked the man about others who had made claims. "Sir, if I gave you a couple of names, Tauson, for instance, and Wetherford, could you—"

"Son, you'd have to see the manager about that. I can't give out no personal business. Next."

The two stepped outside. They decided Bob would stay back to try to get a word with the manager while Jubal scouted out the town. Bob didn't think he'd have much luck prying information, but it would be worth a try, so they agreed to meet back in camp later in the afternoon.

Jubal cocked his thumb back and fired a shot at Bob with his index finger. Bob faked a shot to the heart, then Jubal proceeded up the street, only to be stopped with a shout. The mountain man caught up to him and held one hand to the side of his mouth as if he were about to impart a secret. "Listen, pardner. A-ah," he stammered. "You're not ashamed of me, are you?"

"Ashamed, why? What about?" Jubal frowned.

He paused, then blurted, "Ah, well, shoot. You know, all that palaver about my time in the war, how I hightailed it to greener pastures, you know all that kid's nonsense."

"Forget it. You did what you thought was right." Jubal stuck out his hand, they shook, and Bob proceeded back toward the claims office. He turned once again, hands over his heart as if wounded from Jubal's previous mock gunplay. Jubal had to smile at the big guy's sense of humor. He also thought in some ways he knew exactly what Bob had gone through. There had been a number of times at Morning Peak when he had wanted to drop everything and run for his life.

TWENTY-THREE

Jubal passed the local post office on Main Street, a building with a high U.S. MAIL facade and an American flag waving off the porch. Thin vertical bars encased the windows from inside, and the building sat alone as if it were grander and more proud than the other wood structures on the street. Jubal wondered if it would be possible to send a note to Judge Wickham. Stepping inside the building, he noticed a wall of small wood boxes with tiny windows. Jubal figured it was so mail would be easily visible. "Excuse me, sir. I wonder if you could help me."

"I can probably help you with anything relating to the mail, but I don't lend money and I don't have a daughter you can marry, so what's your pleasure?"

"Sir. I need to send a note to someone in Cerro Vista, New Mexico. I wonder how I go about that."

The kindly postmaster smiled. "Do you have the note with you?"

"No, sir. I haven't written it yet."

"Well, cowboy, once you've written the note you simply give it to me. I'll sell you a stamp, you lick it, stick it on the envelope, and I mail it for you. Simple, huh?"

For a second, Jubal wondered how to continue.

The older man chuckled. "You don't have a piece of paper, do you? Or an envelope? How about a pencil or pen?" The postmaster lowered his voice. "Can you write?"

Jubal quickly said, "Ah, yes, sir, I write quite well."

The clerk reached under the counter and produced several sheets of paper, an envelope, and a pencil. "You can stand there by the WANTED posters and write 'til sundown."

Jubal moved along the oak counter until he was standing beneath several notices proclaiming several hundred dollars' reward for information about a certain Jack Stanton and another for the dead-or-alive capture of a desperado named Miguel Cavallo.

Jubal had a tough time concentrating with these outlaws staring down at him.

Judge Wickham,

I hope this note finds you in good health. When last I saw you, your color was the shade of this paper. I hope your health has improved.

As for me, I disobeyed your wishes to stay close by in Cerro Vista. Sir, I am not asking for a pardon or sympathy but simply understanding.

I was doing okay until your shooting. Something about the gracious supper earlier in the evening, the company and your welcome, that, simply put, overwhelmed me after your wounding.

I am, sir, not much of a scholar, so please forgive this poor attempt, but I will try to do whatever it takes to apprehend the villains who shot you and bring them to justice.

Regards to your family.

> I remain your loyal servant,
> Jubal Young

Jubal slid the envelope, paper, and pencil back to the center of the counter.

"How did you do, youngster? Everything hunky-dory?"

"Yes, sir."

"Are you going to address the envelope?"

"Ah, yessir, I forgot." As Jubal wrote the address of the Wicks Hotel, he asked the clerk, "Sir, if someone wanted to send a letter to me, how would they do that?"

"Well, son, you put a return address on the envelope. You have an address, don't you?"

"No, sir, I don't. I'm just sort of wandering about in these parts."

"You could rent a post office box for a dollar a month or if you don't expect a lot of mail you could just say on the envelope, 'care of general delivery.' How's that?"

"Fine and thank you, sir." Jubal started to leave.

"Are you forgetting something, sonny?"

"Ah, yes, sorry, what do I owe you?"

"Penny for the stamp and I'd have to charge you another penny for the paper and envelope. Fair enough?"

"Yes, sir. More than fair, thank you . . . and the use of the pencil?"

"Just consider that courtesy of the U.S. government."

Jubal felt good having gotten the burden of a guilty conscience off his chest. He hoped Judge Wickham would accept his apology and explanation in the tone and manner in which he intended.

By the end of the day, Jubal felt he knew nearly all of the various dwellings in the immediate vicinity. He'd made a rough mental sketch of the places where he had seen people and where they camped. Trying to keep track of a bunch of prospectors became a tiresome job, but the idea that he could best the raiders of the farm kept him going.

After a long day, Jubal and Bob were at last back at their campsite, a number of fires glowing throughout the surrounding woods. They stirred their vegetable stew and spoke of their endeavors.

"The claims man wouldn't tell me a whole hell of a lot. He didn't really want to say anything. Went on about claims being private. I did a bit of weepy storytelling about my brother and a death in the family. He finally looked it up but couldn't find anything on Tauson, William F., or Wetherford, Peter. You say you had a good look around and didn't see any signs of them, right?"

"Right." Jubal stirred the stew with a long stick. "Let's drift back into town tonight, late. See if those devils are sticking close to what they know, boozing and trouble-making."

Around ten-thirty that night, Jubal and Bob walked into town to find a group of men raising a fuss outside the

Good Chance Saloon. As they approached, Jubal saw two of them rolling on the ground, throwing wild fists, while bystanders shouted encouragement. Neither man seemed very fit and the fight didn't look as if it would lead to anything. Bob and Jubal stepped around the panting figures.

Inside the music hall, merrymakers crowded the grimy floor and lined a second-story balcony. A piano man, being generally ignored, struggled with his songs. Jubal and Bob skirted along the walls of the large room, trying to see as much as they could without being seen.

"I'll stand you to a beer, son. Wait here." Bob elbowed his way through the drunks and soon-to-be drunks to get to the bar, his bald head bobbing above the throng.

As Jubal waited, a woman approached him. "New in town?"

Jubal nodded.

"Uh-huh. You looking for a good time, handsome?"

"Good time, sure, I'm having a—oh, you mean . . . No. Sorry."

She drifted away, calling over her shoulder, "Your mustache is weeping, sonny."

Jubal's hand flew to his upper lip, coming away with a dark smudge. He felt an urgent need to get a look at himself. On the far wall between two pillars hung an ornate mirror tilted to one side. Jubal made his way through the room and stared at his clouded image. A faint walnut stain colored his upper lip. He wet it with his tongue, then scrubbed it with a finger.

"What's you doing, fella? Come in here to drink with the men, or are you some kinda dandy what comes in to just use the mirror?"

Jubal turned to see a young man about his own age holding a foaming glass of beer in one hand and a cigar in the other, his cattleman's hat towering above Jubal.

"I asked you a question, cowboy," he said. "Are you looking for trouble?"

His sudden temper surprised Jubal, like he was looking for a fight. "Looking for trouble?" Jubal responded. "No, why would I do that?"

The stranger looked around to make sure his buddies were behind him, hearing every word. "Don't smart me. I'll rip off that girlish pin on your hat and fix it onto your goateed face, you hear?"

Jubal waved him off and moved away through the crowd. He could hear the young man bellowing and the chorus of catcalls coming from his friends. It was difficult to do, to walk away, but he certainly didn't want to draw attention to himself. He reached up, touched the brooch on his hat, and smiled.

"Where you been, Jubal? Was looking for you." Bob handed him his beer.

"Oh, I just took a gander at myself in the mirror. I thought my disguise was slipping." They clinked glasses, Jubal taking a sip of the warm liquid. It tasted good, mysterious, filling his mouth with sensation. As he swallowed, there came a light need to cough, but the fluid coated his throat. He started to feel a strange relaxation. "It's good, I'm surprised."

"Surprised, why?"

Jubal didn't want to tell Bob it was his first beer. "Oh, I don't know, surprised they would have this good a beer, way back here in the hind end of nowhere."

Bob looked at Jubal quizzically. "Have you drank before?"

"Oh, sure, lots," Jubal answered, maybe a little too quickly. The two drifted back toward the wall so they could survey the room. When they decided they'd seen enough, they started toward the door.

"You were rude to me, cowboy," came the familiar taunting voice from earlier. "My friends made fun of me 'cause of you."

"Who's this," said Bob, more like a statement than a question.

Jubal pointed at him. "Oh, it's a lad who seems to be in charge of the mirror."

"You just aching for it, ain't you?" said the stranger.

"Aching for it?" Jubal looked at him again. "Let's go outside." He put the half-full glass on a table and pushed his way out through the swinging doors.

They walked out to the dirt street, the men from the previous fight long gone. "What I am aching for, sir, is to see the smirk on that rotten-boy face of yours wiped off. I've done you no harm, minding my own business. You're half drunk and wanting to show off for your drunk friends. If I was somehow rude to you, I apologize. So turn your country ass around, and you and your girlfriends call it a night."

It surprised Jubal how calm he was; he actually felt good. A part of him wanted to lay into the provocative yokel, but he thought the time just wasn't right. Jubal had nothing against him, he was a young man itching for a fight, trying to prove he was a fully grown man. Jubal stuck out his hand.

"Shake, partner. Let's call it a misunderstanding, okay?"

"You hear this, guys?" The man glanced back at his friends. "Wants to shake and chicken out."

Jubal turned and smiled at Bob. "Let's call it a night."

It really did take a lot of gumption to walk away from a fight.

TWENTY-FOUR

The duo hung around the Poverty Gulch campsite for a week without spotting Wetherford or Tauson. It made them restless.

"There's a bunch of different mining sites around this here gulch," Bob said after their seventh consecutive fruitless day. "What say we split up and scout the various spots?"

"Sure, but as you said when I first met you, a body doesn't want to be standing up to the likes of Tauson or Wetherford alone."

Bob thought about this. "Damn if you aren't right, son. Let's get a move on, we've done nearly all the scouting we can do here. Let's stick together."

Unfortunately, they were running low on money. Jubal had almost none, and Bob had enough to last only three or four days. The animals wouldn't understand short rations and neither would they, so they had to make a decision.

"You want to try our luck at mining?" Bob asked.

"I don't look forward to getting down in a deep hole and shoveling rock, if that's what you're saying."

"It would only be for a few days, maybe a week," answered Bob quickly. "I've heard you can make a good number of dollars working the company mines."

The following day they signed on at the Ajax and, along with nearly fifty other men, descended into the shaft. Dust hung like fireflies, seeping into every pore, even though Jubal wore a neckerchief around his mouth and nose.

After the first week, as they stood outside the mine entrance waiting to be paid, Bob declared, "Life is too short to devote to this sort of slavery. Perhaps we should call it a career."

Jubal had been thinking the same thing. "Well, Mr. Bob, if you insist. I was just beginning to like it. The sweat, the camaraderie, the grinding dust. But to be serious, I understand that for very little money we could pan for gold along the creek, be outside, work for ourselves—find a spot that wasn't staked and have at it. What do you say?"

Fresh air sounded great to Bob. They headed up high into the hills to begin their attempt at placer gold mining.

After several hours they ran into a friendly old-timer on his way back down the mountain. He made time to explain the process of panning.

"Find yourself a spot where you've come upon some quartz. Something that looks like it fell off a ledge 'cause of an earthquake or some kinda upheaval years ago. If there's a crick nearby, all the better. Look for a place where the stream changes direction or stands still like a backwater—"

"Don't you just pan in the water?" interrupted Bob.

"No law against it, son, but you'd be best spending your time in a little used-to-be streambed close by. Otherwise you might as well take to being a mucker."

Jubal and Bob glanced at each other.

"Oh, I see you've tried your hand at that," the old man added. "Anyway, dig to a solid area, then spread that there dirt, about half a shovelful, into your pan."

They looked once again at each other.

"You didn't bring a shovel, did ya?" The old man grinned. Without waiting for their answer, he reached over to his pack and tossed a small shovel at their feet. "One dollar, cash money."

"You got it," Jubal said.

The prospector continued. "Hunker down next to the streambed and flip half a shovel of dirt into your pan, then dip a corner into the water. About a pint, I reckon. Then make the whole kaboodle kind of like soup—"

"Soup?" asked Bob.

"Yep, then scoop up more water and whirl the whole shebang 'round and 'round, then slowly let some of the soup slip out over the edge. Continue 'til all the regular rock and gravel have been slurped over the edge. Get it so far?"

Jubal felt as if he understood up until then. Bob looked mystified.

"Well, sir, get her down to just a swath of dark red sand—almost black. Then drain the water to get the sand even all over. Gold is heavier than gravel and rock, and will settle at the bottom. If you got yourself five or six little sparklies, fine. Don't depend on the sun. Take your pan into the shade—if it still glitters, it's the genuine article. Make yourself a horsehair brush and sweep it gentle-like over the dried findings, and you can generally pick up your lode. Store it in a leather pouch and you're off and running. If your spot gets thin and played, move on." He paused, and said finally, "Don't forget the dollar. For the shovel."

The two greenhorns paid the old man his dollar. It worked out to fifty cents for the shovel and the same for the lecture.

The duo unsteadily continued upstream. Jubal hoped all of this would get him closer to Pete Wetherford and William F. Tauson.

They bought enough provisions to last a month with their few dollars and moved their camp high into the hills.

The first week of placer mining proved frustrating, even an outright disappointment. Bob stumbled his way through the day. They finally devised a method where Jubal stayed in the water and did the initial pannings, then Bob would take the red and black leavings and store them in a large bucket for further exploration.

By the end of the tenth day they had accumulated what they thought to be about an ounce and a half of dust.

"My good man, I think it's time for ole Bob Patterson to have a couple of beers, what do you say?"

Jubal straightened his back. "I suppose we could journey into town for a decent meal and a beer. Let's go in the morning. I'll try and pan as much as I'm able the rest of the day to build up our little sack of dough."

That evening, Jubal didn't feel much like a king, but there could be no doubt about the heavy little pouch underneath his pillow. It represented a week and a half of work, and it was very real.

Before their journey into town, Jubal and Bob rode high into the mountains for target practice. In a small canyon facing away from the town below, they tied off their horses and walked deep into the crevasse.

Bob had a big old Colt .45. He thumbed back the hammer. "An old-timer once told me that two gunners fixing to shoot it out are usually inside twenty feet." He fired off a round at a piñon and missed by several feet, pulled back the hammer once again, and in that way fired several more quick shots in a crouched gunfighter position. All the rounds missed high and wide. He was hopeless.

Jubal had Audrey in a battered holster at his right side. He pulled his coat back and laid his thumb lightly on top of the hammer, his fingers not quite touching the burnt handle. Bob yelled, "Draw," and Jubal's fingers pulled up on the bottom of the grip as his thumb cocked the weapon. With knees slightly bent, he fired as the piece became level with his waist. The rock split in half. He reached across with his left hand and ripped his palm across the hammer and kept the trigger depressed, firing off all six rounds as he fanned the piece with his left palm. It was fairly fast and, more importantly, accurate.

"Any questions?"

"You're right handy with that piece. How's about another knife-throwing session?"

Jubal agreed and they proceeded to throw at a tree that had overgrown its purchase at the side of the canyon. Jubal was pretty good inside ten feet or so. He could stick the blade eight out of ten times, but it became more difficult when the long-bladed knife had to rotate in the air more than once. Bob could also throw underhanded, so that the sticker didn't tumble in the air but slid out of his hand quickly with a long stride. This, Bob explained, was the "desperadoes' death throw."

"You sling it just like you would a rock. Underhanded."

Jubal thought maybe it was exactly that, in more ways than one.

Their little sack of dough, as they called it, netted them right at $28 from the local assayer. Bob, pleased with his half of the take, bounced up and down on one leg like a child. "I got to have me a beer, son."

"Bob, it's ten in the morning." Jubal laughed at his antics. "Let's meet back here at the assayer's office at noon, then decide about eats. What do you say?"

They agreed. Bob hightailed it over to the Good Chance. Acting drunk, he waved to Jubal and zigzagged his way up the saloon steps.

Jubal unhitched Frisk from the rail outside the assayer's office. He rode Frisk the length of Bennett Street and stopped at the general store to inquire if anyone knew about sluice boxes and how to build them. He had been told by a mine worker that a sluice was a better way of getting to the gold.

He killed time admiring various weaponry under a glass display case. As he bent over to get a closer look, someone jostled him from behind. He turned without rising up, astounded at the rudeness of people. Jubal saw only the man's back as he continued chatting with another fellow on their way out of the store. Just another hurried soul in a town full of unfamiliar people.

The clerk at the counter directed Jubal to Faulkner's Livery, where a man named Lou could help him with instructions about a sluice.

Jubal led Frisk to the blacksmith to adjust a shoe, then stood in the open barn door watching the heavy rain that had begun to fall. To pass the time, he sharpened his long-bladed knife with the smith's stone, then, with the man's permission, tossed the bone-handled piece accurately into a heavy hitching post.

Lou turned out to be a nice fellow who dutifully sketched a picture of a sluice with all the dimensions. Jubal rode Frisk back down the street toward the general store for supplies.

Outside the store, he glanced at a large clock on a pole outside the bank. Eleven-thirty. If Bob was still in the tavern, he was well on his way to being stiff with drink. Jubal strapped his purchases behind the saddle and took his time walking Frisk back toward the saloon. Maybe he would simply wait outside the drinking establishment and give the bearlike man his time to imbibe. He stayed on the steps a few minutes but then decided to see if Bob was, indeed, in the tavern.

As he started to enter the Good Chance, he took a quick peek over the swinging doors and spied Bob at a far table, his sweaty bald head shining like a beacon. Jubal pushed the doors open, started in, then stopped. Bob sat with two men. One of them, his back to Jubal, was the rude man from the store.

Jubal now recognized him. The gray-haired Billy Tauson.

Jubal eased back out onto the sidewalk. He stumbled on the rotting planks, finding himself seated in the dirt street. Several passersby probably thought him to be drunk. He shot to his feet, running down the street to Frisk and the saddlebag with his pa's pistol. As he neared the horse, he slowed himself. He knew Tauson's location; no need to panic. He retrieved the .44-caliber and tucked it firmly in his belt, hidden beneath his coat. Mounting Frisk, he rode slowly back.

He steadied himself by carefully going over the things he knew. Tauson was previously acquainted with Bob Patterson, and there was bad blood flowing between the two. That would explain the tension at the table.

Tauson had also never seen Jubal up close. The fleeting image of a young man darting about the farm, taking potshots at him, hadn't registered in any meaningful way, Jubal hoped. Plus, he was now adorned with his fresh new mustache and goatee.

But most importantly, Billy Tauson wouldn't be expecting company.

TWENTY-FIVE

Jubal moved Frisk to a hitching post in front of a dry goods store. Slipping between two buildings, he made his way to the alley behind the tavern. He climbed the outside stairway to the second floor and let himself in the door. A short hall opened onto the mezzanine looking down to the floor of the tavern. The balcony swept around three sides of the tavern, with a half dozen rooms opening onto the banistered walkway.

He positioned himself from above so he could see the table with Bob and Tauson. A Mexican also sat with them; the man rose and made his way to the bar to reorder.

Staying close to the inner wall, Jubal made his way toward the steps leading to the tavern floor. Mountain Bob's nerves were showing. He sat hunched forward as if listening to each word Tauson said to him. Jubal was certain Bob was unarmed, but from all that he had seen and heard about Billy Tauson, that probably wouldn't matter.

For a moment Jubal considered whether he should get a lawman to intercede, in order to reduce the chance of gunplay. He had made certain promises to Judge Wickham. Or maybe this was the correct way to subdue this bastard. Come at him head-on, not try to finesse the thing. Perhaps attack in a way that the notorious Billy Tauson would understand. Let the devil get his due.

A young woman came out of a room in front of Jubal and glanced at him as she straightened her dress.

"Are you ready for a second go-around, handsome?"

The woman's inquiry startled Jubal, but he recognized her from the other night. "Ah, well, yes, ma'am. I mean, not exactly. I was looking for the gents'."

"Back down the hall by the outside door. Are you sure you wouldn't like a Saturday virgin, good-looking?"

Jubal had no idea what a Saturday virgin was, and it must have showed in the way he looked at her.

She smiled at his expression. "I'm just starting work. Fresh as a schoolgirl, all yours for a drink and two dollars." She cocked her hip and placed one hand around a breast. She ran her other hand slowly up, down, and against the outside of her leg.

Rather than looking appealing, she came off as kind of ridiculous, but there was something about her that seemed bright. "Could I buy you a drink and just kind of, well, the two of us just hang about for a short while?"

"Sure, hon. But it'll still cost you the same."

Jubal paid her, then turned his back to the raucous doings downstairs. "You see the red-mustached man sitting with two other men at the table, just to the left of the pillar?"

"Yeah, the dense-looking big guy?"

"He's a friend and we had a bet as to who could get drunk the fastest and find the most beautiful . . . girl. I just want to tease him a bit. Maybe disrupt his serious talk with those two gents he's speaking with. Okay? Will you play along?"

"Yeah, sure, but you gotta buy me the drink first."

He gave her the money and watched Bob sweat at the table as Jubal waited for his lady of the evening to return.

She arrived back with a pair of beers, as if looking forward to the charade. "By the way, my name is Pauline. What's yours?"

"Jack. Jack Older."

"What do you want me to do, Jack?

"Just go along with whatever I do. Right?"

"Yeah, right." She put one arm around Jubal's waist and felt the pistol tucked in his belt. "Well, you're packing 'round your middle. How about down here, Long John?" She reached low in Jubal's crotch and gave him a gentle tug, then laughed. Not unpleasantly.

Jubal just took a sip of beer, wrapped his arm around Pauline's shoulder, and started down the stairs, still feeling the sensation of her gentle tug.

"Bob Patterson!" Jubal shouted. "You old warhorse. How you doing?" He extended a hand in greeting. "You remember me? I'm Jack Older!"

"Jack Older—" Bob looked stunned. He glanced at Tauson and dropped his head.

"This here is my sweetie, Pauline. Say hello to my friend Bob Patterson." Jubal looked at Tauson. "Who's your lady friend, Bob?"

Disgusted, Tauson breathed a long sigh of annoyance. "Who's this jackass, Ginger?"

Jubal thrust out his hand like a rube. "Name of Jack Older. Pleased to meet you, and you are?"

"None of your beeswax, sonny."

Jubal's plan was to distract Tauson long enough so he could get the drop on him. Jubal set his beer on the table. His arm still around Pauline, he faked a cough and went as if to retrieve a handkerchief from his inside coat pocket, feeling for the burnt-handled .44. To his surprise, Pauline was gripping the gun from outside of his coat. He couldn't get to it.

Tauson tapped his fingers on his half-filled glass. "Bob, why don't you tell your asshole buddy here to take his painted whore off to another room somewhere and leave us be?"

"Hey, hold on, there, mister," Jubal said. "No need to be rude. Pauline and I are fixing to tie the knot. Why, heck, Ginger is gonna be my best man, right, Bob?"

Bob remained seated, his hands holding the edge of the table, ready to spring. Jubal waved his arms in a parody of someone who was upset, trying to get Pauline's death grip around his waist to loosen up.

"Bob, tell your gray-haired friend here what a sweet gal Pauline is, and have him say he's sorry for his remarks."

"Jube, I'm in trouble." Bob glanced quickly at Tauson. "That is to say, Billy, I mean Mr. Tauson, wants . . . oh, shit, he's going to kill me."

Jubal dropped his arm from around Pauline's shoulder and briskly forced her away with his hip. "That right, Mr. Beeswax? You gonna kill my friend Bob?"

Jubal watched Tauson's hands, still on the table.

The Mexican on Jubal's left slid his way slowly away from the table. "I'll be moseying along, Señor Bill. *Adiós.*"

Jubal didn't take his eyes from Tauson, but called out to the Mexican. "What's your name, amigo?"

The man kept walking slowly backward until he stumbled into the back of a chair. "Manolo."

"Where you know Mr. Beeswax from?"

Manolo snickered weakly. "We do business about claims of gold and such. No funny stuff. Just business."

"Have you ever been south, around Cerro Vista?" Jubal never took his eyes from Billy Tauson's hands. He hadn't recognized the Mexican from the confrontation on the street or the raid on the farm, but there had been a lot of confusion both days. He could have been one of the horsemen.

Jubal was cursing himself for having his coat buttoned. He motioned for Manolo to come back closer to the table.

"Señor, I never been anyplace like Cerro Vista. I swear on my sainted mother. Why you ask, please?"

Pauline had moved away from Jubal's side, and he could sense Bob trying to ease his chair back from the table. Jubal now shifted his gaze to Billy Tauson's eyes. The man seemed relaxed but with a growing sense of suspicion.

"You know, Manolo, some time ago, a group of cowards and lowlifes raided a farm up in the high foothills east of Cerro Vista. These selfsame scum murdered a whole family. Raped two of them. Burned their farmhouse and outbuildings."

Tauson glanced downward at the mention of the deaths and fire.

"You know anything about that, Manolo?" Jubal closely watched Tauson, whose mouth had the beginnings of a slight grin.

Manolo spread his arms wide in an innocent gesture. "Ah, señor, I swear on all that's holy—"

"Manolo, step back away from the table and call it a night, *comprende*?" Jubal interrupted.

The man stumbled as he once again walked backward. "Gracias, señor. Gracias."

The packed tavern quieted, both the drunk and the sober all very aware of the tableau taking place in the middle of the room.

Tauson's hands hadn't moved. "What's the reason for all this rigamarole, mister? Or should I say 'sonny'?"

Bob began weeping.

"'Sonny,' will do," Jubal said, "or you could call me Jubal."

Tauson gave a slight nod. "How fast are you, sonny?"

"Accurate." Jubal didn't blink.

"Accurate?" Tauson smirked.

"I'll put two into your chest while you scatter your quick shots around the room."

Tauson tapped all ten fingers on the beer-streaked table, trying to intimidate Jubal. His right hand moved toward his drink. "May I have a last sip, *angelito*?"

Jubal didn't know the term but nodded in agreement.

"*Velorio de angelito.*" Tauson grinned. "Wake for a dead child." He took a sip, dropped the glass, flipped the table onto its side, and dove to the floor.

Jubal moved to his right behind Bob's chair as Tauson fired wildly from around the corner of the table. People screamed, ducked behind the bar, and scattered out the front door. Jubal dug his pistol out from his belt, having second thoughts about provoking Billy Tauson into a gun-fight. *Well, like it or not, we're in with both feet now.*

Pauline curled into a ball at the base of the overturned table, gasping for breath in between blurting a string of expletives describing Tauson's lineage, his penis size, and the dubious profession of his mother.

TWENTY-SIX

Bob Patterson was lying faceup, hands frozen across his chest. Blood pumped between his fingers as he muttered a prayer. Jubal was stretched out on the floor next to him, facing the direction of the overturned table.

". . . Forgive us our sins as we . . ." He stopped speaking as Jubal felt his forehead. There began a long slow pouring out of air from Bob and a dry clattering rattle. His eyes were fixed on the ceiling and his pupils were dilated. Jubal moved his fingers to Bob's neck, then noticed the blood had stopped.

He was gone.

Jubal thought Tauson must have crawled away while he was tending to Mountain Bob. People were still calling out, with the occasional sprint toward the doorway. Jubal, using his elbows, moved up behind Pauline and touched her ankle. She screamed and kicked out at him. "Pauline, it's all right. It's me."

"Goddammit. You scared the hell out of me. What? You want your money back, for Christ's sake?"

"Take my hand. I'll get you out of here. Just take it." Pauline sniffled a few times while Jubal looked over the top of the table. A number of people were still crouched, seeking a safe haven. The bartender had a shotgun and was bent over the polished wood service gate. When Jubal finally caught his eye, he motioned to the man with open hands and shrugged as if to ask, *Which way did he go?* The white-aproned barkeep pointed up the stairs to the second-story balcony. Jubal grasped Pauline's hand and pulled her to her feet, wrapping his free arm around her waist, half carrying her out the front door. After charging across the street with her, he sat her down on a bench in front of a haberdashery.

"Sorry about this, miss. As soon as you catch your breath, hightail it for home."

"That is my home."

"Where?"

She pointed. "The bar. The room you saw me come out of, number three."

"Is it locked?"

She nodded.

"Is there a back window?"

"There's a door with a window in it that leads out the back of the building to a walkway that runs to the back stairs."

Jubal remembered seeing the walkway, probably so the women would have access to their rooms when the bar was closed. "Do you have your key?"

Pauline took from around her neck a pink ribbon that had been threaded into a large skeleton key.

"Will this unlock all of the rooms?"

She wrapped her arms around herself and nodded again. "Is he dead? The bald man with the red mustache?"

Jubal chewed his lip. "Afraid so."

He made his way to the back stairs and ascended them, then crawled along the walkway, looking in the windows. When he made it to room two, he spied Billy Tauson with his back to the inner wall, his left arm wrapped around an older woman's neck while his right held his pistol to her head.

Jubal made his way back through Pauline's room and crept along the balcony away from room two. When he was about halfway over the bar, he hissed a couple of times until the barkeep finally stepped out from beneath the balcony.

"He's in room two," Jubal whispered. "With an older woman held hostage. I think if you distract him with a knock on the door I can get him from behind, okay?"

"That's Mary, damn it to hell." It sounded like the barkeep might be sweet on her. "Maybe we should wait for the sheriff. He's up in the hills arresting some wife-beater."

"I don't know. This guy looks desperate."

"All right," the bartender said. He started up the stairs, frightened silly.

"Hey. I'm Jubal. What's your name?"

"Mike."

Jubal nodded, then signaled Mike by tucking his gun under his arm and holding up all ten fingers, twice.

The barman understood and began a silent count. Jubal did the same as he slid through room three to the walkway, crouching beneath the door marked with a number two.

At the count of fourteen, the waiting seemed an eternity. At seventeen Jubal heard a loud knock. Praying Tauson would face the woman toward the interior door, he broke the window. "Drop the gun, Billy, or I'll kill you."

Tauson spun away from the woman and snapped a wild shot as Jubal fired back, hitting Tauson in the right forearm.

"You wet-behind-the-ears piece of dog shit." He dropped his weapon. "You can't do this." His left hand gripped his crippled arm. "Ah, Christ a-mighty, you bastard, I'll kill you." He danced from foot to foot, circling the room.

Mike stepped into the room and threw one arm around the woman, the other still holding the shotgun, his apron sporting a vivid trail of blood left by one of Tauson's pain-induced spins.

"Why did you shoot that poor bastard downstairs?" Mike said.

Tauson looked up. "'Cause I felt like it, jackass."

Mike handed the shotgun to the woman and slapped Tauson hard across the face. "Don't talk to me like that, in my place. You got it, cowboy?"

Tauson attempted a feeble swing of his uninjured arm, which prompted a kick in the shin from Mike. Tauson dropped to one knee.

"Who's the jackass now, fellow?"

Jubal stepped in and jerked Tauson upright. "Let's take a walk downstairs, Billy." He walked his man down the tavern stairs and righted the table where they had been sitting. Jubal took off his coat and draped it over Bob Patterson's face.

"You must feel like a big man, killing a soul like ole Bob."

There was no answer, just a back-and-forth rocking. Billy Tauson keening away, eyes screwed tightly shut, tears streaking his face.

"You killed my family, at the farm you used to own. Why?"

Tauson ignored Jubal's question. "I need a drink."

His pain was evident and Jubal so enjoyed it. It was a small thing, but satisfying in a peculiar way. The events at the farm and the ruckus on the street in Cerro Vista all came sweeping past Jubal.

Hard to believe, but he had him. Billy Tauson was his prisoner. He smiled. The man didn't seem so full of himself now, doubled over in pain. Sweat beaded on his forehead, a haunting look to his eyes.

"Bob here"—Jubal motioned toward the dead form of his friend—"told me an interesting tale about your wife, Mr. Tauson. Said she ran off."

Tauson rubbed his upper arm. "Leave the past to its memories, sonny."

"We have plenty of time 'til the sheriff gets here. I was just wondering if there's a body somewhere on the Young family farm that doesn't belong there."

"As I said, farmer boy, leave the past to rot on its own." Tauson writhed in his chair.

Jubal rapped gently for attention with his father's pistol on the edge of the table. "Did you kill her, Tauson? How about it?"

Tauson kicked out with his boot toward Jubal but fell way short.

"Nice try, Billy," Jubal said. "I guess that meant yes."

"Leave me alone, dammit. I need something for the pain. A drink. I'll pay." He let go of his busted arm and fished inside his vest pocket. He tossed several coins onto the table.

"Tell us about your wife, Tauson. Then maybe we'll get those drinks."

Tauson did not try to hide his discomfort. The demise of the man's wife really wasn't of interest to Jubal, but he thought if he could get Tauson talking about the farm and why he had instigated the raid, it would help Jubal understand the meaning of the whole episode. Tauson abruptly called out for a bottle of rye whiskey and water.

Mike gave no answer, just leaned against the bar, the shotgun at his fingertips. "You scared my friend Mary, you bastard. You get nothing 'til the youngster says so."

Tauson went back to drumming his left hand on the tabletop. "My wife was having a to-do with one of my employees."

Jubal smiled broadly. "A . . . to-do?"

"I made the mistake of telling him I was tired of her. I was just funning, but the fellow was a crazy son of a bitch and—"

"Who was this crazy man, Billy?"

"Oh, for the sake of being loyal I can't say."

"Pete Wetherford?"

Tauson continued his nervous tapping. "Petey and Sara were having at it most every day, then one evening around mealtime she disappeared. I looked for her around the place, up in the woods, out toward Morning Peak. Couldn't find her. I finally waked some of the hands and we searched nearly the whole five hundred acres. I ended up with Pete Wetherford and a couple others north of the farmhouse in the woods.

"We were spread out when I hear a voice to my left. It's Pete. He calls out, 'Let's try this meadow yonder.' Sure enough, she was lying there in the dim of night all messed. Dead as a winter flower. Me and the cowhands dismounted and stood around. I covered her bare grimy legs. Then this voice from behind."

"'It is necessary to the happiness of man to be mentally faithful to hisself.' I read that once. Some educated clown talking about coveting a neighbor's wife, least I think that's what he meant.

"It was Pete Wetherford. He hadn't gotten off his horse. Just looked down at us and poor Sara. Then he started singing some damn spiritual and rode off. Crazy bastard. Tried talking to him about it, but he'd never say anything. Just stare at me with that half a crooked grin of his. I've never been scared of any man, except that one. Doesn't seem human. I tried getting rid of him a number of times, but he just wouldn't go away. He'd kill me in a minute if he knew I told anybody about all this."

"Where did you bury your wife?"

"In a glade at the edge of a stand of pines."

It sounded to Jubal like it was very close to where he had buried his family. Imagine Pete Wetherford being responsible for all those deaths, and all in the same hallowed ground. "Mike, bring Mr. Tauson his bottle." Jubal spun his father's pistol around his finger several times. Audrey had served him well.

"I was there on the street," Jubal said, "the day you and your buddy Pete confronted my father. But of course that wasn't enough for you, was it? You had to go a step further."

"This is all very amusing," Tauson said, eyes shifting. "But I'm done talking." Tauson put his good hand on the arm of the chair and rose. But when he heard the double click of the hammer on Jubal's .44, he eased back down. "All right. What is it?"

Jubal leaned forward slightly. "Retribution, justice, revenge. Maybe a bit of groveling."

"I don't grovel." Tauson looked bored. "Why should I, and for what?"

"Murder."

"I didn't mur—"

"Don't say it, Tauson." Jubal struggled to control himself. "Do you hear me?"

Tauson's upper lip dampened.

Jubal glanced around the room, which was now deserted save for Mike.

"Where's your friend Wetherford?"

"Dead, I suppose, I don't know."

"Liar."

"We all lie from time to time, but in this case, as I said before, I don't know—"

Jubal reached under the table and cracked Tauson hard on the knee with the pistol.

"What in hell are you doing? Dammit." Tauson let go of his damaged arm and reached to massage his knee.

"Keep your hands where I can see them." Jubal carefully weighed how to proceed. "Some time ago, you and my father spoke outside of the land office in Cerro Vista, New Mexico. You threatened him because he gained control of your land through auction. It was done fair and legal after you fell behind on your taxes . . . but 'say your night prayers,' you said. I heard you."

"So?"

"So, later you sent one of your cohorts, a certain Mr. Crook Arm, of Ute or Navajo lineage, to follow us home. You knew where we lived. It had been your former home, but you wanted to scare us, didn't you?"

"Once again, I don't—"

"Shut up! Dammit."

"Listen, son. Yes, we'd come out to raise hell and put a scare into you folks, but I had nothing to do with anything . . ." Tauson searched for the right word. "Illegal or rough. I told those old boys to settle down and cool off. Leave the women be. But they'd have none of it. They just went ahead and did what they damn well pleased."

"That's what your cousin said."

"My cousin?"

Jubal put a little extra effort into his intense stare.

"Ty?"

For the first time, Jubal sensed Tauson had begun to unravel. "After you left him wounded on the farm, he waited for your return. When you didn't come back, he finally got astride his horse and made it halfway into Cerro Vista, where I found him, lying bundled up in pain beside the road."

"How is he?"

"How in the hell you think he is, Billy?"

"I'll have to get in touch with his mother." Tauson paused. "Why you so riled about Ty Blake, for Christ's sake? You gave us hell with that little peashooter. You were the one who shot him."

"Yes, sir, I surely did, but here's the difference. I didn't leave him to die after promising I'd return, then ride off like a snake in the night. As he lay dying, he ratted on you, Mr. Tauson. Told the doctor, deputy, sheriff, and a priest the whole thing."

Tauson shifted. "We had a difficult night, things happened in the hills that evening. We couldn't get back to the farm like I promised. I had a terrible fall."

"Really? Tell me about it."

"Petey got hisself killed along with a Mexican. They did a stupid thing."

"Uh-huh."

"Not much to tell. They both fell off a cliff. I went down that rock face trying to see if they were alive, but it weren't any good. They were both kilt."

Jubal smiled, enjoying the man's gift for spinning a tale. He was startled by a voice from his right.

"Young man, what's going on here?" A man with a metal star pinned to his vest stood a few feet away, relaxed, hands at his side. "By the way, in case you're wondering, I'm Tom Cox, the sheriff."

Jubal nodded. "This man, William F. Tauson, is wanted in Cerro Vista, New Mexico, for triple murder, and is also responsible for the body you see there on the floor, name of Bob Patterson." He paused. "If you have a telegraph, you could confirm the Cerro Vista deaths with Wayne Turner, U.S. Marshal for that territory."

"And who might you be?"

"I'm the son and brother of the deceased, sir. My name is Jubal Young."

The sheriff swung a chair around and straddled it, but didn't move any closer. "When did this triple murder take place, son?"

Jubal still hadn't moved his gaze from Tauson. "The tenth day of this past April, sir, about noon. This coward and his gang killed my family. Raped my mother and fourteen-year-old sister."

"Hold on there a damn minute. I didn't rape any—"

Jubal swatted Tauson heavily on the knee again. "Keep those hands where I can see them, Billy."

Tauson's eyes watered.

The sheriff signaled to the bartender. "Bring me some writing materials, Mike."

The mustached barkeep scurried out from behind his workplace with a tablet and pencil. The sheriff glanced around at the quiet room. He noted all pertinent information from Jubal. The names and dates of the various events, Ty Blake's deathbed confession, the shootings of Sheriff Morton and Deputy Ron. The shoot-out at Judge Wickham's house and Jubal's unsuccessful attempt to join Wayne Turner's posse.

"You're not going to do anything stupid, are you?" the sheriff asked Jubal as he ran his hands down the inside of Tauson's coat and pants pockets, looking for a weapon.

"No, sir, but I can tell you he'll leave here either in shackles or a pine box."

"Fair enough. You hear that, Mr. Tauson? I overheard enough of your conversation to believe something serious took place back in New Mexico and that you were somehow involved. Also, what about this body here on the floor? What happened?"

Tauson shrugged. "This kid pulled down on me. He didn't give me any choice, he just dove down to the ground behind Ginger."

The sheriff held up his hand. "Ginger?"

Jubal spoke up. "That was the nickname of ole Bob. He was helping me chase down this rat. Unfortunately, he caught one that was meant for me." Jubal fought back a lump in his throat. "This lout and a man name of Pete Wetherford raised a lot of hell in and around Cerro Vista—"

"This little twerp blames the whole thing on someone who isn't even here to defend hisself 'cause he's dead."

"Who else is dead?" asked the sheriff.

"Pete Wetherford," answered Tauson nervously.

"That true, youngster?"

Jubal smiled. "No, sir. I tracked Wetherford and another, all the way up here, from just north of Cerro Vista. He's alive, all right, and somewhere here in the Cripple Creek district."

The sheriff seemed to be taking in the complexity of it all. "I'm gonna wake up Ned Grant and have him send a wire to this Marshal Turner. It might be a while afore we hear back." He looked at Jubal. "You be okay?"

"We'll be fine." Jubal nodded at Tauson. "Won't we, Billy?"

The sheriff walked to the bar and spoke for a moment

with the bartender, then returned. "I've asked Mike to help keep an eye on the situation, son. He's fairly handy with that scattergun, so be careful. Okay?"

"Yes, sir. I'll not do anything hasty, you can rely on it."

The sheriff's departure once again left Jubal and Tauson contemplating each other. Tauson finally peeled back his torn shirtsleeve. Gazing at his wound, he slipped his kerchief from around his throat and tied it snug around his bloody arm. "You're a funny little half-growed-up boy, you know it?" He grinned. "Sitting there with your *pistola* all proper-like. But in the meantime, I got to go. Nature calls."

Jubal nodded.

"Come on, dammit. I'm going to wet myself."

"Go." Jubal once again ratcheted the hammer on the pistol as Tauson started to rise from his chair.

Tauson slid back down. "I thought you said to go."

"I did."

"Then why the stupid play with the pistol?"

"Go where you are."

"What do you mean?"

"I mean, if you hear the call of nature, answer it."

"Where?"

"Right where you're sitting, pardner."

The more Tauson struggled with his bladder, the more Jubal felt uncomfortable. He'd had a bellyful of bad feelings for one night. "Mike, where can this man take a piss?"

Mike still had the shotgun draped across the bar. "You can step out to the back alley."

"Let's take a walk, Billy."

Once outside, Tauson faced away from Jubal and took care of his needs. "Do you hafta stand there looking at me?"

"No, I don't hafta, Mr. Tauson. But if you're inclined to run, I want to make sure old Audrey does her duty and puts a little lead pellet in the back of your head. Can't tell you how much I wish you'd try that. A side of me would love seeing you kick your life away on that nasty soaked ground. You're a bully. Probably always been. You encouraged your band of drunks to scare a family of perfectly innocent souls."

"Nobody is perfectly innocent, sonny boy."

Jubal's face flushed. He fired twice into the ground, close to Tauson's feet. The man leapt into the air, both knees pumping to try and keep from being hit.

"My sister was an angel, you bastard." Jubal closed the ground between the two of them in several quick strides. Grabbing Billy Tauson's shirtfront with his left hand, he drove his pistol hard up to the older man's throat. "Don't speak another word to me, ever. You hear me?"

Tauson nodded, a gagging sound coming from his throat. A voice called out from the back door of the bar.

"It's Mike. You all right? I heard gunfire."

"Everything's fine now. Just a little misunderstanding."

Jubal whispered into Tauson's ear as he marched him back into the bar, "Never, ever, and I repeat, never, meet my eyes."

Tauson dropped his head.

Jubal frightened himself. He had come very close to killing Billy Tauson. He could feel himself changing and he didn't like it.

"Thou shalt tear out the teeth of the dragon and trample the lions underfoot . . ." As Monte Cristo had read in the Bible, so shall it be. The passage gave the Count his supposed right of vengeance. It bothered Jubal that he was so quick to bestow his own transgressions on Edmond Dantès.

TWENTY-SEVEN

They sat for several hours. Avoiding Jubal's gaze, Tauson looked at Bob's body. "Your partner was a coward. You know that, don't you?"

Jubal switched his grip on the pistol from the handle to the barrel and swung the piece, once again, viciously into Tauson's protruding knee.

"You rotten son of a—" Tauson rocked back and forth, both hands flat on the table.

"There are worse things than not being brave."

"You and I will have a serious date one day," Billy gasped. "You hear me, Mr. Young?"

"Uh-huh, that's what your friend Pete Wetherford told me just after I jiggled that log he held on to so desperately."

"You were there? No, you weren't. Where were you?"

"After he and Jorge fell, you walked around the crevasse and came back. You stood talking to Pete's brother,

Al. I tucked myself safely under the log bridge hidden by branches. My rifle was pointing up, only a couple feet from your crotch. I thought about pulling the trigger. Wish I would have, but on second thought maybe it'll be better to see you and Pete swinging in the breeze for your escapades. I don't really know . . . and by the way, you didn't go down that rock face to see that Pete and Jorge were 'kilt,' you pathetic liar."

"If Wetherford is alive as you say," Tauson said, "and you followed him up here, he's without a doubt looking for me." Tauson kept avoiding Jubal's gaze. "And when he finds me there's gonna be a hellish debt to pay around here. You can trust me on that, Mr. Young."

Maybe, thought Jubal. But so far he hadn't been able to trust William F. Tauson on much of anything.

At three a.m., the sheriff and a tired deputy came back to the Good Chance. He came directly to the table and found a sleeping Billy Tauson.

The sheriff kicked his chair hard. "Time to wake up." As Tauson stirred, the deputy snapped a set of leg irons around his ankles, then secured them to the shackles the sheriff had applied to his wrists. "You're in for a long trip."

The man turned to Jubal. "Heard back from your friend Wayne Turner. Here, I'll let you read what he says." The sheriff handed a folded telegram to Jubal.

To Sheriff Tom Cox of Teller County, Colorado.

Sir, received your wire in regards to a William F. Tauson who has been accused of murder here

in the environs of Cerro Vista, New Mexico.
Please hold said individual until my arrival by
train at 4 p.m. later today.

> Signed,
> Wayne Turner
> U.S. Marshal

p.s. as per your wire, I understand a Mr. Jubal
Young might have had something to do with
apprehension? Hard to believe.

He laughed. Yes, difficult even for Jubal to believe,
but there he was, William F. Tauson, taking shackled baby
steps, dragging the chain from his leg irons as the deputy
led the tall gray-haired man out of the Good Chance.

Jubal looked around the tavern, then followed the men
into the street.

The sheriff wrapped his right hand around Tauson's
forearm.

Tauson grunted in pain.

Jubal found Frisk and rode out of town toward his
campsite. He thought the revenge Bob had desired over
the years toward Billy Tauson had become, in reality, much
harsher than Bob had imagined. What was it Tauson had
said? "Your partner is a coward." Bob hadn't been the
bravest, certainly, just a gentle soul who didn't have the
same sense of responsibility toward justice that burdened
Jubal, and Jubal didn't consider himself brave. Throughout the long night it had never occurred to him that he
had been doing anything except what was required of him,
what he had set out to do some six weeks earlier.

In a peculiar way, Bob had been his responsibility. Yes, the man was older and maybe more versed in the ways of life, but—and this was what bothered Jubal—he was an innocent. Jubal thought it would have been difficult for him to change the path the two of them had pursued, but he should have tried. After all, it was his crusade, his pursuit. Bob had come along because Jubal really hadn't thought out his dream of revenge against Billy Tauson, and in the end it had cost the big fellow his life. Jubal would have to live with that.

That responsibility, the weight of obligation.

He made his way back to the partially deserted campsite to sleep a few hours. Breaking camp as the sun rose, he bundled his few belongings, including the placer mining tools Bob had left behind. He loaded everything on Frisk's broad back and headed into town. He found Bennett Street and finally the sheriff's office.

Jubal looked around for a spot where he could keep watch for Marshal Wayne Turner's arrival, settling on a nearby run-down building. He tied Frisk out back and stationed himself, hunkering down on what was left of the porch.

Tauson said Pete Wetherford would be trying to find him if he was alive, and that there would be "a hellish debt to pay." With all the commotion at the Good Chance, Jubal was certain that if Wetherford was in the district, he would have heard of it.

If Wetherford showed himself and tried to get Tauson out of jail, Jubal wanted to be a part of any hell-paying. He leaned against the dilapidated building and cleaned his father's pistol.

Beef cattle were being driven along Bennett Street, about fifty head, their loud protests at being hurried along awakening Jubal, who had fallen asleep with his back to the rough siding. A recurring dream lingered, something about a game and his family, when they were in Kansas five or six years ago. He tried to remember but couldn't. Something about numbers.

He silently addressed his father. *I got the leader, Pa.*

He also pledged that Tauson definitely would not be the last.

TWENTY-EIGHT

Their home in Kansas had been modest but full of love. Pa would be gone most days, traveling, selling harnesses and various gear to outfit the average farmer. His territory had been most of Kansas. They often passed the time with numbers. The game had been devised by Jubal's mother, and the idea was to see who could guess how many beans were in a jar or a tin cup. Jubal marveled at how his family could be so easily amused. Pru would almost always initiate the game, screaming, "Firsts, firsts, please, Ma, please!"

They were in the middle of a game one evening when Jubal's father came home from his travels with a red welt above his left brow that gave his face an uneven look. Jubal had never seen his father injured. He'd always seemed immortal.

"We're going to have to consider that farm out west I told you about," Jubal's pa said to his ma.

"Why is that, Jube? Did you have problems with Hank again?" She ran her hand gently over her husband's brow.

"*Afraid so, Bea. 'Fraid so. It's serious this time, we came to blows.*"

"*Oh, Jube, are you all right?*"

Jubal's father went to the highboy for a bottle of scotch whiskey. He looked so sad perched that way, squeezing the neck of the bottle. "I really made a mess of things this time, Bea. Really upset the old proverbial apple cart for good."

Jubal and Pru played checkers while their parents sat in the corner of the living room speaking in quiet tones. Pru had won her third game in a row when Jubal heard his mother's strained voice. "Oh, my God. Jube, no, how did it—" She turned. "Children, go to bed, please. Now."

He'd gone to bed but had not been able to sleep. Something had happened with his father. He ended up being around the house a lot after that. He fiddled around in the garden, painted the window sashes, redid the flower beds, but, most importantly, met with ugly men in suits and ties who came to the house to hold long, noisy meetings in the living room, sometimes far into the night. Jubal remembered the man Hank. He had been a fellow who presented himself as cocksure.

It had been a hot summer in Kansas. Jubal was almost fifteen when the company his father worked for had invited employees' families and friends to an end-of-summer picnic.

A tree-lined lake provided an idyllic background. Toward the end of the day, the head of the company stood and made a brief speech, thanking everyone for their hard work and loyalty. As he began winding down, he was interrupted by a voice in the crowd.

"*Tug-of-war, tug-of-war.*"

The fellow Hank stood up, trying to exhort the crowd. "Tug-of-war. Salesmen against harness makers. Tug-of-war."

It took a while to get organized and eventually the two reluctant groups came together and discussed the rules, most of them trying to be good sports about the game. As it happened, ten fellows in sales and eight harness makers made up the teams. Jubal was recruited to his father's side. They stretched the knotted rope across a small creek leading down to the lake. Someone tied a handkerchief to the rope in the center of the little creek. Jubal was second in line, close to the creek's edge. It wasn't deep, only a couple of feet, but the stream ran muddy over a rocky bottom.

The sales team made a good effort of it, but the superior strength of the harness makers eventually pulled the first three members of Jubal's team into the creek. There began good-natured laughter, and then from Hank a slightly different tone.

"Hey, Jubal, what happened to your boy? Was he trying to learn to swim?"

The elder Young ignored Hank and dutifully helped Jubal out of the quagmire. "You okay, son?"

"Yeah, Pa, sorry about getting all nasty. I tried pulling, but they were just too much for us, weren't they?"

"Yeah, they were, Jube. But we tried."

Hank walked up. "Too bad about that, sonny. But it's all in the growing up, ain't it? Maybe next year you'll come pull on our side, be with the winners."

Jubal's father stiffened as Hank gave him a big phony wink and strutted away.

"That jackass will be the death of me yet," his father muttered. Of course, it didn't turn out that way exactly.

Jubal waited across the street from the sheriff's office on Bennett. Marshal Wayne Turner said he would arrive on the four p.m. train from Antonito, and Jubal felt he needed to be there to see his new acquaintance, Mr. William F. Tauson, safely in the hands of the marshal.

He dug his ma's Bible from his saddlebag and sat back down on the weathered porch. He looked for a passage on revenge or salvation, but stumbled onto a line that he thought amusing: "Righteousness and justice are the foundation of your throne." So if he took this literally, having caught Billy Tauson, he was being rewarded with this hard seat under this broken-down porch for his righteousness.

My throne is low, but my spirits aren't.

He felt good; the capture of the man had left him in fine fettle, although the word "capture" didn't feel right for what had taken place. "Apprehension" seemed too literate, and to "take captive" sounded like it might come from a pirate's tale. Maybe "detain" would work best.

It had a certain adult sound to it. Jubal Young the Detainer, the scourge of the West, fighting injustice wherever he found it. Tracking down predators, hyenas, ne'er-do-wells, and gallantly releasing them to the authorities.

His daydreams made him smile, but a sober reminder brought him back. There were at least two more villains to be detained—Pete Wetherford and the man he was reminded of each morning when he arose and tried to stretch his midriff—Chief Crook Arm and his damnable arrow. Actually, he thought Crook Arm more than likely was not a chief.

Jubal's sister Pru loved calling their father "chief," always behind his back, and only in Jubal's presence. They would titter and make fun of Jubal, Sr.'s gruff but loving voice. Pru would parade around the barn, her small fists planted firmly on her hips, her face screwed up into a make-believe belligerent frown.

"Jubal, if I've told you once, I've told you . . ."

In chorus, Jubal and Pru: ". . . nearly a godforsaken thousand times." He would then point to her and she would say, "Milk those cows, tend those sheep."

"We don't have any sheep, Pa," Jubal would respond.

"I know that, smarty. I just wanted to see if you were paying attention. Hoe that garden, pick that corn."

"It's too early for corn, sir."

Pru would deepen her frown. "Don't talk back to me, boy."

Joining their voices once again, they would intone, "Your father knows best, darn it."

Pru always had her head on a swivel when she made fun of her pa. Running to the barn door, she would look both ways, then turn dramatically, wiping make-believe sweat from her brow. "When I get married, I'm going to be just like mom, you know, whip-smart, but with a voice like pa's, full of authority and wisdom. Though sometimes when I forget to help ma with the dishes and he scolds me, I wonder about his wisdom."

Then she would daydream about her life as an adult.

"I'll have three children all at once, and I'll have them in the field, where I won't have to miss a day's work. I'll name them Pru One, Two, and Three. If they are all boys, so much the better. With names like that, they'll learn to fight at an early age. My husband will be six-foot-four and protect me from my willful brother, who is as lazy as a sow. I'll fight for women's right to vote and I'll run for mayor and governor at the same time."

One time Jubal called out with his hands cupped around his mouth, "What about a man's right to bear arms?"

"Yes, I'm for it, I think a man should have bare arms and a bare backside."

She stopped and held her hands over her mouth in embarrassment as Jubal called out, "Bare backsides, bare backsides."

He would never see Pru married, never be godfather to her children. He had been denied the pleasure of her tall, straight countenance on her wedding day. That radiant smile, the sense of play and joy of life.

He had been denied that by a number of fools who had thought their need for fun was greater than the rights of three loving people.

TWENTY-NINE

The marshal, when he finally arrived, strutted down Bennett Street like a man going to his own wedding. Shirt fresh, boots shined. His badge, usually worn on his vest and tucked away, now appeared prominently on the outside lapel of his smart jacket. From the attention he was paid by the various passersby, it seemed the man had achieved satisfaction from his appearance.

Jubal walked to the other side of the street and fell in step alongside Marshal Turner. "Good afternoon, sir, lovely day, wouldn't you say?"

Turner was lost in his own image. "What the hell? Oh, it's the young shootist, come to gloat."

Jubal chose to ignore the remark. "How's the judge doing, Mr. Turner?"

"I guess you're going to be a pain in my behind the rest of the day, aren't you?"

"No, sir, I'm not." Jubal continued walking beside

the marshal. "I just wanted to inquire of Judge Wickham's health. How is he?"

They reached the front of the sheriff's office. The tight-lipped marshal paused, looked at Jubal, then entered and shut the heavy door behind him.

Jubal returned to his run-down structure and slid his back down the side of the porch. He was still determined to see Tauson be ridden off to the train. He was baffled as to what he had done that had so agitated Marshal Wayne.

It was close to an hour's wait when Sheriff Cox and Marshal Turner came out of the building. They spoke for a while before the deputy appeared with Tauson in tow. The group loaded their chained prisoner into a buggy and took their seats. Jubal was determined to get an answer from the marshal.

"Maybe you didn't hear me before, Mr. Turner, but I asked about the judge. How is he?"

"I heard you, schoolboy. The man you shot, Al Wetherford, is in the hospital in Albuquerque. He's gonna live. As for the judge, he'll make it, too, no thanks to you."

They rode off toward the train station with Tauson trying to look his haughty best, under the circumstances. Sheriff Cox was the only one to acknowledge Jubal, winking at him as the group disappeared down the dirt street.

"'No thanks to you'?" Jubal repeated aloud, wondering what the heck that meant.

He had no idea how to proceed, thinking maybe he'd hang around until Sheriff Cox came back from delivering Tauson and the marshal to the train station. He then changed his mind and took off.

Jubal walked Frisk slowly down the dirt street, passing the post office, wondering when or if he would hear from the judge. He liked the man. Judge Wickham seemed unusually honest, and while thinking of the judge and his family, it was an easy jump for Jubal to let his mind wander over the body and soul of one Cybil Wickham. He imagined her soft hair, smile, and mischievous frame. A wonderful group of particulars wrapped around a humorous and quick mind. He passed Faulkner's Livery where he had been yesterday to find out about a sluice for panning gold.

Well, that would have to wait. First he needed to talk to a fellow he had heard of, a certain Greek, a man named Mr. Apoptic.

The dark establishment reeked of chemicals and other dank scents. A thin man, his sleeves rolled up, dried his hands on an overused towel and asked Jubal how he could be of help.

"I came about Bob Patterson."

The man looked puzzled.

"He was probably brought in early this morning from the tavern. Gunshot wound to the chest, a bit of ginger-colored hair and sideburns. . . ."

"Ah, yes, and you're here to . . ."

"Pay my respects and take care of his funeral if I'm able."

The man directed Jubal to a chair across from a dark wooden desk.

"Is Mr. Patterson a relative, Mr. . . ."

"Young, Jubal Young. No, we are just friends. Or, I mean, we were friends before."

"Mr. Jubal. I know you would like to see your friend Bob well taken care of, wouldn't you?"

Jubal thought he'd like not to be called "mister," and especially not "Mr. Jubal," but then, what the heck was the difference? "Yes, of course, but I've been caught a little short, so it'll have to be a modest event."

"Event?"

"I mean, I'm not sure what all this entails, as I've never taken part before—in a funeral, I mean."

The man leafed through a ledger. Jubal suspected the man already had a figure in mind and was just posing.

"Beloved friend Bob." He took on a serious look. "Could be nicely interred for, I think, around one hundred"— he glanced up to see how Jubal was taking it—"and thirty dollars. Mr. Jubal, would that suit?"

"That includes a box, I mean, a casket and all?"

"Yes, of course, the very finest carved rosewood receptacle we have. That would include a charge for a carriage to the cemetery, crepe for doors—"

"Could you scratch around and find something a little more plain? You see, Bob didn't go in for anything fancy . . . wouldn't feel comfortable in anything too ornate."

The funeral director moved his pince-nez glasses up closer to his eyes as if looking at the fine print. "How would one hundred and ten suit friend Bob? Think he might rest comfortably at that bargain rate? Of course, that would be all-inclusive. Preparation, a shroud, engraved plate, gloves for friend Bob, opening the ground—"

"What's a shroud?"

"I assume since we're talking a value-conscious 'event' that you wouldn't be buying friend Bob a new suit. A shroud is what they wear at a church choir. It just covers the front."

Jubal paused. "Can I see him?"

"Yes, certainly, give me a minute, please."

The cost of death surprised him.

Bob looked pale. Mouth open, hands locked across his chest. "I'll leave you alone," said the funeral director.

Jubal heard the door click behind him. The dark room, with several covered forms on long, flat tables, did not spark his curiosity. It was cold. It smelled strange. Jubal looked at the stark mound that had been a laughing, fun-loving human being just hours before. He pulled the sheet down to Bob's waist and took one last look, then rested his hand on Bob's vest pocket. He felt the hard surface of Bob's gold watch that he had been so proud of. Also in the pocket were a couple of gold coins. Jubal pocketed the watch and money.

It would all go back to Mr. Funny Glasses in the end, but Jubal thought it best if it passed through him first. He didn't want to interrupt his search for Pete Wetherford, but Bob Patterson's funeral and his own need for food and provisions would have to come first.

THIRTY

Jubal passed a shop with a trio of metal balls hanging from a sign that read WALT'S HOCK AND TRADE. While Jubal was looking in the window, the man he assumed to be Walt came to the door.

"How you doing, son?"

"Oh, fine, sir. I've got a watch I need to sell."

"Sell or hock?"

"Sell, I think. What's 'hock'?"

"It's when we loan money on an item, like a watch."

"I think I just need to sell this, sir." Jubal took out Bob's watch and handed it over.

"A Swiss copy. What did you think on getting for this piece, sonny?"

"It were pa's and I hate to let it go from the family. I'll need a right good number for it, sir."

Walt opened the back of the watch and squinted at an inscription. "Was your pa's name Patterson?"

Jubal nodded, trying to look sad.

"I'll give you thirty dollars for it. It's not stolen, is it? I'm not going to get some fella in my shop a-yelling at me that I've got his timepiece, am I?"

"I can assure you, that will not happen."

Jubal decided to return to the livery to ask for directions to the sawmill.

An old-timer with a wad of tobacco in his jaw, upon regarding Jubal's sketch of the sluice, offered to accompany him.

"A man could describe a sluice to you 'til sundown and you'd still not understand the lay of it. . . . Look here." The bent old miner laid out a series of planks and drew his own sketch in the soft ground. "You need a gentle angle along here so the water and your filings will filter down. . . ."

It took a while, but in the end Jubal purchased his lumber, bundling it so Frisk could drag it, and then proceeded into the hills to try and make a living.

It was frustrating work. The sluice he built worked better than the way he and Bob had panned, but it would have been much easier with two men.

The ten-foot-long apparatus slanted at a thirty- to forty-degree angle. The high part was about four feet off the ground, then it angled down close to the surface of the stream. Narrow one-inch riffles, there to catch the gold, created a series of dams along the length of the sluice. Jubal would pour dirt from the streambed onto a screen that caught the larger of the rocks. The water then flowed into the top of the sluice, washing down past the little dams, the theory being that as Jubal shook the whole trough, the heavy gold would settle into the strip of burlap placed in the bottom of the channel.

After a while the screen would become clogged with material that wouldn't track down the length of the apparatus, and Jubal would stop and clean it out. He would also be careful to glean the small, heavy sparkles stuck to the burlap at the bottom.

After a week of sluicing, he figured he had enough of a stake that it would be worth making his way back down the mountain. He hid his sluice behind some pine trees and headed for the assayer's office.

"Eighty-seven dollars, mister. What's you gonna do with all that cash?"

"Bury some sad memories."

Jubal paid the funeral man and saved himself five dollars by hooking Frisk to the carriage wagon with flower-etched windows. They headed up the long hill to Pisgah, a run-down cemetery at the top of a verdant mound overlooking the tight little valley.

Mr. Apoptic, a preacher for hire named Reverend Everett, and Jubal stood silently after a short few words and benediction. The funeral director signaled for Jubal to begin filling in the damp grave. It had rained the previous night, and the sides of the grave were washed down, the wooden casket settling halfway into a puddle of mud. Jubal carefully tamped the shoveled earth alongside the box and proceeded to fill in the wet hole, wishing he had Bob's five-dollar gloves.

Mr. Apoptic and Everett disappeared down the hill with Frisk and the black-filigreed wagon, Jubal briefly considering charging the pair a fee for using his horse on their way back.

He had many thoughts along those lines, mostly about injustice and greed. Jubal stopped himself from feeling put-upon and morbidly sorry for allowing people to take advantage of him. He resolved to be more tough-minded and resolute, and to direct his feelings in more positive directions. *Here I am, worrying about a trifle in terms of rudeness by this bastard Greek funeral director and a for-hire illiterate preacher, while my friend Bob lies at the bottom of a wet grave—his fingers still locked across a cold chest. Heaven help us.*

Frisk stood, head down, still harnessed to the funeral wagon.

"I hope you were satisfied with the service, Mr. Jubal." Mr. Apoptic appeared at the back door of the home. "I had to charge you, of course, for the ice to keep friend Bob comfy. I also took the liberty of advancing Reverend Everett ten dollars extra for his thoughtful address. I felt confident you would agree and reimburse me for my foresight. In beloved friend Bob's memory."

Jubal unhitched Frisk and dropped the weighty harness to the ground. "Mr. Apologetic, your foresight and taking of liberties with my money has astounded me. I would have thought people in your position, dealing with folks who have lost those they care for, would be a little more sensitive. Would you like to take a ride with me to the Methodist church? We'll ask the kind Reverend Ev whether he received a gratuity or not. What do you say? It's worth an additional ten dollars to you if he says yes."

The funeral man ducked back inside his dark house and slammed the door.

Jubal rode Frisk back into the street. He withdrew his pistol and hit the large reception-room window with the butt end. The glass crazed into a beautiful star shape. He knew it to be childish, but it satisfied him.

Jubal passed a school that looked closed for the day. A few boys played hide-and-seek, their shouts of joy as they searched out their playmates a delight to Jubal's ears. He pressed on without really knowing where it would lead him, and even considered riding through the various shanty-towns and calling out Pete Wetherford's name, like a child.

But justice wouldn't happen that way.

Jubal,

"Beauty is truth, truth beauty. That is all ye need know."

Your note was refreshing and found me in both good spirits and fine health. I walk a little further each day and my appetite has returned.

Both Marlene and Cybil are doing well and send their regards.

I hope you'll excuse the beginning of this note's partial quote from John Keats. It is one of my favorites and held me in good stead, my years on the bench.

You have a way about you, young man. Your

honesty and forthright behavior will, I think, be the bedrock of your life's work. Whatever that turns out to be.

I am flattered you took my incident of physical harm to such heart. Cybil described to me your sensitive help with Doc Brown and how her own woozy behavior led to her comfort and support by you. My most humble gratitude.

If you will be kind enough to indulge an old man, "heed ye these morsels of ancient wisdom"?

Stop constantly putting your life on the line, dammit. I know you have been through much and that you are headstrong and independent. But Jubal, my son, think about the consequences of your actions, please. I understand your need for revenge but if it jeopardizes your life, is it worth it?

I am reminded of a recent confluence of Cervantes scholars; we stood on a dusty street trading quotations. Praying that I achieve at least a credible semblance of exactitude, I quote Sancho Panza to his riding companion. "Good Christians should never avenge injuries." My beating of Pete Wetherford notwithstanding, I believe in this.

I'll not belabor the point but know that we all care for you, especially one undergraduate of my acquaintance. By the way, this particular wayward student sends her regards and has enclosed a note sealed from her doddering father's inquisitive eyes.

Please take care and weigh the consequences of revenge carefully.

Yours truly,
Hiram Wickham

p.s. wondrous to hear that Marshal Turner brought William Tauson back from Colorado. There was news from the marshal that Tauson had killed another man in a tavern up your way. I didn't know if you knew of the Tauson incident but there you have it.

Jubal turned Cybil's note over in his hands. It had been folded along with the judge's envelope and sealed with wax, scented as if soaked in rosewater.

Jubal,

Several days after daddy's attack, a U.S. Marshal came by to see Father and inquire of his health. I overheard him talking about you having followed his band of townsmen, his "posse," for quite some time, then headed out north on, as he described it, a "wild goose chase."

We are all still shaken and apprehensive about that nightmarish evening.

I would like to take this occasion to explain my sickening behavior that evening. I hope you understand that the sight of my strong-willed father, helpless on that bloody table, was overwhelming.

Jubal, your complete concentration and steadfast manner with Doctor Brown created an atmosphere of enormous love and caring for another human being. Thank you.

Marshal Turner has stopped by several times and is somewhat a pest. He insisted on describing to me how he wounded Al Wetherford in the street in front of our house and other feats of derring-do throughout his career. I have less than zero interest in him and his oily hair.

I'll close now, hoping this note finds you in close proximity to transportation back to Cerro Vista and people who care for you.

                                    Regards,
                                    Cybil Wickham

p.s. may the wild geese be chased south to our warmer climes.

He held Cybil's scented note to his nose again before heading back into the mountains. It pleased him that he had made such good friends. He was touched that Judge Wickham thought so much of him. He hoped he would be worthy.

Cybil. How could this creature possibly know so much about him, and how was it that she could put into words things he had privately thought of and run through his mind about her? It was as if she could gaze into his heart. There was no doubt he admired her, and now his determination to continue his search was, if anything, more resolute.

Marshal Turner. An extraordinary expression of humanity. The man might not have come right out and said he'd captured Tauson, but since he brought him back to town he could just leave the rest to people's imagination. As for telling Cybil of his shooting Al Wetherford on the street in front of the Wickhams', it was . . . ridiculous, Jubal thought.

In some regard the greasy-haired marshal's behavior with Cybil was understandable. Jubal himself was smitten. It also became clear that he and Marshal Turner had become rivals. *Now I've got trouble on both sides of the law.*

THIRTY-ONE

Pete Wetherford felt tired. His companion Ed Thompson acted like a dolt and moved too slowly. They rode almost nonstop for several days.

"Why do we need to put so much distance between us and Cerro Vista, Pete?" Wetherford's driven behavior baffled Ed.

"Why you suppose, idiot? We're wanted. My brother Al's been shot dead. We plugged the judge, I killed the sheriff and probably the deputy. We're wanted for those drunken events at the farm. Not to mention our little stop-over in La Majestad."

Ed looked blankly at Wetherford.

"The village where we spent the night, stupid."

"I don't like the idea of riding this here pony not knowing who the hell it belongs to, I'll tell you that."

Wetherford thought this funny. He rode in silence for a while, then sidled up next to Ed with his mount. "If you don't shine up to that there cayuse, why don't you slip off her and give her a good slap on the butt? She'll head on back to La Majestad right quick, that way it would relieve all your worries about being hung for a horse thief."

Ed didn't know if Pete was kidding him or not. "You know well as I they don't hang folks for horse thievery anymore. Just concerned 'cause I'm wondering what you did back at that . . ."

"La Majestad."

"Yeah, that town. What you did to that old gal."

Wetherford didn't know whether to satisfy Ed's curiosity. The man was beginning to annoy him. "When you were waiting by the mesa for me, what did you think? That Pete's a crazy one, he's gone back to kill that señorita, sure as hell? Was that drifting around in that pea brain of yours?"

"Nah," protested Ed. "I just don't want the law taking me down for something I didn't do." He glanced over at Wetherford. "Did you do her?"

Wetherford laughed. "When I got back to the shack, she was gone, along with one of the horses. So, yeah, she probably rode into that burg and told someone she had a rollicking good time the previous night, but now she regretted it and would someone please chase after a couple gringos, one who has a big smile plastered across his face? Hell's fire, man, we're a hell of a way down the road. No one's gonna catch us—shake off your willies. Outside of that, we could just parade up and down old La Majestad or Cerro Vista until Christmas. There's just a couple villages 'round these parts that don't need to see the likes of Pete Wetherford and a certain scared-shitless Ed 'Mama's Boy' Thompson."

Ed reined in his horse and waited for Wetherford to do the same. "No need to talk to a fellow like that. I was just asking, is all. Jesus."

"You want to trail out of here on your own, Thompson, have at it." Wetherford jerked his horse around. "Your problem, Ed, is you got no sense of fun and very little patience."

"Don't be talking to me about patience. I told you and Al on the street before we ambushed the judge's house that we should hold up. Try and get the fellow to come out on the porch so we could fix him good. But no, you gotta ride down there spraying away at everything in sight. I said to Al that I seen a couple fellows coming down the street. What is it with the Wetherfords? Whatever you want to do, you just do it? Like it don't make no never mind what other folk might be thinking or wanting? Now you got us in trouble for raping that Mexican gal and stealing her horse. Lord knows what else."

"The Wetherfords don't take kindly to folks who want to criticize or talk ugly." Wetherford looped his leg over the saddle horn and took a hard look at his riding crony. "Thing is, Ed, I guess I really don't like you much. Trail your butt out of here before I lose my temper."

Ed's long stare angered Wetherford.

"Go on, git. Tell your story while you ride away." Wetherford took his pistol from the holster, holding it loosely. "Questions?"

Ed mumbled while turning his horse.

"What did you say?" Wetherford called out to him. "Did you call me a name? Spit it out, man."

Ed spurred his horse northeast into a gallop through the foothills.

Wetherford wheeled his mare, Brindle, back onto the trail to Poverty Gulch. He figured it was closer to five miles than ten. The confrontation with Thompson had been, to Wetherford's way of thinking, inevitable. The man brought him low in spirit. They hadn't really been friends in Tauson's group, anyway, and it was pure happenstance they had hooked up after Wetherford's escape from the Cerro Vista Jail.

Wetherford had snuck back into town several days after the jailbreak looking for whiskey and ran into Ed at Casa Rey. They had decided to ride north together looking for Billy Tauson and his promised gold deal.

"We'll all be rich as Midas, boys!" Tauson had shouted, back when he had described his claim and how he wanted the fellows to stake their titles adjacent to his so they could control a whole continuous patch of free-flowing riches. "I'll buy your claims and you fellers will work for me, 'cause I got the seed money. Don't worry none about being cheated. I'll take care of you, I promise."

Yeah, Wetherford thought. He would promise in the same way one would to a gal, "I'll be your sweetie forever, hon." Wetherford knew Tauson would do him dirt if he got the chance, even though he was smart and had an enterprising soul. A good person for Pete to hook his future to.

If he stayed alert, Pete Wetherford could do well with Billy Tauson.

Wetherford rode through a wooded draw, pulled up, and twisted around slowly in the saddle. Something felt strange, but he couldn't put a finger to it. As he started to alight from his mare, a rifle shot blew off a small tree branch just above his head.

Wetherford ducked under his horse and tried to get the lay of the surrounding area. A copse of trees stood up the side of the mountain to the east. Behind him, only open trail. To the west, a steep rocky descent to a stream below. The shot seemed to come from above and to the east. He knew who had fired it.

He tied Brindle to a sapling and unsheathed his rifle, a Spencer carbine.

He waited, knowing Big Ed would be nervous, since his first shot had missed. He would move soon, Wetherford was sure of it. Another bullet ricocheted off a thick piece of shale some ten or twelve feet to his left. A crouched figure darted between the trees and dove behind a log perpendicular to the slope.

Crawling up the grade, Wetherford watched the distant log, stopping where a large rock gave him protection from the shooter. Lifting the rear brass sight to adjust for the rise in terrain, he framed his view, pulled back the hammer, and waited.

"Hey, Ed? Jesus, man. What the hell you doing? I know you're kind of miffed at me, but Christ, can we talk about it? We been riding buddies for quite a spell now. I gotta admit I go too far sometimes, but . . . losing Al and all . . . can you give a fellow another chance, pardner?"

The beginnings of a clump of hair starting to rise above the bark of the tree. Then an ear and a forehead. As the eyes came into view, Wetherford squeezed off a round from the Spencer. A billowing array of shredded bark exploded next to Ed Thompson's head, accompanied by the man's shriek. Ed rolled out from behind the log, both hands holding the side of his face. He staggered down the slanted ground while Wetherford levered in another round, cocked the Spencer, and fired, thinking this time maybe he hit the area of Ed's left hip.

He tried to decide whether to inspect the body that was now slowly rolling down the steep hill or continue on his way. He gave a satisfied grunt as he watched Big Ed's limp form continue its lazy descent.

Brindle kicked up a fuss. The gunfire had unnerved her, but as he drew close, she gave a snort as if welcoming him back. Wetherford smiled and mounted, a gratifying conclusion to an irritating problem.

THIRTY-TWO

The thought of shouting out a murderer's name in a tent city appealed to Jubal still, even though the consequences could be dire. It seemed on the surface downright silly, but perhaps it would be effective.

Jubal went back and forth about the idea, going from wild enthusiasm one minute to humbling fear the next. Finally, he decided he'd try it on some of the close-in communities, the ones where he might get support from the local townspeople if trouble arose. He rode into the hills.

Then again, perhaps it wasn't such a good idea. It was near to suppertime, and most of the campers would be fixing their eats. People might be annoyed at his bellyaching during their meal. Perhaps he'd give it some time.

He realized he missed Cybil more than ever. She seemed so wise and confident. He wished she were there to counsel him.

Jubal turned back toward town. The sun had begun to set and from his hillside he could see a soft purple light descending on the community. It wasn't such a bad town after all. He and Mountain Bob had shared some fine times. He would have to drop a note to the gal Anne at Anne's Good Eats to tell of Bob's sad demise.

As Jubal got closer to town he could see a number of people in the street. A crowd had gathered, a few of the people pointing south toward a lone horseman stumbling along on the main street. Jubal spurred Frisk into a gallop. The man was not sitting atop his mount but was being dragged by his horse as he clung to the saddle horn.

By the time Jubal arrived, several townsmen were trying to untie the man's right hand from the metal and leather horn protruding from the front of the saddle.

"Ease him up a bit onto his feet to take some pressure off his hand." This from a gruff fellow who had put himself in charge.

Jubal tied Frisk to a hitching post and joined the gawking crowd.

Clothes torn and caked with dirt, his face and hair matted with blood, it looked as if the horseman had been hit by a tree trunk, with large crimson-tinted shards of wood embedded in his head. He was keening like an infant, and blood oozed down his left side.

Jubal stepped forward. "I think he's been hip-shot."

"You the expert on gut-shot? Shut your face and give us a hand here."

Jubal put his right arm around the man's waist from the back and gently lifted him. He surveyed the man's hand. "Look at that, would you?"

"So what?" The tough talker glanced at the rider's hand.

"It's black, he's lost the use. Circulation's been cut off. It would be best to try and rub some blood back into that hand before we cut him loose."

"All right, Doctor. Whatever you say. Damnation. Everybody's an expert, holy Jesus."

Jubal continued to prop up the bound horseman. Jubal's head was close to the back of the man's right ear. "Who did this to you, mister?"

The man breathed deeply. "I did."

"What do you mean, you did?" Jubal moved his feet to get a better purchase as the gruff man massaged the horseman's forearm.

"I wrapped my arm with my belt and secured it to the saddle horn. I couldn't mount the horse. . . . Too weak, she dragged me for days and hustled along, 'til I stumbled into this place. . . . Where are we?"

Massaging the man's forearm had restored some of the color. Jubal unsheathed his bowie knife and passed it, handle first, to the man massaging the arm. He sliced through the wounded man's brass-studded belt and Jubal lowered him to the ground. "You're in Poverty Gulch, my good man."

The horseman's eyes grew large. "Oh, shit. Tell the law to look after me or I'm a goner for sure."

Before Jubal could ask him why, a man calling himself Doc Ward arrived with Sheriff Cox. The doctor had the man moved to the porch of the dry goods store while the lawman bent over him to ask a few questions.

Jubal couldn't hear everything that was said, but

toward the end of the conversation he heard the five-star peacekeeper repeat the name "Pete Wetherford." Along with other townsmen, Jubal carried the wounded man to the doctor's office.

Sheriff Cox trailed behind. "Seems like every time I see you, son, there's a lot of blood. What gives?"

"Guess I attract disaster, Sheriff. Some people surround themselves with flowers; I'm destined for stinkweed."

Cox chuckled.

They arrived at the doctor's office and the men laid the moaning patient on the examining table.

Jubal stepped back out into the street with the lawman.

"Do you know this dunderhead, Slim?" Cox asked him.

"Can't say I know him, but I'm pretty sure he's one of Billy Tauson's gang of rascals. I recognized his checkered vest."

"Care to join me, son?" The sheriff took out a cheroot and a safety match.

"No, thanks. Never acquired the habit. Suppose if that fellow lives through his ordeal he'll have some things to tell us about . . . Pete Wetherford."

"He already did." The sheriff struck the match on the butt end of his pistol and lit his cigar. "Said he and Pete were heading up this way to Poverty Gulch to do some mining when, out of nowhere, Pete shot him, left him for dead. Robbed his money, then rode off. Says he don't know why. Supposed to be friends."

"If he's anything like the rest of his 'friends,' he wouldn't know the truth if it was packing double behind him on his saddle. I'm going to take a little look-see around town, near the tents. Try and spot our Mr. Wetherford."

"I'll get a note off to that Turner friend of yours and join you up around Twin Pines. Just before that flat meadow where the tents are. Don't do anything hasty, buckaroo."

Jubal tipped his hand to his hat and urged Frisk into a slow trot. He liked Sheriff Tom Cox. Seemed like a respectable man. Still wore his blue Union Army pants, but with a fringe-laden buckskin jacket and Union Army scarf. Jubal tried counting how many years Tom would have had those pants. *Lord, near to thirty years. But the man doesn't look that old.* Jubal calculated this would have made him twenty or younger during the war.

He rode the main thoroughfare, and then started up the mountain.

It was near dark by the time Sheriff Cox joined him at the trailhead marked by matching pine trees.

Tom Cox pointed across the open space. "There's a temporary saloon set up in the trees on the other side of this meadow. Let's take a look."

As they rode across the wide meadow, Jubal asked Tom about his trousers.

"Thanks for asking, Slim. Truth is, my daddy served in the cavalry. Had a couple pair. When he passed, ma inherited these on down to me. Probably looks a might ridiculous, but I guess folks 'round these parts have kind of gotten used to the look."

"My pa served too, but he wore out his gold-stripers years ago." Jubal had only a vague memory of Jubal, Sr., in his uniform. "He'd dig them out from time to time and parade around a bit. 'What you think, Bea? The tunic covers the waistline right smart,' he'd say. And then my ma would giggle and point silently toward the wardrobe."

The saloon tent, rigged by an enterprising barkeep, was not much more than a hank of long canvas stretched between two trees and open on three sides. A bearded musician seated at the far end plucked a banjo while a couple of tired-looking ladies scooted around with pitchers of beer. Close to a dozen tables were spread out, each with its own kerosene lantern. Thirty or forty patrons huddled about, drinking their suds.

Sheriff Cox signaled for Jubal to follow him to the makeshift bar, merely a couple of long planks stretched between two barrels. Jubal stood at the far end while the sheriff walked slowly through the crowd, looking for unfamiliar faces.

"What you have, old-timer?" This from a thin fellow wearing a white apron and a ridiculous-looking ten-gallon hat.

Jubal didn't really want a drink but thought maybe for the sake of appearances he should have something. "I think maybe a glass of beer. Make that two glasses, if you would." He watched as the sheriff continued to walk among the patrons. When the beer arrived, Jubal paid and took a sip. Wasn't bad, he thought, for an old seasoned beer drinker like himself.

The bartender stood in front of Jubal polishing beer glasses. "Where you in from, pard?"

"Ah, well, here and there, sir. Mostly down Cerro Vista way."

"Where's that?"

"South, in New Mexico."

"There were a rascal in here, I think it was last night, from New Mexico, strange dude. Looked as if he were spoiling for trouble. You know the type. Always taking harm at everything a person might say to him. Mean eyes."

"Did he have black hair, long dark coat, sort of a nasty grin?"

Someone at the far end of the bar called out for service. The barkeep held up a finger to Jubal. "Hold on a spell, youngster. Got a customer down there. I'll get back to you."

Jubal felt as if Wetherford might be close. His reverie was interrupted by an angry voice at the other end of the makeshift saloon. The space grew quiet, the banjo player continued awhile, then gradually petered out. Jubal took his beer and stepped out of the tent, skirting behind the open canopy.

"You got no jurisdiction up here. I'm a law-abiding citizen having a drink, trying to mind my own self. Why you pestering me for?"

Judging by the murmur from the surrounding miners, they all seemed to agree the drunk was within his rights. Jubal glanced around the tent. Not many friendly faces.

"Say, there, Walker," Sheriff Cox said. "That is your name, isn't it?"

"Yep, my mama gave me that name." The big guy looked around at his drinking mates. "I'd be obliged for you not to wear it out."

The sheriff took a step closer. "Walker, I explained to you some two weeks ago about you drinking, then going home and beatin' the shit out of that ninety-pound wife of yours. I'm not going to tell you again, you hear? I approached you in a friendly way, but you want to make a spectacle of yourself and let all these good folk hear how much of a cowardly bully you are."

The red-faced man was close to exploding.

The sheriff waited.

Controlling his temper, Walker revealed a gap-toothed grin, then poured his beer slowly on Tom Cox's boots while glancing about the room.

The sheriff slapped the glass away and drew his pistol in one swift move.

"Everyone stay seated." Sheriff Cox called out to the barkeep, "If you want to stay open the rest of the night, no more drinks for Mr. Big Mouth Walker, agreed?"

"You got 'er, Tom, whatever you say," the bartender called back.

Tom directed his talk back to Walker. "Why don't you call it a night, big boy?"

Another man, definitely drunk, came up close behind the sheriff. "Why don't you kiss all our behinds, lawman?" He poked Sheriff Cox in the back with a long-barreled six-shooter.

A chorus of "Oh, shit" echoed in the crowded tent.

The drunk with the gun spouted a litany of grievances, not just about lawmen but about the rigors of gold mining, the cold winters, and life in general.

Jubal drifted toward the back of the tent, remaining in the shadows, choosing his moment. When it arrived, he stepped out of the darkness, drew his pistol, and got behind the drunk. He forced the barrel into the man's ear so he could hear the unmistakable sound of the hammer being cocked.

"Drop that piece or your head comes off, cowboy," Jubal whispered.

Sheriff Cox turned and disarmed the drunk, slapping him hard across the face with an open hand. "Henry, you're getting to be a pain, you know that? How many times have I taken this weapon from you?"

"Too many?" The drunk tried to focus.

"That's for damn sure." The sheriff cracked open the six-shooter and spilled the brass cartridges into his hand, then tossed them out into the black night. "Folks, listen up. I realize a lot of you are from out of town and are here to make your fortune, but you don't have a license to act up. You work hard, and want to relax, but you can't break the law." He waited to gauge the response. Most of the drinkers seemed to acquiesce and went back to their beers.

"Hear me out. We'll shut this circus down and you'll have to hoof it into town for your beer." He paused, turning back to Walker, and tapped him in the chest with Henry's empty pistol. "As for you, wife-beater, the next time you cause a ruckus, your butt is behind bars. You *sabe*?"

"Hey, what about my hogleg, Tom?" This from Henry.

"You'll get it back from the barkeep at the end of the night, okay?"

"What if I needed it afore that, I'd just be stuck, wouldn't I?"

"As drunk as you are, if you were called out in a gunfight you'd never clear your holster. Now sit down and shut up."

The sheriff handed the empty six-shooter to the barkeep and told him to keep watch on it until Henry sobered up. Tom and Jubal made their way to the saloon exit, the barkeep following them to the edge of the tent.

"Hey, Slim. Didn't you want to hear about your friend from New Mexico? The way you described him, kinda mean grin, all nasty black hair, sounds like your buddy, uh . . . what's his name?"

"Pete?"

"Yeah, that's it. Said he was heading up the mountain, do some sifting for yellow with his partner, if he could find him. Billy something or other."

Jubal and Sheriff Cox glanced at each other. Jubal thanked the man and the two walked to their horses.

The sheriff mounted first. "You put yourself in a tough position back there, Slim. Pulling down on that clown Henry, you looked a mite too comfortable with that shooter of yours."

Jubal didn't answer, just fiddled with Frisk's reins.

"Thing is, youngster, I appreciate what you did. Don't misunderstand me, but don't get too comfortable unleashing that weapon. You might be forced to shoot someone, take a life someday. You hear?"

He agreed with a nod, resisting the urge to smile.

Sheriff Cox turned his horse back toward Poverty Gulch. "After all that, we hear that your 'friend' Pete Wetherford is in the area."

Jubal followed the sheriff back in the direction of the gulch. They rode in silence until Jubal called to the man, "Somehow, sir, I don't think my 'friend' Pete had gotten word that Billy Tauson is in jail. He's going to be hunting around creek beds and panning sites, asking about him, and the more he asks, the more people will know which way he's headed. He's going to leave a trail, the bastard."

As they picked their way down the dark foothills, Jubal's thoughts drifted back to his father and the reasons for the move from Kansas.

His pa stood by the closet, running his hand reverently over his Civil War tunic. "Bea, I've caused a man to die." They briefly touched. "It was an accident, but nevertheless, he's gone. It's tough to live with that."

Jubal's mother hugged her husband. "Jube, dear, Hank passed away? Wait while I get the children to bed."

His mother scooted both him and Pru into their bedrooms. After she quietly bade him good night, Jubal crept back to the heavy oak door and cracked it open. His parents stood at the entrance to the hallway in a tight embrace, his father weeping. "I never liked that jasper, but I had no real intent. Like I told you the other day, it was just a scuffle, then he fell. His head . . ."

"What's to become of us, Jube?" his mother said. "You know we've spoken of this before, and it's always the same, you have to face it."

"I know, sweetheart. But I'm certain my days in the harness trade are finished. We may have to consider a move out west . . . that land sale."

THIRTY-THREE

Bastards seemed to run in Pete Wetherford's family. He could recall a number of uncles, cousins, and the like who, even if trying to be kind, were out-and-out sons of bitches.

Wetherford moved his way up the steep embankment alongside the creek. He'd seen a number of miners, all waist-deep in cold water, shoveling and rattling their sluices, trying to eke out a living. He'd decided, potential riches or not, it was not the life for him. Perhaps he'd let those yokels do their panning, then relieve them of their riches in order to save them a trip down the mountain to the assayer's office. *Why, Lord's sake, it would be almost like a community service.*

Dismounting, he knelt down next to the stream and dipped his head into the cool water, trying to shake off his hangover. The tented saloon with its warm beer and rotgut whiskey had been a mistake, but like most promises he made to himself, his pledge to ease off the drinking proved difficult. He recalled a distant relative, Uncle Arnie. The man hadn't drawn a sober breath in twenty years, and then one day Pete's ma got a letter addressed to his long-departed father, telling of Uncle Arnie's passing.

> Arnie was taken from us on the 12th of August in the year of our Lord, 1876. Gunned down by a cowardly bank guard while our beloved was innocently fiddling with his own Colt pistol. The blessed Lord has seen fit to take his sainted soul back to the promise land.
>
> Love always,
Verna Wetherford
>
> p.s. can you send us a small passel of cash money to hold us over?

Pete remembered his ma practically pissing herself when she read the letter. She carried it around with her for days. Dragging it from her apron pocket, she held the paper with one hand while clamping the other across her mouth, always ready to explode in delight.

Once, before going out on her nightly haunt, his mother asked if he remembered an Uncle Arnie.

"Was that the old man who always smelled so bad?"

"Yeah, son, that's the one. He were a right bastard."

Wetherford felt he'd gone about as far up the mountain as he dared in the fading light. Earlier, an old-timer cooking his beans for the night attempted to regale him about an event that had happened recently in town.

"I heard you asking that no-good busybody on the next claim over about a friend of yours. What's his name again?"

"Tauson, Billy Tauson."

"Can't rightly say if he was the one, but as you described him, kinda early gray hair, could've been him."

"Yeah, just get on with it."

"I was having my weekly allowance of beer when all a sudden hell's fire breaks out. The screaming and shouting . . . well, the long and short of it were that some buckskin-clad cowboy got hisself seriously killed, dead. This dude what kilt him, the gray-haired vaquero, was hauled away by the sheriff. The sheriff arriving I didn't actually see. I'd left during the gunplay and heard about the rest from prospectors."

"Okay, old-timer. Thanks for the story, guess I'll be drifting."

The old man stoked his fire with a long stick. "The damnedest part about the whole rigamarole was this kid, heck fire, he couldn't a been over eighteen. He pulled down on this gray-haired fellow like he was born to the gun. Just calm as you please. Way I heard it, the older gunner nearly dumped his drawers, he were so scared of this young slinger."

Settling in for the night in his blanket roll, Wetherford was putting the pieces together. If the man the old miner had described was actually Billy Tauson, then he would certainly have to change his plans. The young buck, well, he could be the little nosy bastard from the farm. If he was in fact up here, Wetherford knew he would no doubt be looking for him. The kid would have some gunmen with him, a couple paid hands who Pete knew would need sorting out.

Whenever he shifted his sleeping position, he was painfully reminded of his descent from the log bridge at the canyon on Morning Peak. He went over what he would do to the little shit.

He woke with the sunlight streaming through the trees. He tried to decide whether to continue up the steep trail looking for the elusive Billy Tauson or take the old-timer's story as whole cloth and traipse back down the mountain.

He hoped the kid from that story was the young sodbuster from the farm. Pete could do him in before the kid and his hired guns bushwhacked him in the comfort of his bedroll.

The old miner was working at his sluice when Wetherford came riding into his camp. "Heading toward town, are you?" the miner called out.

Wetherford dismounted and walked toward the elderly man.

The old forty-niner remained steadfast, his free hand moving to his vest pocket, then down to a belt held high on his waist. His hand came to rest on a holster holding a gnarly six-shooter.

"No need for any gunplay, old-timer. Just fork over your sack of powder and I'll be on my way."

"I knew sure as shooting last evening when I was talking to you, you'd be back." The old man took out his gun, his hand shaking with palsy. "You just have that look about you."

"I'll have your tote of yellow, pard. Don't waste my time with a passel of conversation." Pete made a toss-it-here gesture with his hand.

The old-timer stood thigh-deep in cold water. "I'll have to fetch it from my pack." He shivered, looking as if he wanted to steady his hand long enough to take a shot.

"I'll put one right in your forehead, Gramps, afore you can squeeze the trigger. You brushed that vest pocket of yours before you drew down on me. Let's have a look inside."

The old fellow took a small leather pouch out of his vest pocket, along with a gold watch. After gazing down at the bag a moment, he tossed it across the short expanse of water to the ground in front of Pete.

"I'll have that watch, too. Sling it over here easy-like."

The prospector did so reluctantly, then tried to raise his shaking hand to level his gun, but Wetherford beat him, firing twice before the miner's hand reached flush with Pete's waist. He wavered, his arms spread, trying to steady himself. Knees wobbling, he slipped silently into the waiting stream.

Wetherford watched, delighting in the rose-colored patch of water starting to form on the surface of the creek. He retrieved his loot, went through the miner's pack, then mounted and headed downhill to the next claim.

A hundred yards down the mountain, a man working his claim greeted him, saying he heard gunfire and wondered "what was up."

"Your hands, pardner, reach to the blue, let's have your tote."

"What happened to ole Eden?"

"He took an early retirement from panning. Thought maybe he'd rest easy for a spell, visit the kids, play that prissy game of tennis, that sort of thing. Said you might want to join him if you cared to."

The fellow got teary-eyed. "Did you kill him, mister?"

"What d'you think, stupid? I was having target practice and old Eden just stepped in front of the bullets? Empty your pockets, and be quick about it."

He continued down the mountain that way. Of the five people he robbed, only one other tried his hand at gunplay. The man's efforts were rewarded with the same result that the older prospector had experienced. Wetherford now had a smart cache, all in different leather bags, all brimming with yellow dust. He liked mining.

Wetherford waited in the trees above town until just before the closing hour of the assayer's office. He tied his horse in a back street behind the office, then walked past the window several times, looking inside. A heavyset woman wearing men's pants seemed to be the only customer. Pete stood off the porch out of view as the buxom gal came out counting her dollars, and once she disappeared up the street, Wetherford slid through the barred glass door. The man who ran the place had just started to turn the OPEN sign in the window to CLOSED.

"We're done for the day, pardner. Could you come back in the morning?"

Pete contrived a hurt tone to his voice. "Dangnation, I got no place to stay tonight without some cash."

"Sorry, as I said, we're closed. Got to go home, have

my supper, chase the wife around the stove, that sort of thing. I already locked up the safe."

"Sir. If I gave you a sack of yellow on trust, could you maybe advance me a tenner out of your pocket 'til morning? Could you manage that?"

"Highly unusual, but let me see your poke." The man opened a spring-loaded latched gate to his barred cubicle and donned a green isinglass eyeshade.

Wetherford dug out one of the small leather bags and laid it on the glass counter.

Instead of opening the bag to examine the gold dust, the man turned it over in his hands several times. "You a friend of old Eden Jones?

Pete didn't understand. "Why you ask?"

"'Cause this bag belongs to Ole Man Jones."

Wetherford tried to be dismissive. "Oh, hell, you're right. The old guy asked me to do him the favor of cashing in his find, since I was coming into town anyway. I better give you mine just to keep things straight." Pete retrieved another bag from his pocket. It seemed fairly new and common-looking. He casually tossed it toward the man. "How did you know that was ole Eden's poke?"

"He's one of the few old-timers who experienced the gold rush in California sometime in the forties. See that ink drawing on the buckskin?" He held the bag up to the light and pointed out a cartoon drawing of a money bag with a dollar sign in the middle, the number 49 below it. "That's how I know it's his. Did he give you a note saying it's okay for you to have this and cash it in?"

Pete reached below the counter as if to retrieve a note and came up with his pistol. He laid the barrel of the piece on the edge of the glass countertop. "It wasn't so much what he gave me but what I gave him. Keep your hands right there above the cabinet top and slowly ease your bones over to the gate and open it real gentle-like."

"What, are you crazy? You're right in the center of town. You shoot me and the whole community will descend on you like flies on dung." Nevertheless, the man raised his hands high.

"Ease your arms down so folks can't see you from the street. Finish turning that CLOSED sign over. Lock the door and blow out that kerosene lamp. Hustle, now, quick." Pete followed the movement with his gun. "Now open up that safe. Put the cash and what dust you've got in this saddle-bag." Pete tossed the bag he'd slung over his shoulder toward the man.

The safe was a large affair with two wide double doors. Pete moved behind the counter and jammed the gun into the man's liver. "Make it quick, Mr. Assayer."

The shopkeeper hurriedly loaded the saddlebag with money from a drawer and some fifteen small bags of gold dust.

"Now move back behind the safe, and be brisk on it." It was a spot of bother, having to tie the man up instead of shooting him, but it was true, a gunshot in the middle of town would create havoc for him. Best to take the time and do it proper. "Take off that belt"—Pete glanced around the tight space—"and that dandy's tie, give it here."

Once he had the tie and the belt, he instructed the man to lie on the floor on his side. Wetherford wrapped the leather belt securely around the man's crossed ankles. Next he bound his hands behind his back with the tie, looping a loose end through the belt. He looked quickly around the back room of the store and found an oily cleaning rag, which he stuffed unceremoniously into the assayer's mouth, but not before the man spit out his thoughts.

"May the wrath of the devil rise up out of the depths and smite you a paralyzing blow, you no-good, lazy rapscallion."

Huh. That's a new one. Better give this jackass a swift kick in the gut, just in case "rapscallion" means something heavier than it sounds. So he did.

It was near to dark, the setting sun casting the trees with a soft feathery glow.

Wetherford had taken the assayer's horse. With a short hank of rope, he tied it to his own mare's saddle horn. With two horses he could trade off, making better time— the trailing horse resting, not burdened with Pete's two hundred pounds.

It had been a productive day. By this time Pete could assume the trembling souls who had recently contributed to his larder of riches would have united and traipsed down the mountain to tell their sad story to the sheriff. Wouldn't it be funny, he thought, if the group ran into Mr. Assayer as he hobbled down the street, ankles and hands still tied, making strange muffled sounds through the cloth stuffed in his mouth? Pete laughed at the image.

With the demise of old-timer Eden Jones and the other miner who had decided to be brave but been too slow when it came to gunplay, Pete decided to hightail it back toward New Mexico and folks he knew. He was running low on friends, what with the passing of Ty Blake and brother Al, not to mention the lately departed Big Ed Thompson.

Wherever Billy Tauson was, he would just have to wait to be gifted with Pete Wetherford's presence.

He had plenty of money, a warm feeling about the men he'd killed, and best of all, no ties. No one and nothing to latch onto him, and a free conscience. He felt good as he headed south, humming along at an easy gallop. *"Duh dum de dum da dum. That sav'd a wretch like me! / I once was lost, but now am found, / Was blind, but now I see."*

In the distance, a rumble from a far-off thunderhead. But Wetherford didn't hear it. He was too busy celebrating his amazing grace.

THIRTY-FOUR

The gunfire came from close by. It seemed to come down the mountain, and Jubal first sloughed it off as drunken celebrations. He stoked his fire and wrapped his bedroll over his shoulders. Frisk stirred, not reacting well to the echoing shots.

He'd chosen his spot on the mountain well, much higher than most of the miners. Since he didn't have a legitimate claim, he decided he'd best distance himself from the pack. It also helped not to hear the endless questions. "What you doing, son? Are your parents up here with you?" Or, "You look too young to be prospecting, you should be in school." *They're probably right about school,* he admitted.

Jubal knew as soon as this hunt was over he would need to further his education. Maybe something back east, possibly in the area of Boston, where a certain erudite young lady of his acquaintance would be residing. That, he thought, would be something to look forward to.

He planned on dragging the sluice he had built out of the woods and start panning. Then he would scout the various creeks and streams in the area for a couple of days, looking for Wetherford. He thought alternating the routine would keep him fresh.

The morning light found Jubal once again feeding his sluice. He selected this site for the quartz deposits scattered around the immediate vicinity. Their presence, as an old-timer suggested, was evidence of gold in the area.

Around midmorning, as he emptied his gold-finding apparatus for the fifth time, he asked himself if it was really worth the bother.

He didn't mind the work. In fact he liked it; lathering up a sweat reminded him of home. But there was always the nagging feeling he wasn't doing enough in his pursuit of Pete Wetherford. He fought for a while with his sense of discipline, going back and forth between wanting to pack in the silly panning for gold and the terrible need to find Pete. He was determined to tough out the schedule he had set for himself—two days of panning to make a living, two days of looking for Pete, then back to panning.

As he worked in the middle of the stream, he kept going over the possibilities, playing a game of throwing out the large worthless rocks caught up in the riffles of his sluice. He said to himself if he discarded ten rocks the size of a marble without spying a small sparkle of gold, he would, as penance, five times lift the log that sat on the shore.

Once, he tallied thirty required lifts of his log and waded to the bank, but instead of doing the prescribed lifts he'd promised himself, he sat on the log and flipped the last stone into the air.

Maybe this panning business was just too much of a distraction, keeping him from his pursuits, or maybe it was the other way around and his dogged quest for justice kept him from making his fortune. In any case, he was dispirited. He lifted a lone rock to his eye, wondering if the answer might be hidden in the hard interior of the ancient piece. To his surprise, a small glitter was attached to the rock.

He retrieved his leather bag with its pitiful layer of gold dust sprinkled along the bottom and tried to chip the sparkle from the rock with his fingernail into his cache. It wouldn't budge. Jubal took the stone to the streambed and tried washing the mud from it. As the caked dirt came away, he realized the tiny gold particle he'd seen had disappeared and become one with the entire stone. He was holding a gold nugget the size of one of ma's biscuits.

It didn't take long for Jubal to break camp. He left his sluice standing in the middle of the stream, a scribbled note impaled on the handle: *This apparatus is my gift to whosoever wants it. May you prosper and may the mountain bear thee fruit—although you would probably prefer gold.*

The ride down felt endless. He was anxious to have his nugget appraised. He passed a deserted claim, clothing and equipment strewn about as if a bear had ravaged the camp. Jubal rode on and came upon a man sitting forlornly, head in hands, next to the stream, staring into the distant trees.

"Hello . . . how you faring?"

The man turned away, seeming not to want to talk.

"Anything you need? Food? What's the matter?"

The man waved his arm in a limp fashion, as if trying to dismiss Jubal.

"Suit yourself," Jubal said, and urged Frisk on.

As the path curved abruptly into the trees, the man cried out.

"He robbed me, the bastard, then went off singing some fucking spiritual like he was descended from heaven. That were a month's work he took. Ahhh, shit."

Jubal looked back. The shaken worker trampled the ground like a wild man putting out a fire.

He reined in Frisk. "Do you need a ride into town, mister?"

The victim looked up in surprise. "What . . . what do you want?"

"Do you need help, a ride into the gulch?"

"I've worked my whole life, then a ruffian with rotten breath and a nickel-plated shooter takes my savings and tries to bum-diddle me." He walked toward Jubal, his hands spread. "Can you imagine, I'm forty-five years old and I never felt no man's hands on me." He shivered, completely dumbfounded.

"When did this happen?"

"Don't rightly know, maybe yesterday. Ah, hell, what's the difference? I'll ride into town with you, thank you."

Jubal eased Frisk near to a tree stump and the shaken worker mounted behind him. They followed the trail bordering the creek and hadn't gone a hundred yards when the man slid off the back of Frisk's rump.

"I'll walk, I don't feel comfortable riding double." He

seemed embarrassed. "Got to get to the sheriff. See if I can't get that rotter throwed in jail."

"What brings you into town, big guy?"

Sheriff Cox seemed surprised to see him. Jubal smiled at the lawman and gestured outside the jail to the prospector from the mountain, sitting slumped on the bench. The two stepped outside just as it started to rain. Main Street was awash, the water starting to form small rivulets. The sheriff held his hand out into the downpour.

"What's eating at you, pal?"

The man glanced up. "A fellow did me wrong, Sheriff. He surely did. Robbed me like I was a piece of bear droppings. He . . . Well, never mind. He robbed me, on my claim, of a month's panning."

"When did this happen?"

"I been in such a state, I can't rightly tell you. Probably yesterday."

Sheriff Cox looked to Jubal. "You're the third one to come off the mountain with the same tale. You're lucky."

"Lucky? How in hell you figure that?"

"The shooter killed two miners and robbed a number of others, including yourself. Yeah, you're fortunate you didn't go to battle with that desperado. He'd a killed you sure as kittens are cute. Come on inside and I'll take a statement from you. What's your name?"

"Call me sucker."

Sheriff Cox and Jubal laughed as the sheriff gestured for the man to step into the jailhouse. "Well, Mr. Sucker, please enter."

As the man described his assailant, Jubal was sure it

was Pete Wetherford. The physical description, the sheer ruthless behavior—it had to be him. Wetherford had cut a path of death and malice through the countryside, and Jubal wondered if it would all lead to him. He had no doubt Wetherford would kill him without hesitation. He would need to stay vigilant.

The street had quite a slope to it, the water rushing along as many small tributaries before eventually melding into one watercourse. The rutted dirt road became difficult, and he was reminded of his hellish ride with Frisk down the raging waters in the arroyo.

As the downpour lessened, Jubal darted across the street, leaping carefully over the beginnings of the small river in the middle of the roadbed, to stand under the awning of the assayer's shop. The sign above the door read GOLD APPRAISED AND BOUGHT. PROPRIETOR STEVEN WILLS. In the window of the door, a CLOSED sign with note attached: *Regret, the shop will be closed for several days, sorry. S.W.*

Later that day, Jubal heard from the sheriff that the fellow Ed Thompson, who had been dragged into town by his horse, would live.

Jubal and Sheriff Cox had become fairly good friends and, when the rain finally stopped, Jubal asked the sheriff to visit Ed with him. The rain finally stopped, bringing out the sun along with the locals. The shops and stores buzzed with a variety of miners and prospectors, all intent on spending money. Jubal remarked to Sheriff Cox how prosperous the town appeared to be.

"Yeah, I suppose you could say that. Except it also has

a lot of yokels who are flat on their asses, so anytime you have that kind of disparity among folks, you'll always have trouble. Grousing about wages, unhappy about their lot in life. A kind of constant woe-is-me mentality. You get my drift?"

Jubal thought maybe he understood. "Then you have guys like Pete Wetherford," he said, "robbing and killing. Makes for an unhappy combination, I guess." They continued walking along a street with a mix of proper houses and occasional shacks and tents.

The doctor had arranged for Ed to be bedded in a home for the infirm. Ed sat propped up in an easy chair, head swathed in bandages. A shirt open at the front revealed an array of dressings across his waist and chest.

Sheriff Cox sat beside him on a couch. "How you holding?"

Ed Thompson's eyes darted around the room. "The doctor says I need plenty of rest."

"Ah-huh. Well, this young'un wants to talk to you. He's one of the folks who helped you when you slid into town."

"I don't feel much like talking, if you don't mind."

"I do mind, dammit," Sheriff Cox said. "You came into town bullet-shot and whimpering. I want to know what happened."

Jubal introduced himself to Ed and started to tell him his story. He saw the man's eyes shift from looking at him to checking his left hand as if he'd never seen it before. "In April of this year, a group of cowardly bastards rode into our meadow, killed my family—"

"Why you telling me all this sad tale? In April I was

up in Alamosa, ranching with Billy Tauson. You could ask anyone. I swear, cross my heart."

"Who had your vest?"

"What?"

Jubal watched the man's eyes. "Your vest. It's very distinctive, what do you call it?"

"My vest? I don't understand."

"Your checkered vest was at our farm that day. I saw it, and you were there, too. Don't deny it."

"How you gonna act, coming in here at a man's sick-bed making accusations about my behavior? I didn't do nothing wrong. So I have a colorful checkered vest, so what? It was that crazy bastard Pete Wetherford started it." The big lummox of a man started crying, head down, fists buried into his eye sockets.

Sheriff Cox got up from the couch and grabbed the man by the chin. "Listen to me . . . fellow. Look up here at me."

Ed Thompson finally looked at the sheriff.

"I'll drag your lanky butt out of that comfy chair and deposit you down at the jail, you understand me?"

Big Ed agreed to cooperate.

Jubal began once again. "Where's Pete Wetherford?"

"We were heading into Cripple Creek here to try and find Billy Tauson." Big Ed took a breath. "Supposedly to do some mining. Gold. Hear tell there's plenty around."

Jubal thought of the nugget he had squirreled away in his pocket.

"I don't have no idea where the bastard is. Hell's fire, he shot me with no warning. I hope he's in hell." He tried to shift his weight in the chair. "You got to look after me,

Sheriff. That bully will come into town and back-shoot me sure as heck. Tried to sweet-talk me . . . then, ah, hell."

Sheriff Cox nodded, signaling to Jubal they were leaving. He glanced back briefly at Ed Thompson and slammed the door. They walked toward Tom's office.

"What do you think about all this?" Jubal asked.

"Pete ambushes this phony Big Ed, rides on into town. Stops for a drink at the tented bar, goes up the mountain, kills a couple innocents, robs a handful of prospectors, then what?" Tom arched his brows in mock surprise. "That's right, you didn't hear the best part. After all that, he came down here late in the afternoon, tied up the gold assayer, took his stash out of the safe, and rode off with the man's horse."

"All this happened in the last few days?"

Sheriff Cox nodded. "The fellow is a handful, I'll tell you."

Jubal couldn't imagine what would get into a human being to get in such a state as to commit so many crimes. *I'll continue looking. I just don't know where to start.*

"How about I buy you supper?" Tom put his hand on Jubal's shoulder. "I got a few things to clear up. Meet you five-thirty at the Big Pan."

Jubal agreed, thanked the man, and walked down Main Street. He felt reasonably certain Wetherford would not have stayed anywhere close to town. He seemed to be a loner, always on the move. He'd be hard to find. *Even when I find him, what the heck am I to do about it? Challenge him to a duel? But some way I will kill him.* He could feel his attitude hardening further.

He continued walking as the shop owners rolled up their awnings, closing for the day.

The man from the post office waved to him as he locked his office door. "Hold on, there, scamp, I got something." The man darted back inside his office and came back with a letter held high in the air. "This thing's been reeking up my place for several days. Lord a-mighty. What's your lady friend do? Write with rose oil?" He seemed to enjoy that he could deliver the letter to Jubal. "You are Jubal Young"—he glanced down at the address— "Terror of the West?"

Jubal couldn't imagine what he was talking about. The clerk pointed to the penned address on the front of the letter.

Jubal Young, Terror of the West
c/o General Delivery
Cripple Creek (Poverty Gulch), Colorado

The man handed the letter over. "I'd hold on to that old gal, she's got herself a sense of humor, and a dandy supply of bouquet perfume. . . ."

Pleased, Jubal sauntered up the street whistling "Clementine." He found the Big Pan and waited for Sheriff Cox on the wood plank sidewalk. He turned the letter over in his hands several times, touching where she had touched, wanting to open it, yet also treasuring the moment of anticipation.

THIRTY-FIVE

Dearest Jubal,

Your letters have all gone missing. Rumors are adrift that bears are stopping the U.S. mail trains and rifling through various correspondence searching for ones that are the sweetest.

We all know how bears have a sugary tooth so I'm sure your notes would have been the first taken. You are excused but just *bearly*.

Jube, please forgive my attempts at humor. Dad is feeling good, goes to the hotel every day, and is generally back to his opinionated self. Mom sends regards as she works in her garden.

I'm writing primarily because I have a problem. I have to go back to school soon and I don't see how I can do that without setting eyes on the People's Purveyor of Peace once more before I'm swallowed up in academia on the east coast. I don't really mean to make fun of your quest, but please write.

Marshal Wayne Turner sends his regards. (Just kidding.)

> Fondly,
> Cybil Wickham

p.s. my bedroom window looks east, I can see Morning Peak, where Daddy told me your family lived. Please hurry back to Cerro Vista, there are people here who miss you.

"You look as if you're on another planet, youngster," Sheriff Cox said, startling Jubal. "Is it good news?"

He quickly stood. "Ah, yes, sir. Good news, sure, from my girlfriend, or I should say my could-be, hope-to-be friend. She's a girl who is more than a just a friend, but maybe not quite a girl, yet. She's a girl, but not yet a girlfriend."

"Well, the fact that she can get you to rattle on like that means she's probably as nuts about you as you are about her. Come on, let's get dinner, Romeo."

They were halfway through their meal when Jubal told Tom of his nugget find.

"Holy Jesus, sounds huge. Where do you keep it?"

Jubal patted his pocket and looked around the restaurant. About a dozen miners were enjoying their meals, but no one was close by. He unbuttoned his pocket and glanced once again around the eatery. Unfolding his fist on the table, he revealed the nugget. He placed it on the black-painted table, where it looked like a ripe moon on a dark night.

Tom reached slowly across the table. "May I?"

"Sure."

The sheriff held the piece close to the candle on the table.

"I've never seen a nugget this big; not many people have. Holy . . ."

"What do you think it will assay at?"

Tom bounced the piece in his hand. "It feels to be something over a quarter pound. Worth a whole hell of a lot more than just the sheer ounce value."

"I don't understand."

"Let's say there's four ounces of gold here. The ounce weight would be around a hundred dollars, but this nugget could be worth four or five times that because of its rare size—and, I might add, it is truly beautiful."

Though Jubal realized the nugget could be of great monetary value, that meant very little to him. It paled in comparison to his constant ache for retribution.

Jubal slept in the blacksmith's barn. The rain had brought moisture into the building, making the straw damp and smelly. In the morning he rubbed Frisk down, then walked over to the jail. He waved at Sheriff Cox. "Morning, Mr. Jailer, how's it going?"

"Passable. Yes, tolerable and passable. How's by you?" Sheriff Cox sipped coffee from a tin cup.

"Everything you just mentioned, along with restless."

Sheriff Cox motioned to the coffeepot on the iron stove. "Help yourself."

Jubal took from the shelf a cup that looked as if it could stand a good washing, but, being polite, he poured the black coffee. "I've been thinking, Tom, about an idea I had concerning our Mr. Thompson."

"And?"

"What would you say to my bundling him up in the bed of a buckboard and hustling him down to Cerro Vista to stand trial along with Billy Tauson?"

"You're a persistent devil, aren't you?" Tom paused. "I don't have any jurisdiction over that brute. Only thing he's done wrong, as far as I can tell, is get hisself all shot up. Yes. Take him away. Think you can handle him?"

Jubal set the vile-tasting coffee down on the stove. "How can you drink that? It tastes like—"

"Horse piss?"

"Come to think of it, yes."

The sheriff offered no excuses other than explaining the whims of being a single man in his busy world. "What was your plan about Big Ed?'

"No real plan, just get a mattress, build a little tent of sorts over the buckboard, harness up Frisk, and light out." Jubal hoped this was making sense. "I saw an old wagon in the corner of the blacksmith's barn. Figured I could buy it cheap, have the smithy anchor a twenty-foot chain to the end of the side plate, then secure Big Ed with an ankle shackle from my friend Tom Cox."

Sheriff Cox smiled. "For someone without a plan, you sound like you've got it pretty well figured out. Why the twenty-foot chain?"

"That way I don't have to worry about old Ed wandering off. He can do his business along the side of the road without me having to lock and unlock his tether constantly."

"Sounds good. Strangely enough, I never heard back from your buddy Marshal Turner, so if anybody is going to secure your Big Ed, I guess it's gonna have to be you. I can deputize you, but it'll only be good in this county. I could give you a note, though, to cover yourself, explaining the situation. Might help. When did you plan on leaving?"

"Don't know. What do you think of Thompson's health?"

"He's a sugar tit, the bastard. He looked fit enough now, far as I'm concerned."

Firm in his plan, Jubal headed out for the black-smith's.

"What I thought might work, sir, is a bolt through the back of the sideboard near to the tailgate. The chain link could be secured by the bolt and then onto the shackle around the fellow's leg. But first I'd need to know what you want for that buckboard in the corner of the barn."

The smithy guffawed. "That old thing? If you pay me twenty dollars, I'll be glad to get rid of it. I'll even grease the axles and straighten out a few flat spots in those rims."

"I'd need a harness for Frisk."

"We'll rig up something. I'll have her done by tomorrow night 'round five, okay?"

Jubal spent the rest of the day provisioning for the trip. He bought hardtack, a side of bacon, coffee, sugar, and, because deep down he was still a kid, several handfuls of hard candy.

He needed a mattress for the back of the wagon for

Thompson to lie on. He solved that problem by borrowing a stiff canvas mattress cover from the jail and stuffing it with straw from the blacksmith's barn. He confiscated additional yardage of canvas from the back alley of a store that had just replaced their awning. It would suffice as shelter for him at night, as well as protection for his patient-prisoner, Mr. Ed Thompson.

The following day he got the ankle shackle from the sheriff and took it to the smithy, who welded it to the twenty-foot chain, then bolted the other end to the wagon.

He was getting close.

The smithy told him he would have the rims straightened in another hour. Jubal left the mattress and awning material in the buckboard and went back to the sheriff's office.

"All set?" Cox asked.

"Yes, sir."

"Do you want me to accompany you to see Ed? That yehoo will probably kick up a fuss when he sees what's happening."

Jubal agreed that he would more than likely need help. After settling up with the smithy, Jubal harnessed Frisk and they all headed to visit with Ed.

"I wrote you this letter, put it on official county stationery."

To Whom It May Concern—

This letter is to inform all, that the holder of this document, a certain Mr. Jubal Young, is a deputy of Teller County, in and around the town of Cripple Creek, Colorado. This deputy is authorized to transport one Mr. Ed Thompson to the environs of Cerro Vista, New Mexico, where Mr. Ed Thompson is wanted for multiple counts of murder.

Sheriff Tom Cox of Teller County, Colorado.

"Of course, the crux of it is that it isn't worth much once you get outside the county. But it might help."

They pulled up outside the house.

"Raise your right hand."

"What? Oh, yes, the deputizing." Jubal dutifully raised his right hand while the sheriff read over him. He felt he was now a deputy in Teller and Cerro Vista counties. All he would have to worry about now was the half dozen or so counties in between.

Sheriff Cox stopped Jubal at the door. "We need to make this short and to the point. No explanations or bullshit. Is the ankle shackle open?"

Jubal nodded.

"All right, here's the key. Don't lose it. You snap the shackle closed as we load our Mr. Thompson on board. The folks inside won't know what's going on—and don't tell them. They'll recognize my badge and will damn well stand off. If we have to carry the bastard, we'll do that. Remember, no explanations. Just 'This is official business,' right?"

"Right." Jubal admired Sheriff Cox's tough approach.

A matronly woman greeted them at the house. The sheriff looked down at a piece of paper he'd retrieved from his pocket as if it were official business. "Where is a . . . Mr. Ed Thompson?"

"Mr. Thompson is still feeling poorly. Can't stand proper. He's in the kitchen having supper."

They shouldered their way into the country kitchen, where six people sat around a large wood table. Sheriff Cox looked at Jubal. "Chair and all, okay?" Jubal agreed as they each sidled next to Thompson and picked up his chair.

Ed, with a large hunk of cornbread in his mouth, gripped both sides of his chair arms and protested. "What in the name of God are you doing?"

They didn't answer, but turned sideways to get through the kitchen entry. Hustling across the parlor, they kicked the front door open and stopped on the porch to catch their breath.

"I'll have you prosecuted," Ed squealed, and looked closely at the sheriff. "Why you doing this? Tell me, am I arrested? For what?"

"A number of things, namely being a sloppy eater." Ed's front was covered with soup stains and cornbread crumbs.

They took their burden down the short flight of steps and next to the tailgate of the wagon. Jubal snapped the shackle around Ed's right ankle, then closed the padlock. Accompanied by Ed's howling, they lifted him off his chair and into the buckboard. Sheriff Cox took the seat next to Jubal as they headed for the jail.

"Jubal, once you let me off, don't stop 'til you're well out of town, you hear?"

"Yes, sir." Jubal urged Frisk on. She seemed to be at home with the wagon harness buckled around her.

They paused in front of the jail. "I'll say adios, amigo.

You got your letter. Let me know how things turn out, will you?"

"Yes, sir, I certainly will. And thank you for being a friend."

Sheriff Cox looked back down the street where they'd just come from. A group of four people were heading their way. Two men, a woman dressed as a nurse, and the matronly gal from the home. "Better scoot, son. It looks like I've got some explaining to do."

"Come on, girl. We've got a long ride ahead." Jubal clicked his tongue at Frisk and snapped the reins on her broad back.

THIRTY-SIX

Wetherford had intended to head more directly south, keeping just west of the Sangre de Cristo Mountains, but instead, after leaving Alamosa, he veered by chance southwest and found himself in the San Juan Mountains. He began following the railroad tracks and ended up in the small community of Chama, New Mexico.

He provisioned, spent the night in a small boarding-house, and, after getting specific directions to Cerro Vista, set out once again. The land flattened, and though ranges of tall, difficult alpine masses still endured, they were mostly surrounded by flat plains that seemed to link to one another.

He enjoyed his days, not in a hurry to get anyplace in particular. He'd been ruminating lately about a plan for a holdup, maybe the First National in Cerro Vista. He figured the town deserved it. Although other than Judge

Wickham, none of the locals had done him dirt, that didn't mean they wouldn't if given the chance.

Revenge. It reminded Wetherford of the man his drunken mother said was his father. Although, to be fair, she did always preface her exhortations of the brothers' lineage with the apologetic "That's your father . . . I think." She had named the children "Wetherford" but never bothered to marry the fellow, and by the time the youngsters asked about him, he was long dead of mysterious causes. One day Al had asked his mom about "Mr. Wetherford."

"What about him?"

"Ah, nothing, Ma. I just wondered when he was coming back. He seemed kind of nice."

"Nice? Are you funning me, boy?"

"He gave Petey and me those toy guns. He seemed sorta okay."

"Listen to me, son. Just because some overnight stayer gives you some half-assed toy don't make him nice." She went to the door of their one-room shack and gazed out at the yard strewn with debris. "He were a regular. Just rode up one day an entire stranger, paid me well, and came and went without a fuss. But that don't make him no saint. You hear?"

The boys nodded but didn't understand what their mother was going on about.

"He's actually closer than you think. You boys take a walk with me, come on."

They each took a hand as they walked with their mother across a dark open field into a wooded area sloping down to the Rio Grande.

"Your Mr. Wetherford and me got to fussing one night. Not in the cabin but out here in the field. He could get full of the devil 'cause he were a morphine-eater. He'd also been drinking right smart for the better part of the day and was talking rough."

She stopped and shook her fist at the dark sky.

"Told me about a wife he had, and a couple little rotters running about. Said it like he were proud he had the obligation of a real marriage and the runabout freedom to come over here from Farmington and play around like it made no never mind to me." She paused, as if trying to hold in her anger, then made a show of spitting with gusto. "Not saying the bastard owed me anything, and I ain't making no apologies about who I am and what I do to feed you little shits, but the man done me dirt. . . . Drunk always, he was. Slapped the shit out of me, then said, 'I'd apologize, but you probably wouldn't understand.' Why wouldn't I know when a grown man knocks me about? Then he says I 'wouldn't get it' if he was to say he was sorry. Would you explain me that? Would you?"

Al moved behind his brother for shelter. "I'm scared, Ma, when you talk like that. All I said were that Mr. Wetherford was 'kind of nice,' is all."

"He's right yonder a-moldering away. Why don't you go over there and tell him how much you miss him? Go on, in a nice loud voice tell him. You'll have to speak up, though, 'cause Mr. Lucas Wetherford is a couple feet under God's green earth and he don't hear so well these days."

The brothers huddled closely together as their mother

walked over to a mound of unusually long grass and once again spit heavily.

In the years since, Pete could recall a half dozen times when he and Al had talked about that night. The peculiar thing was they both remembered it the exact same way, Al always describing their mother as "crazy as a March hare barking at the moon."

She had stood in that vast field, carrying on as if her anger alone could bring back her man Wetherford. Her silhouette dancing over the uneven earth, her fists raised to the skies in mad defiance.

Revenge. It seemed to work for his mother.

Wetherford crossed forty miles of flat, mesa-dotted land, skirted the end of the San Juans, and headed east toward Cerro Vista. He held a huge stash of bullion and cash from the prospectors and the fool at the assayer's office. He toyed with several ideas of what to do with it—principally thoughts of women, booze, and unmentionable pursuits.

But beyond that he knew he should consider land. That one valuable item that everyone wanted to possess. The dream of vast chunks of grazing land for herds of cattle, verdant fields of maize and hay, and him all wrapped in the comfort of a cozy farmhouse.

He chuckled out loud. He'd have a harem, maybe half a dozen floozies doing their salaams for him while he ate an onion-covered steak and drank imported wine from somewhere in Europe. He liked the layout of the farm that Tauson's group had attacked. Once he found that little shit who'd unbalanced him off the log at Morning Peak, he'd do him in, then show up at the land office to plead his case for recovery. *I'm really too upset about losing my relatives, sir, to go into it in detail, but what would be the procedure to gain title of my old uncle Jubal's place, the Youngs' farm?* Maybe it would be ridiculous, but stranger things had happened.

First, he considered he would have to dispose of his make-believe uncle's skinny sodbuster son, Jubal Young.

THIRTY-SEVEN

Jubal Young, Terror of the West. He had to admit it had a certain ring to it. Cybil's sense of humor always seemed based in her own reality. *Does she really think of me as a terror?* Jubal smiled, it made him feel good to reminisce about her. Why she enjoyed his company, he didn't really know—it wasn't as if they had shared a great deal of time together.

He walked next to Frisk, his right hand looped casually into her bridle. It had been three long days since they'd left Cripple Creek, the both of them hoofing it in order to lighten the load. The soft earth made it difficult for Frisk to pull the heavy wagon.

Ed Thompson remained quiet, calling out occasionally for a break to relieve himself. But all in all, he was fairly well behaved.

Jubal's attitude toward his pursuit of the gang members had changed over the last couple of days. Instead of the fiery, energetic passion that had consumed him early on, he now felt more contained, as if it were his life's work, and worthy of the patience, to do it right. Patience. A word that would have been at the end of a long list of things he hadn't possessed several months ago. But he was determined to try. Like the ever-patient Count of Monte Cristo, Dantès had spent fourteen years in prison. Once he constructed his escape, he persevered and found his treasure. *Of course, mine is a mere pittance. But I will become resolute.*

Each day started the same, his first thoughts being of Pru, ma, and pa. Then the slow realization that they were gone and that part of his life was over. This would be followed by a brief summary of the Tauson episode in the saloon, sometimes the memory of Ty Blake, then Bob's funeral and the Ed Thompson story. Only then would he allow himself to think of the good things in his life—Cybil, her parents—notwithstanding the Mrs., who didn't seem to cotton to him. And lastly his nugget. He was anxious to have someone assess it, tell him what it was worth. It had certainly come at an opportune time, this chunk of gold.

They headed east, closer to the Sangre de Cristo mountain range. "The Blood of Christ." The legend had it that each evening as the sun set the Sangres would turn briefly red in order to show respect for the sacrifice of Christ, the flash of light reflecting off the array of piñon and aspen, or in the winter the snow turning a vivid pink across the mountainous expanse.

Jubal would stand on a rock pinnacle, gazing east to the range as the sun set behind him. A brief moment in the fading light, every night. Although he did carry his mother's Bible, Jubal had never considered himself religious, but there was always something sacred about that small piece of the day.

Pru had called it "God's painting."

"God plays with turning the evergreens just slightly red or pink each evening, taking a look at it, trying to decide when She should make a decision. Do you think people would even notice, Jube?"

Jubal and his chained prisoner stopped overnight in the shade of some cottonwoods. A small stream wound its way east toward the Rio Grande.

"How about releasing me so I can stretch my crippled leg, pard?"

Jubal continued to fix their meager supper. "You're just fine the way you are, Mr. Thompson."

"Hell's fire. You don't have to call me 'mister,' son. 'Ed' is good enough.

"I meant it in a facetious way, Thompson."

Ed picked up the long length of chain and rattled it against the tailgate of the wagon. "What's that mean, 'fish-us'?"

Jubal considered this. "It was mostly meant to belittle the fact that you could be called a 'mister,' after all that you did." Jubal paused. "So I facetiously refer to you as 'mister.' It's one of those things one doesn't really mean. One says it in jest."

"You mean like an insult?"

"Yeah, kind of like that."

Ed Thompson continued to pace, twenty feet out from the wagon, then twenty feet back, the chain rattling a dull clunking sound in the dirt. "Shoot, I thought we was getting to be friends, the two of us."

Jubal scooped a portion of the soup into a tin bowl and walked it over to the wagon. "When I referred to you as 'mister,' what I am really saying is 'asshole.' I am making fun of the fact that a grown man could be persuaded to participate in the taking of three innocent lives. . . . You want this soup or not?"

"Yeah, thanks. As I said to you a couple times already, it were Pete Wetherford that did all the dirty stuff."

"Why didn't you stop him?"

"Stop Petey, boy? Not a chance. Look what he did to me. For no damn reason at all, shot the living daylights outta me up there in the mountains. . . . My hip is paining me something terrible."

Jubal walked back to the soup pot and stared at it briefly while Ed slurped away at the thin broth. For some reason, this angered him. Jubal moved to his saddlebag and retrieved his father's pistol, then turned toward Ed.

"She was fourteen years old, my sister." He fired into the ground close to Ed's feet.

"Jesus, save me! What're you doing?"

"She was the finest, most innocent person I've ever met." Jubal fired again, splintering a chunk of wood from the sideboard close to Mr. Ed Thompson's hand. "She wanted to study and marry and have children, you bastard." Jubal emptied the pistol in the air around Ed's crouched form. "I should just kill you right here, but you know what, you rotten son of a bitch? She's going to save your miserable life."

Ed held his hands in front of his face.

"She would have said, 'He can be redeemed.' For what? I can't imagine. But I'll obey what I know she would have pleaded for. Climb back into that wagon and don't let me hear anything else from you. You hear?"

Ed shuffled his way to the tailgate and crawled into his nest with nary a word.

Each day seemed much like the last. Jubal spotted the old water tank where Bob Patterson had waited for him. It seemed a hundred years had passed since then. They were close to Antonito now, the mountains to the east looking the same as the day Jubal passed through Bob's old stomping grounds. He knew he would have to stop and speak to Anne.

A number of horses were tied to the restaurant's hitching post. Jubal pulled the wagon around to the back of the modest frame building.

"We gonna have us some store-bought vittles for breakfast?" Ed Thompson rattled his chain as he moved in the back of the wagon.

Jubal dismounted the buckboard and stretched. "I'll see. Depends on how my storytelling goes." It surprised him how nervous he felt going into the eatery. A half dozen ranchers sat spread out in the restaurant, so Jubal chose a table tucked in a corner of the room.

He waited patiently for Anne, wondering how he would tell her about Bob. She finally came from the kitchen, humming and joking with the patrons. She settled her plates and scanned the room, finally spying Jubal alone in the corner. Her broad welcoming smile slowly faded as she made her way between the tables.

"You came to bad-news me, didn't you?"

Jubal had trouble meeting her intent gaze. "I'm afraid so, Anne. I don't rightly know how to begin."

"What'll you have?"

"What do you mean?"

"For eats. The last time you were here, you had hotcakes and coffee. You left me a quarter. What'll it be, the same?" She stood erect, a small pad from her apron pocket poised below her pencil.

Her stoicism confused Jubal. "Yes, the same, please." She walked back toward the kitchen, and it wasn't more than thirty seconds before loud thundering sounds of pans falling or being thrown came from the rear of the restaurant. One of the men sitting at the counter slipped through the kitchen's swinging doors to offer help. Jubal stood, not knowing what to do. The man who had gone to the kitchen returned and addressed the group of diners.

"Everything's fine. Anne said she just took a header. Said coffee's on the house." He took a tall pot of coffee and proceeded around the room, filling cups. He got to Jubal. "Anne says to take your story elsewhere. She don't want to hear it."

Jubal drifted outside and sat on the wooden sidewalk while the restaurant emptied. Soon, the CLOSED sign had been put on the front door, probably by the coffee man. Jubal tried the door and found it unlocked. The place was empty and he took his original seat in the corner.

Anne was still in back. He listened for any sound from her. Silence first, then a small noise—the scraping of a dish or a piece of silverware being tossed into a tub of water. An occasional sniffle, an exclamation of anger.

She finally came out of the kitchen, a plate of hotcakes slathered with butter and syrup balanced on her right hand, in her left a pot of steaming coffee. She slid the plate in front of Jubal and pulled out a chair opposite him.

"Don't mind me. Eat, Slim."

Jubal dabbed at his food. "I don't really know how to begin."

"Did he suffer?"

"It was fairly quick. No, I don't think he suffered." His eyes welled.

"Who?"

Jubal stirred the syrup with his fork, the butter melting into a yellow stream blending into the maple concoction. "A gent Bob used to work for, named William F. Tauson." Jubal tried to drink the coffee, but it wouldn't go down. "Originally, Bob told me he'd had trouble with Tauson, and that he wanted to settle up with him. We ran into him at a saloon in Cripple Creek, Colorado."

"Bullshit."

"What?"

"When Bob left here, he said to me that you were a troubled youngster and that he wanted to help you. I knew Bob." She paused, trying to control her breathing.

Jubal watched as she massaged her throat, trying to rub away the lump of grief. "He wouldn't have confronted this Tauson. He would have thought about it, oh, hell, yeah. Dreamt about it, maybe told the world what he would do to the man. But I know Bob . . . knew Bob. He was talk unadulterated, sweet Jesus. Talk, and that's all." She covered her face. "The poor big dummy." Her hands moved to her eyes. "He hooks up with a sad-faced snot, trying to be the big man, and gets hisself, what, pistoled? Stabbed?"

"He was shot." He could barely get out the words. "Died real quick."

"He deserted from the army, got the holy bejeezus scared outta him." She pounded her small fist into her opposite palm.

"He told me." Then Jubal waited for her to speak.

"He must have liked you, kid. I guess that says something about you. Bob was a sensitive soul. Fact he would open up to you is surprising."

"We were riding one day, him talking about sleeping outside, then all of a sudden he started weeping. Went on about scooting for home, hiding out. . . . I held the shooter Tauson 'til the sheriff came and hauled him away. Justice—"

"So you held the guy 'til the law came. Why didn't you shoot the bastard? Don't answer that. I don't want to hear your crap about what you did and what someone else did. Bob's dead. Did you bury him?"

"Yes, ma'am. I sure did. Gave him a decent funeral."

"There's nothing decent about a funeral." She broke down and cried into her folded arms on the table. "I loved him. Can you understand that?"

"Yes, ma'am. Is there someone I could get to stay with you, a relative or such?"

She didn't answer, just pointed toward the door.

At the exit, Jubal turned and tried to comfort her. "I really liked—"

"Did you get the watch I gave him?"

He paused. "No, ma'am, in the confusion and all . . ."
She silently waved him out the door.

Jubal suffered some after his meeting with Anne. He knew
Bob didn't have the gumption for the kind of confrontation that Billy Tauson posed. He should have convinced
Bob to go back to Antonito, his life of washing dishes and
his relationship with Anne. She'd been tough, pegged him
pretty well, he had to admit. He felt she was aware of him
laying it on about Bob's former relationship with Tauson,
and especially the question about the watch. Why, he asked
himself, didn't he tell her the truth?

Pure truth, like pure gold, needs refining.

Pa had said that to him one day. "It's like when you
tell a white lie, Jube. You stay as close to the gospel as possible, but you shave a little off here, and you add a little
something there. Before you know it, you've got yourself
a whopping good tale. Don't get me wrong, son, I'm not
advocating you tell lies, but to make them stick, stay near
to the gospel as possible."

He loved his dad, but the man did have some peculiar
notions.

In the case of Anne, Jubal thought he'd done the right
thing, even though she threw him out. He'd conveyed the
news in the only way he knew. But he still felt bad. He'd
lied when he didn't really have to.

The thing about guilt, Jubal reasoned, is it doesn't
let up. Hunger, pain, happiness . . . one can control those
things. But guilt is unrelenting, ever-present.

He continued to push ahead, trying to understand
why he had lied to Anne about the watch. Why couldn't

he have simply said he didn't have enough money to bury ole Bob so he had to sell his watch to help with the expense of it?

Maybe, he thought, doing the "hock" thing would have been better. At least that way he might have redeemed the timepiece later.

They had been on the road near to two hours. When Jubal turned the wagon, Ed woke from his nap.

"What's going on there, son? Feels like we're headed back around."

"We are. I forgot something back in Antonito."

"Yeah, like my breakfast?"

Jubal drove on without answering. What he had forgotten, he finally figured out, were his manners and common sense.

By the time Jubal returned to Anne's Good Eats, the lunch crowd had dispersed. Once again, the CLOSED sign sat tilted in the window. Jubal knocked and then tried the door—locked. The rear of the building had a small shed attached, where Anne sat in the doorway on a short stool, a large pot full of potatoes between her legs.

Peeling knife in hand, Anne looked up at Jubal with red-rimmed eyes.

"You're too late for lunch. Grill's all cleaned and shut down. I banked the fire and hauled out the garbage. What was it you wanted? Forgiveness?"

Jubal rolled a stump used for splitting kindling up close to the door and straddled the splintered log. "No, ma'am, being forgiven is not on my list of wants." He rustled his boots among the wood chips on the ground, trying to figure out how to start. "In my haste and embarrassment this morning, I forgot to give you something Bob wanted you to have."

Anne expertly peeled her potatoes while Jubal continued his halting speech.

"I don't remember if I told you, but Bob and I did some prospecting."

"You did?" Anne replied in a sardonic tone. "What now, Bob left me a sack of dust?"

Jubal fished into his vest pocket. "Not dust, a nugget. Bob's last words were 'Anne's. Jubal, it's Anne's.' Bob patted his vest close to his heart, then he . . . passed. I'm sorry." Jubal handed the nugget to the woman and eased himself up from the stump.

Anne took the craggy chunk of gold in her two hands and examined it, then looked up at Jubal, her eyes wet. "Big Bob . . ." She paused. "The old galoot had been kind to me."

Jubal watched as Anne fiddled with the paring knife.

"We talked of getting hitched, then finally decided it was more interesting to live in sin. It were no stranger to me."

"What was no stranger?"

"Sin." Anne gently stabbed at the potatoes floating in the sun. "A fellow named Colonel Baker brought me and several other girls out from Philadelphia to entertain the yokels during the gold rush in California. I guess that's finally what attracted Bob and me, we were both youngsters when our lives changed, and not necessarily for the better. Colonel Baker died on the trail down toward Santa Fe, left us stranded." She let loose a mirthless string of profanity. "We screwed our way north to Denver on a wagon train. Believe me, kid, that were a wake-up call. I bummed around Denver for a few years. Dance halls, colored lights—mostly red. Then married some jasper who wanted to explore the Far West." She stopped as if overcome, then finally blurted, "I had a child. He lived for near to year two, then died of diphtheria. Guess it were payback for all my dirty deeds. Mr. Ronson, the baby's father, blamed me. The bastard. You know what it feels like to be beaten by someone who's twice your size?"

"No, ma'am, I don't." Jubal knew something about pain but decided he would keep it to himself.

"Well, saint that I was, I decided that Ronson and his bad breath, body odor, and rank personality would be better off living a separate life from yours truly." She began once again to peel her potatoes.

"I'm sorry, Miss Anne. I don't know what to say."

"'Sorry' is good enough. Ole Ronson had a few dollars saved up. Went missing soon after he beat me. All the locals thought it a shame. Except Bob, who was the onliest one to ask me how I got the swollen face and busted lip. They found Karl Ronson out in the high desert, his dick missing along with his money and clothes, just lying there innocent-like, naked as the day he were born, staring up at the noon-day sun. I built this place soon after. For a spell there, Bob were my only customer, but over the years its changed. I went from being the black widow to simply Anne.

"He was such a love, that guy, and the interesting thing is, Bob couldn't write. . . ." She paused. "But he managed to scratch my name on this shiny piece of earth. Funny, isn't it?"

Jubal realized he had made a mistake, had gone too far in his zeal to make things right.

"Misspelled and everything." Anne traced the carved three letters in the nugget with her finger. She tossed the nugget back to Jubal. "Drag your sorry butt out of here and take your chunk of absolution with you."

"But Bob wanted you to have—"

"I wouldn't feel right about taking that, knowing Bob didn't really inherit it over to me," she said thoughtfully. "Grow up, kid. You can't buy your way into heaven, being a polite snot-nose don't earn you no Pearly Gate points." Anne pushed herself up from her chore. "I loved that big slob, but no way in hell his last thoughts were on me. I'm real enough to know that. Shove off, cowboy." She swiped her eyes quickly with her apron ends and, with the load of peeled potatoes hefted to her waist, she walked briskly into the restaurant.

Jubal made the few steps to the wagon and clicked his tongue for Frisk to resume their journey. Anne seeing through his little farce had taught him something about being truthful. Trying to solve the discomforts of life only sugarcoated disappointments.

He had carved the name *Ann* with the best of intentions.

THIRTY-EIGHT

Hope seemed to be in the air, and Jubal started to think they would reach Cerro Vista that day. He started early, just before first light. After an hour he could hear moaning from the back of the wagon. "What is it?" he called out.

"May I speak?" asked Ed in a contrived weak voice.

Jubal preferred not to spend the day angry. "I don't want to hear any nonsense from you. Nothing about who was at fault, who did what. You're a grown man, you know right from wrong, live with it."

"I need coffee. I'm hurting. Ain't there nothing to eat? Why didn't we have breakfast?"

"Because, to use your own words, 'there ain't none.'"

"Why you being 'fish-us' again?"

"'Cause I 'ain't' got the patience to be polite, Mr. Thompson. We should be in Cerro Vista around noon. If you're lucky, the jailer there might rustle you up some steak and beans."

"Really?"

"No, not really. I'm just being 'fish-us.'"

They trudged on into the rising sun. Near to noon-time, old Sol was high in a bright blue sky. Jubal could see for miles as he scanned the eastern horizon. Morning Peak rose out from a thin layer of clouds, and a haze of smoke from a hundred woodstoves drifted above the town of Cerro Vista.

To his right, cutting a path nearly parallel to them and heading toward town, Jubal could just make out a lone rider leading a packhorse. He watched as the man stopped and surveyed the countryside, then changed direction and headed due south. *I suppose he figures the town isn't worth seeing, or maybe he's saving time, skirting the tiny burg. Well, cowboy, you're missing a sweet little village. Come on back and give Cerro Vista a second chance.*

Jubal urged Frisk across the rough earth. He was pleased to be so close to the end of his journey, but there was a nagging, just at the edge of his memory. Something about Sheriff Cox and the assayer. It had to do with what Pete Wetherford had taken from the shopkeeper's office. Gold, money . . . right there on the tip of recollection. *Darn it.*

The troubling thought stayed just beyond his grasp as they rode into Cerro Vista. A number of people stared at the wagon and its strange cargo.

Jubal turned onto Paseo Segundo in front of the hotel and proceeded toward the jail. "Won't be long now, Ed. You'll be able to talk to your former boss Billy Tauson. You two can cook up some tale of how you were pressured into raping and killing. Yeah, tell a jury about a desperado named Pete Wetherford, how he forced all of you to travel out to the Young family property to do your deed. Maybe tell them you were simply an 'unwilling observer.'"

Big Ed stayed silent.

"Explain how you were held at gunpoint while Petey did his rotten work." Jubal looked back at Ed.

The man seemed crestfallen, his legs dangling lifelessly over the edge of the tailgate.

As they pulled in front of the jail, Jubal jumped off the buckboard, checking that Thompson's chain and leg irons were still well and truly intact. "Be back in a minute, Ed. Are you comfy?"

Ed turned and sneered.

The adobe structure was just as he last remembered. Even Sheriff Morton's memorabilia remained tacked to the wall. Jubal's reverie was interrupted by the new peace officer, who introduced himself as Fred Dale and asked if he needed help.

"Yessir, I surely do. Name's Jubal Young. My family was . . . taken." Jubal found it hard to say the word "murdered." "In April, at our farm, just east of town. I have one of the perpetrators in my wagon."

"I'm aware of the event, son. Let's go have a look." The man took an envelope out of his desk drawer and followed Jubal into the street.

The sheriff looked at the mess of a man tethered to the back of the wagon. He gave the long chain a solid jerk.

"Damnation, that hurt. Why you have to go and do such a thing?" shrieked Ed.

"Shut your pie hole." The sheriff looked to Ed to make sure he understood his instructions. "I'm going to read a bunch of names. You call out when and if I come to yours. Understand?"

Ed didn't really agree, just remained silent.

"Billy Tauson." The sheriff looked up with a half grin, waited, then went ahead. "I didn't think so, he's already inside. Pete Wetherford."

Nothing.

"Jorge Morales? You don't look like a Jorge. Al Wetherford? No? Ty Blake—you're a little bright around the cheeks to be the late Mr. Blake. A certain Indian, Crook Arm? Okay, how about Edward Thompson, does that ring a bell?"

Big Ed lifted his arm in a halfhearted gesture to signify that yes, indeed, he was the aforementioned Ed Thompson.

The sheriff once again rattled Ed's chain. "Where's the key to this medieval contraption?"

Jubal unlocked the shackle around Ed's ankle and stepped back. The sheriff grabbed his prisoner by the scruff of the neck and marched him into the jail, Jubal following.

Ed sat across the desk from the sheriff as the lawman folded the paper he had been reading from. He placed it deliberately back into an envelope.

Jubal leaned against the rough adobe wall. "If you don't mind my asking, where did you get the list, sir?"

The sheriff propped his legs on the desk. "Don't mind at all. Seems our Mr. Tauson, who now makes his home in a seven-by-eight-foot cell just beyond that door, decided he wanted to unburden his heart. Signed a full confession naming all the actors in our little drama.

Excuse me, son. I don't mean to make light of your memories. By the way, condolences on the untimely demise of your family."

Jubal thanked him and headed for the door. "I'll probably be at the hotel if you need me, Sheriff."

"Probably?"

"I had a job and bed there. Whether they're still available, I just don't know."

"Well, I still have two cots available in the back, if you're interested."

Jubal smiled as he let himself out. "I've done that, sir. I'd prefer open air to another night in the hoosegow."

Jubal spoke with the manager of the hotel, who welcomed his return. They walked back to his old room.

"Yes, standing orders from Judge Wickham. 'If that wayward scamp comes back, give him his room. Set him to work and send a messenger for me.' I think maybe the judge likes you, son."

Alone in his old room, Jubal sat on his bed.

It was dark but still too early to sleep. Jubal stretched out on his cot and stared up at the *latillas*, the thin poles stretching across the ceiling, looking like a virgin forest, each pole carefully selected and set into the adobe. Jubal wondered what it would be like to have a job where the most taxing part of the day hinged on deciding how much bark to skin from these *latillas* and what to leave for rustic authenticity.

Cybil would know. It was the kind of commonsense problem she'd be good at solving. Jubal swung his legs off the bed and slipped into his boots.

The walk to the Wickhams' house took only a couple of minutes. He walked right past the huge structure, stopping near the tree stump where he had waited when Al Wetherford pounded up the street on horseback.

He kept walking, continuing down Calle Piñon. Most of the homes were lit, their warm lights washing the lawns and trees in an amber glow. At the end of the street, where he had seen the three horsemen dancing their mounts in a deadly frenzy, he turned. A hundred feet farther on, a dusty path led back parallel with Calle Piñon. It wasn't really an alley but a well-worn dirt trail at the rear of the houses on the adjoining street, used mostly as a shortcut to Paseo Segundo, where the hotel was situated.

He walked silently back toward the Wickhams' and heard conversation coming from one of the neighboring homes. It sounded friendly, a family together after a bountiful supper, children being wrestled and cuddled by a loving father and mother.

A soft breeze moved the evening air. He came to the garden where he and Cybil had first met. The kitchen window where Mrs. Wickham had let her presence be known was lit, but was now absent of her mother-hen awareness. A glow in the window on the second floor caught his eye. He saw a shadow move across the thin curtain and stop, a flickering light behind the image outlining a slim figure standing in the middle of the room. Jubal watched, fascinated that this could be Cybil. He stood transfixed as the form slowly began to grow in size until, outlined against the curtain, the figure parted the thin cloth and appeared to gaze into the night.

Cybil stared into the dark evening.

Jubal wanted to dive for cover, knowing if she saw him something would change in their need for each other. He stood without moving, wondering if she could feel his presence. She bent down, raising the window a foot or so, took another glance into the night, and disappeared back into the room.

He found himself holding his breath, a sudden guilt pressing through him. He questioned why he should feel that way, especially since he'd committed no offense. After all, he hadn't shimmied up the kitchen roof's drainpipe, nor had he crawled up the sloped shingles to her window. Neither had he peered over the sill through the open window to her bedroom. And yet the guilt persisted. The light slowly diminished and the house became dark. Jubal moved slowly up the path toward the hotel.

A man wavered over Jubal. A white mist drifted behind his head, appearing as if he were on a mountaintop. Both hands rested quietly on the butts of two .44 pistols, stuffed into twin holsters. Long black sideburns made his face appear lean; a dark mustache under his crooked nose outlined a mean mouth, curled down at the corners. He smiled sardonically.

"I told you what I was going to do to you, didn't I?" With his right hand he swept back his long black hair. "Well, it's time, boy." His body shook as if he had no control. "You knocked me off that log bridge, you little bastard. I promised I would do you." He took a long circular walk, his head still in the mist. He wept when he once again stood over Jubal. "You killed Al, my brother, and got my buddy Billy Tauson throwed in jail. You little bastard." He stomped both feet and raised his head to the heavens. "I'll remember you. You hear, I'll remember!" he shouted. The noise reverberated as if screamed into a vast canyon. "I did your mother and that brat sister of yours." He disappeared from view, the scuffle of his boots getting louder as he made ever-tightening circles, repeated over and over.

Then he was back. "Look here what you did." He took off his buckskin jacket and displayed his bloody arms. Dropping his pants to show a sharp bone protruding from the side of a purple bruised leg, he became hysterical. With his pants still around his knees he drew both pistols and made as if firing them. Mimicking loud bullet sounds, he rocked his pistols up and down, childlike, pointing at the sides of Jubal's head.

Jubal found himself trying to explain to Pete that his brother Al was among the living. He could hear his shouted words atop the foggy mountain. "Al is alive somewhere, wounded but alive. Doesn't that count for something?" *Why am I asking this vision of madness for forgiveness?* He woke with a start. Propping himself on his elbows and peering into the blackness, he heard gasps—his own.

THIRTY-NINE

Carl Buckles lived a few miles south of Cerro Vista in a shack where he sold stolen property, a ramshackle adobe hut with a hundred-mile view, perched on the crest of a butte overlooking a rambling stream. Wetherford had dealt with him a few times and tolerated him, although he knew better than to turn his back on Mr. Buckles.

Wetherford had decided at the last minute not to traipse smack-dab into the center of Cerro Vista without first knowing the atmosphere in town. He made his way up the steep butte.

"Pete, I could have plugged you an hour ago," Carl said. "My boy, you make a lot of noise coming up that hill. What's with that packhorse?"

Wetherford continued up the rise. Once at the top, he doffed his hat and wiped the sweat from his brow. "How you making it, Carl? Everything hunky-dory?"

"Can't complain. Me and Omaha doing just fine.

Funny you showing up at this time. Your brother Al came by about a week or so ago. Sold him a couple of shooters—"

"What?"

"Yeah, Al, your brother. Sold him a couple of pistols."

"Holy Christ. Al? You sure?"

"What you mean, am I sure? I know a Wetherford when I see one."

Pete sat down on a stump in Carl's messy yard, trying to wrap the news around his addled mind. "I thought he was dead. Lord a-mighty. Al alive."

"Hadn't heard nothing about his death. He told me, when I asked about his bent-over shape, that he'd taken a round in the gut in a bar squabble. Spent some time in the hospital down Albuquerque way. . . . What you need, Pete? Did you come by to pay Al's credit I advanced him?"

"Yeah, I'll settle up with you, Carl. What do you hear down Cerro Vista way? Are people hereabouts still looking for me?"

"I don't think they're out scouring the hills trying to catch sight of you, but there's a new sheriff, and course that puffed-up Marshal Wayne Turner. Yeah, they'd like to nab you, but nobody's beating the bushes."

Wetherford shrugged, then lit a cigarette. "I came up here wanting to ask you where I could get a couple men to ride with me. Had a certain bank I want to visit, if you get my drift."

Carl paced back and forth in front of his shanty. "I'd go myself, but I promised my old lady that I would give up that life."

"How is Omaha, anyway? I always liked that gal."

"Fine, just fine, giving herself her weekly bath down the stream a ways. Speaking of water, Al's over in Agua Diablo taking the cures. Soaking in the mineral baths trying to get his self right." Carl yelled out to his wife, who was making her way up the path next to the stream. "Omie, look who's here. It's Pete, remember? Al's brother."

An enormous woman already, Omaha looked even bigger wrapped in a colorful native blanket. She waved at Pete. "Looks tired. How you making, big Pete?"

"Making good, Omie, and you?" Wetherford asked.

"Omaha makin' bread, deer steak, makin' good."

After a heavy meal and an ample quantity of rotgut whiskey, as Omie called it, they sat next to a blazing fire. Omaha passed a strand of beef jerky to Pete. "I have a friend, Indian, actually, named Wild Pony. Says her brother Crook Arm is looking for work."

"I know Crook Arm, he rode with us for a while. He's a good hand. Where is he?"

"Hanging out up north of Cerro Vista in a cave," said Carl. "Just up past Big Rock on the river's east side. Been there about a month."

"What do you hear about Billy Tauson?" Wetherford asked. "Some simpleton up Colorado way said he was taken by some gunslinger in a saloon."

Carl wrapped his arm around his wife's neck and pulled her close. "Yeah, I heard that Turner brought him back from somewhere up north, but I hadn't heard anything about a shooter."

"This old prospector said the guy pulled down on

Billy Tauson in a tavern. Kept him sitting next to a dude that took a round to the chest, they were there half the night 'til the law came and pulled him away. If it's that little chump from Young's farm, I'll—"

Carl seemed to awaken at the mention of Young's farm. "What you know about that set-to at the farm, Pete?"

"No more than anyone else, why you ask?"

Carl threw a log on the banked embers of the fire. "I hear tell that was a right mess. Couple women got raped and kilt. Some farmer got hung. You involved, Pete?"

"I think you know better than to ask me particulars like that, don't you?" Wetherford gave him a look of warning.

"Yeah, I do, Petey. Sorry. Just that everybody knows you and Al were there. Of course, that's why your former boss Billy Tauson's in jail, isn't it?"

"If you knew I was there, why did you ask?" Wetherford exhaled loudly. "Oh, hell, it don't make no never mind. Things kind of got out of hand. But Al and I ended up suffering for it. That, I don't forgive."

He spent the night, settled up with Carl for Al's debt, bought some ammunition for his Spencer rifle, and lit out for Agua Diablo.

Jubal awoke his first morning back from his long trip feeling drowsy and out of sorts. He dressed and then reported for duty, as it were, in the lobby of the hotel.

"Well, until we can figure out exactly what your status is, whether you're our handyman or what, have breakfast in the employees' kitchen and I'll come and get you directly, okay?" The hotel manager was busy and the last thing he needed was to deal with Jubal.

As he sat having tea and oatmeal, he heard a familiar voice.

"Where's that prodigal child?" Judge Wickham appeared in the doorway of the small room. "Weren't you told to keep your hind end in and around the environs of Cerro Vista, young man?" The judge scowled.

Jubal smiled and rose from his chair. "Yes, sir, but I've never been good with geography and such, I hope you'll excuse me." They embraced. "How's your health?"

"I'm feeling better by the day. Come with me, youngster. There are folks you need to say hello to."

Jubal followed the man into the dining room, where Cybil, Mrs. Wickham, and Marshal Turner were having breakfast. When Cybil saw Jubal, she dropped her fork and half rose from her chair. "My God . . . Jubal?"

The judge loved the fact that he could surprise his family with Jubal's presence. "You've met the marshal, haven't you, Jubal?"

The two men shook hands solemnly, then Jubal acknowledged Mrs. Wickham and finally Cybil.

"Miss Wickham, so glad to see you. Shouldn't you be back east?"

Cybil brushed away the egg crumbs from her dropped fork. "Yes, I was meant to go this week, but, well, it's a long story. How are you? I'm just so shocked to see you. Daddy said he had a surprise for us this morning. Oh, excuse my manners. Please sit."

Jubal looked to the judge, who grinned and pointed to an empty chair across from Marshal Turner. Jubal thought it to be ironic, having breakfast with the love of his weary life and his rival for her affection.

"Marlene, pass our wandering pioneer that bowl of hash. Jubal, would you like some eggs or hotcakes?"

"No, thank you, sir. These potatoes and such are just fine."

"I hear you brought in one of those varmints from the raid."

"Yes, sir, a certain Mr. Ed Thompson."

Cybil sipped her tea. "Was he one of the ringleaders?"

"No, I don't think so, just a cowboy who made some mistakes."

Turner swiped his mouth with his napkin. "The real boss of the gang was the one I secured from Colorado a while back, William F. Tauson."

"Wayne, how did you happen to hear about that fellow all the way up there in Colorado?" Cybil asked.

Jubal had to swallow his gall at Cybil's use of Turner's first name.

Marshal Turner folded his napkin carefully. "You see, Miss Cybil, lawmen have a kind of community bind, in that we try and keep feelers out to our brethren. In this case, I had been in touch with an officer named . . . well, his name isn't so important. The point is, we help one another all throughout the West. I happened to be in touch with this lawman . . ."

Jubal loved that he was repeating himself.

". . . and he described this certain hombre he had in custody. I put two and two together, caught the train to Colorado, and managed to incarcerate this Tauson desperado."

Mrs. Wickham chimed in. "Jubal, you must be very grateful to the marshal for his work on this case."

Jubal chewed on a piece of toast and found it hard to swallow. "Oh, yes, ma'am. The marshal has done a workmanlike job. Yes, indeed." He glanced at Cybil, who was looking back at him with such affection he nearly burst. "In my limited travels I find people of Marshal Turner's experience along with folks like Sheriff Tom Cox of Cripple Creek invaluable. As the marshal says, it's the community spirit that's important. Everyone pulling together. Right, Wayne?"

Marshal Turner grunted in the affirmative. The Wickhams smiled, continuing their breakfast.

Later on the hotel porch, the Wickhams said their good-byes to Turner and left Jubal leaning against a pillar. He watched as the family started down Calle Piñon. Suddenly Cybil stopped her parents. Jubal saw her speaking with them, then she hurried back toward him and the hotel.

As she approached, she grinned broadly. "I am so pleased to see you. I had to tell a little fib to my parents about a lost embroidered hankie." She glanced down the street to where the older couple were just turning into their home. "Can we sit here and chat?"

Jubal wiped down the porch swing he had painted earlier in the spring. They took a seat and Cybil pedaled the white planked flooring.

"I've missed you," she said. "What if Daddy hadn't brought us over for breakfast and surprised us, what would you have done? Just hung around here at the hotel hoping

I might pass by and you could wave hello? Didn't you want to see me?"

"I suppose the real problem is, when I see you sitting near 'lover boy' I get the willies. Guess I'm just jealous. You say in your letters—"

"That I care for you, in case you don't read my letters accurately, Mr. Young."

"Okay. Then I see you with, in your words, 'oily hair,' and I'm confused."

Cybil smiled. "So you *do* read my letters. Jube, listen to me. I've said this before. My parents like Wayne. He's polite, brushes his suit, and, ah, yes, combs his hair, but— and this is important—he's their friend, not mine. Okay, Mr. Jealousy?"

Jubal smiled and reached for her hand. "Thank you." He couldn't look at her. He felt he didn't deserve her, felt she was way above him in intellect and maturity, yet in spite of all that, he knew they were right for each other.

Cybil continued to move the swing with her feet.

"What was all that law-community nonsense Wayne was spouting on about?" Cybil asked. "Did you understand what he was getting at? The fact you had to finally supply the name of the sheriff he was supposedly working with seemed peculiar."

Jubal told Cybil the whole story. As they talked, they enjoyed the passing array of locals, some of them shopping, others simply taking in the day. Cybil squeezed his hand. "I truly felt stupid when you asked if I should be back east. On the way over to the hotel for breakfast, mom and I had a kind of set-to about my travel plans. I had told my parents earlier in the week I wasn't feeling well and that I wanted to stay a few days longer. Guess why."

Jubal put on a dumb look. "Because you wanted to hang out to see if your sweetie pie would come back from the wars?"

"Jubal Young, that's the most conceited, arrogant, exaggerated—"

"You left out honest."

"Fraudulent."

"Not deceptive?"

"Self-important, not to mention self-serving."

"Lovable?"

"All right. I'll grant you it was lovable that you saw through my little deceit with my parents." Cybil softened. "What would you say to a quick walk in the countryside? There's something I would like to plant on that smug little kisser of yours."

Jubal met her eyes. "For the life of me, I can't imagine what that would be."

They left the hotel porch and walked east toward Morning Peak, unaware of a lone rider leading a pack-horse, passing just behind them on his way north toward Agua Diablo.

FORTY

Wetherford liked taking chances. He could very easily have skirted around the west side of town to get to the waters, but he didn't like hiding out or dodging the authorities. He rode through town as if he owned it, nodding from time to time at the various passersby.

Agua Diablo, the Devil's Water, was north of Cerro Vista about five miles. Not a town, but just a few tents scattered along the streambed and a couple of ragtag shacks. Other than that, it was simply a natural hot spring that the locals proclaimed had healing powers. Women weren't excluded from the waters, but most of the men would bathe in the nude, so it was very close to being exclusive.

Wetherford led his two-horse caravan to the far end of the bubbling waters and secured the horses in the trees, then walked back to check on the various bathers. Steam rose from four areas along the riverbed where the water was deepest. Each pool had a number of elderly men, standing in water chest-high, staring blank-eyed into the near distance. Al Wetherford sat by himself in the last pool, slowly twisting his head from side to side, his right arm stretched high in the air.

"What's you reaching for, Al, the heavens? It's a far piece." Pete grinned, circling around, trying to see through the mist.

"Is that you, Pete? Boy, I didn't think you were in the area. Where you been?"

Pete sat on the edge of the bank and took off his shoes. "Oh, here and there. I've been mourning your death these past couple fortnights. Your head popping out of that mist makes me wonder whether maybe what I heard about you dying in the street that night was true."

"I felt like death was traipsing pretty close to my sorry behind for a while there. They carted me down to an Albuquerque hospital. Once I started feeling a little better, I shined on to this ugly nurse. After that, it was easy as pie."

They grinned.

"Brother, pie can be tart sometimes."

"Yes, it's true. What we do for love. She brought me fresh clothes, I relieved her of her money, and I was on my way, down the back stairs. Poor ole Magdalena yelling out the hospital window, 'Stop that man, he made off with my virginity!'"

Once again, they enjoyed Al's account.

"She didn't actually say that, but she might as well have. Come on in, these warm waters will set you right."

Pete took off his clothes, laid them on the bank. Took his pistol and held it high out of the moisture as he gradually submerged himself. He secreted his .44 in a small crevice in a boulder that protruded from the stream. "Yeah, I was up at Carl Buckles's place yesterday to see if I could round up some hearty souls for a little adventure I had in mind. Then old Buckles says, 'Your brother Al was up here a week or so ago.' Hell's fire, I nearly had a stroke. It's good to see you, son."

They spoke for some time, Al admonishing his brother for not coming back for him in front of Judge Wickham's house, and Pete explaining that Ed Thompson, now deceased, had told him Al was dead.

"How'd Ed get it?"

"Ed decided he was the baddest man alive and I had to dissuade him of that notion."

"Where did that happen?"

"Up around Colorado way, near to Cripple Creek."

"What were you doing up there?"

"Looking for Billy Tauson."

"Tauson is in jail here in Cerro Vista."

"Yeah, I heard tell—"

A voice from the bank of the streambed startled them. "Hey, you guys. It's two dollars for the herbal waters. I'll settle up with you when you get out."

Pete looked at the grizzled man, his shirt off as if to show his sturdy build. He held a double-barreled shotgun casually in his arms.

Pete called out to the proprietor while moving toward his hidden weapon in the boulder. "No need to wait around, fellow. Just drop the two dollars on my pants there on the bank."

"What did you say? I didn't get it."

Pete reached his pistol and, keeping it shoulder-high, began walking out of the water. When he got to where the water was only knee-high, he pointed his weapon at the man and spoke calmly to him. "Take two dollars out of your pocket, without moving that scattergun one inch. Lay the money carefully on my pants, then toss that shotgun into the water."

"What? Are you loco? I run this here concession. You got to pay me for using the waters."

"Who says?"

"Seth Watkins, that's me."

Pete cocked the six-shooter and took several steps closer to the man, raising his weapon slowly toward the man's chest. "Suit yourself, Seth. I'll put two in your nipples afore you can wheel that buck-shooter around this way. But favor yourself. Either do as I say—put the two dollars on my pants and toss that weapon into the water— or get ready for the Holy Ghost. It don't make no never mind to me either way." Pete smiled pleasantly.

The man's eyes darted back and forth between Al, who was still chest-deep in the water, and Pete, who was now standing within arm's length of him.

"It's two against one. What's a fellow to do?" He looked to Pete as if asking his permission to weasel out of his predicament.

Pete broadened his smile. "The dude in the water doesn't have a gun, unless you count his dick." He began a disingenuous chortle. "So it's just the two of us and the two dollars you owe me. Let's see it."

The man slowly set his shotgun down on a stump, reached in his pocket for the two dollars, set those on

Pete's trousers, and turned once again, making a careful move toward his weapon. Once he had the piece cradled securely in his arms, he started to walk away.

"You're forgetting something, Seth, and because of that I'm gonna ask you to also pack up your duds and your tent if you have one and skedaddle out of here, but not before you complete what we agreed upon, which I'll not repeat."

Seth Watkins stood with his back to Pete. "You wouldn't shoot a man from behind, would you?"

"Make a funny move and see."

The man rocked back and forth in his boots, then finally raised the shotgun slowly over his head and tossed it into the water.

Pete winked at Al and turned back to Seth. "Don't you feel better now, relieved of the burden of having to decide if you were going to get yourself killed?" Pete walked up behind Seth and whispered in his ear, "You got ten minutes. I don't ever want to see you around these parts again, you hear me?"

"My wife, what—"

"I'm being as kind as I can be. Send your wife down here to keep us company whilst you pack up."

"I've got a good little business going here. Everybody knows Seth."

"Don't come around here anymore. I'll hurt you real bad and do some ugly things to the little woman, agreed?"

Seth looked to Pete, then walked away.

"Hurry, now, you only got ten minutes." Pete went back into the water. "I hate a bully, don't you, Al?"

Pete told Al his plans for raising cash and asked if he

was interested. After hearing a "Hell, yes" from Al, Pete mentioned Crook Arm.

"He's a good enough hand, but where the hell is he?" Al said.

Pete explained to Al that Omaha had told him of Crook Arm's whereabouts. They decided their soak was over, and soon set out for Big Rock and the completion of the trio that was to become the infamous Día de los Muertos Banditos.

Cybil and Jubal sat next to a meandering stream. Cyb had indeed planted her lips on Jubal's kisser.

"You know you'll have to marry me, don't you?" she said.

"I thought it was the man's prerogative to make that decision."

Cybil ran her hands along her long legs, straightening the wrinkles in her skirt. "I think, if truth be told, women make their men feel as if it's their choice, but in reality it's always a woman's decision."

"But when you say I'll have to marry you, it sounds as if you're confident that I would want to."

"I know you want to be with me . . . that's apparent." Cybil smiled.

"Am I so easy to read?" He tried to look hurt.

Cyb poked him in the ribs. "Oh, it's a combination of reading and what you might call observing what is undisguised."

"I realize that when we are together, I tend to . . . apologize. I don't seem to be able to help myself, I guess I haven't the control I feel you deserve." He wondered how his deepest secrets could be so transparent to this person. "I would marry you in a minute if I had a decent job or an education, or, for that matter, two dollars for the marriage license." *Unless you consider that tarnished lump of yellow.*

She gazed at him. "It's so good to see that apple-pie face of yours again."

"What would you say if I told you I saw you when I returned before you saw me?" Jubal tossed a rock in the streambed.

"You mean when Daddy brought you into the dining room? What are you getting at, Mr. Wandering Deputy?"

"Ah, never mind. It was just a crazy thought. Forget it."

She made a fist with her right hand and punched Jubal lightly on the shoulder. "You will sit by this streambed 'til it freezes over if you don't tell me what you're speaking of." She put both hands on Jubal's chest and pinned him against the sloped bank.

"I thought you ladies of eastern education were taught manners and—"

"Decorum, cotillion dances. Wrestling, also." She was bent over him, her arms still pinning his shoulders to the grassy verge, her face merely inches from his. "Give, or I'll put a death grip on you."

"Uh-hm. Death grip." He rubbed his chin as if contemplating something. "Sounds interesting. . . . It's not such a big thing. I saw you last night."

Cybil released his shoulders. "Last night? When?"

"I was out walking"—he sat up and wrapped his arms

around his knees—"and found myself in the pathway behind your house."

She gasped.

"I wanted to be close, I wanted to see you."

"You just happened to find yourself lurking behind my house. . . . But where was I? In the kitchen with Mom?"

He shook his head and pointed upward with a finger.

"I was upstairs? In the sanctity of my room?" She poked Jubal in the ribs with a sharp finger. "You are a degenerate, Mr. Junior Lawman, and should be arrested. . . . Was I dressed?"

"Nope."

"You're lying. You weren't there, were you?"

"I was kidding. You were dressed, stood in the center of the room, and then came to the window to raise the sash. You then parted the curtains and stood for a moment thinking of me."

She howled and settled next to him on the grassy bank. "I did think of you last night." She held his hand. "I don't remember when, maybe it was when you were behind my house."

"I felt as if you knew I was close. I wanted to toss a pebble at your window and wish you good night."

"You should have, Jube. Who knows?"

They looked at each other and kissed softly.

"I think I should be getting back. Mom's going to be asking questions about that 'embroidered hankie.'"

They started back toward town, arm in arm. "We'll be with each other someday, Jube. I love you and know you'll be kind."

Their heads together, Jubal buried his face in Cybil's hair. Her arms around his waist, she tightened her hold on him.

The Wetherford brothers found Crook Arm right where Omaha had said he'd be—sitting in his rock cave, smoking peyote. Through a long, painful explanation of what they were planning and what was expected of him, Crook Arm's expression never changed. With an elaborate system of rocks and pebbles laid on the floor of the cave, Wetherford showed the Indian how much he would receive from their planned robbery.

Crook Arm grunted his assent and explained through sign that he didn't have a horse, that he had gambled it away. They showed him the assayer's mount from Cripple Creek. The man sprang onto the animal's back and raised his fist high into the air, screaming something that sounded like he was in a great deal of pain.

The brothers looked at each other, wondering if they had made the right decision with this wild man.

The *tres hombres* rode into the courtyard of Miguel Lopez, an old man waving to them.

"*Hola, amigos.* What can this ancient hombre do for you?"

"Masks. Scary ones, *comprende?*"

"Ah, yes. Sí, señor. Masks I have. Día de los Muertos is not 'til November but I have for you many masks."

"I still don't understand why we need masks, Pete. Hell, the townics all know us, we're wanted for everything from rape to murder. Why bother?"

"Al, my good fellow, you haven't any romance in your soul. The right mask will scare the bejeezus out of these poor clerks, wait and see." He raised his hands high in the air and made a creepy sound.

They paid Lopez for three masks and started to leave.

"Señors, I would like you to take with you some of Rosa, my wife's, special food."

Lopez went into the kitchen and came back wrapping in paper a half dozen fried hotcake-looking pastries. "Very good, corn flour and chile chicken cooked in wood-fire pit. Is good, señors. Eat on your way to your destination."

They saluted the old Mexican and rode off. Pete turned to Al after a short time. "Did that old man say eat these on the way to your 'destiny'?"

FORTY-ONE

Jubal and Cybil managed to extract themselves from each other before reaching the center of town. They stood at the corner of Calle Piñon and Paseo Segundo. "Is my hair mussed, Jube?"

"It looks as if you just jumped out of bed, Cyb."

She smiled, a bittersweet look to her. "I know you're funning with me, but be serious, please."

"You look beautiful. No one would know that we just walked a mile wrapped tightly in each other's clothes."

Cybil glanced around at the passerby, then playfully stuck out her hand as if to shake. "Mr. Young. It's been a pleasure spending this fine morning with you."

They shook hands rather formally.

"And you, Miss Wickham. I trust you are busy packing for your sojourn back east?"

"Yes. I'm leaving in the morning, Jube, and I have so

much . . . stuff. It will take a team of mules to get me to the station."

They smiled, both glancing around, wondering if it would be safe to kiss once again.

"Will I see you tonight?" Jubal asked.

"Let's try."

They once again shook hands, enjoying the fun of the little drama, and parted.

Jubal watched from the hotel porch as Cybil walked the few paces down Calle Piñon. It had been a fine morning and Jubal was anxious to get to work, to bury himself in the pure splendor of hard honest labor.

He thought maybe it would be fun to help Cybil pack, to pester her about what she was taking back to school. "What are these for, Cyb?" He would hold up a lacy chemise and act innocent. Then reach for— His thoughts were interrupted. Something about what Cybil had said about packing. Try as he might, he couldn't remember. It wasn't the packing, but the way to get to the railroad station, what had she said? "A team of mules."

It all came flooding back. A team of horses. Two. The image of the lone rider when Jubal was coming into Cerro Vista. The man who was leading a packhorse. Cripple Creek's sheriff Tom Cox's explanation of the theft of the assayer's horse after the robbery.

Pete Wetherford was in the vicinity of Cerro Vista. Jubal was sure of it.

The trio of gunmen neared the outskirts of the northern border of Cerro Vista.

"We're all clear where to meet afterwards? The fork

in the road at Morning Peak?" Pete made a sign to Crook Arm with his spread fingers indicating a fork.

Crook Arm acknowledged with a grunt.

"You think he'll understand what's needed, Pete?"

Pete smiled and patted brother Al on the back. "If he does half of what's asked of him, it'll do."

They parted just before reaching the cantina. Crook Arm proceeded along a back alley toward the hotel while the brothers continued to Paseo Segundo. They moved past the jail, and Pete wasn't able to resist a call out to the open rear window, "Hey, Billy! How's it swinging, boss?" He laughed, and there was no reply.

Al shifted in his saddle. "Let's try and concentrate here, Pete."

They rode along Paseo until they were across from the land office, then donned their masks and set their cowboy hats on top of the full headpieces. Pete's mask was made of stiff papier-mâché, painted a bright red, the eyes black-rimmed and dead-looking, while the mouth was frozen in a crooked sneer. His hat was stuck up high on his head, secured by the rawhide string under his chin. Al's white-painted skull sported red and black circles for eyes, the open lips adorned with rotting teeth, the nose hole and hollowed-out cheeks painted bloodred.

Al glanced at his pocket watch. "About a minute."

They glanced around at the few locals walking along the wooden sidewalk, some looking astonished at the two men, while others waved as if trying to get into the spirit of things. Al nodded and they moved up the street. When they were a hundred feet from the bank, smoke began coming from the back of The Wicks Hotel.

The masked pair proceeded down the street, taking their time.

Farther along, a few locals ran toward the stable in the back of the hotel. Someone called out "Fire!" as the two masked men tied their horses in front of the bank, waiting until the people in the building were alerted. In a short time, a half dozen souls came streaming through the double doors looking back down the street at the now-crackling flames.

The brothers walked into the emptying bank.

"*Hola, amigos.* We're here for the pesos. This is a robbery. Fill these bags *mucho pronto.*" Pete didn't even attempt to make his Spanish sound authentic. They brought out two canvas feed bags and the bespectacled clerk behind the cage began stuffing them with money. Only four people remained in the bank—a customer, the manager, and two tellers. Those not busy emptying the till stood with hands raised, keeping watch on the masked gunmen.

Pete motioned for the hostages to move toward the back room, tying the manager to his desk chair and stuffing a kerchief in his mouth. The woman who was the customer he locked in a clothes closet along with the frightened tellers. He then went back to Al and the business at hand.

Business was brisk at the hotel. Jubal had been given the task of helping the maid fold sheets in the basement, and though it wasn't his favorite pastime, he was certain it was only temporary. His thoughts were of Cybil and their conversation on the street just before parting. "Will I see you tonight?" "Let's try." It had a sign of hope to it.

He was startled from his absorption by the maid asking a question. "What? Sorry, I didn't understand what you said, miss."

"Listen, *por favor.*"

Jubal heard yelling and footsteps on the floor above them. He went up the basement stairs. At the top, people moved quickly from the lobby onto the front porch.

A women's high-pitched voice screamed, "Fire!"

"Is it in the stable?" Jubal asked.

"Yes!"

Jubal's one thought was Frisk. He ran outside to find one end of the barn where Frisk was stabled consumed by heavy flames.

Jubal darted into the barn and began releasing the horses into the courtyard. Frisk was five stalls down close to the fire. Jubal couldn't get to the gate, as the flames had caught the dried wood and begun climbing, so he crawled over the slats separating the stalls until he reached her. She was dancing at the flames licking at the stacked hay in the corner.

He kicked at the horizontal planks separating Frisk's stall from the adjoining one. Finally breaking the top board, he grabbed her halter and encouraged her to jump the last two planks. They did the same to the next stall, finally able to make their way through the smoke into the now-busy courtyard.

"Did you let those horses out, son?" the manager asked.

"Sure did."

"Good job. My God. I thought I was seeing ghosts when you came out of that dense smoke. Christ, I don't know what I'm gonna tell Judge Wickham."

Jubal looked over the man's shoulder back down the alleyway toward Tres Paseo. "Look, it seems there's another fire close to the jail, just up the street at the cantina. Something's going on."

While leaving the bank, Pete and Al saw the second fire Crook Arm had started, at the back of the cantina.

"Shit fire, there's people running around like headless chickens. It's working, Pete."

"Damn, boy, you look scary, what with that stupid sombrero sitting atop that skull. If I didn't know it was you behind that getup, I'd be shaking like a coyote in a wolf's cave."

"Let's hightail it, Pete. Come on."

"I can see the jailhouse doors open. The sheriff's probably carrying water to one of the fires. Let's take a minute for some tit for tat."

The brothers quickly rode down the street to the jail. Pete tossed his reins to Al and dashed into the outer office of the lockup. Gathering the two wastebaskets and an armload of paper folders from the bookshelf, he kicked in the door leading to the barred cells. He spread his papers around the loose logs next to the wood-burning stove and lit them. He took off his long coat and fanned the flames. The dried logs and papers burned well. It was only a few minutes until the *latillas* covering the ceiling began smoldering. The straw used for insulation between the horizontal logs and roof was soon fully alight.

"Hey, what the hell's going on? This some kind of joke?"

Pete raised his hands high and spoke through his

sneering papier-mâché lips. "Everybody loves a joke now and again . . . Billy."

"Pete Wetherford? Why you doing this?"

"Guess." Pete walked toward the broken door, the smoke starting to thicken.

"Don't leave us in here, Petey. Lord God a-mighty."

This was a different voice. "Who's calling?"

"It's Ed Thompson, Pete. Don't do this. Help me, please, for God's sake."

Pete looked back into the smoke-filled room. A figure moved in panic behind the bars. *But Ed Thompson's dead, has been for quite some time.* He walked slowly from the jail, his coat dragging behind, and got back on his horse.

Three fires burned now, and one of them had a voice that spoke from the dead. The brothers turned their mounts back toward Calle Piñon and Judge Wickham's house.

Because the shed Jubal shared with the two other workers was close to the stable and in danger of burning, he took the time to get his possessions out. He dropped the grain sack filled with his clothes behind the front desk counter and ran toward Calle Piñon. Jubal knew something dangerous was going on.

Al was upset. "Christ, man, you're gonna get our butts fried. First the bank, then you wanted 'tit for tat' at the jail. Where we heading now? We're supposed to meet Crook Arm at the East Fork."

"I got to settle up with His Honor the right nasty Hiram Wickham. Crook Arm can wait 'til Christmas. I never did intend to divvy up with Mr. Powwow nohow."

The streets were peppered with horses, wagons, people running. Jubal saw the sheriff and Marshal Turner in front of the jail. Flames leapt twenty feet in the air, fully engulfing the structure's roof. Several bodies lay on the sidewalk in front of the adobe building.

The whole town filled with smoke. Horses were loose, trotting unattended, trying to distance themselves from the fires. Relieved he had taken the time to secure Frisk in an orchard behind the hotel, Jubal reached the Wickhams' front gate, where he could see horses in the back alley. He had a moment of reflection, thinking this was the second time Frisk had gone through a session of fire in a barn.

The Wickhams would have to be deaf not to have heard the commotion. But the house seemed strangely quiet.

FORTY-TWO

"What is it you want from us, Wetherford?"

Pete stood in the doorway of the Wickhams' kitchen. Al crowded in behind him in the narrow passageway.

"You beat me when I was feeling poorly up on Morning Peak. I intend for 'satisfaction.'" He dragged the word out, enjoying his sense of power. He looked at Marlene and Cybil huddled behind Judge Wickham. "Maybe the word is 'satisfy.'"

Jubal listened at the judge's front door. Something told him things weren't quite right. He wanted to open the door without knocking but knew he'd feel a fool if he did and everything in the house was fine.

Pete motioned for Judge Wickham to move to one side. "You with the pretty ribbon in your hair, come here."

Cybil walked tentatively across the kitchen floor.

Judge Wickham spoke in a loud voice. "Now, listen, Wetherford, leave my family alone. We have some money stashed away. Take it and leave us. For God's sake, man. Have you no self-respect?" He stomped his foot in frustration. "If you need a hostage, take me!"

Pete looked at the judge. "Why would I take a withered bag of wind like you when I could have this fresh, unspoiled maiden?" He wrapped his left arm around Cybil's waist and pulled her in close, his pistol pressing tightly into her stomach. "You look kind of innocent. Are you . . . unspoiled?"

Cybil spat in his face and struggled to free herself.

"Al, watch these old farts while I take care of this one." Pete slapped Cybil hard, knocking her into the hallway.

"Are you some kind of a debauch?" This from someone behind Jubal. "Creeping around Cybil's house?"

He turned to see Wayne Turner smirking. Jubal held a finger to his lips and whispered, "I just heard Judge Wickham getting angry with someone. I think it's Pete Wetherford."

"You're always hearing and seeing things, aren't you, shooter?"

"Why the fires?" Jubal gestured with his arm at the surrounding smoke.

"It's been a dry summer."

"Three fires all at once?" Jubal cocked his head at the lawman.

Marshal Turner took a step toward the door. He cupped his hands around his eyes, pressing against the

engraved glass panel of the door. He peered in, then suddenly stepped away. "There are two of them. They got
Cybil. Get help. Go get the sheriff."

Marshal Turner leapt off the porch and crouched down,
fumbling under his coat for his pistol. A scream came from
the back of the house as Jubal tried the knob of the front
door—which was locked. He drove his elbow through the
etched glass, cleared the broken shards, reached in, and
unlatched the door. Moving along the hallway, he could see
a shadow against the far wall, someone in the kitchen.

Standing with his back to him at the kitchen entry was
Al Wetherford.

Jubal's first instinct would be a shot to Al's back, but
if the round went through his body, it would endanger
whoever was at gunpoint in the kitchen. Jubal saw Al had
positioned himself half in and half out of the doorway so
he could keep watch on the hallway and the kitchen both.

Jubal eased himself behind the stairs and released
the long-bladed knife from its scabbard, hoping his few
practice sessions with Mountain Bob would now pay off.
Hidden behind the uprights on the banister railing, he
waited until Al glanced down the hall. He could hear the
angry voice of Judge Wickham as Al turned his head back
toward the kitchen.

Moving into the hall, Jubal took a long deliberate
stride toward the kitchen door. He threw the knife at the
broadest part of Al's back, but just as the blade completed
its first full rotation, Al moved. He had bent slightly forward and down, the knife slicing through the top of his coat
collar, ripping open the back of his neck and sticking with

a resounding *thwack* into the door casing. Jubal covered the remaining distance in an instant.

He slipped Ty Blake's nickel–plated .44 from his waistband and pressed it against Al's bloody neck. "One little sound from you, jackass, and daylight will come streaming through that pumpkin head of yours. What'll it be?"

Al nodded and held his weapon chest-high with just his finger. The pistol swung gently by the trigger guard, and Jubal disarmed him.

"I'm hurt bad, pard. I can feel the wetness on my back."

"You'll live, it's just a nick."

Al moaned.

A lucky throw, Jubal mused. *Practice made almost perfect.*

"Where's Cybil?" he whispered to Judge Wickham, holding the gun out to him.

Judge Wickham took it and answered quietly, "I heard a scream. It sounded as if it came from out back, by the path."

"Are you okay holding him, Judge?"

The judge pushed the barrel of Al's pistol hard into the man's chest. "I'll be fine. Careful with Cyb."

Jubal made his way back out the front entrance, then ran to the side of the house, where he met Marshal Turner creeping along, glancing through the kitchen windows.

"She's gone!" Jubal shouted. "Wetherford went out the back door with her. The judge has Al at gunpoint." He sprinted past the startled lawman and headed toward the walking path stretching up toward Paseo Segundo. One of the horses he'd noticed earlier was missing, and a pair of papier-mâché masks lay crushed on the dirt path. Jubal continued up the trail toward the hotel. A number of people milled about in front of the building.

Heavy smoke thickened the air. The stable behind the hotel was fully engulfed in flames. Jubal made his way past the onlookers and scrambled around to the orchard to find Frisk. It looked as though she had fought her restraints, rebelling against the smoke that swept through the orchard. The sky was a dirty gray, the wind carrying most of the smoke east, obscuring the mountains.

He grabbed Frisk's mane close to her withers and vaulted onto her back. He rode out in pursuit, stopping an older man and his wife to ask if they had seen a horseman with a young girl. The old man shook his head as if it were a peculiar question, given the turmoil in the streets.

Jubal trotted Frisk in a circle to loosen her, then galloped down to the jail, finding the sheriff crouched over the burnt bodies of Billy Tauson and Ed Thompson.

"Sir, Judge Wickham is holding Al Wetherford at gunpoint at his house. Brother Pete's got Cybil held hostage somewhere, and Marshal Turner is wandering near the house, Lord knows where."

"Is that who's behind this mess? Pete Wetherford?"

"Yes, sir."

"You say the judge has Al?" He paused, looking behind Jubal toward the hotel.

Marshal Turner was marching Al down the street toward the jail. "You, there, why didn't you do as I said?" Turner called out to Jubal. Drawing closer, he continued to shout, pushing Al violently into the waiting arms of the sheriff. "This jackanapes needs to be locked up, Fred." He then looked to the skeletal remains of the jail. "Jesus wept, what happened here?"

Jubal turned Frisk in a complete circle, looking for Pete and Cybil on horseback. No sign of them, only people wandering the street.

"These fellers started at least three fires, Marshal," the sheriff said. "Where in the hell have you been?"

"Why?"

It looked to Jubal as if Turner resented the sheriff questioning him, but the sheriff continued. "While you were out roaming around, that jackass Pete Wetherford started these fires to cover up the fact they were robbing the bank. What did you think, all those separate fires started on their own, all at once? I asked you a question. Where you been?"

Frustrated as the two upstanding lawmen squabbled, Jubal turned and moved past the men.

He had no idea which way to go. Where, he asked himself, would Pete want to be—to fulfill whatever twisted dream he had about Cybil? The man probably had tied her to the saddle. In his haste to get to Frisk, Jubal realized he had ignored signs of which direction Pete might have gone. Jubal reversed his direction and headed back toward the Wickham house.

From the base of the tree where the horses had been tied, a set of hoofprints led west across a vegetable garden and between two houses on the street behind the Wickhams'. Jubal led Frisk on foot around the garden and out onto the adjoining street. A woman standing with a child in her arms looked across the open expanse to the east, gazing at the transformed sky.

"Excuse me, ma'am. Have you seen a big cowboy on horseback in the last few minutes? Maybe with a young girl, she's probably tied?"

"Sorry, just came out of the house a moment ago to watch the smoke and fire. What happened?"

Jubal looked back toward the darkening skies. "Lord only knows, ma'am." He started up the street toward Paseo Segundo and the hotel.

"I did hear some shouting a while back, down toward Paloma."

Jubal turned Frisk and headed back down the street toward the crossroad La Paloma, at the far end of which stood a large residence known to most residents in Cerro Vista as the Dove's Nest, a house of ill repute situated at the edge of town. Jubal had never seen the place, but it might be something that Pete would be drawn to.

"You're a total bastard, you know that, don't you?" Cybil, her hands tied in front of her, struggled to loosen her bonds. Pulling a rope lashed tightly to the saddle horn of a dapple-gray mare, Wetherford led them into the stable behind the Dove's Nest.

"You make my nether regions swell with joy when you speak, sweetness. So keep it up. I know this will be difficult, but you'll have to endure a few minutes without me while I talk to my compadre about a room for the two of us, so we can fulfill your dreams."

Cybil struggled once again with the rope around her wrists and waist. "I have only nightmares about you."

Wetherford took several steps toward her, moving his hands slowly up and down around his loins. "You heard

what I said, how those sweet words stir my ole Johnson."
He hissed, posing with his hips thrust out. "If I hear you
carrying on, I'll come back out and shoot you right smack
in your belly button, got it?" He stood beside Cybil's left
leg, running his hand under her long dress and up her bare
thigh until he felt her tense.

"Keep away from me." She bent her leg, ready to kick
him in the face.

He stepped back and once again rubbed himself.
"Mind what I say," he hissed. Pete walked toward the
barn door. "My ma used to call women like you 'bitches.'
Haughty, kind of pretty, and full of themselves, but in the
night when the devil lights his fires . . . they change to
vixens."

"Your schooling concerning women is sorely lacking."

Wetherford started back toward Cybil. "Never you
mind about my getting on with women. I'll beat your face,
missy." He continued toward her.

"Of course you'll beat my face, that's what you do,
because you're afraid to be a human being. Tie me up like a
pig sent to market, then try to terrify me with ugly threats.
That's what little children do because they don't know
any better. But you're not a child, that's what makes you
so pitiful. I'm scared to death of you, of what you'll do to
me. . . . Even you must be shocked at your behavior." She
struggled to keep her composure. "No one can go through
life so out of control and not have at least one thought
about what it is they're doing." Cybil stopped to catch her
breath.

Wetherford stood in the gray light of the stable, small
particles of dust floating in the air. The mare pawed the

floor, causing the matted straw to give off a musky stale-
ness, the only other sound the occasional snorting of the
mare.

"You stand there rubbing yourself like a five-year-
old, do you actually think anyone would be attracted to
something like that?" Cybil stopped and wept, her head
bowed, nose running. "You provoke people so you'll have
an excuse to beat them up or to rape them or in some way
diminish them so that you'll feel better about your . . .
miserable self."

A bird flew under the eaves of the hayloft sitting high
above the stable floor. It called a few times to its mate in
a soft cooing sound, then fluttered in a wide circle and
escaped through a gap in the top of the structure.

"Let me go, please." Cybil's voice broke. "I'll do . . . no,
I won't do . . . just, please." She sobbed for a minute, then
tried to pull herself together. Wetherford stomped around
the stable muttering to himself, finally shouting at her.

"Who gave you the right to say I'm some kind of
child? You haughty rich girl. Talking about women and
such. I do what I like 'cause it pleasures me. I got my own
rules and if so-called proper folks don't like them, they can
kiss my behind. . . . What do you mean, I don't think about
anything I do? You calling me stupid . . . I ain't no sissy
boy. Treat everybody the same, men and women . . . afraid
of nothing."

Cybil raised her head. "Why do you have me trussed
up this way? Because you're afraid someone might say no
to you? A woman outside of a whorehouse might actually
have an opinion about you that you couldn't handle."

"You got a . . . got a . . . right smart mouth on you."

Wetherford surprised himself when he stammered. He usually didn't allow anyone to talk to him like that. He was glad it was dark in the stable. He felt his face reddening. His impulse was to jerk the girl off the horse and punish her. She had made him stammer and he didn't like it. But he hesitated, forced a chuckle, then latched the large double doors behind him.

Jubal turned on La Paloma and headed west. The sun turned the sky a soft pink, the smoke changing the light from bright blue to a rosy hue. The row of houses thinned, and a crude sign haphazardly stuck in the earth at the side of the road showed a white dove winking an eye and flying toward the end of the road. The combination of smoke-filled light and setting sun made the house shimmer as if it were suspended in midair, balancing delicately on what appeared to be a band of water.

He stopped up the road from the two-story Victorian and slipped off Frisk's broad back. There were very few houses other than the lone frame building for at least a hundred yards. He moved off the road, tied his horse to a cottonwood, and walked through a copse of juniper toward the dwelling. Sparrows and robins bickered in the branches above him as he made his way carefully toward the back of the Dove's Nest. The light softened, diminishing any color remaining, changing the trees and bushes into gray silhouettes.

Jubal stopped at a clearing overlooking the side of the house and several outbuildings, along with the stable and a broken-down windmill. He could hear music from the house, a spirited rendition of "Dixie" on an out-of-tune piano. Jubal hadn't any real way of knowing if Wetherford was there, but it seemed to be of his speed and want. He sprinted toward the side of the building and pressed himself against the aged shingles.

The sound of horses and men's drunken voices came from the road. A hitching post at the front of the house would soon be occupied by the partying horsemen. They would see him; he had to move.

The largest of the adobe buildings in the compound was an outdoor privy. Jubal stood on the side farthest from the house, having decided he would hold on until the light had truly diminished.

"What's you doing, cowboy? Trying to get a free peeka-boo?" A woman of thirty or so came from the outhouse lighting a cheroot.

"Ah, no, ma'am. Just looking for a friend."

The woman's spangled red dress matched her bright crimson lipstick. Her eyes were blackened under the brows with lashes that seemed inordinately long. "What's your friend's name, hon?"

"Ah, Pete. Yeah, goes by Pete. Sort of."

"Pete sort of? Ahh, you're cute. There's a customer talking to Willy D. Tall, dark hair, looks like the devil's helper . . . that your friend?"

"Yep, sounds like old Petey. If you're going back inside, miss, don't say anything to old Petey. I'm trying to surprise him, okay?"

"You're a funny little young'un, you know that?" She took a long drag on her square-cut cheroot. "If you're looking for a trip around the world later, look me up. Ask for Lavern. Deal?"

"Deal," Jubal said. He moved farther back on the property next to an open toolshed, crouching down next to a double plow and trying to figure out what to do next. Behind him, the stable's long east-pointing shadow darkened a group of piñon. A large cottonwood close to the Rio embankment sheltered him as he dodged to the far side of the stable. He felt he was safe for the time being, but then his expression changed and he took off angry.

"I can't have you making a fuss in here, Pete. You get my drift? Got to look out for my regulars. I'll let you use the apartment in the back, but nothing loud and unruly."

"Look here, Willy D.," Wetherford said. "I never did you no dirt and don't intend to start now. I need a place to lay low 'til the middle of the night, then I'll be gone. In the meantime, I got my nuptials to take care of. This heifer is kind of new to the ways of bump and diddle, so she might be shouting for joy, but that shouldn't bother your class of quick finishers, should it?"

"Upstairs to the right, last door facing the stairs, windows got a good view of the Rio Grande and another one south toward the cowshed." Willy D. tossed Pete a key. "You can either watch the sunset over her shoulder while you do her or contemplate your early days doing the sheep in an old red-painted barn."

Willy D. thought that to be quite funny as Wetherford pressed a handful of coins into his outstretched paw.

"I never affaired with no sheep, Mr. D. Watch your mouth." Pete headed out toward the stable and his talkative virgin.

FORTY-THREE

Jubal eased his trim frame between the corral fence and the edge of the stable. It would be dark in another half hour and easier to move about.

The back of the stable faced south, showing wear from the sun. Jubal could see the stable layout between several slats of weathered boards. "Unused" would be the best way to describe it. Several empty stalls on the left smelled of moldy hay and the structure lacked any hint of fresh manure.

A wide weathered plank at the back of the structure, decayed at the bottom, came away easily from the vertical studs. It would be more prudent to go in the back rather than expose himself at the stable door, facing the house. He slid quietly through the opening and was surprised to hear the movement of a large animal. He crouched in a dusty stall, listening.

A horse stomped a hoof several stalls away on the

right side of the dark stable. A few stripes of light filtered through gaps in the stable boards, making eerie patterns on the earthen floor. Jubal listened again. The animal breathed heavily, and just under that sound he heard a faint cry. A woman's whispered catch in the throat.

The soft weeping of Cybil Wickham.

Jubal wasn't sure if she was alone. He eased his pistol from his belt, straining to see in the dark, and took a chance.

"Cybil?" he whispered.

A quick intake of her breath. "Jube?"

Staying crouched, Jubal made his way along the bank of stalls to where she was, then slipped the circle of rope from the top of the stall door and eased in next to her horse. He looked up to her on the mare. "Are you all right?"

"He said he'd kill me if I made a sound. . . . Are my parents okay? Are they harmed?"

"They're fine," Jubal said. "Slip off that horse. I have to get you out of here."

"I can't. I'm tied, Jube."

Jubal took out his knife. In the dim light, he carefully ran his free hand up the saddle, then cut the ropes holding Cybil to the saddle horn. He helped her slide off the mount. She was trembling.

"Hold me tight, Jube." She buried her face into his collar. "I was so afraid." She finally took a long breath and sighed. "I think I'll be all right. Get me out of here, please."

"We'll ease out the way I came in."

As they started out of the stall, the mare tossed her

head, pawing the straw-covered earth. Jubal raised a finger
to his mouth. "Someone's coming."

A muted, high-pitched voice struggled with a spiritual.
The sound came from the direction of the house's back
porch and seemed to be getting closer. Cybil started toward
the back of the barn.

"Wait," Jubal said. "There isn't time. Stay in the
back of the stall behind the horse. Take this." He handed
his knife to her and tossed his hat onto the floor of the
enclosure. "Give me your hair ribbon."

Cybil took the wide, pale ribbon from her hair and
handed it to him. Jubal mounted the horse as the singer
came closer.

*"Amazing grace! (how sweet the sound) / That sav'd a
wretch like me! . . ."*

Jubal slumped down in the saddle after looping the
ribbon with a large bow around his head and tying it under
his chin. He coaxed the mare sideways so the light would
catch the top of his bowed head, and waited.

Pete Wetherford unlatched the stable door.

*". . . I once was lost, but now am found, / Was blind, but
now I see."* Pete lingered before entering. "Are you ready
for me, darlin'?"

The door bounced against the side of the barn and
sprang back. Pete was silhouetted against the smoky sunset, the sky a muddy red band behind his head. Mustard-
colored stripes melted into the vanished sun, burnishing
the horizon in a soft orange.

"I have something for you, sweet lips." He stepped
into the barn. "Don't be hanging your head, darling. Old

Pete will take care of you." He took out a bowie knife. "I changed my mind, dumpling. I'm gonna let you fly back up La Paloma Street to Calle Piñon, and fall into the arms of that rotten man you call 'Daddy' . . . how's that, sweetness?"

When Jubal heard the door slam open his first impulse was to confront Pete head-on, but with the light being so dim, he decided to wait until the man moved closer. He could hear Cybil once again behind him, trying to muffle her sobbing. Jubal thought that might be good, at least it came from the right general direction. He kept his head down, praying that in the soft light Pete would see only a faint image of a figure on horseback.

"I done me a lot of terrible deeds today, sweetness." Pete waited, as if trying to make a decision. "I can smell lilac water perfume coming off you, hon. . . . If you ask me gentle-like, I'd be pleased to carry you up to the second-floor room my friend Willy D. gave us and per-form a wedding ceremony with you. Course, it wouldn't include a preacher, but it would be the start of a new life for you . . . you can trust me on that." He hummed the spiritual again, but didn't move.

The barn door suddenly slammed shut. "Whoo-ee. That scared the snot out of me." He laughed and resumed his humming. "I was letting the beast out today. You and me could start a family, sweetness. You know how that goes, don't you? You lie in bed all coy and innocent . . ."

Cybil's sobbing grew louder. Jubal strained to see across the darkening stable floor.

"Don't worry, missy. Like I said, I'm gonna turn you

loose. You believe in fate and all that? You don't have to answer, I can hear your misery. Old Pete had the scare of his life today, want to hear 'bout it? I'm sure anything regarding my pain you'd want to listen to, right?"

Cybil continued her crying.

"I take that as a yes. I was in the jail talking to my former boss, who was unaware of his approaching death. When out of the past comes this voice of a fellow who has been dead for at least a month. . . . Yeah, big as life comes this countrified sound. You want to hear this story, don't you?" He interpreted Cybil's weeping as assent. "Reason I know he was dead was, I put him in that particular way." He stopped to listen to Cybil for a while. "Still interested in this, sweetness?"

When she didn't answer, he continued. "Anyhow, this voice at the jail got me all jiggled up. Pete has scared feelings sometimes too. Wouldn't say that to just anyone." He kicked the loose straw on the stable floor. "You said some hurtful words to me, darlin'." He tried to slough it off, his confession to her. "I can only think that maybe I've done enough disruption for one day. Strange thing, when I heard this Ed Thompson, it reminded me of an old fellow I had to string up on the side of a barn. I won't put you to sleep with all that story nonsense, but that farmer didn't beg for his life like Ed did, just called me every name in God's blue skies. It were funny as all hell. He were a tough old bastard." He stood waiting. He was hard-pressed to know for what . . . a sign, a word.

The silence in the stable finally broke when he continued his humming, then moved toward the old mare.

A voice that was definitely not the girl's startled him.

"That's far enough, Wetherford."

He stopped in the center of the stable floor, the last of the evening light casting the shape of a cross, creating a soft double band across his chest. Jubal cocked his weapon and rested it on the top of the saddle horn.

"If you move, I'll kill you. So don't tempt me." When Wetherford mentioned Jubal's father and the way he had died, it was all he could do to keep from killing the man right there, but unprovoked, he knew it would be a mistake that he couldn't live with. Jubal could tell that regardless what Wetherford was saying, Jubal was still undecided about what he was going to do. But there was one certainty. He couldn't live with Cybil's disapproval. He had to be careful. The words "it was funny as all hell" echoed in his head.

Wetherford snorted hard, bending over to rest his hands on his knees, in spite of Jubal's threat. "It's the"— he paused—"the sodbuster. Well, damn all. If this isn't the funniest thing. Where's the slut, farmer boy?"

"Just pay close attention to what I'm saying, Pete. If you doubt that I'll kill you, make a quick move and see."

Jubal had no sooner spoken than Pete made a darting, childlike move to his left, then back the other way. He giggled and squatted down, spun in place several times, and ended up with both hands clasped tightly around his groin. Through his merriment he hissed to Jubal.

"I moved a-plenty and you didn't fire. Wonder why. Remember what I told you when I was laying all beat up on the mountain? I said I'd do you. You're a coward, boy. You're afraid to pull that trigger 'cause you was raised up to do the right thing. You're not gonna shoot me because you don't have the eggs, señor. The *huevos*. Stones. You're a mama's boy. By the way, she had nice teats, your mom." He reached quickly under his coat, making a gunfighter's move, laughing hysterically.

Jubal fired twice, the first round catching Pete in the stomach, the second a little higher in the center of his chest.

Revenge.

Jubal swung his right leg over the saddle horn and slid easily onto the ground, brushing Cybil's ribbon from his head. He never took his eyes from the stretched-out form on the stable floor. He could hear only soft gurgling sounds, and then nothing. Jubal approached cautiously, bent on one knee, and ran his hand along Wetherford's belt for a weapon. It wasn't there. Wetherford was not armed.

Jubal heard voices coming from the back of the house.

"Who's out there? What's going on?"

"It's all over!" Jubal shouted. "Give me a minute." He stood over the body and felt no remorse, only vindication. He wondered if the folks outside had been Pete Wetherford's friends. If so, would they consider Jubal's act self-defense if Wetherford was unarmed?

Jubal walked back to the mare. In the saddlebag, he found Pete's Colt revolver. He checked the chamber and found it full. He tossed it on the ground next to Pete's body, then took a quick look out back for Cybil, who he thought would be at least halfway home by now.

Jubal walked to the double stable doors and pushed them open. A crowd of men and scantily clad women, several with lanterns, stood in a semicircle staring at the building.

"Pete Wetherford is inside, he pulled down on me. It wasn't of my choosing."

He led Frisk back through the woods to La Paloma Street, finally coming to the path trailing behind the Wickhams' house. A pale light from the kitchen illuminated the back garden area. A shadow moved across the curtained view. A figure appeared at the door.

"Who's there?" Judge Wickham opened the door only partially.

"It's Jubal, sir."

"Come in, youngster. Lord God almighty. Are you all right?"

"Yes, sir, and yourself?"

"We'll manage. Come in, come in. We're sitting around the table trying to make sense of this night."

Jubal appeared in the doorway of the dining room and Cybil walked shakily into his arms. As they embraced, Jubal looked over her shoulder and spoke to Mrs. Wickham.

"How are you doing, ma'am?"

She cocked her head slightly at Jubal. "Let's just say I've had better days."

Judge Wickham pulled out a chair for Jubal and offered tea. The atmosphere at the table was heavy with relief.

"We, as a family, wish to thank you, young man, for the splendid job you did retrieving Cybil from that renegade bastard—"

"Hiram, please. Your language." Mrs. Wickham flicked

her teaspoon in the air, gesturing toward Jubal. "What were you thinking, young man? To bring your family's story into this household . . . you nearly got all of us killed."

"Marlene, that's not fair. Jubal didn't instigate this debacle, far from it. He's as much a victim in this situation as we are."

She bolted from her chair. "I won't have it, do you hear? I won't have him in this house. My God, Hiram. He's just killed a man."

The table went silent, and Jubal rose. "Excuse me." He made his way out the back door to the sound of the judge and his wife shouting at each other. By the time he'd reached the alley, Cybil was right behind him.

"Jube, please wait. I apologize for my mother. She's completely wrong. She's simply trying to sort out her fear and this horrible night. Please, Jube. Stop, don't run away, please."

Jubal paused next to Frisk. He fooled with her bridle, self-consciously adjusting the buckles.

"How did your mother know that I shot Wetherford?"

Cybil placed both of her hands on Jubal's shoulders. "Because I told them."

"But you were gone by the time I shot him."

"I ran into the woods, then stopped when I heard gunfire. I don't know what I would have done if you had been shot, so I went back." She paused and wept. "I couldn't see very well, but I stood by the open slat until I heard you call out to the people behind the house."

Jubal wondered if she had seen him take Pete's pistol out of the saddlebag.

He thought maybe he would never know.

Jubal wondered if he had accomplished what he'd set out to do. Were things better in his small world? He had to admit to himself that the revenge he'd promised was unfulfilling. He was afraid a hollowness about it all would haunt him.

He didn't much like who he had become. Would his old friend, the Count, have had those same feelings? What were those words that Pete kept singing?

"I once was lost, but now I'm found. Was blind, but now I see."

EPILOGUE

Al Wetherford had the dubious distinction of being the only one of the Tauson gang who stood trial. His days were short-lived.

The Ute Crook Arm was found dead behind the land office, his Día de los Muertos mask still in place. It seemed he'd grown fond of setting the fires and was in the process of igniting several stores when Marshal Wayne Turner not so bravely shot him in the back.

Cybil left for Boston, but not before she and Jubal filled their time together with promises of being re-united.

Frisk carried Jubal east toward Morning Peak and the farm. The cottonwoods and aspens, in full color, had weathered the long summer. Grayish yellow clouds crowded the eastern skies. Raindrops the size of small marbles pelted the rutted path.

Jubal stopped under a cottonwood by the stream and

watched the storm create small dust devils, then smother them with God's tears.

He guided Frisk up through the trees just north of the burnt homestead, where the family was buried. The small makeshift cross was on its side. Jubal adjusted it and took a moment for his family, then walked Frisk farther up into the pines. The heavy clouds released a torrent of rain through the native grasses, washing dust from the rocks that littered the ground. He looked for nearly an hour for the grave of Tauson's wife, thinking perhaps he would give her a proper marker. On the way back down, he noticed Frisk had stepped on a broken rock. A blue-green stone, revealed, like a lump of dull glass with sky-blue tint. Jubal dismounted, took the piece, and rubbed it hard against his saddle blanket, seeing a luster coming through flaky dust. Then he noticed an eroded slope nearby was alive with gray-green and sky-blue rocks. He knew what they were, his mother's petite brooch having the same type of embedded stones. She had prized it, because it had been a gift from Jubal's father in Kansas on their wedding day.

Turquoise.

The brief shower left the trees and native grasses glistening. The last vestige of sunlight struck a brilliant rainbow that seemed to settle in the open meadow next to Jubal's former home. The charred remains still endured as a stark reminder of the long, disastrous events.

Jubal went into the root cellar and found his mother's papers. He came upon the envelope his sister had left for him. She had written it in the spring and given it to their mother to keep for Jubal's birthday in August.

He was now eighteen, and had difficulty getting there.
The crumpled paper still held a faint hint of rose oil.

A coyote walks its winding path,
I hear a raven's caw.
This land.
I feel the mountain breeze, I touch the rocky earth.
Oh, land I truly love.
An elk trumpets its mournful call. As eagles circle prey.
This land is wildly loved.
A boy walks these man-sized hills. This girl child
watches in envy.
A brother is warmly loved.
The vibrant earth sprouts vivid green. The snow
melts to water.
This girl becomes a woman.
Oh, sun, slow your rapid arc.
These mortal souls would extend their days.
Oh, life I dearly love.

ACKNOWLEDGMENTS

My sincere gratitude always to literary agent Noah Lukeman for his persistence and invaluable insight (some of which I actually used).

At Simon & Schuster, I give special thanks to my editor, Anthony Ziccardi. Andrea DeWerd, thank you for pulling everything together. Kevin Smith, your positive feedback was most appreciated. Thank you, also, to Louise Burke, Alex Su, Esther Paradelo, Liangela Cabrera, Dave Cole, Lisa Litwack, Jean Anne Rose, and Renee Huff. Damn, it really does take more than a village.